ELIZABETH GAGE

Against All Odds

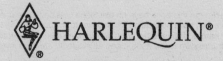

D0286473

HARLEQUIN®

TORONTO • NEW YORK • LONDON
AMSTERDAM • PARIS • SYDNEY • HAMBURG
STOCKHOLM • ATHENS • TOKYO • MILAN • MADRID
PRAGUE • WARSAW • BUDAPEST • AUCKLAND

RECYCLED PAPER

ISBN 0-373-83366-0

AGAINST ALL ODDS

Copyright © 1998 by Harlequin Books S.A.

Intimate © 1984 by Donna Huxley
Number One © 1984 by Donna Huxley
A Stranger to Love © 1984 by Donna Huxley

This edition published by arrangement with Harlequin Books S.A.

® and TM are trademarks of the publisher. Trademarks indicated with ® are registered in the United States Patent and Trademark Office, the Canadian Trade Marks Office and in other countries.

Printed in U.S.A.

The critics praise

ELIZABETH GAGE

A Glimpse of Stocking

"Has blockbuster written all over it."
—*Chicago Sun-Times*

Pandora's Box

"Meticulously researched and engrossing, the novel glows with perceptive characterization."
—*Publishers Weekly*

Taboo

"*Taboo* is steamy, romantic fiction
at its absolute best. Juicy romance doesn't
get any better than this."
—*West Coast Review of Books*

In 1988 Elizabeth Gage burst onto the fiction scene with the shocking *New York Times* bestseller, *A Glimpse of Stocking*. Bought at auction for the highest price ever paid to a first novelist, *A Glimpse of Stocking* was translated into eighteen languages and launched Elizabeth Gage as a popular author with a uniquely powerful style. Gage followed *A Glimpse of Stocking* with *Pandora's Box, The Master Stroke, Taboo* and *Intimate*, all national bestsellers with rave reviews and sales to match. Her latest, *Confession*, a June 1998 title from MIRA Books, continues the series. She will publish *The Hourglass* with MIRA in March 1999. The three Harlequin Presents novels offered in this collection, written just before *A Glimpse of Stocking* made its mark, showcase the unique Gage combination of complex characterization and compelling storytelling.

The critics praise

ELIZABETH GAGE

A Glimpse of Stocking

"Has blockbuster written all over it."
—*Chicago Sun-Times*

Pandora's Box

"Meticulously researched and engrossing, the novel glows with perceptive characterization."
—*Publishers Weekly*

Taboo

"*Taboo* is steamy, romantic fiction at its absolute best. Juicy romance doesn't get any better than this."
—*West Coast Review of Books*

In 1988 Elizabeth Gage burst onto the fiction scene with the shocking *New York Times* bestseller, *A Glimpse of Stocking*. Bought at auction for the highest price ever paid to a first novelist, *A Glimpse of Stocking* was translated into eighteen languages and launched Elizabeth Gage as a popular author with a uniquely powerful style. Gage followed *A Glimpse of Stocking* with *Pandora's Box, The Master Stroke, Taboo* and *Intimate,* all national bestsellers with rave reviews and sales to match. Her latest, *Confession,* a June 1998 title from MIRA Books, continues the series. She will publish *The Hourglass* with MIRA in March 1999. The three Harlequin Presents novels offered in this collection, written just before *A Glimpse of Stocking* made its mark, showcase the unique Gage combination of complex characterization and compelling storytelling.

INTIMATE

INTIMATE

CONTENTS

CONTENTS

CHAPTER ONE

PORTER Deman swung his desk chair abruptly to face the young woman before him. A sigh of irritation passed his curled lips.

'You're making this very difficult, Anna,' he said quietly. 'Difficult for yourself.' His cajoling voice was tinged with an undertone of menace which sent a cold chill down Anna's spine.

The springs of his chair groaned quietly as he rocked, his eyes exploring the gentle waves of Anna's auburn hair. The office was silent, its calm disturbed only by the distant thrum of computers printing out sheets of data for waiting secretaries.

Shocked into speechlessness by the insolence of his proposal, Anna Halpern stood livid and trembling with outrage before the man who contemplated her.

'I...I can't believe this,' she said finally, her voice threatening to break under the strain of her position. 'I've worked here for four years, and no one has had occasion to complain about me. Quite the contrary, in fact. And now you come along. You've only been here six months, and...'

'But I'm here now, aren't I?' he drawled, self-satisfaction glimmering in his cold grey eyes. 'So you'll have to deal with that fact. That's what I've been trying to explain to you for weeks, Anna. But you don't listen, do you?' Again he sighed with feigned exasperation. 'And you see where your obstinacy has got you.'

Anna stared in helpless wonderment at the figure before

her. His thinning grey hair immaculately tonsured so as to
conceal the onset of baldness, Porter Deman was dressed
as usual in an obviously expensive three-piece suit whose
fine lines minimised the slight paunch around his waist. He
was the very image of complacent wealth and influence.
His tanned face and taut skin bespoke long hours spent at
a health club in a deliberate effort to hold off middle age.

The day he had replaced Tom Green as manager of
Anna's research department at N.T.E.L., she had studied
his cold eyes and abrupt manner, and concluded that he
might be a demanding boss. But in the last month she had
realised how catastrophically she had misjudged him. Ever
since the first evening he had invited her to dinner, in his
oddly dictatorial way, she had begun to fear him. And gradually, as though inevitably, it had come to this.

'Well?' he asked. 'I'm waiting to hear what you have to
say for yourself.' His lip curled ironically as his eyes slid
over her slender shoulders, coming to rest languidly on the
sleek curve of her breasts under the silky fabric of her
blouse. With studied impudence, he allowed his stare to
stray to her hips, and downward along the rich line of her
thighs, before returning his gaze to her deep emerald eyes.

'What I have asked of you,' he drawled, 'is not only
quite simple, but also essential to the good working relationship I must have with you. It is a very common thing,
I can assure you, and not at all worth staying awake nights
over. But, as I've tried to make you understand, it is necessary.' His eyes bored into her. '*Necessary*,' he repeated
darkly. 'You don't seem to comprehend the meaning of the
word.'

'Necessary,' she retorted, her anger boiling over, 'that I
should go to bed with you, simply because I work under
your direction for this company?'

'Now you're putting words in my mouth,' he corrected
with a slight smile. 'It's simply a question of a close per-

sonal relationship facilitating an efficient professional one. You state it far too bluntly.'

'That's beside the point,' Anna said firmly, controlling her revulsion with difficulty. 'I know what you mean to say, so there's no sense in denying it.'

'Listen, Anna,' he warned. 'I understand that this all may seem strange to you. It may seem unfamiliar, since you've apparently led a rather sheltered life, but you're simply going to have to wake up to a simple truth. This is,' he said, weighing the words deliberately, 'the way things are done, the way the world is. Now, you'll just have to learn to play the game according to the rules, or get out. I mean what I say, now.' Severity resounded in his deep voice.

She felt herself flush under the insolence of his exploring gaze and the unbearable arrogance of his words.

'I...I need this job,' she said quietly, her courage flagging. 'Can't you understand? I can't afford a change of jobs at the moment. I need the income in order to keep financing my sister's education. She doesn't have anyone else. I simply can't afford to be fired, because of your...'

He smiled, his eyes glistening dewily with undisguised desire. 'That's exactly my point,' he said. 'You can't afford to go against the grain, so why spite yourself by refusing to do what I ask? If you had had an open mind about things weeks ago, you would never have got yourself into this fix in the first place. Things would have fallen into place, and you wouldn't have had a thing to worry about.'

His tone became more cajoling as he stepped around the desk toward her. 'Think of it this way,' he said. 'I'm not an unattractive man, if I say so myself. I'm not so bad to look at, am I?' He smiled, his finger stroking her hair.

Unnerved by his nearness, Anna stared beyond him at the painting behind his desk.

'Is it so terrible,' he went on, his finger straying gently to her shoulder, its meandering movement leading ever

downward, 'to think of sharing a little closeness with me?
A little human tenderness?'

Anna shuddered, her nerves crying out in exasperation
as the cloying scent of his cologne filled her nostrils. His
hands closed around her waist, pressing warmly at the
creamy flesh under her skirt.

'That's not so bad, is it?' he whispered, his lips touching
the soft hollow of her neck. 'There's no one here. We're
alone. Why don't you relax and let yourself go, just this
once?'

'Take your hands off me!' Her tense voice resounded
warningly.

'Don't destroy yourself,' came his low murmur, 'out of
silly stubbornness. Don't be a little fool. I can make you
happy.'

Unable to bear his touch an instant longer, she stepped
back a pace, her eyes still locked to the meaningless form
of the painting on the wall.

She heard a stifled growl of frustration, and felt his hands
grasp her purposefully.

'Come on,' he whispered, his lips approaching her own.
'Give me what I want, and I'll take care of you.'

'No!' she heard herself cry as the limits of her self-
control exploded. The image of her upraised hand seemed
a dream before her tormented eyes, but the resounding slap
she had planted square in the centre of his cheek was no
dream, as the tingling in her palm made perfectly clear.

He stepped back, the growing anger in his cold eyes
alloyed by a shadow of genuine shock which gave Anna
an inner spark of satisfaction, despite her panic.

He sat down behind the desk, a sore red spot beginning
to colour his cheek.

'You shouldn't have done that,' he said. 'You have made
a big mistake, young lady.' His eyes glistened with fury.

'You gave me no choice,' Anna said quietly, her hopes

collapsing inside her breast. 'I…I can't give you what you want. It just isn't in me. You had no right…'

'Your explanation comes too late,' he said darkly. 'I'm afraid you've succeeded in destroying what chance remained for you to solve this…dilemma.'

'What are you saying?' she asked, the colour leaving her cheeks.

'It's quite simple, Miss Halpern,' he smiled sardonically. 'Your days at N.T.E.L. are numbered. I would say, as a matter of fact, that time has about run out for you. A pity, too. You were so happy here, and your work was appreciated. I shall never understand how certain people can simply throw away what was most important to them.'

'I can report you,' she told him, her thoughts racing to find a weapon she could use against him. 'Sexual harassment is against the law. My work is well known here, and I'll be taken seriously.'

Porter Deman chuckled, shaking his head.

'It's been tried,' he said. 'It never works when the executive involved is important. And I am important, Anna. Far more important to this company than you. I'm sure you're somewhat aware of the lengths your employers went to woo me away from Cambridge Manufacturing. You see, they need me—they need my abilities. And even if your complaints were taken seriously enough to introduce the shadow of a doubt into my colleagues' minds, you would still lose your job. No one likes a troublemaker, Anna.'

'I'll take the chance,' she retorted.

'Go ahead,' he laughed. 'Be my guest. Speak to Charles Robbins, or even the President. Speak to anyone you please. You'll see. You'll be greeted warmly, and you may be lent a sympathetic ear. But in the end, no matter how much your superiors seem to be on your side, you will be politely asked to change your tune or pick up your pink slip. It's a man's world, Anna. If you try to fight it, you'll be wasting your time. But,' he added, a darker look cloud-ing his grey eyes, 'I wouldn't advise that.'

'Why?' she asked, her hatred and contempt threatening to overwhelm her fears.

'In any case, you're through at N.T.E.L. But if you should be so foolish as to cause me any embarrassment, I can assure you I am capable of a revenge that won't end overnight. I can quite easily see to it that you don't work anywhere in this business. Ever.' He smiled smugly. 'Do you follow me?' he asked.

'I'm sure you overrate your influence,' Anna said tartly.

'If I were in your shoes, young lady,' he warned, 'I wouldn't take the chance of finding out.'

Pale with anger and hurt, she stood for a long moment regarding the reclining man behind the desk. His cold, nearly colourless eyes looked out at her like those of a serpent, expressionless and dangerous.

At last she sighed. 'I would like to know,' she said, 'what makes you think you have the right to ruin other people's lives, when they've never done a thing to you, simply be-cause of your pathetic, cheap desires.'

Anger showed in his pupils. 'Get out!' he growled. 'You'd better start seeing to your things—you'll be leaving us soon!'

Anna closed the door quietly behind her, determined not to allow her anguish to attract the attention of the other employees. Porter Deman was left alone in the silence of his office, his chin resting on his hand, his eyes staring before him with an expression of alert intensity. For an instant a look of concern clouded his grey irises. Then he reached for the telephone.

The green eyes which looked out at Anna from the ladies' room mirror had a haunted expression. Even the emerald glow of her irises, normally the most striking feature of her face, seemed blunted by the pressure of the emotions she fought to control. The creamy complexion of her cheeks shone pale under the harsh fluorescent light, making the flowing auburn tresses of her hair seem unusually dark by contrast.

Grateful for the solitude of the empty bathroom, Anna stared intently at her image, struggling to put this morning's events into some sort of perspective.

'Calm down,' she told herself firmly. 'You're all right. Nothing has changed.' Despite his sinister demands and threatening behaviour, Porter Deman was surely bluffing. If he made a serious attempt to have her fired, she would simply defend herself with the truth. Her four years of invaluable service to N.T.E.L. would carry considerable weight in comparison with the unsupported claims of one executive who had joined the company only recently.

And she would not hesitate to tell the whole truth, she resolved. No amount of embarrassment could prevent her from exposing Porter Deman for the contemptible bully he was.

With a rueful smile she thought of the unpredictable and even rash personality which lurked under her calmly efficient exterior. Her stinging slap had surprised her as well as its victim, for in her years at N.T.E.L. she had grown accustomed to keeping her impulsive nature in check, in the interest of her sister's security as well as her own.

In the mirror her admirably sensual figure was highlighted by the silky fabric of her blouse. The gentle swell of her breasts, shaken now by the short, nervous breaths she took, still glimmered with feminine grace. Despite the crawling of her skin, her image remained vibrant and healthy, as though lit from within by the stubbornly independent personality whose wrath Porter Deman had unwittingly tempted.

'Anna,' a voice startled her suddenly, 'are you all right?'

As Debby Johnson's short figure came into view next to her own, Anna realised she must have been too preoccupied to hear the other woman come into the room. Debby's bright brown eyes, normally glinting with mischievous good humour, were clouded by concern as she put a hand on her friend's shoulder.

The sudden appearance of a friendly face was a welcome release after the tension Anna had just experienced, and she smiled gratefully.

'I didn't see you come in,' she said. 'I must have been lost in thought.'

'What did Deman want?' asked Debby, her intuition startling Anna.

'Oh, nothing much,' Anna replied. 'The usual.' She was uncomfortably aware that her flushed cheeks and tense demeanour contradicted her casual words.

'He didn't say anything to upset you, did he?'

'Not particularly,' Anna lied, determined not to refer directly to the disturbing scene that had just taken place. 'Why should he upset me?'

'Listen,' Debby pursued, her brow furrowed in concentration, 'I don't want to pry, Anna, but I've noticed how edgy you've been every time Deman has shown his face these past weeks. As a matter of fact, I've been meaning to talk to you about him. He's dangerous.'

'I suppose you're right,' Anna agreed ruefully. 'But he doesn't scare me.'

'That puts you in a league by yourself,' Debby frowned. 'Things haven't been the same around here since Deman showed up. He's got a lot of people pretty frightened.'

'How do you mean?' asked Anna. But her glance at her friend's troubled features left little doubt as to what was in her mind.

'I'll tell you what,' said Debby, 'let's have lunch and

talk this over. I have a feeling we can enlighten each other about Porter Deman, and maybe do something about him.'

Anna hesitated, weighing her reluctance to talk about what had happened against the obvious advantage of confiding in someone she could trust.

'All right,' she said at last, reasoning that if Porter Deman had made his threat in earnest, she might soon find herself in desperate need of an ally.

The corridor seemed crowded with secretaries and research personnel as Anna and Debby approached their office. N.T.E.L.'s normally quiet workings often burst into a sudden tumult of activity just before the noon hour, as reports had to be completed, letters signed, and meetings hastily terminated.

'Hey there!' came a familiar voice behind Anna as she passed the elevators.

Turning to see the perpetually laughing face of Bob Samuels, the company's Vice-President in charge of Research, Anna smiled in greeting. As luck would have it, her momentary inattention to the busy corridor before her sufficed to cause a small collision, and she found herself immobilised by two powerful hands which had closed around her slender arms.

'Sorry,' she heard a deep voice say as she turned to face the tall form she had nearly bumped into. Looking upward past the deep chest at the level of her eyes, she met a dark gaze whose trace of irritation was combined with a glint of amusement.

'Excuse me,' she said, annoyed as much by the mockery in the ebony irises looking down at her as by her own clumsiness, 'I wasn't looking where I was going.'

'My fault,' Bob interrupted, coming to a halt beside her. 'I shouldn't have distracted you, Anna. You haven't met Marsh yet, have you?'

'No,' she answered, darting a diffident smile of inquiry at the stranger who stood before her.

'Well,' Bob laughed, 'this is as good a time as any, since I've caused you to literally bump into each other. Marsh, this is Anna Halpern, one of our research geniuses. Anna, meet Marsh Hamilton. He's working on our contract with Arons and Birnbaum.'

'How do you do, Mr Hamilton,' said Anna, covering her embarrassment with an air of detached politeness.

'Call me Marsh.' The black eyes staring down at her shone with easy familiarity amid the strong lines of a sun-bronzed face. A large hand grasped her own in self-assured friendliness as she noted the dark brow and chiselled jaw which heightened the aura of daunting male strength surrounding Marsh Hamilton.

'Marsh's firm is collaborating with our own legal department on Arons and Birnbaum and some other accounts,' Bob explained, adjusting his glasses with his accustomed nervous energy. 'We're attempting to give him first-class treatment, since he's been kind enough to work with us personally. It's not usual for a partner in the firm to roll up his sleeves, so to speak, and dig into contract details with our young lawyers upstairs.''

'I enjoy it,' said Marsh, his eyes not leaving Anna. 'Gives me a chance to get out of the office. Besides, I think it makes for a better result if your people can connect Feuerbach, Smith and Hamilton with a face.'

The face of Marsh Hamilton would be hard to forget, Anna reflected. Underneath its veneer of calm amiability, one sensed a mixture of sharp determination and unlimited energy which seemed almost reckless. It was the face of a man whose self-confidence had long since triumphed over any obstacles life might have placed in his path.

No wonder, she decided, that he was already a partner

in his firm, although the strong lines of his face suggested he was still in his mid-thirties.

'I'm afraid contracts aren't my department,' she said, feeling her senses tingle under the caress of his probing gaze. 'Nevertheless, welcome to N.T.E.L. I hope your work with us goes well.'

'I don't anticipate any problems,' he smiled, not bothering to conceal the frank interest palpable in his expression. 'I expect we'll be seeing each other around, Miss Halpern. Perhaps running into each other would be a better way to put it.'

'I'll try to look where I'm going next time,' Anna laughed a trifle nervously.

'I'd be interested to know more about your research work,' he added. 'It would help me to understand N.T.E.L.'s inner structure.'

'Drop in to our office any time,' she invited. 'Debby or I would be happy to give you a tour, although you might find it somewhat boring.'

With a sudden glance around her, she realised that the throng of employees crowding the corridor had engulfed Debby. The fascination exerted by Marsh Hamilton's imposing form had made her forget her friend's very existence.

'I'll try to take you up on that,' said Marsh. 'I'm quite sure I wouldn't find it boring.'

'Well,' Anna stammered, unnerved by the enfolding stillness which seemed to immobilise her in his presence, 'goodbye, then. It was nice meeting you.'

'So long,' came his deep voice, its timbre seeming to echo the daunting warmth of his regard.

As she started off down the corridor, Anna could hear Bob Samuels engaging Marsh in conversation. But a sixth sense told her that the stranger's alert glance remained fixed to her receding form, and she could not suppress the disturbing feeling that she was fleeing him toward the safety of her office, like a frightened prey before an aroused predator.

Shaking off the impression with an effort, she pushed open the door and hurried to her desk. This morning's jarring events had distracted her from urgent work awaiting her and the employees working under her supervision. There was no time to lose.

'You can't let him get away with this,' insisted Debby, speaking in low tones so as not to be overheard by the other patrons in the crowded café. 'Can she, Barbara?'

Barbara Moore nodded, her pale blue eyes suffused with sympathy. 'Debby's right, Anna. If someone doesn't stand up to him, there'll be no end to this.'

Anna smiled to acknowledge her friends' support. Debby Johnson and Barbara Moore, themselves best friends and each the other's closest confidante, had made Anna welcome since her first day on the job at N.T.E.L. Their valuable advice on company programming and the processing of information had made Anna's first months of work a pleasant and exciting experience. And now that Anna had been given greater responsibility and was their office supervisor, Barbara and Debby were far from envious, but more cheerful and supportive than ever.

Unlike her rather plump, impish friend, Barbara was a tall, willowy young woman whose shy demeanour and delicate beauty seemed to bring out the best in all who knew her. She touched Anna's hand concernedly now, as though feeling in her own breast the insult her friend had suffered.

'I'm not sure what I can do,' Anna sighed. 'If Deman isn't bluffing, I'm going to be fired on some pretext or other. But I don't know what it will be, or when it will happen.'

'Look,' said Debby, 'the important thing is that you acted

properly. You did the right thing. You have nothing to feel bad about, except the insult of being threatened by that lecher. But now you have to go on doing the right thing. If you don't blow the whistle on this creep, he's going to terrorise every girl in this department, and get away with it. Think of everybody else, Anna.'

'But suppose they don't believe me?' Anna said thoughtfully. 'Deman seemed certain that the executives would take his word over mine.'

'You have to take that chance,' Debby insisted. 'But you may be too worried about it. Nobody around here is more respected than you. I think they'll take your word over his, even if they don't have the guts to fire him.'

'Who should I see?' Anna asked hesitantly.

'Well,' Debby sighed, 'there's no sense going to the President, he doesn't know you. You can try Chuck Robbins. He's in charge of Personnel, so it's really his problem. Or Bob Samuels: he's a good man, he would be fair. Also, he knows your work.'

'But that would be going outside channels,' Anna objected. 'Bob is in Research. I don't think he would know what to do.'

'I guess you're right,' agreed Debby, darting a glance at Barbara, who nodded uncertainly. 'Try Robbins, then. But don't wait: call him this afternoon. See him right away, if you can. If you tell him that Deman is going to try to get you fired, he'll know what's going on. What do you say?'

Anna sighed, chagrined at the prospect of admitting to an executive she knew only slightly that she had been the victim of harassment. Debby's words rang true, however. Chuck Robbins had the reputation of a demanding but fair boss. Nevertheless, Anna reflected with an involuntary shudder, there might be truth in Porter Deman's words. Perhaps the battle was lost already.

'All right,' she said determinedly. 'It can't do any harm,

even if it doesn't do any of us any good—least of all me. Porter Deman promised me I would never find work again if I said anything about this.'

'All the more reason,' insisted Debby, 'to go to Robbins. If he's warned before anything happens, he can use his influence in your behalf. After all, who's to say that Deman won't make good on his threat regardless of what you do? You might as well have someone on your side, Anna. Isn't that right, Barbara?'

Barbara nodded weakly. Since the beginning of the conversation, Anna had noticed, Barbara seemed even more diffident and quiet than usual, and her face bore a pained expression.

'I'm going to have to go,' she said. 'I have a call to make before I go back to work. I'll see you in the office, okay?' She squeezed Anna's hand gently. 'It will work out,' she said. 'You'll see, Anna.'

As she watched Barbara's slender form wending its way among the restaurant's crowded tables, Anna felt a pang of sympathy for her. Barbara was such a sweet, gentle creature. If something like this ever happened to her...

All at once the truth glimmered in Anna's mind. Barbara had disappeared through the revolving door. As she turned back to Debby, she could see a look of sad confirmation in the woman's brown eyes.

'You mean...?' asked Anna.

'That's right,' said Debby. 'Barbara. Deman has been putting the same number on her that you're getting now. She's such a sweet girl, so vulnerable... She's no match for him. She really needs the job. It's an absolute crime!'

Waves of impotent sympathy for Barbara shook Anna, who thought with horror of Porter Deman's cruelty.

'That's why she just left,' Debby continued. 'I knew she wanted me to tell you. Don't you see, Anna? She doesn't have your strength. That's why it would mean a lot to her if you talk to Robbins. You'll be doing it for Barbara as well as for yourself.' Abruptly, she laughed. 'And maybe for me. I know I'm not good-looking, the way you two are—that's why he hasn't bothered me. But if somebody doesn't do something, he'll get around to me eventually. I know his type.' Her face darkened. 'It isn't sex he's after: it's power. He gets his thrills out of terrorising women. The physical part is the least important.'

'All right,' Anna said firmly. 'Before I leave work today, I'm going to call Chuck Robbins. I'll make an appointment to see him.'

'That's the spirit, Anna,' Debby smiled. 'He'll listen to you, don't worry.'

'Whether he listens to me or not,' Anna frowned, 'he's going to get an idea of what's going on around here.'

But in Debby's eyes there was more sympathy than hope, Anna reflected.

As she walked the short block separating the restaurant from N.T.E.L.'s headquarters, Anna was nearly oblivious to the throng of traffic and pedestrians around her. Chicago's bustling Loop seemed even more vibrant than usual on this crisp autumn day. An El train roared overhead as Anna waited for the light to change. In the distance she could see Lake Michigan, its blue expanse broken by a solitary sail. The enormous public parking lots adjacent to the Art Institute heightened the impression of urban vitality crowded close to the Lake's cold, choppy water.

With a firm smile of determination Anna approached the revolving doors leading to N.T.E.L.'s spacious lobby. Her thoughts absorbed by the turn of events which now menaced the job she had pursued with pleasure for four years, she imagined herself telling the unpleasant truth to a shocked Charles Robbins.

On one hand, Porter Deman's behaviour seemed absurd

and almost laughable. One reads about sexual harassment in the newspapers, Anna thought, but when one meets it face to face in the form of an arrogant, ageing executive, it seems both pathetic and ridiculous. Porter Deman had received the brisk slap he richly deserved. Although her meeting with Chuck Robbins would be intensely embarrassing, the ordeal would be well worth her trouble.

On the other hand, she thought with a suppressed shudder, the loss of her job at N.T.E.L. would be a crisis requiring immediate and perhaps desperate action. The slightest gap in her earnings would upset the delicate balance which maintained her own life while paying her sister Sally's college tuition.

Five years ago, when she had first moved to Chicago, life had been far simpler, for she had only herself to consider. She was fresh out of college, and looking for an interesting career. The family was safe and happy in Bloomington, and Sally was a freshman in high school.

Then abruptly, with Dad's crippling heart attack and Mother's illness, life had changed. Anna was still haunted by the memory of the two of them forcing smiles through their pain, and of her mute understanding that the impossible tragedy of losing both parents to incurable disease was actually to befall her. As the medical bills mounted, prompting concerned talks with the family's attorney, Anna realised that she must help Sally accept the inevitability of becoming an orphan at the age of seventeen.

In the fearfully short space of two anguished years, Mother and Dad were both gone. Both their daughters had been forced to grow up quickly—too quickly, in Sally's case, Anna had feared.

But somehow she had managed it. Sally had finished high school with good grades, and since Anna was now a resident of Illinois, she had agreed to attend college in Chicago, where the tuition was mercifully low. The urban university was certainly not the bucolic college campus Anna had wished for her sister, but it was better than nothing at all, and Sally had seemed to honestly want to be near Anna. The two sisters called each other often, and their relationship seemed cemented by the tragic circumstances that had left them alone in life.

Despite the strain on her meagre finances, Anna was delighted to be able to assure Sally of the advanced education she herself had enjoyed under happier conditions. Her salary increases at N.T.E.L. had somehow kept pace with the high cost of living, and in another two years, when Sally was on her own, Anna would be proud to think that her parents' wishes for their younger daughter had come true.

But now the loathsome scheming of Porter Deman threatened to jeopardize everything. Sally held a part-time job already, and could not possibly earn more without sacrificing the precious hours required for her studies. If Anna were to lose her position at N.T.E.L., she would have to find work at a comparable salary without delay.

'It can't happen,' she thought determinedly as the elevator stopped at her floor. 'I won't let it happen.' Whatever Chuck Robbins' attitude might be, she would somehow make him see the truth.

'I told you we'd be running into each other.' A deep voice startled her from her reverie, and she looked up to see Marsh Hamilton standing before her in the carpeted corridor.

'Mr Hamilton!' she exclaimed with a little gasp of surprise. 'I didn't see you. I guess I was lost in thought again. This is turning out to be a busy day.'

'Marsh,' he corrected, his black eyes holding her with their penetrating gaze. 'Remember?'

'Marsh,' she smiled. 'Yes, of course.' Her diffident glance once more encountered the hint of mockery in his

expression. But warm friendliness was evident in his relaxed demeanour as he returned her smile.

'To be entirely truthful,' he said, 'I was hoping I'd cross
your path again today.'

Still a trifle stunned by his sudden appearance, Anna
could think of no response.

'You might be able to help me out with something,' he
went on. 'If you'd be willing, that is.'

'Of course,' she smiled, 'if it's in my power—which I
doubt. I'm just a small cog around here, you know.'

'I don't feel I quite have a handle on the flow of information within your company,' he told her. 'You seem to
me the sort of person who would have a good understanding of it.'

'That's an overstatement,' Anna laughed, doing her best
to suppress the tingle of fascination she felt in his tall presence. For the first time she noticed the careless waves of
black hair over his tanned face, their expanse accentuating
the roguish energy which harmonised mysteriously with his
air of taut determination. 'I know where our data comes
from, and where we send it, if that's any help. Would you
like to see how our office runs?'

'No, I won't interrupt your work,' he answered, 'since
you say it's a busy day. How about dinner tonight?'

Taken aback by the abruptness of his invitation, Anna
struggled to collect her thoughts.

'This is rather sudden,' she replied weakly. 'Are you sure
you wouldn't do better to speak with someone else? I mean,
someone in a more responsible position?'

'Positive,' he said simply, his slight smile betokening
amusement at her hesitation. 'Eight o'clock?'

'Really, Mr...' she began.

'Marsh,' he insisted, his teasing grin widening.

'Marsh, then,' she said, exasperated by his bluntness no
less than by the undeniable ferment his powerful presence

was creating in her senses. 'I'm afraid I really couldn't make it tonight,' she went on, her thoughts returning to the unpleasant interviews she must have with Charles Robbins. Against the background of this morning's events, it seemed essential to maintain an attitude of grim concentration. Marsh Hamilton's disturbing effect on her could hardly contribute to the mood of determination she sought.

'Tomorrow night, then?' he pursued. 'Really, you'd be doing me a favour. Will you be busy?'

'No,' she admitted. 'But are you quite sure...'

'For the second time,' he interrupted, 'yes, I'm sure, Anna. May I call you Anna?'

She nodded in consternation. 'It's awfully nice of you,' she said, 'to invite me...'

'It's settled, then,' he concluded simply. 'Eight o'clock?'

'All right,' she gave in. 'Let me give you my address.'

She could feel the caressing warmth of his gaze upon her as she fumbled in her bag for a piece of paper. After hurriedly writing her address, she held it out and watched his large hand cover it.

'It's on the near north side,' she explained.

'I'll find it,' he said without looking at the paper which had disappeared into his palm. 'I'll be looking forward to seeing you.'

With a calm smile he took his leave of her, and she went into her office, still disconcerted by the gamut of emotions she had been through in one short morning. Coming on the heels of the disgust and exasperation occasioned by Porter Deman's threats, Marsh Hamilton's handsome form and obvious interest in her had shocked her senses. But there was no denying the frank attraction she felt in his presence, she reasoned, and no sensible pretext for refusing his invitation.

Perhaps, indeed, things would be straightened out by tomorrow night, and she would be in a more relaxed frame of mind. If, that was, her meeting with Charles Robbins accomplished its purpose.

With a deep breath she reached for the telephone, hoping that his secretary would be able to fit her in for an appointment as soon as possible.

As though to nip her hopes in the bud, a memo caught her eye on the desk before her, and she returned the receiver to its place without completing the call.

'Please come to my office tomorrow 10 a.m.,' the memo read. Charles Robbins' hasty signature was scrawled under the message.

For a long moment Anna sat in silence, regarding the blunt words before her. She had not dealt directly with Charles since a new research assistant had been hired for her department several months ago. In her four years at N.T.E.L. she had never received such a message summoning her to his office.

Suddenly the image of Porter Deman's cold eyes entered her consciousness. Perhaps she had underestimated the immediacy of his threat. Perhaps, after all, he was not bluffing.

CHAPTER TWO

CHARLES ROBBINS' physiognomy had always seemed to Anna the very incarnation of the Middle American man. With his greying hair, his amiably rounded features, and the slight bulge of his midriff, Chuck called up images of lazy Saturday afternoons, noisy children, and a front lawn not yet mowed, because Dad was watching a baseball game after his hard week of work. Indeed, Chuck's friendliness bordered on sheepish diffidence as he reluctantly gave orders to his assistants and secretaries. Although he did his work well, and had dealt with many a delicate crisis in Personnel, the gentle look in his blue eyes always seemed to betoken the secret wish that he were somewhere else, reclining beside a fishing pole by a stream perhaps, or watching from a lazy porch swing as his children played.

But this morning Charles Robbins' apologetic smile was not in evidence as he ushered Anna to the chair before his desk. His expression was pained as he settled himself into his swivel chair and cleared his throat.

'Anna,' he said uncomfortably, 'I wonder if you could tell me whether you've ever had occasion to use our computers on the WR-3-A material.'

'WR-3-A?' Anna repeated in perplexity. 'Isn't that military?'

'It's arms sales and agreements,' he informed her. 'The Middle East, to be exact.'

'No,' she said, wondering what on earth such a subject had to do with her own difficulties. 'Our department hasn't

touched a military subject in my four years at N.T.E.L. That
would be the fifth floor, if I'm not mistaken—Mr Panar-
iello's department. Why do you ask?'

'You're quite sure,' he insisted uneasily, 'you've had no
contact with that material.'

'Absolutely sure,' she answered firmly.

'Well,' he sighed, 'this is very difficult for me, Anna.
Very embarrassing. A whole series of print-outs from that
file has been found in your desk. So,' he cleared his throat,
'I'm asking you how you think it might have got there.'
He hesitated before adding superfluously, 'Series A 16.'

'It's impossible,' Anna responded, 'I don't have any use
for that material, nor do I have clearance to pull it in the
first place. It couldn't have been in my desk, unless there's
some mistake.' Too late, she began to realise the import of
Charles Robbins's words.

'Anna,' he sighed, 'this is really very difficult, very painful for me. Please, don't say anything now until I'm finished.' He twisted uncomfortably in his chair. 'N.T.E.L. is,
as you know, an information processing company. Our clients confide data in us for analysis, and our job is to advise
them on the patterns and implications of the information
we study. It is, of course, essential that the client trust in
our absolute confidentiality. Our reputation is based on that
trust.'

His gaze was directed through the tinted panes of the
windows to the skyscrapers along the horizon. At intervals
he darted a glance to Anna's eyes. 'Naturally,' he went on,
'as big as we are, one of our most valued clients is the
Federal Government. In order to fulfill our Government
contracts, we have to work with classified material, so our
personnel has to be organised in terms of security clearance. If an employee is found to have handled material for
which he or she was not cleared, that employee has to be
let go—immediately. The reputation of the entire company

is at stake, of course, so, inhuman as it seems, I must say the rule is necessary.'

He looked at the file on the desk top before him. 'Now,' he went on, 'this material was pulled from the computer under your personal access code. 1289, isn't it?'

Anna nodded, realising what had happened, and that it was impossible to prove her innocence.

'The classification code was punched in, of course, or the computer wouldn't have responded,' he said. 'Although you didn't have clearance for this material, you know the company well enough to be aware of the various classification codes.' A forced look of anger came over his naturally friendly features. 'I have no choice but to let you go, Anna—I'm sure you realise that. But I know what motivated your action. Who put you up to it, so to speak. I think,' he added, 'I'm in a position to say that if you give me that information, it will go easier for you.'

Anna sighed. It was obvious what had happened. Porter Deman had simply used her access code to pull the WR-3-A material, had had it printed out, and brought it straight to Charles Robbins.

'May I ask,' she said, 'who discovered this material in my desk? Who brought it to your attention?'

'You know I can't tell you that,' he answered, irritation in his voice. 'Naturally I have to protect the source against possible reprisals. Besides, it doesn't make any difference who found it; what matters is that it was there. Now are you going to tell me why you wanted this file?'

Bitterly, Anna pondered the efficiency of Porter Deman's strategy. There was no way she could defend herself convincingly.

'I never pulled that file,' she said simply. 'I would have no reason to look at it, and I never did look at it. There's either some mistake, or...or I don't know what.'

Charles Robbins sighed. Plainly, he had expected just such a denial.

'So,' he said, 'you don't intend to tell me who put you up to this?'

'No one put me up to anything,' she retorted, angered by the tone of his words. 'I've never seen that file.'

'Then we're at a standstill, aren't we?' he said.

Desperately Anna searched her memory of the company's operations to find a way of exposing Porter Deman's treachery. But it was impossible. He had clearly acted immediately, so that she would be accused of a security breach before she had time to report his harassment to Charles Robbins, or anyone else. Now the classified file was a *fait accompli*, and her own explanation of the situation would sound like a desperate and improbable attempt at self-defence.

'I'm afraid,' she said simply, 'I can't enlighten you about this. I've worked for this company for four years, and never had any problems. I know nothing about the file you're talking about. Beyond my own work record and reputation within the company, I can't offer anything to support what I say. It happens to be the truth, however.' Bitterly she heard the hollow ring of her words.

Chuck was staring at her with a perplexed intensity.

'Anna,' he said at last, 'I'm going to have to let you go. You can understand, of course, why that is unavoidable. But in view of your spotless record with the company, and my personal regard for you, I'm going to take a chance. I may regret it, but I can't help believing it's the right thing to do. I'm going to notate this as a termination due to employee incompatibility in your personnel file. I will not mention the present episode. This will give you the opportunity to find work in this field, or at least in computers. Of course, any mention in your file of a security breach would be disastrous to you.'

She nodded quietly, too hurt and angry to thank him for his magnanimity, yet grateful for his gesture.

'But before I do so,' he added, 'and in view of your excellent work for us, I want to give you one last chance to tell me what's behind this business. I'm ready to listen to whatever you have to say.'

Anna sat uncomfortably in the massive leather chair before his desk. What was the point of saying anything? Porter Deman had been diabolically clever.

Nevertheless, the thought of Barbara and Debby, and all the other women who might someday share her unfortunate fate, drove her to speak.

'Mr Robbins,' she began, 'I can see that it's too late for me to defend myself in a believable way, beyond pointing out that everyone at N.T.E.L. knows me well enough to see the...absurdity of this accusation. But I'll tell you what I think is behind it, for your own information.'

He regarded her in silence, awaiting her explanation.

'This is embarrassing for me as well,' Anna went on, 'but I'll say it anyway. I was asked by one of our executives to do something improper. Something that didn't have anything to do with the company, but improper in any case. I refused. When I did so, I was told that my days here were numbered. And now, as you can see, I'm being fired.'

'Which executive? What sort of impropriety?' Suspicion vied with acute interest in Charles' troubled eyes.

'I don't feel inclined to mention the person's name,' Anna sighed, 'since I'm leaving you anyway, and since an accusation coming from me obviously wouldn't carry much weight. Perhaps you'd better investigate the situation for yourself.' She took a deep breath. 'The impropriety...has to do with the fact that I'm a woman.'

In consternation he turned once more to look at the skyline, his lips pursed, before returning his gaze to her.

'You're talking about harassment,' he said, articulating the words with a grunt of displeasure.

Anna made no response.

'But you won't say who the culprit is.'

'I'd prefer not to.' Despite her determined tone, she felt herself flush in embarrassment.

'When did this ultimatum, as you describe it, take place?' he asked.

'Do you mean...?'

'I mean, when were you told you were going to lose your job, as a consequence of not going along with this improper proposal?'

'Yesterday,' Anna replied. 'I had intended to make an appointment with you right away, but I got your memo before I could call your secretary. The...situation,' she added, 'had been going on for some time before it reached the point of this threat.'

His eyes were riveted to the file on the desk top before him.

'Anna,' he said, 'nobody likes it when the word harassment rears its ugly head. We know it takes place occasionally, but we don't like to admit that it could happen here.'

'It came as quite a shock to me, too,' Anna said ruefully.

'You're not understanding me,' he frowned. 'Coming as it does on the heels of this very serious security breach, your explanation is not very convincing.'

'I know,' she began. 'I already...'

'And there's another thing to consider,' he interrupted, his pained expression betraying the annoyance he felt in his inquisitor's role. 'This file was pulled over a week ago. The employee who brought it to me had hesitated for several days—out of regard for you, I might add, and disbelief—to make its existence known. Now how do you explain that all this started long before the so-called ultimatum you describe?'

In silence Anna weighed the importance of his words. Porter Deman must have found a way to pre-date his pulling of the file from the computer's memory. Anna herself could not imagine a procedure which could override the machine's automatic dating mechanism, but Deman, she knew, was a past master at programming.

On the other hand, she thought, perhaps he had in fact pulled the file days before his final confrontation with her, as a weapon to be kept in reserve against her. Perhaps, in his calculating cruelty, he secreted such evidence against all his prospective victims.

Clearly there was no defence of herself that could compete with the power and expertise of such a twisted mind.

'Well?' Charles Robbins asked.

'I can't explain that,' she replied. 'I know only that for four years I worked here without any problems. Then this business started. When I refused to do what I was asked, I was told I would lose my job. Now it's all over.'

Despite the expression of exasperated stubbornness on his face, Charles seemed to be weighing her words carefully.

'A name would help, Anna,' he said at last with visible discomfort. 'It might help a great deal.'

For a long moment Anna hesitated, her hopeless outrage and involuntary shame threatening to reduce her to silence.

'You suggested,' he prodded, 'that I investigate the situation for myself. Now, a name...'

The memory of Barbara Moore's delicate vulnerability decided Anna at last to speak.

'Porter Deman,' she said abruptly. 'And for your information, Mr. Robbins, I'm not his only...victim.'

Hardly had she begun to pronounce the distasteful syllables when the man before her began to shake his head. With pursed lips and furrowed brow, Charles seemed at once to want to interrupt her and to blot out what he had heard.

'That's going a little far, Anna,' he said reproachfully. 'Porter Deman is a very valuable man to this company. We went to great lengths to acquire his services. He has a spotless reputation in the field, and no one has ever accused him of anything even approaching what you're talking about.'

'I wouldn't know about that,' Anna replied. 'I only know that my troubles started when he joined this company. And as I say, I'm not the only…'

'All right,' he cut her off. 'You've said what you wanted to say. And, as I've told you, the situation leaves me no choice but to do what I must do. I'll make good on my promise to keep this problem out of your personnel file. As I see it, nothing remains but to wish you the best of luck in whatever you choose to do.'

'Thank you,' sighed Anna, standing up to leave. Clearly, his haste to end the interview betrayed the incredulity he felt, or wanted to feel. His hands were tied within the company, and they both knew it. Porter Deman had won. There was nothing left but to admit defeat.

'Anna,' he stopped her, 'I really am terribly sorry about this.'

'So am I,' she said, her hand on the doorknob.

'If I can be of any help in any way…' He had arisen, the friendly contours of his overweight body and rumpled suit contradicting his rigid expression.

'I'll get along,' she responded proudly. 'But there are other women in the company who need your help, Mr. Robbins. I'd suggest you give some thought to them.' She closed the door behind her.

Charles Robbins settled exhaustedly into his desk chair. The worst part of this job, he reflected, was letting people go. So embarrassing. So contrary to his helpful nature.

How could she do it? he wondered in perplexity. Of all people, he never would have suspected Anna Halpern of being a security risk. She was the very bedrock of her department, and that was why she had been promoted to supervisor two years ago. The thing strained credulity. Yet there was no denying the evidence.

'Well,' he sighed, 'it's impossible to know what motivates people. She seemed so stable, and now she comes out with this cock-and-bull story...

'What's the use?' he thought, reaching to touch his intercom button. 'Such a good-looking woman, too. I'll be sorry not to see her around any more.'

'Yes, sir?' squawked his secretary's voice, amplified by the intercom.

'Who's up?' he asked.

'Mrs Adamson is here. Then Mr Foley, then Bob Hamer, and the Miss Moore who called you yesterday.'

'All right,' he said. 'Hold them all. Just a minute.' His finger still pressed against the button, he stared blankly before him. If there was one thing he had learned in business, it was to anticipate the unexpected. At all costs, one must cover all the bases, and spread responsibility evenly. Never sit on top of a situation alone.

'Sir?' Perplexity resounded in the female voice.

What the hell, he decided. Let's be on the safe side.

'Get me Porter Deman,' he said aloud.

Two hours later Anna sat disconsolately at the table in the dining nook of her flat, contemplating the unfamiliarity of the muted midday sounds filtering through the window. Never since she moved in had she been at home on a week day. The unaccustomed atmosphere, combined with the strange faces of the noontime passengers on her Michigan Avenue bus, was intensely disconcerting, and she had to struggle to control the panic that threatened to take possession of her.

Silvery motes of dust floated lazily in the sunlight streaming in the window. The only sound in the room was Anna's turning of the want ads pages, and the quiet friction of lead against paper as she circled the jobs she intended to apply for.

Determined to remain calm and retain her concentration at all costs, she had bought the latest newspapers at the counter in N.T.E.L.'s lobby, glancing for a last time at the banks of shiny elevators and plush expanse of carpet before pushing through the revolving doors to the sunlit street outside.

A few minutes' study had revealed that the *Tribune* and *Sun-Times* contained the same basic listing of available jobs in computer operation and information processing. As soon as she had made herself a light lunch, she would begin making phone calls in preparation for what would undoubtedly be an exhausting siege of interviews.

Only one course of action made sense, she reflected. There was no point in alarming Sally immediately with the news of her firing. Sally would be upset and, in all probability, would generously insist on suspending her education in order to go to work full-time herself. But things had not yet reached that extremity. The severance pay which would arrive from N.T.E.L. in a matter of days would suffice to finance Anna's rent and the loan payments for Sally's tuition—for a few weeks. If Anna could manage somehow to find a position comparable to her supervisor's job at N.T.E.L., it might be possible to survive this crisis without disturbing the routine that had governed the two sisters' lives for the past two years.

Thank heaven for Charles Robbins' leniency, Anna thought with a shudder. If he had not decided to leave her personnel file free of Porter Deman's grotesque accusation, she would have no chance of finding a responsible job with a salary sufficient for Sally's tuition. Even as things stood, though, it was unlikely that as a new employee somewhere else she could command the salary she had reached through her pay raises at N.T.E.L.

'Let's hope for the best,' she said to herself as she circled another want ad, 'and not get panicky.' Clinging to what remained of her pride, she recalled the first weeks after her mother's death, when it had seemed impossible to earn enough for herself and Sally at the same time. She had used her wits to cope with things then, and she would do so now.

A shiver of anger interrupted her disciplined reasoning as she remembered the cause of her troubles. She imagined Porter Deman seated comfortably in his office, pursuing his work day as though nothing had happened, while the woman he had victimised pored desperately through the want ads in search of a solution to the crisis he had created. The thought of his impunity, and of his complacency, was infuriating. In all probability it would never occur to him that he had nearly ruined a woman's career. His only regret would be that he had not succeeded in intimidating her into giving herself to him physically. And now, as he sat in the swivel chair behind his executive desk, he was probably wondering who his next victim might be. Or perhaps deciding to renew his exploitation of someone familiar. Perhaps Barbara...

With a shudder Anna suppressed the image of Porter Deman's perverted sensuality and triumphant arrogance. He had won his battle, and was more than welcome to the turf he controlled. She would be far better off somewhere else.

She had not had the courage to discuss the reason for her dismissal with Debby and Barbara before leaving the office this morning. Despite their supportive kindness and questioning looks, she had told them only that the inevitable had happened, and that she needed time to think.

But what was there to think about? Charles Robbins was now in possession of all the information needed to launch an investigation that might expose Porter Deman and exonerate Anna. But his irascible, unwilling demeanour was ample evidence that he had no such intention.

Briefly Anna had toyed with the idea of taking legal action in her own behalf. If N.T.E.L. were forced to justify her termination in a civil suit, the fact of her innocence might somehow be established. Porter Deman's hand must surely be visible behind the denunciating of Anna, even if, in his malicious cleverness, he had had someone else to do his dirty work for him.

On the other hand, she thought resignedly, Porter Deman had anticipated just such a move on her part. Her credibility as a plaintiff would surely be compromised by the classified file planted in her desk. In order to claim that she was a victim, she would first have to prove she was not a thief and a security risk. And where was she to find the time, not to mention the money, for a legal battle of uncertain outcome? Her memory told her that litigation concerning harassment was a complex, controversial affair in which victimised women were anything but assured of success.

Only one course of action made sense, she told herself. She must find another job immediately, and put the past behind her. Perhaps there was a way to root out and eliminate the evil that Porter Deman had brought to an unsuspecting company—if, that was, the company as a whole was truly innocent of such goings-on—but nothing could avenge his victims. And Anna was among them. There was no changing what had happened; only the future mattered now.

Finding the silence of the flat intolerable, Anna quickly ate a container of yogurt and began telephoning prospective employers in the downtown area. Searching her memory of the Loop's busy streets, she resolved to fill out applications at three locations within walking distance of each other. After boarding the Fullerton Avenue bus, which was sparsely filled with passengers dressed in casual clothes, she began to plan what to say in her interviews.

Of course she would be asked why she had left N.T.E.L. Since Charles Robbins had notated employee incompatibility as the reason for her termination, the best course was to tell a story not far from the truth. Although formerly happy at N.T.E.L., she would say, she found it impossible to work with a new department manager who had been hired six months ago. Her personnel file, along with Mr. Robbins' written responses to enquiries from prospective employers, would, she hoped, reflect her raises, her increased responsibility, and her good work record.

Four hours later she was aboard her bus once more, in the company of the same preoccupied rush-hour faces she had grown familiar with over four years. Time had permitted only two of the interviews she had planned. As expected, the personnel managers she spoke to seemed impressed by her credentials, but spoke of a lower salary than she had in mind. Nevertheless, they noted, her abilities seemed to promise rapid advancement and an increase in pay. She would be contacted, they claimed, after the weekend—'one way or the other'.

'Which means not at all,' she thought now as the bus stopped in front of her building, 'unless I get the job.' Whoever had said that looking for a job is the hardest job in the world was certainly right, she reflected. The unfamiliarity of offices never before seen, the lengthy applications, the enquiring faces of strangers whose need of help never seemed as urgent as one's own need for a job, made for a profoundly exhausting afternoon.

After a few moments spent poring anew over the newspapers, in search of companies to contact tomorrow, Anna made herself a cup of tea and thought without enthusiasm about what to make for dinner. For a long moment she sat staring blankly at the bland furnishings of the flat, and listening to the city's busy sounds outside. The sinking feeling of alienation brought on by unemployment haunted her as she reflected on the hubbub of activity all around her. Everyone was working, rushing to a job, taking the bus or subway, stopping for lunch at a café, buying new clothes... The whole metropolis maintained its tumultuous rhythm through the people it employed. To be sitting at sixes and sevens, alone in this flat whose perpetually gathering dust and persistent leaking tap were her only companions, seemed intolerably lonely.

Perhaps, she decided, a phone call to Sally would cheer her up. She knew Sally was to leave the city this weekend for a visit to her room-mate's family. Now was as good a time as any to telephone her and enquire casually about her plans, without, of course, mentioning the truth about her own situation. The prospect of hearing a friendly voice, after this day of atrocious solitude, was comforting.

As she reached for the receiver, a thought stole over her mind with such suddenness that her hand stopped in midair.

She had forgotten that she was not to be alone tonight after all.

'Marsh Hamilton,' she whispered to herself, cursing her absentmindedness. 'He'll be here at eight o'clock!'

Without a glance at the wall clock in the kitchen she stood up and hurried towards the bathroom. There was ample time for a shower and shampoo before Marsh's arrival, but the idea that she had nearly forgotten all about him lent an involuntary urgency to her movements.

The image of his probing black eyes and calmly determined demeanour followed her into the bedroom, and she shuddered briefly to think of the shocks her nerves had suffered throughout this eventual day. But it was not without a trace of silent expectancy that she dropped her dress into the clothes hamper and began thinking about what she would wear tonight.

She had underestimated the amount of time she would need to get ready, for she had barely finished dressing and brushing her hair when the buzzer sounded.

CHAPTER THREE

ANNA glanced for a last time at the swirled mane of her auburn hair in the bedroom mirror before hurrying to the door. The pale green fabric of the dress she had chosen, silky and iridescent in the light of the vanity lamp, was a perfect counterpoint to the creamy complexion surrounding her deep green irises.

She had wondered briefly whether the sleek garment was too revealing for her first private encounter with a man so direct and virile as Marsh Hamilton. But she reflected in all honesty that his dauntingly firm features and hard body had attracted her interest from the outset, and she wanted to look her best for him. Besides, after the depressing events of the last two days her self-respect dictated that she take pride in her healthy beauty.

The door opened to reveal Marsh standing calmly under the pale light of the hallway, the light raincoat over his arm glowing against the dark-toned business suit he wore. Again Anna was astonished by his erect, imposing stature. The outlines of his taut thighs and hard shoulders were visible under the fabric covering them, so that one might mistake him for an athlete dressed in business clothes rather than a professional man.

'So you found me,' she smiled.

'It wasn't difficult. I grew up in this town, so I know the North Side pretty well.' The expression in his dark eyes was unfathomable in the dim light.

'Please come in,' said Anna, standing aside as he entered the living room with long strides.

'Something told me you might wear green,' he said, throwing his coat on a chair and turning to her. For the first time she noticed the small florist's box in his large hand. 'Let's see if this goes with it,' he added, producing a lovely white orchid tinged with blue and green. 'May I?'

'You shouldn't have,' she protested as he pinned the flower to her dress, his long fingers working expertly. 'It's too beautiful.' A breath of the crisp outside air had entered the room with him, and as his clean male scent reached her nostrils she began to feel the potent force of his nearness. Its influence was immediate, and frankly delightful.

'There,' he said, ignoring her words. 'I think it suits you fine. You look beautiful, Anna.' There was blunt admiration in his compliment, and she recognised once more his habit of coming directly to the point.

'You're nice to say so,' she said, trying to forget the electric intimacy of his touch. 'I'm afraid I may have over-dressed for our evening.'

'Not at all,' he smiled. 'You'll be the toast of Pierre's. Do you like French food?'

'I love it,' she said, visualising the elegant façade of the legendary establishment in Michigan Avenue's most wealthy block. 'Pierre's will be a new experience for me. My budget has never allowed me to do more than pass it on the bus.'

'Good,' he said, regarding her with undisguised appraisal.

'Perhaps you'd like something to drink?' she asked, blushing slightly under his probing gaze.

'Whatever you're having,' he said.

'Please sit down,' she invited, turning to move towards the kitchen. His tall form seemed to dwarf the small living room as he scanned its furnishings.

'Nice place you have here,' came his deep voice from behind as she filled two glasses with ice and opened the whisky bottle she kept on hand for guests.

'Thanks,' she called over her shoulder. 'It's not very elegant, but I like this neighbourhood, and my bus stops right outside the door.'

'I see you take your work seriously,' he remarked, pointing to the computer magazines and journals on the coffee table as she set down the drinks.

She shrugged, not eager to explain the fact that she had lost the job which had caused her to cross his path two days ago. 'I find it interesting,' she contented herself with replying.

'Did you always want to work in computers?' he asked.

'Actually, I majored in Economics in college,' she recalled. 'The computer courses I took were in the nature of a hobby. Then, when I started looking for work here, I sort of fell into the job at N.T.E.L.' Impelled despite herself to change the subject, she asked, 'How about you? Did you always want to be a lawyer?'

'Always,' he said. 'I went through a five-year Law programme here at the University so as to get college over with in a hurry. Then I went to work for the District Attorney, to gain some experience in criminal law. As it turned out, I stayed with them for eight years. Then I joined our firm.'

'Have you switched to corporation law, then?' Anna asked.

'No. I'm working on this N.T.E.L. contract because John Feuerbach is tied up at the moment. Normally I handle the criminal work for the firm. I stay in contact with my old friends from the D.A.'s office, and run into them in court pretty often—on opposing sides, now.' His lips curled in a slight smile, and Anna noticed for the first time that the clean line of his jaw was marked by a tiny scar.

'Looking at this?' he grinned, touching the spot with a long finger. 'That's one of my souvenirs from my days as a prosecutor.'

'What happened?' asked Anna, unable to contain her curiosity.

'Well,' he said, 'some of us used to work closely with the detectives on stake-outs. When you deal with organised crime, you have to be careful of your legal footing. I often helped in arrests. I got this,' he pointed to the scar, 'when one of our targets decided not to go quietly. It was my own fault, really. I should have stayed in the background. But we were outnumbered, and we had to get them while the evidence was right there.'

'And did you?' she asked. 'Get them, I mean.'

'Oh, yes,' he smiled ruefully. 'But they ended up on the street again in no time. That's one reason I finally got sick of being a prosecutor. We got plenty of convictions, but the criminal justice system wasn't equipped to handle organised crime. The big boys could always hide behind plea-bargaining or some other protection. So I decided to go out on my own.'

'Has it been…satisfying for you?' asked Anna, a trifle disconcerted by the penetrating eyes that regarded her as she spoke.

'Yes, I'm happy with the law,' he concluded easily. 'It's a complex sort of business, full of ambiguities. But quite often I have the chance to really make a difference for someone who's in trouble. Someone who might have fallen on hard times without my help. What about you?' He changed the subject abruptly.

'Me?' Anna asked hesitantly.

'Is your work satisfying for you?' His black eyes were upon her with their teasing intensity.

All at once she sighed to think that it was impossible to hold back the truth any longer. She was sitting here with him under false pretences, and the very reason for their dinner together had fallen away with her job itself.

'It was…satisfying,' she began uncomfortably.

'What do you mean?'

'I know this is going to sound strange,' she said, forcing a rueful smile. 'I left N.T.E.L. this morning. I'm not working there any more.'

'You're kidding!' Incredulity vied with intent curiosity in his quirked brow and alert eyes.

'I wish I were kidding,' she sighed. 'The fact is, Mr Marsh—that I'm worth less than nothing to you as a source of information about the way the company works. I suppose I should have thought of a way to inform you of what had happened, so you wouldn't have had to go to the trouble of coming all the way over here. But I was so busy today…' She felt her cheeks colour with chagrin.

'What happened?' he asked simply.

'It's…it's not something I'd prefer to talk about,' she replied. 'Let's just say it wasn't working out, so now I'm looking for something else.'

'Well,' he smiled, 'the world certainly is a fast moving place. If I hadn't bumped into you in the corridor at N.T.E.L. and invited you out tonight, I might never have met you at all. I guess I made it in the nick of time.'

Anna had the distinct impression that he was prepared to respect her reticence regarding the loss of her job, and indeed had other things on his mind. But the false position she found herself in was nearly intolerable.

In silence he watched her, as though in speculation as to her inner feelings.

'So you see,' she went on, avoiding his eyes, 'there isn't really any reason for our meeting. If you'd like to change your mind…'

A low, amused laugh escaped his lips.

'Is something funny?' she asked, disturbed by his un-flappable calm.

'No,' he said. 'Nothing is funny. I'm laughing at my own luck. If I hadn't encountered you when I did, I wouldn't have known that you existed. Instead, I'm sitting here admiring a beautiful woman who's wearing the orchid I brought her. And in half an hour I'll be the envy of every man in Pierre's dining room.'

Again she felt herself flush as his laughing eyes rested upon her.

'You're sure, then,' she asked, 'that you don't mind…?'

'I think we can be honest with each other, Anna,' he smiled. 'I didn't invite you to dinner to discuss something I can easily find out for myself at N.T.E.L. And I'm sure you were, and are, perfectly aware of that fact. I wanted to see you.'

Diffidently Anna glanced at the bronzed skin around his sharply intelligent eyes. The lines of his face and square contour of his jaw were alive with a masculine interest he had no intention of concealing. For an instant she imagined his handsome features drawing close to her, his powerful hands encircling her as he bent to join his lips to her own. But she banished the thought. There was little point in dallying over the sexual charms of a man who might disappear from her life as quickly as he had entered it.

'I ventured to hope that the feeling was mutual,' he went on. 'Perhaps I was premature. That's not a good thing in a lawyer.'

'I'm sure you're a fine lawyer,' Anna admitted, only too aware that the secret recesses of her body had responded tumultuously to his presence even before he had invited her to dinner.

'Enough said,' he laughed, raising his glass. 'Shall we drink to the beginning of a beautiful relationship?'

She joined him in his toast, suppressing as best she could

the confusion in her senses. Only this afternoon she had been hurriedly walking the noisy streets of the Loop in a desperate search for a job to replace the one she had lost under such unforgivable circumstances. And now it seemed as though the world were a kaleidoscope which, in a single turn, could throw everything into a completely different position. The memory of N.T.E.L and her current difficulties were overwhelmed by the bewitching male attractiveness of Marsh Hamilton, who sat before her now like a lithe athlete, poised for any movement the game might require of him. It was difficult to imagine herself feigning invulnerability to his daunting charms, for already an impudent quickening of her traitorous body sent its dangerous thrill through her mind.

As he helped her on with her coat, the light pressure of his strong hands sent quivers of delight along her shoulders and down her back. Indeed, she thought, Marsh Hamilton seemed a man who thought and did as he pleased. He was doubtless in the habit of overwhelming any obstacles that stood between him and his desires. She had to warn herself to be careful in his company.

The shadowed intimacy of the booth Anna found herself in at the unfamiliar restaurant was hardly calculated to decrease her attraction to the compelling form of Marsh Hamilton. His tanned hands seemed particularly dark against the white tablecloth which glowed under the recessed lights, and again Anna had to admire the stunning virility of his long limbs and authoritative demeanour.

'Have you ever tried a *menu dégustation* in a place like this?' he asked.

'I've never been in a place like this,' Anna laughed.

'I think you'll like it,' he smiled. 'It's an assortment of small items, not too overwhelming for the appetite, and it gives the chef a chance to show off his skills. Shall we give it a try?'

Anna nodded happily.

'And a light white wine,' he added. 'That will leave us plenty of room for dessert, which is really an art form here.'

'I don't know whether my waistline will stand it,' she laughed. 'But for Pierre perhaps I'll make an exception.'

'That's the spirit!' he smiled, the teasing glimmer in his dark irises caressing her in the shadows.

Anna was unprepared for the complex and brilliant variety of the dishes brought by the decorous waiter, who faded into the background between courses, returning only to refill their wine glasses. And each surprise experienced by her palate was accompanied by something new to learn about Marsh Hamilton. He spoke of himself with simple directness, revealing the facts of his life in a detached and humorous manner. Clearly the needs of his pride and ambition had long since found satisfaction from his abilities, for there was no trace of egotism or unfulfilled longing in his personality.

His late father, he said, had been a successful small businessman in Chicago until the postwar recession forced him to sell out.

'He was a smart man,' Marsh explained, 'but his excitement over his own products made him forget the hard facts about overhead and taxation in those changing times. The recession took him by surprise and he couldn't pay his debts. He ended up by working the rest of his days for the competitors who bought him out. It was a sad fate for an ambitious fellow like him.'

He shrugged. 'And I'll have to admit,' he added, 'it made its mark on me as well. After what happened to Dad I made up my mind that I would know all the facts before making any decisions in whatever line of work I chose. The law, it turns out, is just the field to keep me on my toes.'

'Why is that?' asked Anna.

'The name of the legal game is research,' he explained. 'A trial lawyer who's worth his salt never asks a question in court without knowing the answer beforehand. He has to realise that his own witnesses are as unpredictable as those of the opposition, and may be hiding any number of embarrassing facts from him. If he doesn't learn to cover the ground thoroughly before going to trial, he's going to find himself losing cases he should have won.'

He laughed. 'But I don't know why I'm telling you all this,' he said. 'You work in research yourself, so I'm sure you know the pitfalls.'

I thought I did, Anna reflected ruefully behind her smile. The confident man beside her was clearly in the habit of reaping triumph from his professional efforts, and was a stranger to the role of victim. Yet his sympathetic demeanour suggested that he understood those who had fallen prey to life's injustices, and had dedicated himself to helping them as best he could.

'Down at our office,' he went on easily, 'they call me No Surprises Hamilton. I'm such a stickler for detail and preparation that the clerks dread working with me!'

'I'm sure they're happy when their efforts help you to win a case,' said Anna.

'I want them to be proud when we win,' he nodded. 'Every case is theirs as much as mine. Some of them see their research as scut work unrelated to the outcome. I try to make them understand that each piece of information they dig up may make the difference between winning and losing. The good young lawyers learn to appreciate that fact in a hurry. The client's whole life may depend on it.'

'The next time I need a lawyer, I'll know where to come,' Anna laughed, realising uncomfortably that even the talents of a Marsh Hamilton might prove unavailing in her present crisis—assuming for the sake of fantasy that she could afford his firm's fees.

'I hope I won't have to wait that long to see you again,' he said, his deep voice enfolding her with its quiet tones. Again she felt the curious power of his gaze. Alive with penetrating insight it nevertheless rested upon her like a gentle touch, lithe and warm, inspiring her confidence even as it stirred her senses. A stern perfectionist where his work was concerned, Marsh Hamilton had no need to withhold the frank admiration he bestowed upon Anna so naturally.

The impression was heightened by his sympathetic attention to her account of her own past, which culminated in the untimely deaths of her parents and her continuing devotion to Sally. Strangely, Marsh seemed to take for granted the determined strength with which Anna had coped with her situation, as though he already knew her well enough to assume that no crisis could shake her confidence in herself. Retaining his silence regarding the reason why she had left N.T.E.L., he seemed willing to wait for her to discuss it in her own time.

'I have an idea,' he said as Anna sipped the rich coffee that had brought the meal to a close. 'Let's take a walk outside before we drive back. That way we can work off a little of Pierre's cooking.'

'That's the best idea I've heard all evening,' she laughed. 'The dinner was wonderful—and well worth the diet I'll be going on tomorrow!'

The lights of Michigan Avenue sprang into view with particular gaiety as they stepped out into the brisk autumn air. To the right was the long upward slope leading to the river and the centre of the Loop; to the left the elegant shop-lined blocks adjacent to the Water Tower.

'Ever been to Paris?' asked Marsh, taking her arm as he led her through the shadows of the trees lining the sidewalk.

'No,' Anna smiled. 'I've always wanted to see it.'

'We Chicagoans have always made a lot of noise about Michigan Avenue resembling a Paris boulevard,' he said. 'I never really believed it until I had occasion to go over there on business. But it turns out to be true after all. With these wide sidewalks and trees, and the vista from the river down to the Outer Drive, it really resembles some of the big streets on the Right Bank.' He laughed. 'Of course, the Parisians don't have a big lake right beside the city where they can go sailing or windsurfing whenever they want.'

'I don't imagine they have a Daley Plaza, either,' said Anna, 'with a hundred-foot Picasso sculpture looking down at everyone who passes.'

'Spoken like a true Chicagoan!' he laughed. 'You're probably right. There's no place quite like the Loop on earth. Do you like art?'

'Mmm,' she nodded. 'I often used to take my lunch to the Art Institute and spend some time there before going back to work. I have a favourite gallery where I sit and restore myself when I'm feeling tired or harassed.'

'Modern?' he asked. 'The one upstairs, with the Matisses, and Picasso's *Mother and Child*?'

'How did you guess?' she laughed.

'You mentioned Picasso before,' he explained, 'and I seem to remember that that particular gallery has quite a few comfortable benches. It's a bright, cheery sort of place, isn't it?'

She nodded, startled by his intuition. In a dauntingly short space of time he was creating the impression of having known her intimately for months or years. The unseen sparks flowing from his strong hand along the flesh of her arm did little to lessen the feeling. Without urgency or undue forwardness, he was somehow opening her to him, dissipating her resistance so that an unspoken inner closeness sprang into life along with her sensual response to his touch. She knew that this intoxicating caress of his voice and eyes might soon be joined by the probing enquiry of his lips and hands, and she had to remind herself that she still did not know him well.

But somehow it did not matter. Her street was dark and sleepy as Marsh pulled the car to the kerb and turned off the engine. Without a word he drew her to his deep chest, his knowing fingers guiding her along the path of her own willingness, and kissed her with an intimacy that stunned her senses.

His lips explored hers softly, their gentleness contradicting the storm of sudden warmth they spread through her slender limbs. The muscular hands covering her back had no need to force her, for her body knew how to mould itself to his own powerful frame in the darkness. With a little shock of delight she felt his earthy male scent suffuse her. The inflaming touch of his body seemed to expand and multiply the already disturbing visual image of his taut attractiveness.

'You have soft skin, Anna,' he whispered, his lips brushing the tender flesh of her neck and earlobe with maddeningly teasing effect. She felt herself begin to strain against him in a daunting flurry of desire, and her eyes closed as his hard man's limbs held her closer still. Astounded to find herself joined so intimately to a stranger who had emerged from nowhere as her personal life was entering a period of painful upset, she nevertheless let herself go to the wild longing which flared in her every nerve.

The heat of his embrace, so direct and authoritative, bespoke his indifference to whatever obstacles might conspire to separate her from his own desire. He seemed to know all he needed to know about her: that she returned his passion and wanted him already. And so it was with relaxed assurance that he released her, and felt her body rest languidly against his own, too faint with pleasure to recede from him.

'There's one thing on my mind,' she heard his deep murmur against the lush mane of her hair.

'Mmm,' she sighed, still absorbed in her fascination. 'What?'

'If you won't be at N.T.E.L. any more, how am I supposed to get through my days there?' She felt his smile in the lips that kissed her forehead. 'It's going to be pretty dull,' he added.

She nodded, pained by the thought of the desperate days of job-hunting that awaited her. The light touch of the hands cradling her shoulders sent waves of lulling warmth through the naked flesh under her dress, making her worries seem curiously remote.

'Well,' he murmured, 'they can't make me work at night, can they?'

'No,' she smiled, her fingers straying absently over the shirt covering his deep chest. 'They used to make me work at night, but then I was never the partner in a law firm.'

'What will you do now?' he asked.

'Find another job,' she sighed. 'As fast as I can.'

'I imagine you'll be pretty busy,' he remarked, a trace of teasing humour in his voice.

'Probably,' she agreed.

'Not too busy to get to know me a little better,' Marsh said quietly, his hands slipping to her spine to press her closer to him.

Anna could only nod for acquiescence, for the raw eruption in her senses under his knowing touch fairly took her breath away.

'I'll tell you what,' he went on. 'I have to go out of town this weekend on business, but I'll be back on Sunday. How long has it been since you've visited Old Town?'

'A long time, I'm afraid,' she answered, visualising Wells Street and its charming array of shops and cafés. Although the famous area was virtually within walking distance of her flat, her work had prevented her from exploring it for many months.

'Why don't I pick you up Sunday afternoon?' he asked. 'We can take a walk around, perhaps listen to a friend of mine who plays the guitar in a place down there, and have some dinner.'

'It sounds wonderful,' Anna smiled.

'Two o'clock?' The whispered words brushed the soft skin behind her ear like a caress.

'I'll look forward to it.'

A muted inner voice warned that the days ahead would require harsh self-discipline, and that troubling disappointments were probably in store for her. Time was of the essence, and she must allow nothing to disturb her concentration on the business at hand. But as she reclined in the strong arms that held her, as though resting in the quiet eye of the sensual storm that had nearly carried her away only moments ago, she banished all negative thoughts from her mind. Indeed, Marsh Hamilton possessed an invader's power to storm every barrier blocking the path of his desire. In this charmed moment she could only nestle in the bewitching shadow of his strong will. The future would take care of itself. Tonight was hers.

A mile across the dark city the wall clock showed nine-thirty. The office was deserted, except for Joe, the old custodian, who was certainly on another floor.

The bright green glow of the computer display had a festive look under the subdued light. The machine hummed quietly, having received its code, displayed its content, and accepted the change in instructions. Gone for ever was the message it had carried, lost now in a maze of circuitry which was all too capable of forgetting, when told to do so.

A tanned finger touched the keys while a watchful eye verified the appearance of the new text on the display.

'*In addition to the security breach, which constituted immediate grounds for dismissal, it is my unfortunate duty to report that this employee offered improper personal favours in exchange for a promise not to terminate or to prosecute. Regrettably, it was not possible for me to establish the circumstances leading up to her improper query of classified computer data, or the identity of the person or persons for whom this material was intended.*

'*It is with deep regret that I communicate to whom it may concern this unfortunate occurrence...*'

Signed 'Charles Robbins' and pre-dated, the text took its place among the computer's thousands of files. When requested, it would be printed up by an unsuspecting secretary and sent out along with whatever letter Chuck might have dictated. The only eyes to see it from now on would belong to the anonymous employers who asked for the dossier.

How wonderful a thing a computer can be, when one knows how to use it properly! It accepts instructions docilely, and transmits the desired material with the automatism of a robot. It is a perfect servant.

There is an entire world in those circuits. A world of information, of people, of events at my fingertips. And under my control.

Now she'll know how far my power extends. Now she'll realise how foolhardy she was to attempt my wrath. To think of her confidently writing us down as a reference! Let her wonder, then, when no one will hire her. Let her suffer, and learn her lesson. How many tears will flow, as the weeks and months go by. And I, only I, will know.

Straightening his tie with quiet care, Porter Deman turned off the fluorescent lights, closed the door and moved towards the elevators.

CHAPTER FOUR

THE Art Institute's Modern European gallery was wrapped in its usual silence as Anna sat on a padded bench before her favourite painting. Here and there she could see a determined art student standing near a sculpture, making careful notes on a legal pad for a course paper. Across the large room, a group of schoolchildren sat on the floor in unaccustomed silence as their teacher pointed out the playful intricacies of a huge canvas. A few young couples strolled languidly about the gallery, hand in hand. Two or three solitary figures sat on benches in the hushed, still air, seeming meditatively closed upon themselves among the colourful works of art.

'I wonder if they're like me,' Anna wondered. 'Here because they have nowhere else to go.' Her last interview of the morning having taken her to Monroe Street, she had crossed Michigan Avenue's sunlit, busy expanse to have a light lunch in the Art Institute's cafeteria. And now, with an hour left before her next appointment, she had mounted the two long flights of marble steps to the room whose paintings were like old friends.

Five years ago, having just arrived in Chicago, she had sat excitedly in this quiet atmosphere, sensing underneath its calm the vibrant hubbub of the metropolis outside. When Sally had come to enrol at the university, Anna had brought her here for lunch in the middle of a busy day of shopping and sightseeing. Like her sister before her, Sally had been overwhelmed by the Art Institute's fabulous collection, and had stared in wonderment at the classic originals whose reproduced images she had seen in many a book or magazine.

It was difficult to remain indifferent when one contemplated the peaked swirls of oil glistening under the recessed lights on the surface of a world-famous masterpiece. One felt one could almost see the artist's hand at work, and feel the touch of his muscular fingers on the shaft of his brush. And as one scanned the walls of the galleries, the paintings seemed like caged animals, barely domesticated by their frames, each one a vibrant and mysterious world waiting to lure the spectator's eye inside, to uproot him from his familiar surroundings and set him down in a strange landscape filled with people, animals, trees, flowers from another time and place.

But today it was different. Today even the paintings seemed infected by the sinking feeling that had taken possession of Anna. Trapped in their frames under the artificial light, they hung as though thwarted, imprisoned on the walls. Even Léger's *Divers on a Yellow Background*, which she had always preferred for its humorous tangle of bodies falling chaotically through a dreamlike space, seemed somehow sad. As she gazed now at the large canvas, the faces of the divers looked downright depressed, in spite of their antic positions.

It was Friday. Nearly eleven days of job-hunting now lay behind Anna, their morose passage filled with increasing menace. She was beginning to adjust herself to the irony of this new routine of living, which crowded her days with exhausting activity while seeming to lead nowhere. It was a nightmarish existence, busy and yet futile. But it was not without its moments of excitement. For, at intervals, the face and voice of Marsh Hamilton interrupted the monotony of her days, promising something finer and more thrilling than the glum misfortune of her present situation.

True to his word, he had returned from his business trip to accompany Anna on a pleasant walk through the Lincoln Park Zoo to Old Town. An autumnal crispness had sparked the air between the North Side's old apartment buildings. Her hand rested warmly in his large palm as he guided her across streets filled with strolling pedestrians unperturbed by the sparse Sunday traffic.

Following Marsh's suggestion, Anna had dressed informally. Feeling relaxed and happy in her sweater and jeans, she glanced with frank admiration at the tall form of her companion. The cut of the leather jacket above his slacks accentuated Marsh's powerfully muscled shoulders and broad back. Entirely at home in the vibrant city of his youth, he seemed at once to dominate its landscape and to draw the essence of its stored energy into his own personality.

The delicious smells emanating from the restaurants along Wells Street were particularly intoxicating after their brisk walk, so they entered a charmingly decorated café that Anna had never noticed before. As they scanned the imaginative menu, the delicate sound of a guitar stole through the room, and she looked up to see a slender blond man, dressed incongruously in a handsome three-piece business suit, tuning his instrument. After a brief moment of quiet concentration, he began to perform classical pieces with amazing facility, a fugitive smile touching his calm features as his long fingers coaxed delicately modulated sounds and moods from the guitar.

'Is that the friend you spoke of?' Anna asked amid the delighted applause that greeted the close of his first recital.

'That's him,' Marsh nodded. 'He works in a dance band during the week, comes here on Sundays, and performs occasionally with classical groups in concerts. I met him a few years ago, when I was still with the D.A. His car had been stolen by a group of professional thieves we were investigating, and by a miracle we got it back for him before they could strip it for the parts. It was the first car he'd ever owned, and he was grateful.'

'He's wonderfully talented,' said Anna. 'The piece he just played sounded so familiar. It reminded me of Mozart.'

'No wonder,' Marsh laughed. 'It's a Mozart piano sonata that he arranged himself for guitar. So you like classical music, do you?'

'Very much. Especially Beethoven, Mozart and Schubert.'

'I'll be damned,' he smiled. 'We have more in common than I thought. Do you get much chance to hear Solti and the Chicago Symphony?'

Anna shook her head. 'I'm afraid the tickets are well beyond my pocketbook. But I buy some of his records.'

'Well, I'll take you to Orchestra Hall some time when Solti is conducting,' he said. 'A girl can't go through life without hearing some live music, good and loud.'

'Oh, but I do,' Anna smiled. 'Right here in Old Town. I see Junior Wells and Buddy Guy, and Muddy Waters...'

'You're kidding,' he explained. 'You like Chicago blues?'

'I adore it,' she laughed. 'When the weather is nice, and there's a Sunday afternoon show at one of the clubs here, I sometimes walk over and listen.'

'Alone?' he asked, a wry hint of jealousy in his quirked eyebrow.

'My friend Debby comes along occasionally,' she answered. 'But I've gone alone often enough. Does that surprise you?'

He shook his head. 'There's not much about you that doesn't surprise me,' he laughed. 'Aren't you afraid of a lot of men hitting on you in those blues clubs?'

'Not really,' she said. 'I've found that people come to

hear the music. It's quite safe. Besides,' she added, 'I can take care of myself.'

'I'll bet you can,' he said, his eyes appraising her as he took her hand. 'Something tells me you'd be a dangerous adversary if a person were foolish enough to push you too far.'

'Not so dangerous,' she admitted, ruefully recalling her ineffectual attempt to defend herself against the accusation that had cost her her job.

The guitarist had placed his instrument on a tall stool and disappeared through a swinging door as the small spotlight was turned off.

'I'd introduce you to him,' said Marsh with a slight smile, 'but he's very eccentric when he's working. Between sets he does exercises in the back room to calm his nerves. Whenever I come here he sees me and makes believe I'm invisible. We play tennis together downtown sometimes, and then he asks me how I liked his playing. When he's away from his music he's quite relaxed. I'd like to have you meet him some time.'

'I can see that your work brings you into contact with a lot of interesting people,' commented Anna.

'You're telling me,' he replied pointedly, his large hand cradling her slender fingers as his dark eyes caressed her in the shadows.

'I didn't mean me,' she laughed.

'I did,' he insisted with a gentle smile. 'You know, that independent streak of yours reminds me of the best things about life in this town. It's an unpredictable place, because it's full of talents and personalities from a thousand different places, who all came here for their own reasons. Put them together at close quarters, and the sparks are bound to fly. Exciting things happen. We all talk about Chicago as an industrial crossroads, but to me it's a crossroads of people's destinies.'

His eyes sparkled with sharp introspection as he regarded the lush auburn curls which strayed across the fabric of her sweater.

'Think of it this way, Anna. Five years ago I was the last person in the world to suspect that a beautiful young woman from Bloomington was arriving in Chicago and, by chance, "falling into" a job at N.T.E.L. Wasn't that the expression you used? Time has many surprises in store for us. For the last five years I've been going about my business, never suspecting that my firm would one day do a job for N.T.E.L., and that I would meet that girl from Bloomington only hours before she left the company. If you hadn't bumped into me outside the elevator last week, we wouldn't be sitting here right now. And one day later you wouldn't have been there to bump into me. But you did, and that makes all the difference.'

'I must say I never thought of it quite that way,' Anna admitted.

'Neither did I,' he smiled. 'Until I met you.'

His reasoning, she reflected, had more than a grain of truth. For the cruel fate that had thrown her life into turmoil was inextricably linked with the chain of events that had brought her into contact with the handsome, thoughtful man who regarded her now. But as she returned his smile she had to remind herself that the deep voice which displayed the breadth of his knowledge and curiosity was also a caressing weapon which progressively weakened her resistance to his daunting masculinity. Marsh Hamilton's charms were as varied as his incisive ideas, and their impact seemed to increase with his every word and gesture.

The probingly intimate kiss with which he took his leave of her that night was undeniable proof that there was nothing casual about his interest in her, and that he was well aware of the feelings he had kindled in her in so short a time.

'I'll be through at N.T.E.L. this week,' he said, his long arms locked warmly about her slender waist. 'I'll do the rest of the job at my own office. We're pretty busy at the moment on a number of cases, but I'll make the time to call you. If you don't mind, that is.'

'I'd like that,' she replied, doing her best to conceal the breathless excitement she felt in his embrace.

'You're sure you won't be too busy yourself?' he asked. 'I know you have a tough week coming.'

'I'll make the time to answer the phone,' she teased, her finger grazing the windblown strands of his dark hair.

'That's my girl!' he laughed. The words coiled around her with quietly persuasive force, for already she could imagine herself joined to this attractive stranger by bonds of trust and intimacy. Her future was a mystery whose unknown course Marsh Hamilton seemed determined to alter, and she could see no earthly reason to struggle against him. Indeed, she felt compelled to quell the traitorous longing which inflamed her towards him with heedless abandon at every turn. Her self-respect dictated that she take the time to know him better before investing unrealistic hopes in him.

Such scruples seemed the least of her worries as the days passed. Although she had felt reasonably certain that the new week would bring a telephone call from one of the employers she had seen during her first long days of interviews, Anna searched the want ads for additional jobs she might apply for in the days to come. Waiting by the telephone would be too distressing a business. She felt she had to continue taking action, moving forward, to give herself the very best chance of finding a new job before the money she had earned at N.T.E.L. ran out.

Thus a siege began, marked by a mood of grim determination which was all too frequently interrupted by moments of near-panic. Each morning Anna gathered her courage, dressed warmly, and stepped out into the windy autumn air for another round of applications and interviews. Returning mid-afternoon so as to be at home in case the phone rang, she did her best to remain calm and cheerful. Between trips downstairs to the laundry room, she ironed clothes, dusted tables, vacuumed the floor, trying vainly to prevent her expectant eye from darting to the silent telephone. At last, when the apartment had been cleaned and re-cleaned, the kitchen cupboards reorganised, and her entire wardrobe scrutinised with an eye to what she might wear on her first day in a new job, she admitted defeat and sat down restlessly by the phone.

Surely, if an employer had called while she was out, he would call back late in the afternoon. If the phone did not ring before five o'clock, that could only mean that no one had called all day. Listlessly Anna read magazines, paged through a mail order catalogue in search of a birthday present for Sally, glanced at an old novel from her college days.

Prowling the apartment, she felt like a prisoner of the stubbornly mute telephone. She could neither spend the whole day out looking for jobs, nor remain inside waiting for calls that never came.

Recalling previous job searches, she was uncomfortably certain that a positive response nearly always came within a day or two of the initial interview. After that, one could always be sure that the job had been offered to someone else.

How could it be that the phone had not rung? There were numerous jobs available, and Anna's qualifications were quite impressive. She had a college degree and an excellent work record, including a promotion to office supervisor. Surely each one of the companies she had visited could use her abilities. It didn't make sense. Unless somehow the disaster caused by Porter Deman's treachery had found a way to communicate itself to the employers who queried

N.T.E.L. as her reference. But how? Charles Robbins had promised not to place the accusation against Anna in her personnel file.

Unless he had lied…

'It's impossible,' she shrugged off her fears. 'Chuck doesn't lie. It can't be the file…'

By the end of the week the remnants of Anna's optimistic mood had evaporated, and the prospect of the continued search for work seemed a grim ordeal. Before long she would have no choice but to tell Sally her unfortunate news, and journey to the State unemployment office, hoping against hope that she might qualify for benefits despite the ambiguous circumstances surrounding her termination. The thought of the forms she would have to fill out, and the endless waiting, was nothing if not depressing.

Yet as the tension of her job search became more and more painful, another sort of ferment grew with daunting speed within her breast. For Marsh Hamilton did call, as he had promised. The phone rang when night's calming obscurity had settled over the anguish of Anna's hectic day, and she had to conceal as best she could the happiness that leapt through her senses as she exchanged friendly greetings with him, listened to his news, and expressed forced optimism about her job prospects.

Behind the relaxed humour of his conversation, the deep tones of his voice seemed to carry the subtle trace of the heated embrace that had joined him to her days earlier. His genial words, superficially casual, actually bespoke the increasing intimacy of their relationship. Each sound caressed her ear with a delightful gentleness, and she could feel his lips close to her own even as they spoke into a receiver miles away.

Despite herself she felt a schoolgirl's furtive excitement at this marvellous contact at a distance, and a thrill of discovery at each new thing she learned about Marsh. Struggling to contain the undercurrent of eager acceptance that tinged her own responses, she knew that he heard it nonetheless, and felt herself quicken in anticipation of the next time she would see him.

She was not disappointed, for the charmed weekend that followed seemed to have been taken from an entirely different life, full of sunshine and unlimited hope. On Marsh's arm she explored Chinatown, and tasted the deliciously varied wares at a shabby but renowned dim-sum parlour whose clientele included pilgrims from towns many miles distant as well as local Chinese families. She strolled past the robust, joking vendors on Maxwell Street, and accepted Marsh's gift of a colourful scarf whose blue-green hues took up the deep glow of her emerald eyes. After a quiet dinner in a charming restaurant nestled in the busy streets of Uptown, the couple spent the evening watching a talented theatre company perform experimental plays by local writers.

The city seemed to have come to life under Marsh's easy, sweeping gaze, and its sidewalks were friendly and familiar under his confident steps. But while the stunning vitality of the urban landscape passed before Anna in a heady panorama, her mind's eye was fixed in fascination on the dark figure of Marsh himself.

Even as he displayed his almost encyclopaedic familiarity with the city's byzantine political and social fabric, he drew her out on her own opinions and experiences, his attentive eyes resting on her in calm concentration as she spoke. In no time, it seemed, she had bared her innermost ideas on people and things to him, and come to know the reflective personality which underlay his boundless confidence in the skills he put at his clients' disposal.

Her second full week of job-hunting was worse if anything than the first, and she found herself clinging to her memory of Marsh's last kiss, so soft and intimate, as a lifeline which might blunt the cold menace of her solitary ordeal.

But it was more than a lifeline. The memory clung to her like a bewitching philtre, suffusing her senses by day and haunting her dreams by night. Though her nerves were stretched to their limit in her exasperation over her predicament, a secret yielding stole under her skin at every moment, and when she noticed it she realised that Marsh had not been out of her mind since last she saw him. When she contemplated her tired face in the mirror, the image of his laughing eyes and hard body seemed to look out at her, gently drawing her closer to him, enfolding her in a warm embrace from which all pain was banished.

'Am I falling in love?' she asked herself in amazement, her gaze riveted to the green eyes glowing under the lush curls of her hair.

It could not be. She barely knew Marsh Hamilton, and had no earthly reason to believe her heedless emotions might have their counterpart behind his inscrutable eyes. He was simply a part of this mad maelstrom of events that had upset her existence so suddenly—and nothing more. Later, much later, when life was under control once more, it might be possible to think of matters such as love. But not now.

Yet the taunting question popped ceaselessly into her mind, threatening to eclipse all other thoughts. And she began to fear that where Marsh Hamilton was concerned, she would never be in control of herself.

Now, as she rose from her bench to leave the quiet gallery and hurry through the Loop's busy streets to her next interview, Anna relaxed inwardly, allowing herself to be buoyed by the certainty that Marsh's knock would come at her door tonight, regardless of the day's events. Having

teased her with his promise of a surprise for dinner, he had
told her he would arrive by six-thirty.

'Thank God it's Friday,' she thought with painful irony
as the throng of pedestrians on Michigan Avenue engulfed
her. She had worked hard this week, and earned nothing.
The absurdity of unemployment seemed every bit as de-
structive as its financial perils.

'Control yourself,' she thought firmly. 'Be patient.
You'll find a job sooner or later.' Resolved to avoid panic
at all costs, she hurried towards State Street.

The afternoon's interviews were cast in the same mould
as their predecessors. Mr Morgan, the personnel director
whose office was Anna's last stop, seemed to be reciting a
prepared speech as he repeated words she had been hearing
for nearly two weeks.

'I must say that your qualifications are very impressive,
Miss Halpern,' he said. 'Most impressive. Of course, we
do have to interview some other people before making a
final decision. We'll let you know one way or the other...'

After shaking his hand and expressing her thanks with
as much sincerity as she could muster, Anna walked to her
bus stop with a sense of resignation and relief. The week
was over. Two days of rest were now to be hers.

Pushing through the front door of her apartment building
at last, she was anxious to take a hot shower and erase the
traces of the day's depressing efforts before Marsh arrived.
She inserted her small key in the mailbox and saw the door
open to reveal an envelope bearing N.T.E.L.'s logo.

'My severance pay,' she thought. 'So be it.' The last of
her financial resources were now visible. For another two
weeks, or three at most, she could survive without additional income. After that, her own fate, as well as Sally's,
would be out of her control.

The urgent sounds of the Friday evening rush hour re-
verberated outside as Anna sat in her bathrobe before her

mirror and applied a touch of colour to her cheeks. Feeling refreshed and energetic after her bracing shower, she began brushing the sleek auburn tresses which fell in gentle waves over her shoulders. To her surprise, the face of a vital, healthy young woman looked out at her from the glass. There was something virtually festive in the expectant green eyes and glowing cheeks under her flowing hair. She had to admit that today's frantic activity had been distinctly easier to bear after Marsh's call last night. She was still admired and respected by someone in this large and lonely city—someone whose irrepressible charm could not fail to distract her from her nagging trepidation.

The soft outline of her breasts was palpable under the sheer fabric of the dress she chose. For an uncomfortable moment she wondered whether she had unconsciously selected a garment which would show off her femininity too enticingly. As things already stood, she was finding it increasingly difficult to resist the sensual upset that Marsh was so expert in kindling with his every touch.

'I just don't care,' she admitted to herself in all honesty. Come what may, she needed Marsh Hamilton at this crucial moment of her life, and she was willing to run the risk of painful struggle against his seductive virility for the sake of his welcome support and interest.

A rather urgent knock at the door interrupted her reverie, and she opened it to find Marsh standing in the hallway, his arms full of grocery bags.

'You the lady who ordered the groceries?' he asked playfully.

'Marsh, what have you done?' she exclaimed.

'This is your surprise,' he said. 'And your dinner. I don't think I've taken the trouble yet to inform you of my cooking skills. But now you're going to find out all about them. I'm going to make us a real Cordon Bleu dinner tonight.'

He took off his windbreaker and stood before her in dark

slacks which accentuated the taut strength of his thighs, and a handsome turtleneck sweater. The crisp, vibrant coolness of impending autumn seemed to radiate from him as he smiled into her eyes.

'I should have told you not to dress,' he said. 'But I'll confess that I imagined you'd be looking like a million dollars tonight, and I couldn't resist seeing it.'

'That's all right,' she smiled, feeling the appraising penetration of his gaze in all her senses.

'Before I forget,' he said, reaching into one of the bags, 'first things first. If you'll get me a couple of glasses, we can drink this while it's nice and cold.' He produced a bottle of champagne, its chilled glass beaded with drops of condensed moisture from the warm air, and began peeling the foil around the cork.

'Well, don't just stand there, girl,' he ordered happily, seeing her standing before him immobilised more by admiration for his virile self-confidence than by surprise. 'Let's go! It isn't every Friday we toast the end of the week with champagne!'

The cork popped easily under the pressure of his strong fingers, and the effervescent liquid sent sprays of bubbles into the air as Anna held the glasses out to him.

'Now,' he announced, touching his glass to hers, 'this is how we give a lovely lady a first-class evening after a hard working week. Let me see…'

Feigning perfectionistic concentration, he reached into the shopping bags and began producing a lush array of good things to eat.

'Caviare to start, with a touch of scallion,' he murmured, waving a packet of green onions at her distractedly. 'Then a seafood cocktail. A few shrimps, a little lobster: nothing extravagant, not too many calories. We don't want to jade the palate, do we? Let's see… Oh, yes, Caesar salad. Lots of romaine, not too much anchovy, easy on the Tabasco. Where's the steak, now? Ah, yes.'

He glanced critically at her small oven. 'Just as I thought. An old warhorse like that can't broil. I'll panbroil our entrecôtes with cracked pepper and a nice white wine sauce. Now, what's left?' He peered into the bag. 'Of course: a dash of artichoke heart, a little soupçon of a potato, a stalk of asparagus. And then, to finish, my speciality: profiteroles with chocolate sauce.' He looked up. 'That's what we're saving the calories for. Well, Anna, what do you think?'

She was too touched by his thoughtfulness and playful humour to do anything more than smile. Putting down his champagne glass, he stepped to her side.

'But first,' he said, 'a kiss for the chef. For inspiration.' The warm wool of his sweater enfolded her cosily as he put his arms around her. The cool of the street had left its fugitive trace on his cheek, and his tender kiss, already probing with daunting power the waiting embers which sparked within her, seemed indescribably knowing and intimate. She rested her head on his shoulder, allowing his physical strength to support and soothe her as undeniable stirrings of desire shimmered through her senses. Quietly his hands stroked her back, her shoulders, banishing easily the strain that had possessed her for five days.

'No more dallying,' he said, patting her hip and kissing her forehead. 'Otherwise I'll get distracted and we'll never have anything to eat.'

His alacrity in the kitchen amazed Anna as he picked his way with assurance among her dishes and utensils. Adding the spices he had brought to her own, he produced a superb meal with a series of laughing flourishes. His tall, muscular form dwarfed the space of her tiny kitchen, and Anna could not help admiring the seemingly inexhaustible resources of his skill and confidence. For an instant she reflected in involuntary jealousy on how many other women he might have regaled in this charming way before she met him. In the tight sweater which displayed the depths of his chest, the broad power of his shoulders, he was irresistibly attractive, the very figure of the supremely eligible, brilliant young professional.

The meal passed as though in a pleasant dream, suffused by the aura of enfolding warmth which seemed to emanate from Marsh's caressing gaze and quiet humour. Clearly aware that Anna's week had been difficult, he was offering her an elaborate respite from her troubles, and she was only too happy to accept. At last, warmed by the wine he had served with dinner, she sat by his side on her couch, watching the delicate ripples on the tawny surface of the tiny glass of brandy he had placed before her.

'You're a wonderful cook,' she complimented him. 'It was awfully nice of you to do this.'

'I had help,' he smiled. 'Every chef needs inspiration. If you don't mind my saying so, Anna, you look more beautiful every time I see you.'

With the same enrapturing power that had bewitched her before, his lips touched her own. His large hand slipped softly across her shoulder to graze her cheek, her hair. A flare of sudden heat, having slept insidiously within her since his telephone call, shot wildly under her skin, leaving her faint with pleasure.

Struggling to control unwilling limbs, she touched his long arm with tender affection.

'I imagine you've had a hard week,' he murmured against her temple. 'Here, put your head in my lap.'

Pliantly she accepted his suggestion. Slipping off her shoes, she lay beside him, feeling his strong fingers run luxuriantly through her hair, with an occasional pause to massage her neck and shoulder.

'That's heavenly,' she smiled, her eyes closed in rapt

fascination at his touch. 'But I'm going to shed my hair all over you, like a cat.'

'Never mind,' came his deep voice. 'Just relax.'

His finger grazed her earlobe, her cheek, before returning to the lush swirl of her hair. A great, warm yielding overcame her tired nerves as layers of tension were stripped from her by his caress. Her hand rested quietly on his hard thigh as she lay numb with relaxation under the protection of his presence.

'No jobs yet, I take it.' The stroking tones of his words belied their meaning.

'No offers,' she murmured, gratefully allowing his intoxicating nearness to dim the painful memory he had evoked.

'No offers for a research genius?' he smiled. 'Isn't that what Bob called you? I can't believe it.'

'I guess the job market is tighter than I thought,' she sighed. 'I'll just have to stay with it until I find something.'

'Worried about your sister?'

She nodded.

'I wouldn't, if I were you,' he said. 'Things will work out in time.'

Time, she thought bitterly. *That's what I haven't got enough of.*

'I hope so,' she said aloud.

Again the sliding movement of Marsh's hands forced her worries into remote vagueness. Greedily her body poised itself to his caress, unwilling to let any other impression compete with the pure probing of the fingers which soothed her. Never had the touch of another flesh seemed so magical a balm, so total a remedy. A purring sigh of satisfaction escaped her lips.

'You're right,' he whispered. 'Just like a cat. A big, sleek cat in my lap.'

'Mm-m,' Anna smiled against his thigh.

But his soft rubbing, and the shifting of her limbs on the comfortable cushions, the heat of his thigh against her cheek, were beginning to take on another, subtler rhythm. And before she could consciously notice how strange was this change which took place little by little, and yet all at once a deep quickening in her senses told her that, as surely as relaxation had banished the day's fatigue, desire had come to wash away everything in its path. The muscular caress of Marsh's knowing hands, only a moment ago a quiet stroking which peeled away layers of discomfort, now probed intimately to awaken depths of longing within her.

For a moment his caress, enmeshed in the billowed maze of her hair, continued its languid movement as though unaware of the change that had come over the flesh under it. She lay suspended in her own delight, resting with mute expectation against the hardness of his thigh. But at length, as though in response to an impalpable message radiating from her depths, his hand touched her shoulder, slid easily under her arm to caress her waist, her ribs, the creamy flesh of her hip.

'Did they treat you badly?' he asked quietly.

'Mm-m,' she sighed in rapt contentment, barely able to concentrate on the past which seemed buried by the daunting immediacy of Marsh Hamilton's body and personality. 'Who?'

'N.T.E.L.'

'N.T.E.L. is in my past now,' she murmured, stubbornly determined to solve her own problems without involving him. 'It's well out of my life.'

'So they did treat you badly.' The tender sympathy in his voice harmonised bewitchingly with the ethereal touch of his hands on her slender limbs.

'It doesn't matter,' she insisted pridefully. 'I can take care of myself.'

'I know you can,' he smiled with frank admiration. 'You're pretty tough, aren't you, Anna?'

'When I have to be,' she agreed, unafraid to acknowledge the fiercely independent personality which had allowed her to cope with many a pressing dilemma in recent years. But the thought was banished as she felt herself raised tenderly from her reclining position. All at once it occurred to her that she had merely tasted the fearsome virility of Marsh's hard body.

She knew instantly that her intuition was not wrong, for the kiss that penetrated her now sent a stunning wave of desire through her senses. The fingertips pressed to her spine seemed to burn through the fabric of her dress to the silken nudity underneath. A lithe, goading shudder of pleasure shook her with delicious intensity. The male desire behind his friendly words was aroused in its full force, coiled around her at last, and irresistible.

For a long moment he held her in suspension, his lips and arms joining her to him in paralysing intimacy. The fabric of her dress, loosened by her reclining posture, grazed the gentle swell of her breast, teased the impossibly taut flesh of her nipple, as a powerful hand closed over it. A shimmer of tickling excitement trembled across her stomach, slipping quickly down her thighs so that she stirred against him in a little spasm of delight.

'Damn, but I want you, Anna.' His deep voice penetrated her dizzyingly, forcing her to see in words what was all too palpable under the flesh that strained towards him. She could not yet answer him, for the traitorous response of her body, quickening in his grasp, took her breath away.

Again his lips claimed hers, their searing exploration firing an ache of desire in her depths. She knew that he wanted her to be his now, and his passion might well have carried her away, had he not somehow stemmed its tide and released her. Lying in stunned pleasure against his taut

limbs, she was at once grateful for his restraint and unnerved by the seductive power he had so suddenly un-
leashed.

'I can't stand this any more,' he murmured, a groan of
desire mingling with the sharp determination in his voice.
'Marry me, Anna.'

Her numbed thoughts came to an abrupt halt at his
words.

'But…' By instinct she made an effort to clear her mind,
to find her bearings. But to her surprise, his proposal
seemed so self-evident that she could think of no pretext
for questioning it.

'Isn't this a bit sudden?' she said, smiling. 'You hardly
know me, Marsh.'

'I know you,' he said simply. 'I know you well enough
to want you and need you. I don't have to know any more.'

She had to admit the feeling was mutual, and overwhelming in its hold over her.

'You certainly make up your mind about things quickly,'
she said, slipping her hand into his own with quiet tenderness.

'No,' he corrected, 'you're wrong there. I've had days
and nights to think about it, but even that amount of time
was unnecessary. It's really a question of years, Anna. I've
known a lot of women, but inside I've been waiting for
you all along. And now here you are, every bit as thoughtful and beautiful—and independent—as I always knew
you'd be. I don't need to wait any longer. My mind was
made up for me the first time I spoke to you.'

In silence she lay in his arms, bewitched by the strength
of his desire no less than by the daunting flare of exultation
that leapt within her own breast.

Calmly he stroked her hair, her shoulder, as his words
took their effect.

'Of course,' he smiled, 'as I said to you once, a lawyer

shouldn't be premature. I've walked into your life at a difficult moment, and I realise that. Perhaps you need a little time to think things over.'

Though she was flattered by his cautious words, Anna could not help feeling that her past life was already a forgotten thing, banished by the excitement which had overcome her. The hard body and caressing voice which enfolded her now were joined to the centre of her own personality in a mysterious, enthralling harmony. She could think of no earthly reason not to throw herself into his embrace, abandon the concerns that had filled her solitary life for so long, and give herself totally to the joy of belonging to him.

'But something tells me I'm not being premature,' he said, reading her thoughts with uncanny precision.

She shook her head in agreement with him and in wonder at the jarring novelty of the situation she found herself in. The next moment could bring her a new life by opening a door whose existence was unknown to her only two weeks ago. In a flash of memory she saw herself walking the corridors of N.T.E.L., taking the bus, paying the interest on the loans she had taken out for Sally's tuition, without a thought for her own future. That life of determined routine was gone now, as was the preoccupied woman who had lived it. In this heady moment, the unforeseen path to a happiness beyond words had opened upon her, and in her heart she had already welcomed it. She wanted this handsome stranger, and somehow knew already that he deserved her trust.

She could not say no to him, and she knew it. To do so would amount to accepting an exile from her very self, which was already bound to Marsh Hamilton by forces she could not oppose.

'Say yes, Anna.' His deep voice probed to the very quick of her, opening her to him with gentle insistence, drawing the words of acceptance inevitably outward, so that they trembled on her lips, waiting to escape her in joyful freedom.

'Marsh…' She could hold out no longer. Her moment had come, and she prepared to welcome it.

With a jangling shock the phone suddenly rang across the room, striking her dumb. The ebony irises that held her flicked reluctantly to the instrument.

'You'd better answer it.' A teasing smile spread over Marsh's handsome features. 'I hope whoever it is has a good excuse for interrupting us.'

'It must be Sally,' said Anna, rising to cross the room. 'No one else would call me at his hour.'

Still shaken by the emotions claiming her attention, she picked up the receiver with an uncertain smile.

'Hello?' she said, glancing at Marsh's tall form on the couch.

'Hello, Anna,' came a deep voice. 'Remember me?'

Turning instinctively away from Marsh, she paused for a desperate second before answering.

'What is it?' she asked, searching for words which would conceal the nature of the conversation.

'So you do remember,' said Porter Deman. 'I'm not that easy to forget, am I?' There was a silence over the line as he waited, probably calculating the effect of his words on her. 'There's something important I have to discuss with you,' he said at length. 'Very important—to you, Anna. Perhaps at lunch tomorrow.'

'That's out of the question,' she said coldly. Hadn't he done enough to her? What could he possibly want now? What did he have left to threaten her with?

'Why?' he asked slyly. 'Not working, are you?' His low laugh sent a chill down her spine. 'I mean,' he added with feigned innocence, 'tomorrow is Saturday, isn't it? No one works on Saturday.'

As he paused again, she understood his innuendo.

'Having trouble finding a job?' he asked.

Feeling Marsh's presence behind her, Anna had to fight back the angry words that came to her lips. A muffled chuckle sounded over the line.

'Listen to me, Anna,' he said. 'I can help you, don't you see? Without me, you'll never find work. I'm all you've got. What do you say? Just a little lunch. We'll discuss things. Just a civilised little conversation, that's all I ask. Otherwise...'

'Where?' she asked curtly, at once horrified at his reappearance in her life and relieved to know the source of her troubles. She shuddered involuntarily as she listened to his instructions. Without a word, she hung up the phone, made an effort to suppress the torrent of painful thoughts coursing within her, and turned back to Marsh.

'What was that?' he asked, his eyebrow quirked in perplexity.

'Nothing,' she said, forcing a smile.

'Didn't sound like nothing,' he said.

'It was something...that doesn't matter,' she said, torn between her desire to put Porter Deman out of her mind and the necessity of explaining away his call. 'It has to do with jobs,' she added weakly. 'Another interview.'

Marsh had not moved. The dark intensity of his gaze seemed to annihilate the breadth of the room as it reached to caress her slender form.

'Come back,' he said.

Without a word Anna crossed the carpet and buried herself in his waiting arms. She could neither conceal her upset nor reveal the reason for it, so she contented herself with clinging to the strength of the man who held her.

'My poor Anna,' he murmured. 'They're making it tough for you, aren't they?'

She nodded, fearful of his sharp intuition. His observation was disturbingly close to the unspeakable truth.

'That was a rude interruption,' he smiled. 'Some people don't have the decency to let a man propose to his girl in peace.'

She smiled, buoyed by his humour and by the comforting warmth of his muscular arms.

'Perhaps it's for the best, though,' he added, rocking her gently as he touched her cheek. 'I was putting quite a rush on you just now, and I really do want you to have a little time to think over what I've asked.'

For an answer she slipped her hand into his own. Though he could not realise it, his suggestion had a special meaning to her. She must confront Porter Deman one last time, and learn the depth of the danger he posed, before burying him in her past, where he belonged.

For over a week he had succeeded in influencing her destiny through his malignant conniving. She could not turn back the clock, but she could at least inform herself as to the precise extent of his power. There must be a way to fight him or, failing that, to elude him.

Regardless of what tomorrow might bring, she reflected, it could not come between her and the bright future that had opened out before her tonight. Porter Deman was an obstacle, and no more. Soon he would be out of the way, and well out of her life.

The strong arms of Marsh Hamilton continued to support her, sending their waves of tingling warmth through her senses. Here with him, she was safe. The power of his own personality gave her courage to face the coming day optimistically. Thank heaven, she thought, that he had chosen this difficult time to cross her path, and perhaps to alter its course for ever.

So she rested calmly in his embrace. But she could not see the quick turning of the wheels in his lawyer's mind.

CHAPTER FIVE

'SIT down, Anna.'

Porter Deman rose from his seat as the maître d'hôtel pulled the table away from the booth. With chagrin, Anna realised she would have to sit in the intimacy of a booth with him instead of across a table.

'Drink?' he asked. A waiter had appeared and stood expectantly before her. She sat in momentary confusion, unable to think of an answer to the question.

'Bring her what I'm having,' said Porter. 'And another for me.'

Silence reigned between them until the waiter returned. Draining his cocktail with satisfaction, Porter accepted its replacement and twisted the glass absently.

'I love a good strong drink in the middle of the day,' he said, his eyes scanning the expensive appointments of the elegant room. 'They make a good dry Martini here. Go ahead, Anna, taste it.'

The bitter, penetrating taste of the gin was particularly unpleasant, since Anna had had nothing to eat all morning. She felt a deep inner coldness which prevented her from taking any pleasure in outward impressions.

'I'm glad you could join me,' he said. 'In this beautiful fall weather, nothing could be nicer than to get out of the house and meet a beautiful woman for lunch.' Seeing that she did not respond, he leaned comfortably against the plush fabric of the booth and gazed knowingly at her. 'Have you been enjoying the weather?' he asked.

She remained stubbornly silent, fighting against the tumult of emotions inside her. Even to speak to him, to answer his casual questions, seemed an unacceptable participation in his sick game. Yet what choice did she have? She must find out what he had up his sleeve.

'I would appreciate your getting to the point,' she said coldly.

'Why, Anna,' he protested with feigned disappointment, 'what's your hurry? Can't a man enjoy your company for a little while, on such a lovely day? This is a fine restaurant. We should be conversing, relaxing, having a good time.'

Anna stared deliberately into the dewy swirl of her Martini. The olive sat at the bottom of the glass like a strange undersea creature, tilting slightly as unseen currents rocked it. For an instant she imagined the tiny fruit growing on a Mediterranean tree under a bright sun, unaware that its destiny was to drown in this alcoholic liquid which was incapable of supporting life.

'Let's get this over with,' she said without looking up.

'Anna, you disappoint me,' he grumbled. 'You're so impatient. Why, one would think you don't even want to be here! That's a shame, because this lunch could be the key to your whole future. You should be grateful to me for arranging it. Yes,' he sighed, 'this could be the beginning of a beautiful relationship.'

'You're not amusing me,' she said quietly.

The waiter was approaching the table again, his dignified demeanour reflecting the grave mission of taking his clients' order.

'I won't be having anyth...' Anna began, only too certain that she could not swallow a bite of food in the presence of Porter Deman.

'Bring us both the trout, Charles,' he said smiling, silencing her with a touch of his hand. 'And a bottle of your Macon blanc.'

'Yes, sir,' said the waiter, disappearing silently.

'They do a superb trout here, Anna,' said Porter. 'I know you'll enjoy it. Now, where were we? Oh, yes—the purpose of our little meeting.' He emitted a grunt of concentration on the business at hand.

'I'm a peaceable man, Anna,' he began, 'a friendly man. I can't stand unpleasantness of any kind. Live and let live: that's my motto. It has stood me in good stead in the past, and will, I hope, continue to serve in the future.'

He glanced wryly in her direction. Unable to take her eyes off the glass before her, she sensed the hesitant approach of his tanned hand, and removed her own instantly.

'I'm concerned and disappointed about the discord, the gulf, that has come between us,' he went on. 'When I first saw you, six months ago at N.T.E.L., I said to myself, there's an admirable woman. Not only is she beautiful, but she has such dignity, such obvious self-respect. A man would be privileged to have the friendship of such a person. Yes, indeed, a man would be honoured.'

His grey eyes glittered with undisguised irony in the pale light.

'And, at the risk of flattering myself,' he went on, 'I thought I saw in your eyes the trace, just the soupçon, of a reciprocal interest. Don't deny it, now, Anna. My eyes don't deceive me.' He smiled. 'But that, of course, is nothing to be ashamed of. Can't two working people take a friendly interest in each other?'

How long is he going to beat around the bush? Anna wondered in exasperation. Debby was certainly right: he got his thrills out of toying sadistically with his victims.

'Now,' he was saying, 'everything was going famously, until we had our little…misunderstanding. A very unfortunate thing, that. I truly believe that had you not jumped to certain conclusions, without allowing me to explain myself, to explain the sincerity of my position, our problems would have been nipped in the bud.'

Still staring at the drowning olive in her glass, Anna reflected that the gin would probably dry up the last of its vital juices before Porter Deman made his point.

'And that is why,' he said, 'I felt compelled to take desperate measures, so to speak. I simply couldn't let you go away mad, as it were. I felt, and I still feel, that our relationship deserves another chance. I truly admire you, Anna, and I want to express my admiration by doing my level best to make you happy. All I ask from you is a minimum of co-operation.'

Apparently encouraged that she had spoken at all, he patted her hand with proprietorial tenderness before she could withdraw it. Suppressing a shudder of distaste, she joined her hands in her lap and averted her eyes.

'Is it so much to ask,' he sighed, 'that you reconsider a reaction that anyone would call hasty and ill-advised? Really, Anna, you've been entirely too sensitive. All I wanted from you was a little basic human contact, to make the drudgery of work a bit more bearable for both of us. Now, I'm not ashamed to admit that I'm a man who doesn't give up easily. I generally get what I want in life.'

He paused as the waiter brought the wine. 'Good, Charles,' he said, tasting the amber liquid. 'Here, Anna, try some.' He pushed a long-stemmed glass towards her. 'It's a good year.

'Where was I?' he murmured. 'Oh, yes. Now, Anna, I think you've been entirely too prudish about this whole thing. I'm a reasonable man, and not given to holding grudges. That's why I forgave your little…outburst, in my office. But don't you understand? I couldn't just leave it at that. I couldn't let our relationship end prematurely, on such a sour note. That's why I had to do what I did.'

'Namely?' she asked, relieved that he had finally brought his treachery out into the open.

Porter emitted an ambiguous sound, a sort of sheepish giggle tinged with sly menace.

'Well,' he said, 'I don't want to give away a trade secret by going into the details. Let's just say I took advantage of my expertise in the computer field to—' an involuntary chuckle of satisfaction escaped his lips '—to re-program your job search. It was just a little prank, really, quite innocent when you think about it. But don't you see, Anna,' he went on, feigning deep sincerity, 'I had no choice. You gave me no choice. I couldn't allow you to go away full of bitter feelings. I was determined to repair the damage.'

'The damage you yourself caused,' she said bitterly.

'No, my dear,' he retorted. 'The damage *you* caused, through your stubborn, refractory nature. Honestly, Anna, I don't understand how you can refuse the affection of another person, a person who respects you. Are you determined to go through life entirely alone? No man is an island, you know.'

'If I understand you correctly,' Anna pronounced the words carefully, struggling to face him as dispassionately as possible, 'you've compromised me with the employers I've contacted since I left N.T.E.L. Does Chuck Robbins know about this?'

'Of course not,' he answered with wounded dignity. 'This is a private matter, between you and me.'

'So I suppose I won't be able to find a job,' she murmured, astounded by the malignance of the man beside her.

'Not at all, Anna,' he assured her. 'What's been done can be undone, just like that. With one phone call, I can see that you have a position worthy of your unique…gifts.'

'And what do I have to do? Go to bed with you?'

'Anna,' he whispered, glancing concernedly at the nearby tables, 'must you put such a negative construction on things? What am I? Some kind of monster? I have feelings, too, in case that hadn't occurred to you. Now, I simply want you to give our relationship another chance. If you see reason and do as I say, you'll have a job in no time, and a valuable friend in this business. Don't you see what I'm offering you?'

Before he could continue, the waiter appeared. A trout fillet, bathed in white sauce and garnished with an assortment of aesthetically cut vegetables, was placed before Anna.

'Frankly,' sighed Porter as the waiter faded into the shadows, 'I don't see how you can be so severe about all this. You're a young lady who is badly in need of a friend. You've already made one serious mistake in your profession, and it has cost you dearly. You're going to need help from someone in a responsible position, if you expect to find a decent job. Now, I know you have your sister's education at stake. Why don't you think about her for a change, and swallow your silly pride? You need me, and I need you. Don't you see, Anna? We can't do without each other.'

Suddenly the slice of fish before her seemed terribly forlorn and anything but appetising. She understood only too well what Porter Deman was up to. Like any predator, he was tightening the net around his prey, and gambling that its fear would make it all the more vulnerable to him. There was no denying that he possessed the weapons required to instil fear in her, as he had in other women.

'So it's quite simple, you see,' he said. 'With me, you have security and, I daresay, happiness. I can show you a very good time, Anna. I'm sure you know I mean what I say. On the other hand, without me, you're simply finished. I don't know how else to put it. Now what do you say?'

Her courage flagged suddenly as a wave of hopeless disgust broke over her. There was no point in threatening to expose this new treachery to Charles Robbins, or even in doing so without telling Porter. He would always find a way to destroy her. He had too much power, too much influence. There was no way to fight him.

Somehow she would have to find work without citing N.T.E.L. as a reference. But what if that failed as well? What if Porter Deman continued pursuing her, out of sheer perversity, and found ways to make her lose whatever job she could find? What if he decided to telephone her again at home, to torment her at his leisure?

'I'm waiting, Anna,' he said, apparently satisfied that the impact of his threat was dissipating her resistance. 'Waiting for your decision,' he added severely. 'It's either me or…nothing.'

Leaving her fish untouched, she folded her napkin carefully and placed it on the seat beside her. Unaware of the thought which was taking shape in her mind, he smiled to see her pick up her large wine glass.

Predators expect their prey to expose its flanks in terrified flight, she recalled. When, occasionally, the intended victim turns to face its attacker directly, the stronger predator may be so taken aback by the novelty of the situation that it renounces its meal and searches for a more pliant prey.

Porter Deman could indeed hurt her, she decided. But there was one thing he would never accomplish, even if his campaign of terror went on indefinitely. He would not frighten her into submission. She would not allow it.

'As I see it,' he was saying, touching his napkin to his lips, 'your choices have about run out.'

As Anna's slender arm extended towards him, her hand holding the glass of chilled wine, he watched in mute admiration of her finely formed limbs, for he assumed she was merely gesturing to him. Even when the glass began to tip, he remained motionless, the napkin still held to his lips. Only when the cold liquid soaked the unprotected trou-

sers of his costly suit with a wet slapping sound did he
realise what had happened.

Looking up in shock from his inundated lap, he saw
Anna pose the empty glass on the table before her with
calm deliberation.

She was already on her feet as the waiter approached,
superfluously intending to pull out the table for her.

'Goodbye, Mr Deman,' she said, striding firmly towards
the exit.

'You'll regret this!' she heard his warning voice behind
her. But the maître d'hôtel's respectful face occupied her
field of vision as he held a large oaken door open for her,
and she returned his smile with an even wider one of her
own.

The trees lining the street outside wore the first fiery bloom
of their autumn foliage under the early afternoon sun.
Walking quickly so as to put the greatest distance possible
between herself and the scene she had just experienced,
Anna turned the corner into Michigan Avenue.

She hesitated in confusion, not sure whether to wait at
the nearest bus stop or walk even further away. Unable to
make a decision, she wandered towards the Water Tower,
wrapping her coat around her against the gathering Chicago
wind. Every year at this time the chilled autumn breeze
carried a premonitory hint of the savage winter gusts that
would soon follow. Anna's empty stomach, fed only by one
sip of a Martini, ached with hunger, but she knew her tense
emotional state would not allow her to eat. Though she felt
weak and chilly, the fresh air seemed to brace her with its
energy.

Elegantly dressed men and women passed her, bound for
some of the costliest shops on the Avenue. Ahead, the
other-worldly splendour of Water Tower Place awaited the

scores of customers who would ride the glass-walled elevators to its tiers of boutiques this afternoon.

An older woman stood before the window of a dress shop, clutching the fur collar of her coat to her neck. A young girl, curiously overdressed, strode quickly along the sidewalk, her expensively cut blonde hair flowing in gentle ringlets over her shoulders. A kept woman? Anna wondered. The expensive mistress of a rich man who worked in the city…

Yellow taxicabs rolled heavily by, darting between buses whose motors whined angrily each time they lurched into traffic under the weight of their passengers. The Water Tower came into view, a curiously quaint relic among triumphant skyscrapers, its stone walls glowing like adobe under the bright sun. In the distance, the entrance to the Outer Drive swallowed a stream of vehicles which plunged like hurried blood cells through the city's commuter artery.

Doormen tooted their whistles for cabs under the heavy hotel canopies which protected their guests. Before long, powerful heat lamps would be lit under those canvas structures, to offer the hotels' visitors a measure of comfort as they hurried between the revolving doors and the interior of their taxi or limousine. They would be on their way to dinner, to an evening on the town, to Rush Street, Old Town. Excited tourists, lovers perhaps who had their rendezvous in the hotel, or businessmen, they would give the taxi driver an address…

Only a week ago, Anna reflected, she had been in this very spot on Marsh Hamilton's arm, listening to him joke affectionately about his native city, and feeling her senses fill to overflowing with his dauntless male strength. It was impossible to spend more than a moment in his company without becoming infected with his cheerful self-confidence. The city stretched before Marsh as a glittering, vibrant place awaiting his initiative and his domination. If he had ever known defeat or frustration, he had long since overwhelmed them through the irresistible force of his determined personality.

With a smile Anna imagined how heartily Marsh would approve her drenching of Porter Deman's perverted hopes. It was too bad, in a way, that she could never permit herself to tell him about it. Her moment of courageous resistance was over now, and she must face its consequences. Her future in her chosen career was a thing of the past. Unless she could find a job quickly in some other field of endeavour, the fragile fabric of her own life, as well as that of Sally, would unravel overnight.

But somehow she felt no desperation. The cold liquid that had sent such a shock through Porter Deman's arrogant features seemed also to have taken the edge off her own anxiety. At least she had acted, rather than to have futilely consumed her energies in flight. And she was free to continue taking action, no matter where it led her.

On Monday, she decided, she would journey to the Unemployment Office. After applying for benefits, she would scan the want ads with an open mind. Somehow she would find a position without citing N.T.E.L. as a reference. And she would personally make sure that Sally finished her education—regardless of the cost to herself.

Sally had suffered more than enough already. She would never experience that heady, warm feeling of leaving college for Thanksgiving or Christmas, boarding the train or bus, and coming home to a festive house where the family waited to greet her excitedly, take her bags into her old bedroom, overwhelm her with questions about school… Sally would never know the thrill of seeing those smiling, familiar faces waiting at the station, waving, or forcing back tears as they saw her off for another semester. Uprooted from the home that no longer existed, she could only visit her classmates' parents during vacations.

But she would get her degree, she resolved, without a single interruption. In no circumstances would she allow Sally to toil somewhere as a shopgirl or waitress while her course books sat in useless idleness on a shelf.

Absorbed by her determined reflections, Anna forgot both her hunger and her surroundings. She strolled homeward through Lincoln Park without noticing the eager shouts of the children who played their Saturday games on the lawns between all ranks of apartment buildings and the deserted beach. Only when Fullerton Avenue came abruptly into view did she realise that she was nearly home. The long walk had scarcely tired her, for the upheaval in her emotions had resolved itself into a virtually festive intensity.

Only one more tree-lined block separated her from the flat she had rented five years ago for its proximity to the bus line leading into the centre of the Loop. She could not predict whether her next job would force her to walk each morning to a more distant stop, or even to move to a less costly neighbourhood. It hardly mattered, she decided. Wherever she had to live, she would make a home for herself. Whatever work she did would still be an occupation. Life might be difficult, but never impossible.

'Nice day for a walk, isn't it?' a deep voice startled her as she approached her building. Disconcerted, she looked up from the sidewalk to see Marsh Hamilton leaning in casual comfort against the door of his car. The clear light of the autumn sun shone with golden warmth on his dark hair and tanned complexion. The dark slacks and windbreaker that clung to his hard limbs made him an indescribably handsome vision against the urban background which framed him.

'Yes, it is lovely out,' she smiled, concealing her surprise unconvincingly as she strode towards him. 'I'm afraid I haven't been paying enough attention to it. I must have been lost in thought.'

'Head in the clouds again?' he laughed. 'I hope you didn't bump into anyone on the street.'

'Not until this moment,' she smiled.

'Good,' he said. 'I'd feel cheated if you bumped into anyone but me.'

She accepted the hands he held out to her and stood before him, bewitched as never before by the probing gaze of the black eyes which held her with their teasing glimmer. He did not move from his relaxed position, but merely regarded her at arm's length, his large palms warming her cold fingers.

'You're chilled,' he observed, apparently unaware of the charged heat already tingling through her at his touch. 'You ought to be careful with this Chicago weather. Even on a nice day it will nip you when you're not looking.'

'I'll try to be more careful,' she teased.

'I'm beginning to think you need someone to look after you,' he added, his long fingers cradling her wrists. 'Bumping into strange men in hallways, going out in cold weather without enough warm clothing... You're a woman who needs watching.'

'Perhaps you're right there,' she said, recalling her uncertain attempts to deal with the jarring events of the past two weeks. 'Perhaps I should...'

But her words trailed into silence as his hand, having adjusted a strand of her windblown hair, caressed her cheek with lulling tenderness. Her eyes half-closed in pleasure, she stood transfixed by the seductive power of his nearness.

'I thought you were working today,' she said at last, regarding him curiously.

'I was.' He smiled. 'But I'm not any more.'

'I thought you said your partners were...' she began.

'Busy?' he interrupted. 'Yes, we're busy. On the other

hand, we're always busy. I was looking out my office window at this beautiful sun, and I suddenly had a wonderful idea. I thought I'd check it out with you before putting it into action.'

'Really?' she joked, hoping her banter would disguise the sensual flare his warm hands were kindling under her skin.

'Here's my idea,' he began. 'I happen to know a beautiful lake in northern Wisconsin. It has the clearest water in the whole state, and it's surrounded by thick woods. Birch, maple, oak…a little of everything. Since it's up north, the leaves naturally turn earlier in the fall, so that on a weekend like this it would be quite a showplace. There are lots of trails to walk in the woods, and a person can go canoeing or fishing or whatever else he wants to do around a lake.'

The black depths of his eyes, tinged with enigmatic merriment, came closer as his arms slipped around her waist.

'And, as luck would have it,' he went on, 'there's an inn there. A very pretty colonial place, with nice sitting rooms and quilted comforters on the beds, and no television, and old faded landscapes on the walls, and a dining room with a huge fireplace. It can be quite busy there in the summer, but today it will be nearly deserted. The owner and his wife are friends of mine. They enjoy running the place, and they both have a lot of personality. Of course, they're not at all pushy. They would welcome us warmly, and then fade into the background so as to respect our privacy. Shall I go on?'

Anna nodded, intoxicated by the tale of bucolic peace he was spinning, and reluctant to stop him.

'It's quite simple,' he continued, smiling, caressing her waist with quiet intimacy. 'You and I would make a couple of stops here in town, just to get ourselves ready, and then we would drive north in my car. It would take a while to get up there, even through Saturday traffic, and it would be dark by the time we arrived. But the fire would be burning, and the lights would be on in the lobby behind the veranda, and we'd have a nice hot drink to warm us up. Then, tomorrow morning, we'd have one of Elvira's special breakfasts before taking a long, relaxing walk around the lake. Before you knew it, we'd have the city's noise out of our systems.'

'You paint an awfully pretty picture,' she sighed, already beginning to count the reasons why it could never become a reality.

'I haven't finished,' he said. 'My partners in the firm owe me more than a few favours by now, so I'm sure they would look the other way if we made it a very long weekend. Since you're not working, it would be convenient for you, and of course it would be just the tonic I need. I haven't bothered to take a vacation in a long time, since I had no interest in relaxing somewhere alone. But now I would be with you, Anna, and I doubt that I would take much notice of the leaves or the lake or the inn. I'd concentrate on being the happiest man on earth.

'Of course,' he added with feigned concern, 'the whole thing depends to some extent on your sister. Is she in town this weekend?'

'Yes, I think so,' said Anna. 'But what does Sally have to do with this?'

'Well,' he said, his slow smile widening, 'you wouldn't want to get married without telling your sister, would you? She'd feel slighted if she missed your wedding this afternoon, don't you think?'

'Marsh!' Anna was too overwhelmed by the boldness of his proposal to think of an immediate response.

'Judge Bardwell is an old friend of mine,' he went on with unflappable calm. 'He'd be available to perform a quiet ceremony for us. I'd grab a witness from somewhere, we'd pick up Sally, and then drop her at her apartment on our way out of town. We'd have our time together up at the lake, come back next week, move your things over to my place, and live happily ever after.'

'Marsh, I...'

'After a while,' he interrupted, 'we'd move out of my apartment and into a house. We'd need more room, of course, in order to start a family. How many children would you like, Anna? Do you prefer boys or girls? Personally, I have an open mind on the subject...'

With a furtive glance down the quiet sidewalk, he had drawn her closer to him, and she felt the warmth of his desire add itself to the power of his will in a convincing combination.

'You've thought of everything,' she murmured against his chest.

'I think so,' he agreed. 'We'd help Sally finish college, and of course money would be no problem, since her expenses don't amount to much. In return, she'd babysit for us, I imagine. At some point you might decide to go back to work, if that's what you wanted—but you'd need maternity leave. Yes, Anna, I think I've thought of everything. As I say,' he smiled, 'it seems to me a workable plan. With one proviso.'

'And what is that?' she asked, returning the impassioned gaze of the ebony eyes that held her.

'Do you love me?' he asked.

With a grateful sigh she spoke words that had clamoured to escape her lips long before this moment.

'Yes, Marsh, I love you.'

'And I love you,' he whispered, holding her close to him. 'Shall we give up delaying the inevitable, then?'

For an answer she pressed herself to his hard body as the truth of his words came home to her. The cruel phone call that had prevented her from responding to his proposal last night was no more than a brief delay imposed upon a process which had been gaining momentum since the moment she met Marsh Hamilton. 'You're sure,' she questioned, smiling, 'that you want to saddle yourself with someone who has no job, no prospects…'

'Oh, you'll have a job, all right,' he laughed. 'You'll have your hands full with me, Anna. And your future will be our future.'

Something of his dauntless, cheerful confidence seemed to spread through her own depths as he held her close. And she knew that it had been so days earlier. Though she had struggled alone with her recent difficulties, she could not suppress the intuition that Marsh was somehow involved in her efforts, somehow supporting her from a distance. In her bitter passage from interview to interview, her blunt revelation of the truth to Charles Robbins, and even her blithe drowning of Porter Deman's lingering hopes, she had gathered strength from the bright image of the man who had crossed her path so recently.

Perhaps, in a mysterious way, she had already been looking back on these challenges from the vantage point of her happy future with him. Perhaps she had coped with them so fearlessly because she knew that the solitary existence they menaced was about to be eclipsed by a new life of unlimited promise.

'What do you say?' he asked. 'All we have to do is cross this sidewalk, go up those old stairs of yours, call your sister, and pack a bag. Then the future is ours.'

Anna felt herself turn to lead him into the shadows of her home. His strong arm rested on her shoulder like a steadfast beacon which freed her from every impulse to look backward. Already she was his, and she knew it.

He had taken her key and inserted it in the lock. The heavy door swung open easily.

CHAPTER SIX

'COME on, lazybones, get up!'

Marsh stood over Anna, his hands on his hips, the cheerful smirk on his lips plunged into shadow by the blinding light of the sun behind him.

'Mm-m, in a minute,' she purred. 'I like it here.'

The dry leaves crackling under her on the still-green grass were like a comfortable bed of straw. The cool of the earth under the warm blades of grass was so refreshing that she was loath to get up and continue walking.

'Come on, silly,' he prodded, dropping to his knee beside her. 'We're only up here for four days, so we have to keep moving. We've got exploring to do.'

'Uh-huh,' she smiled. 'Come here, you.' Grasping his shoulders, she pulled him down beside her and kissed his lips tenderly. 'That's adventurous enough for me,' she said.

'I see your point,' he agreed, returning her kiss with an intimacy that left her breathless. His hand strayed over her jacket, grazing the outline of her breasts under the suede, and came to rest beside her cheek. For a languorous moment he stroked her gently, contemplating the lush mane of her hair on its bed of leaves. The auburn waves seemed to take up the autumnal aura of their surroundings, as though Anna herself were a forest creature whose silken fur blended into the hues of the foliage around her.

She was gazing into his eyes with a calm he had not seen since he had known her. A slight smile of amusement on her lips, she toyed absently with the fabric of his wind-breaker, her eyes glowing with a strange, elfin satisfaction.

'Penny for your thoughts,' he said, his finger touching the soft skin beneath her ear.

'I love you,' she murmured.

Marsh smiled, a pained nostalgia coming over his features.

'When I think how long it took me to find you,' he said, 'and to hear you say those words. Five years in the same city, before you finally bumped into me!' With a theatrical shudder he banished the memory.

'I love you,' she repeated. 'You can hear it all you want, now. I love you, I love you, I love you.'

The exultation in her green eyes, framed by the hair splayed over the coloured leaves, was too bewitching to resist, and he bent to kiss her again. Her arms encircled him softly and, oblivious to the remote possibility that someone might pass, she hugged him to her, flexing her slender arms in an affectionate imitation of his own powerful embrace. With a histrionic gasp he made believe she had squeezed the wind out of him. But already his lips had touched the softness of her neck, and she felt his cool cheek against her own. Sandwiched between his warm body and the bed of leaves under her, she felt a mysterious peace enfold her, and lay motionless, her arms around him.

The sun glinted among fiery leaves as the branches of the huge oak swayed above her. Crisp autumnal odours were everywhere. Here at Crystal Lake, just as Marsh had predicted, the fall was considerably more advanced than in Chicago—and incomparably beautiful. Luck had been with them, and the Lake was warmed by fresh Indian summer air so pleasant that one nearly felt tempted to have a swim. The long walks they had taken through the many woods near the inn were like so many purifications, freeing Anna from the city's tensions and from her own painful memories.

Within minutes of her agreement to marry him, Marsh had been on the telephone, making hurried arrangements for a wedding in Judge Bardwell's chambers. Anna, feeling her excitement grow by leaps and bounds, had called Sally to explain the urgency of the situation. It was all happening so fast that her head was spinning as though in a pleasant dream.

Judge Bardwell had done his best to superimpose a stern, judicial expression over his approving smile.

'Mr Hamilton,' he said impishly, 'can you give this court one good reason why you deserve this beautiful woman?'

Sally had stood by, her eyes lit with the puckish satisfaction of the matchmaker, as the brief ceremony was performed. Several of Marsh's colleagues from the firm arrived, laden with bottles of champagne and makeshift wedding presents. The air seemed charged with humour and affection on all sides.

'I'm so happy for you, Anna,' Sally had declared, kissing her sister. 'I know you've made the right decision.'

And in a whirl of activity which left Anna breathless, it was over. She found herself in the car with Marsh, embarked on the long drive to northern Wisconsin. A soft smile played over his lips as she held his hand. The highway flowed under them like a moving ribbon in the cool autumn air. And as afternoon turned to dusk, and the car's headlights illuminated the wooded expanse all around, Marsh and Anna talked and talked, filled with plans for the days ahead and the life together that awaited them. The feelings of release, of unaccustomed calm he had brought her over the past week blossomed now into a great glow of peace and happy expectation in the warm quiet of the car.

At last it seemed everything would be all right. Dazzled

by the sudden transition her life had made from utter desperation to heady excitement, Anna clung to Marsh as the one clear beacon that showed the way to her future. During their late supper at the hotel, she found herself gazing into his eyes with an eager avidity that made her blush.

After tipping the sleepy bellboy, Marsh turned to her, his eyes filled with humour and tenderness.

'Well,' he said, 'Mrs Hamilton, is it?'

'Mrs Hamilton,' she stated, smiling from the bed.

'At last,' he murmured, enfolding her in his powerful arms.

And the last traces of her unhappiness seemed banished for ever by the calm yielding she felt in his embrace. Finally she could accept him, open herself to him without second thoughts, experience the fiery intimacy of his lovemaking without an inner struggle to dominate the emotions that bound her to him. And it was a magical sense of sudden belonging that shuddered through her as she grasped and caressed him, certain at last that she was his for ever.

After what seemed a long dream of pure rapture, pleasure had given way to happy exhaustion in her, and she fell into a sweet, refreshing sleep in his arms.

Now, as she lay on the cool grass, her body warmed by the nearness of the man she loved, she felt a flutter in her senses which was instantly echoed by a subtle quickening in the touch of his flesh against her own.

'Let's go back,' Marsh murmured into her ear. 'We'll explore later.'

He felt her nod, and in a single lithe movement he had arisen, pulling her gently to her feet beside him. His hand rested quietly on her hip as they walked through the crackling leaves toward the inn. The sun shone through the boughs of the trees with a sharp, bracing brilliance, as though in celebration of a holiday from which all care and melancholy were banished. The crisp freshness of the world around them was a harmonious counterpoint to the hidden heat that linked them.

'Anna,' he said with sudden seriousness, 'we've talked a lot since we got up here, but you've never really told me how you came to leave N.T.E.L. I never asked Bob Samuels or anyone else about it, because I thought you'd want to tell me yourself sooner or later. Do you want to talk about it?'

Disturbed by the thoughts his question gave rise to in her own mind, she held herself closer to him.

'No,' she said. 'I just want to be with you.'

'You're sure?'

'It wasn't very important,' she said, 'and it's all over now. Now that I'm with you...'

'Okay.' He smiled, hugging her as they walked. 'As long as you feel you can put it behind you. But remember: we're married now, and you can tell me anything. If they treated you badly, you've got me to complain to, if you want.'

'I'm not in a complaining mood,' Anna laughed. 'I was happy there for a few years, and then not so happy. I don't blame N.T.E.L. itself. It was just a thing that didn't work out.'

She was disturbed to keep her chagrin over N.T.E.L. a secret, at the beginning of a new life, a new commitment to Marsh. But the episode, and the memory of Porter Deman, was too loathsome a thing to bring to mind now. She simply could not allow it to trouble the happiness to which she clung with all her heart.

Besides, she knew how upset and angry Marsh would be if she told him of Porter Deman's vicious, clumsy attempts at seduction. The insult to her integrity would pain Marsh deeply, and she couldn't help fearing that he would make up his mind to punish Porter with some sort of retribution. Now was no time for revenge, and Marsh was a man capable of strong emotions.

But she could not forget Debby's opinion that something should be done to stop Porter Deman, for the sake of his future victims. When her honeymoon was over, she resolved, she would discuss the whole situation dispassionately with Marsh. His knowledge that Anna herself was no longer imperilled directly by it would insure his objectivity. She was more than confident that, with his intelligence and resourcefulness, he would know how to take action against so outrageous an injustice.

They would decide what to do together, she determined. But there was no point in spoiling the peaceful closeness of their honeymoon by pondering so distressing a topic. For now, she coveted all the happiness she could find with Marsh. She must derive strength from her love for him, and try to forget the last and most desperate moments of her life without him.

She stood silent by his side in the warm corridor as he turned the key in the heavy lock. With a muffled swish, the door swung back over the thick carpet and they were inside the room. The bright afternoon light shone gaily through the window, and then vanished in shadows as he pulled the curtains shut. The quiet beige walls, with their assortment of landscapes painted in dark hues, were plunged into darkness. Only a pale rim of light remained at the top of the curtains.

A curiously sensual feeling crept over Anna as she stood in the darkness, her eyes half shut, listening to the sounds made by Marsh's movements about the room. It was as though a deliberate silence had fallen between them, charged by their mutual knowledge of what was about to happen.

Her jacket lay on the chair now, and she had slipped off her shoes. She stood in her bare feet, consciously sensing the silky fabric of her blouse, the tightness of her jeans, on the alert flesh underneath. Her embrace with Marsh outside, in the cool air, had stirred her senses to a sudden tumult of desire, and she knew now that in a matter of seconds her impatient body would be naked again, free to spread its passion to the still air of the room, to melt with abandon into his own heat, to feel its excitement expand against his muscular limbs.

In this suspended moment, every fibre of her was tensed with pent-up wanting. Flares of ticklish passion throbbed under her clothes, clamouring for a release which would not be long in coming.

And that was the secret of the pleasure that taunted and excited her as she stood barefoot on the soft carpet. She felt as though there was a subtle nudity in the room itself, a mysterious nakedness to all the surfaces, the soft sounds, the quiet corners surrounding her. She could feel the taut, vibrant expanse of her own skin, breathing this charged air, and each current that touched the downy flesh of her arms, her legs, her cheek, was itself a knowing caress.

He was coming closer now. With a sort of wild attention she stood with her eyes closed, contemplating this last split second before he would touch her. An inner tremor told her she could not bear it longer.

As though he had read her thoughts, Marsh stood silent before her. His lips were the first part of him to touch her, and for a long moment they stood that way, an intimate, warm kiss their only contact. Although the very soul within her strained so urgently outward that she could barely keep from throwing herself at him with shameless abandon, Anna managed to remain somehow in that throbbing immobility.

Time seemed to hesitate, to wait upon itself and speed up with little jarring thrusts. Now, at last, the surface of his strong, unclothed body grazed her gently, and his hands slid over the fabrics that covered her. For a moment he caressed her hips, her arms, as though his touch were amused, titillated by the clothes that separated him from her. But already his fingertips had reached recesses, slender curves, that quickened so tempestuously under their passage that he knew he must free her now from her coverings.

With subtle expertise the gentle touch of his hands loosened her jeans, her blouse, passed languidly over her back and left her bra hanging undone on her shoulders. Bit by bit, curve by curve, her flesh opened itself to the air under his caress, her increasing nudity seeming a mobile, musical thing which drove them both to a tumult of silent wanting in the darkness.

As hard as she tried to concentrate on this teasing rhythm that stripped her slowly, the haze of desire in which she bathed was too bewitching to penetrate, and she came to herself already naked, her soft skin feeling the hardness of his body against her. The mystery of his man's flesh, so muscular, so incisive, and yet all softened into a sweet gentleness that moulded itself to her own soft curves, hypnotised her. And as waves of response flicked across her breasts, her thighs, her shoulders, she felt herself go to him, press against him with a thousand little shudders. In its wild independence, her body moved with him and spoke to him in a language all its own.

As he bore her easily to the bed, placing her on the soft comforter so gently that she felt almost weightless in his arms, it seemed there was no limit to the terrible intimacy with which he overwhelmed her senses. The profound inner tingle that quickened at the very sight of him, and erupted into waves of passion as his lips and hands drove her to ecstatic heights, was at the heart of her woman's body.

She knew she could keep no secret from the man behind the body that covered her now, in this dark room charged with pleasure. Underneath her visible personality, he knew how to make her talk, through her sighs, the responses of her limbs, in the language that he understood. Such was the penetrating power of her intimacy with him, this sensual delight that fed itself on her love for him. He was already rooted so deeply inside her that he must immediately sense every corner of doubt, of fear, of pain that might separate her from him.

And now, as a greater urgency came over their movements, melding them in an enormous, heated embrace, Anna forgot her cautious thoughts and gave herself to him utterly. Last night she had tasted the heady joy of making love to Marsh for the first time; today she knew the full meaning of belonging to him.

At last she lay quietly in his embrace, calmed and soothed by the weight of the hand resting on her breast, her little gasping breaths giving way to a slow, regular respiration as she rested her head on his shoulder. It was no wonder, she thought, that sensual intimacy was called a knowing of a person. Marsh knew her now, for he had stolen into her very heart, had felt her love fill up her whole personality in response to him. And she could trust him never to abuse the power that knowledge gave him.

Recalling his tactful questions about her misfortune at N.T.E.L., she looked forward to the day when she would tell him the whole truth. It would be wonderful to unburden herself with total trust in this sharply introspective man. But all that mattered now was the wonderful security of being with him, knowing that she was no longer alone, that she would never be alone again.

'Penny for your thoughts,' he whispered.

A great exultation suddenly took possession of her, and she squirmed to her knees beside him, her lips close to his own.

'I love you,' she cooed. 'Now give me my penny.'

His kiss was her reward.

In his own way, Marsh must have sensed the mysterious message of utter trust and commitment carried by the deep

passion of their lovemaking, for in the days that followed
his demeanour reflected a quiet joy in Anna's company.
Few words were spoken between them. Somehow the touch
of their hands and the glances they exchanged seemed to
say all that was required. The meaning of their relationship
was clear to both, and their every gesture was a promise to
depend on each other and to make whatever sacrifices
might become necessary to insure the success of their marriage. Over and over again, they plighted their troth through
the affection in their words, their smiles, and the utter closeness of their lovemaking.

The four days at Crystal Lake passed as though in a
sunlit dream. Like a steadfast partner in their happiness, the
Indian summer warmth persisted throughout their stay. Everywhere they walked, trees aflame with colour stood
stately against the clear blue sky, their leaves fluttering
gently, as though conversing with the breeze that caressed
them. The lake's limpid water was like a magic mirror reflecting not only the rocks of its bottom, but also the brilliant hues of the foliage on its shores. Everywhere their
walks took them, a deep autumnal pungency greeted them,
serving as a poetic backdrop to their own feelings. It was
a change of season, a natural ferment of the woods' life
which seemed to celebrate the change that had brought
them together.

The long drive back to Chicago was not filled with excited conversation, as had been the trip to Crystal Lake.
Instead, as the north woods gave way to rolling farmland,
and finally to the flat vistas of Illinois, a silence made of
pure fulfilment and understanding lay between them, punctuated now and then by a happy remark, a laugh, a caress.

Marsh's apartment, located in a skyscraper that towered
above the Loop, was all that Anna might have expected.
Its tasteful décor, highlighted by functional modern furni-

ture, glass surfaces, and clear white walls, reflected his solid masculinity and his impatience with frills of any kind. He threw open the curtains to reveal a dazzling vista which included the river, the Marina Towers, the Wrigley Building.

'Marsh, it's wonderful!' Anna exclaimed.

'Think you can stand it here?'

'I'll go anywhere with you,' she said, smiling.

With a look of amused concentration, he showed her all the rooms, pausing at the large closet in the bedroom.

'Think you can get all your clothes in there?' he asked with a critical frown.

'Certainly,' she said. 'I don't have that many. My salary has never allowed a lot of buying.'

'That will change now.' He smiled. 'I want you to have a wardrobe that suits your every mood. As long,' he added, hugging her, 'as you don't mind taking those clothes off once in a while.'

It was agreed that Anna would take a cab to her apartment tomorrow to pick up her clothes and a few personal effects. Marsh would have a full day of work, but promised to be home early. In the days to come Anna would see to clearing out her apartment and finding room for everything in her new home. After a good long rest, she would decide whether to look for work.

'The honeymoon isn't over yet,' Marsh assured her. 'We're going to enjoy ourselves. And there's no time,' he added, trapping her suddenly in his powerful arms, 'like the present.'

'Well, how's the newlywed?' asked Marsh's secretary as he entered the office the next morning.

'Never better, Mary. Did you all manage to survive without me?'

'In a manner of speaking,' she sighed.

'Where's John?'

'He's with Harold and a couple of lawyers. They want you to meet them for lunch. It's about a murder.'

'Murder?' Marsh feigned surprise. 'In this town? I don't believe it.'

'Your mail is waiting,' she added as he pushed open the door of his office.

After opening the window to let in some fresh air, Marsh stood over his desk, sorting through envelopes and manila folders and doing his best to recall the state of his case load before he left for Wisconsin. There was work to be done, and he would have to have a talk with his partners about pending cases.

'What's this?' he wondered absently, opening a letter bearing the N.T.E.L. logo. 'Oh, yes,' he stated. In his concern about Anna's difficulties in finding a job, he had had Mary write N.T.E.L. for her personnel file, on the pretext that she was applying for work with his firm. In the excitement of his marriage and honeymoon he had forgotten all about the request. Now he recalled his curiosity as to whether the company had somehow mistreated Anna, and he felt the furtive thrill of the eavesdropper as he prepared to see what her bosses thought of her.

His face became serious as he tossed the secretary's covering letter aside and began to read the computer's file. After a moment he sat down at his desk, reading and then re-reading the words before him.

'I don't believe it,' he murmured, glancing about the room before perusing the file for a third time. Finally he put the letter down and stood up to pace the office.

It was simply too much to take in all at once. Anna, a thief? A security risk... And the other part, the part about offering herself sexually in exchange for leniency. It couldn't be! That couldn't be Anna Halpern, Anna Hamilton they were talking about. It was unbelievable.

God knows, he thought, she did seem terribly upset last week and the week before. It was obvious there was some kind of trouble. And no wonder she wasn't getting anywhere in the job market, with this thing in her personnel file. But an accusation of such enormity! What in hell had she done to deserve this? There must be some sort of mistake. They must have mixed her up with somebody else.

Quickly he turned back to the desk and read the damning document once more. No, there was no mistake. It was Anna, all right. They had all her numbers, her job record.

Marsh stared out the window in perplexity. 'Well,' he thought, 'I can understand why she didn't want to talk about this.' In retrospect, it was clear she must have had some inkling of what was going on. Otherwise, why the air of desperation, of depression, of pained reticence about her termination? But why hadn't she told him about it? What was she hiding? If she was innocent, there must be some explanation for this unbelievable smear. If she was innocent...

Remembering his lawyers' instincts, he tried to imagine the circumstances that could have led to such a thing. But nothing made sense. If it were all some kind of crazy frame-up, then why hadn't they prosecuted her? So much malice breathed through the lines of that text that it seemed inconceivable they wouldn't have had her arrested. Unless they had their doubts...

But the accusation was so unequivocal, so overwhelming. Who would make up a thing like that? Suppose she was guilty, even if the idea strained credulity. Why would she do it? Fear? Blackmail? What about the people who put her up to it? Perhaps they weren't satisfied, when she failed. Perhaps that was who was on the phone that night, when Anna suddenly became so upset.

What had she said? *'That's out of the question.'* And then: *'Where?'* Such secretive talk. She couldn't have been so upset about the simple difficulty of finding another job. She had to know what was going on.

So she was desperate, for whatever reason. She had nowhere to turn. Knew she wouldn't find another job, knew that that thing was in her file. Or feared that it was. And she had her sister to worry about...

'So what did she do?' he thought, sitting down heavily to blunt the realisation. 'She married me.

'That's why she agreed so abruptly. It was the day after that enigmatic phone call. I didn't seriously expect her to agree without a lot of thought, a long delay. I concluded it was love that was motivating her. Perhaps it was desperation.'

He struggled confusedly to adjust his own mental image of Anna to the picture painted by the personnel file. Anna was the essence of honesty, self-respect, pride. The file described someone who undertook illegal behaviour for the benefit of an unidentified conspirator. For money? Or political reasons? Or both... And the offer of sexual favours seemed to indicate either an utterly loathsome personality, or, perhaps, some sort of blind commitment to a cause. But none of this made sense when ascribed to Anna.

With a sinking feeling he suddenly imagined her using him, marrying him through some ulterior motive. It was too fantastic to believe, but it hurt.

'Well, I'll just have to get it out of her,' he thought. It had been one thing to respect her privacy when all he knew was that she was having trouble finding a job. It was quite another to keep silent about so outrageous a discovery.

She would probably have an explanation. There was no sense in getting angry until he had heard her out. But in spite of his resolution to be reasonable, he felt a dark anger in his heart. Whatever the explanation, she had presumed to marry him without ever having confided in him about so grave a matter. She had simply assumed that he was not worthy of her trust.

But surely, if she was innocent, she would have spoken up! As he stood alone in his office, Marsh found it more and more difficult to believe Anna could be blameless, even though the deeds ascribed to her seemed out of character. She must have done something, something blameworthy, to get herself into this mess.

Her image was receding from his mind's eye, becoming less and less familiar, more alien and disconcerting, as he thought over the revelations in the file. He found himself wondering in consternation at his own haste in marrying this woman he knew so little. Perhaps she was motivated by things she had kept from him. Who knew? Perhaps there were parts of her life, her character, that he knew nothing about.

'I want you and need you,' he had insisted in his innocence as he proposed to her. *'I don't need to know any more.'* How hollow those words rang now!

He recalled his unspoken speculations about the men in Anna's life. She was a strikingly beautiful woman, clearly not the type to lead a life without involvements with the opposite sex. There must be a man in this plot somewhere. A contact, a boss—something.

Now he remembered his visceral impression that the person on the phone that night, whose words had elicited such terse replies from Anna, was a man. *'Where?'* she had asked, turning her back to Marsh as she spoke into the phone.

The torments of jealousy began to add themselves to his already painful thoughts. He imagined Anna engaged in behaviour he had never dreamed possible. He imagined her attempt to seduce the boss who had confronted her with the evidence against her. The idea of her offer, her prop-

osition, the expression she must have had on her face, as
seductive as possible… It was intolerable.

'No,' he said aloud, shaking off his suspicions. 'She'll
have an explanation. There's no sense in jumping to conclusions. But, by God, she'll tell me what the hell is going
on, or I'll…'

Suddenly the most disturbing thought of all struck him.
There was Sally. Suppose, for the sake of argument, that
Anna did what she did for money. God knew she needed
it for Sally's education, since their parents' deaths had left
them without a nickel. Suppose she failed to accomplish
her mission and was not paid by whoever put her up to it.
Then, having lost her job, she would have been desperate.
She would not have known where to turn for money.

He recalled his own cajoling efforts to persuade her to
marry him. *'We'll help Sally finish college,'* he had said.
'Money will be no problem.' Obviously Anna had taken
him at his word.

And only last night he had insisted on taking care of
Sally's pending tuition payments immediately, so that his
new wife's lingering financial worries could be dissipated
without further ado. He had laughed off Anna's protesting
complaints about her own insolvency, belittling the very
idea of money and its attendant woes.

'If you want to pay me back,' he had grinned, 'just step
right over here.' The delightful, soft kiss she had placed on
his lips had seemed an almost disproportionate payment for
so insubstantial an amount.

But it could not have seen insubstantial to her, in her
desperate need.

'What a sucker I've been,' he thought. 'No Surprises
Hamilton! Well, I've had the surprise of my life this time.'
As a successful lawyer who was more than vulnerable to
Anna's charms, he had appeared on the scene just in time
to serve as her escape from the predicament she found her-

self in. How fortunate for her that he was walking down that N.T.E.L. corridor at the propitious moment! And within two weeks she had become his wife...

The two images of Anna began to cease contradicting each other. Now he could picture Anna who stooped to illegal and perhaps despicable actions out of desperate loyalty to her sister. Including marrying a man she had just met—a man who was obviously hellbent on marrying her as soon as possible.

'Come on,' he upbraided himself, 'take it easy. Get control of yourself. There's an answer to all this, and you'll find it.'

But the tormenting thoughts that assailed him would not cease their cacophony inside his mind. Angry with himself, with Anna, and with this whole mess which had suddenly thrown his life into chaos, he slammed the desk drawer on the file and left the office.

CHAPTER SEVEN

ANNA heard the unfamiliar sound of Marsh's key in the lock just as she had finished her preparations for dinner. It had been a busy, happy day. After a restful sleep, she had had coffee with Marsh this morning and then journeyed to her old apartment. Its bland, forlorn furnishings, which for so long had been the scene of her loneliness, had the look of relics. The patina of time seemed already to have marked them with a prehistoric aura. They were the personal effects of someone who no longer existed: Anna Halpern, solitary working woman. Now she could move among them with easy confidence, picking out an item here and there to take across the city to her new home, her new life. The rest would soon fade into oblivion as the old flat was rented to a stranger.

It was a heady feeling, tinged with the childish excitement of a holiday. Even the rays of sunshine streaming in the window had lost their faded look, and seemed to radiate from that high place across the city where life had begun anew for her. After gathering her clothes in suitcases and filling a box with the things she needed most, she had helped the friendly cab driver carry it all downstairs. How strange it felt to ride a cab through the Loop! The city seemed so elegant, so vibrantly metropolitan, that Anna could not help experiencing a tourist's excitement as theatres, department stores, famous Chicago landmarks passed by.

After putting her things away in the large bedroom closet

and bureau, she studied Marsh's kitchen. Although the refrigerator was nearly empty, the cupboards and spice rack confirmed the impression made by the meal he had cooked at her flat. He was indeed a good cook, and had had occasion to buy most of the ingredients needed for gourmet recipes. Sitting with a cup of coffee before the magnificent picture window, Anna made a short list of groceries to buy. She wanted to make him something special tonight, to welcome him home to his first evening of married life.

For a few precious moments she sat gazing at the urban vista outside the window, allowing herself to savour the novelty of the situation. She was actually to live here, in this apartment, with the handsome man who had swept her off her feet from the first instant she had seen him. It all seemed too good to be true.

At last, afraid her bubble would burst if she dwelt too long on her happiness, she had gone out to an unfamiliar downtown grocery store and bought what she needed. And now the preparations were finished.

'Welcome home.' She smiled, rising to greet him.

His kiss was less than passionate as he rested his hand on her shoulder before throwing his briefcase on a chair.

'Hard day?' she asked, imagining the busy schedule he had left in abeyance during their honeymoon.

'In more ways than one,' he grunted.

'Would you like a drink?' she asked, feeling her happy mood dissolve under a nameless trepidation.

'I'll make it.' He disappeared into the kitchen. She heard the sound of ice being dropped into his glass.

'I'm making you something special tonight,' she called. There was no answer. Instead, she heard cupboards being opened and closed, the muffled thump of the refrigerator door. After a moment he crossed to the bedroom, drink in hand, without saying a word.

After two minutes that seemed an eternity to Anna, he

emerged dressed in slacks and a sweater, and sat down with a sigh in the chair facing her. His expression was pained, distracted.

'You look tired,' she said tentatively. 'Had a lot of work piled up while we were gone?'

Marsh grunted. 'You never know,' he said darkly, 'what's going to pop up when you turn your back for a second.'

'Is it still the hard case you mentioned last week?' she asked.

'They're all hard,' he said, without looking at her, his jaw set in a rigid, unhappy look. 'The hardest part,' he went on, darting her a significant glance, 'is trying to get people to tell you the truth. Everyone is always hiding something.'

Silence fell again as he finished his drink and strode to the kitchen to get another. It was clear something was wrong. Anna had never seen Marsh's accustomed cheerfulness disappear in so total a manner, and she was forced to reflect that she had not known him long enough to be familiar with all his moods. On the other hand, his demeanour seemed far too enigmatic and even dangerous to be explained by a mere mood. Something must be seriously wrong.

He returned to his chair, giving her an inscrutable glance as he sat down.

'Is something the matter, Marsh?' she asked, unable to bear this stony silence a minute longer. 'You don't seem to be yourself.'

'A lot of people,' he retorted with ill-concealed anger, 'are not quite themselves, I discover. Not quite what they seem.'

'What do you mean?'

'You think you know someone,' he said. 'You think you understand a situation. Then you find out you've been ignorant of the real facts of the case, because someone has been misrepresenting himself, in order to try to hoodwink you. It isn't fun being a dupe, Anna, believe me.'

'I don't understand,' she said. 'What case you are talking about?'

'It's a little closer to home than that, my love,' he said darkly.

'Why don't you tell me what you're getting at?' she asked, flushing under his accusing stare. 'Must you talk in circles?'

'I've been going around in circles for quite some time,' he said, arising suddenly and seizing his briefcase. 'If it hadn't been for one little break, one little accident, I might have gone on that way for ever.'

'Marsh,' she pleaded, genuinely frightened by his words and his scowling aspect, 'what are you talking about?'

'There,' he said, throwing the letter on the coffee table before her. 'Read it for yourself, Anna. Then explain it to me, if you can.'

Fearfully she opened the envelope, although the sight of the N.T.E.L. logo and address already sufficed to tell her that something grave had happened.

At first the impersonal message, headed by her name, Social Security number, and address, seemed merely strange—a curious eavesdropping on her identity, intended to be passed among others. Then the horrifying words of the file began to sink in.

A great chill went through her limbs as she saw the monstrous extent of Porter Deman's chicanery. It had been one thing to realise that she was not finding a new job because Porter had done something, some obscure thing to harm her. It was quite another to see her name vilified, her character assassinated, in the text of this official document. It was as though the whole company, the gigantic N.T.E.L. corporation, had acquiesced in this malignant plan to spread evil lies about her to any employer who would listen.

'My God,' she thought, feeling faint from the shock of seeing the file. 'My God!' But she said nothing. Over and over again, she read the words in stunned disbelief. Distantly, she heard the sound of the ice clinking in Marsh's glass. He had gone back to the kitchen, probably to make himself another drink.

'No wonder,' she thought. 'After what he must think of me now.'

Her emotions seemed to have retreated to a faraway corner of her mind, and warred chaotically with each other. She felt so cold that she thought she must be pale as a ghost. In her numbness she did not notice the tears which ran silently down her cheeks.

She heard his voice as though across a gulf of shadow.

'See what I mean?' he said cruelly, triumphantly. 'You never know what you're going to find out about someone you thought you knew pretty well.'

'Where did you get this?' she heard herself ask.

'What difference does it make where I got it?' he shot back.

'No, I meant…I mean.' Her words came out chaotically, uncontrollably. She had to struggle to determine what she wanted to say.

'It isn't true,' she said at last. 'It isn't true.'

He sat in silence across the room.

'Then what is true?' he asked at length. 'Just what the hell *is* true about you, Anna? You've been lying to me for so long, hiding things from me for so long, I think it's about time you said one true thing to me.'

'I haven't lied to you,' she protested lamely.

'That's a good one,' he laughed bitterly. 'The first time I ever met you, you claimed you were quite ignorant of your company's inner workings. A small cog, you called yourself. Apparently you understated your expertise.'

'That was true,' she said, acutely aware that the document before her contradicted her words.

'But that was only the beginning,' he shrugged off her denial. 'You saw fit to tell me that you left N.T.E.L. because things "weren't working out", as you put it. At the time, I saw no reason to suspect there was anything more to it. I let myself believe that you and the company had simply become incompatible, for some reason of convenience or personality, or whatever. Are you going to tell me that was true as well?'

Anna shook her head. 'No,' she admitted, 'that was not true.'

'Well,' Marsh smiled ironically, 'at least we've made a step in the right direction. Where shall we go from here? Let's see... I've seen your sister, so I know she really exists. There's no point in wondering whether you made her up along with your other lies. And the cheque I put in the mail for her tuition this morning was real enough. As soon as the university cashes it, I'll be able to set my mind at rest on that score. How about your parents? Are they really dead? Are you really from Bloomington?'

'Don't be cruel, Marsh. Please!' The tears inundating her flushed cheeks belied her expression of stunned panic. 'I've never lied to you. I just couldn't...talk about what happened.'

'You'll talk about it now,' he warned. 'And you'd better talk straight, Anna.'

Shocked into momentary silence by the enormity of the situation, Anna tried desperately to think. But the obscene success of Porter Deman's evil design seemed overwhelming. After having cost her her job and preventing her from finding another one, he had managed to come between her and the husband she loved. It seemed every bit as futile to explain herself to Marsh as to convince a prospective employer that the file was full of lies. The letter was official.

It carried the weight of the company itself, and emerged from the endless banks of computers which made up not only N.T.E.L., but the whole business establishment of the city, the nation. How could she bluntly deny what was there in black and white, for all to see?

'I'm waiting,' said Marsh, a sardonic smile curling his lips.

'All right,' she began miserably, 'I'll try to explain.' Every corner of her body, only recently cleansed and purified by her intimacy with Marsh, suddenly curled up on itself, stung by the nausea of her memory of Porter Deman. The evil she had seen incarnated in the file seemed to penetrate her like a poison, making her feel unclean and violated, as though in this very moment Porter Deman's vile hands still reached out towards her. And in truth, had he now found a way to invade the very privacy of her marriage, to transform her loving husband into the hurt, accusing figure who now stared at her without trust?

'None of it is true,' she insisted. 'I can't understand how he…how this happened. They know, at N.T.E.L., that this isn't true.'

'They know,' he mimicked pitilessly, 'that what they themselves had attested to in your personnel file is a lie? You must be kidding, Anna.'

'I mean,' she persisted, 'they assured me there would be nothing in the file, even though they had to…fire me.' Her hand rose to her knitted brow as she tried to sort out the confusing facts thronging her mind.

'But that's exactly what the file says,' Marsh taunted her. 'That you tried to convince them not to make any of it official. You have a lot of explaining to do, Anna.'

'Please,' she sighed, 'let me finish.' But she could hardly find words to describe the miasma of misfortune created by Porter Deman. Though she knew the truth was her only ally, her shame and disbelief paralysed her. How could she explain away so complex and convincing a web of lies?

'I'll tell you,' she said, turning pale, 'what I told the Vice-President when this whole thing began. I never saw the file they claim was in my desk. I never pulled it from the computer. It was…it was all the work of one man. He did this to me. As for the part about attempting to…to seduce…' Her eyes filled with tears once more, and she could not suppress a sob of pain and exasperation. 'This is a lie—a horrid, awful lie.'

'What man?' asked Marsh. 'What are you talking about? Your own Vice-President's signature is under this text. Are you trying to tell me he's framing you?'

'No.' She shook her head, trying to clear the cobwebs caused by this complicated dilemma about which Marsh knew nothing. 'Another man. Someone from N.T.E.L. He tried to force me to…do something improper. When I wouldn't, he told me I'd be fired. The next day I was fired—because of this classified file business. I knew he was behind it, but there was nothing I could do. Mr Robbins didn't believe me, but he said he wouldn't mention the incident in my personnel file, so that I would be able to find another job in the field. Then I couldn't find a job, and…and this is obviously why. He did this—the other man. He even told me…'

'What man?' asked Marsh. 'What was improper? What do you mean when you say he told you? How could Robbins not know about this, since it's over his own signature? You're not making sense, Anna. You'd better start telling a more coherent story. Or is it too hard to make up a thing like this on the spur of the moment? Is that it?'

A curious sensation stole insidiously through Anna. How loathsome it was to be a victim, a prey. The passivity of the role seemed to penetrate to one's very bones. Trapped, immobilised by the staring eyes which demanded that she submit, that she do the will of someone else, or suffer the consequences... A profound, resentful anger began to alloy her terrified sense of guilt. How long was this bondage to continue? How long must she continue to cower under the imperious stares of severe, demanding men?

'I'm waiting, Anna.'

For a cruel instant Marsh's deep voice brought back the memory of Porter Deman speaking the same words as he sat rocking in his desk chair under the painting on his office wall. *'I'm waiting, Anna...'*

She looked up at Marsh. Even the power of her love was not sufficient to dissipate the sudden suspicion she felt. Just like Porter Deman, like Charles Robbins, like all the polite but demanding personnel managers she had had interviews with, Marsh was immured within his prideful man's pre-occupations. He sat there, in his wounded masculinity, turning all his energies to his accusation of her. His pride was hurt by the revelation that he did not possess every shred of information about her private life. He was making no effort to listen or understand, but only to accuse.

'I didn't tell you about this,' she said firmly, 'because it was too horrible, and upsetting, and...' she searched for the word which would describe her state of mind, 'unjust. Perhaps I was wrong, but I wanted to leave it behind me. The charges are false. They were concocted by an executive who had a personal grudge against me. I know for a fact that he is responsible for this file, as he was for the original accusation.'

'Who?' Marsh asked, his black eyes glittering with a light so dangerous that Anna felt a shudder of real fear before him. 'Who did this? What personal grudge? What improper thing?'

Anna shook her head, tormented by his stabbing questions. A great surge of impotent anger possessed her. She could not bear to be humiliated further by the web of lies surrounding her. And even though she knew her resentment against Marsh was not entirely justified, she felt that her agony of useless self-defence must stop somewhere.

'He wanted me to go to bed with him,' she said at last, feeling darkly indifferent to the consequences of her revelation. 'I wouldn't do it, so he took his revenge.'

'Who?' The menacing intensity in Marsh's voice was almost unbearable to hear.

'I told Charles Robbins the man's name,' said Anna, feeling suddenly, pridefully alone. 'I suggested that he investigate the situation for himself. But I see no reason to tell you his name, Marsh. To be frank, it's none of your business. He's the company's problem now. If they let him get away with an ugly thing like this,' she glanced at the tear-stained document, 'so be it. I'm finished with them.'

'But you're not finished with me,' said Marsh. 'Not yet, anyway. If you expect me to believe this story—which seems, by the way, a little less credible with every detail you add—you'd better make a clean breast of it. And I'd suggest you start with the name of the man you say is your accuser.'

His taut limbs seemed coiled in a lethal readiness for action as he sat before her. Anna dared not speculate on what he might do if she gave him the information he wanted. Again she had to remind herself that she did not know Marsh well enough to predict what extremities his anger could force him to.

Besides, she reflected, the important thing was his relationship with her. The punishment of Porter Deman was the affair of N.T.E.L.

'No,' she shook her head determinedly. 'I've told you the truth. You don't need his name. It's not your place to get involved in this, Marsh. I don't know how you came by this file, but...'

'I had my secretary write to N.T.E.L. for it,' he interrupted. 'Before our marriage. I knew you were having some sort of trouble, and since you weren't forthcoming about it, I decided to find out for myself.'

'I see,' she shot back angrily. 'As though it wasn't bad enough to know that there were slanderous documents circulating about me behind my back, now I find that my own husband has been spying on me, as well! You had no right, Marsh.'

'Normal rules were suspended,' he shrugged ironically, 'since the woman I was about to marry lacked the confidence in me to reveal that she was in bad trouble. I thought I might be able to help you.'

'No one could help me,' Anna insisted. 'He'd planned it so that I would be accused of breaching security before I had a chance to complain about his behaviour towards me. There was no way for me to convince my superiors I was telling the truth.'

'There would have been,' he corrected, 'if you had been telling the truth. You could have taken legal action to force them to prove their accusation against you. And when this personnel file came out, which you now claim you were aware of, you could have produced it as clear evidence of malice. That alone would have convinced a judge that you were the victim of a deliberate plot, and had been deprived of your job illegally. They would have been forced to take you back, regardless of what they believed—assuming they were prejudiced. But you did none of those things, and two things resulted.'

'What things?' Chagrined to hear his lucid legal reasoning, Anna began to doubt the correctness of her actions.

'In the first place,' he said, 'you lost your job and your career, since this file made you unemployable. And in the second place,' he said darkly, 'you married me.'

'I don't understand,' began Anna, stung by his conclusions. 'What are you saying?'

'It's simple, my love,' he answered. 'You were lying before, and you're lying now. What I'm saying is that I do not believe you.'

'Marsh!' she cried. 'You can't be serious! I've told you the truth. I was guilty of nothing!'

'But you never behaved like a person who was innocent,' he pursued. 'You behaved like a person who had been caught engaging in illegal conduct, and who moved on to greener pastures.'

'What's that supposed to mean?' As though she had been enveloped by a nightmare that refused to end, Anna saw the shade of Charles Robbins' calm incredulity in her own husband's eyes. *He doesn't believe me,* she thought desperately.

'It means,' he said, 'that you were out of a job, still responsible for your sister's education, and unable to find work. As luck would have it, your considerable charms managed to attract a suitor who had enough means to take care of your financial burdens. A gullible sort of fellow who wanted nothing more than to marry you, support you, and share your troubles. In the circumstances, you saw the line of least resistance, and you followed it.'

'I can't believe what I'm hearing,' muttered Anna, her heart sinking. 'You think I used you? That I married you for the sake of convenience?'

'The shoe certainly fits,' he shrugged. 'Your farfetched story about a mystery man who manipulates the personnel department of a corporation in order to satisfy his personal grudges put a bit of a strain on the imagination. If it were true, you would have sought legal advice. And,' he laughed bitterly, 'I was right there at the time. I'm a lawyer myself.'

'But I barely knew you,' Anna protested. 'I couldn't see involving you in my personal difficulties.'

'You knew me well enough to marry me, though, didn't you?' Angry triumph resounded in his deep voice as his logic coiled pitilessly around her. 'You married the man you wouldn't trust to help you. If that isn't using a person, I don't know what is.'

'You're twisting it all out of shape,' Anna objected in confusion. 'I may have been wrong, and as you say, I probably should have found legal help. But it seems impossible to prove my innocence. When Mr Robbins fired me despite my work record at N.T.E.L., I felt I had no chance. I thought the battle was lost, and I wanted to put it behind me.'

'By marrying me.'

'No!' she cried, forcing herself to meet the black eyes which seemed to grip her cruelly. 'I did everything I could to find a job. Then I found out I wasn't going to succeed and…'

'And then you married me.'

'No, Marsh, you have it all wrong. I was desperate, and I was so ashamed…so disgusted by the whole thing. I just couldn't talk about it. But I married you for the simple reason that I loved you. You must believe that.'

'Why should I?' he asked. 'Since you didn't trust me enough to tell me the truth about yourself then, why should I believe you're being honest now?'

'Because I am!' Anna insisted. 'What I've said is true, Marsh—every word of it.'

'What do you suppose would happen,' he changed the subject, 'if I showed this file to Charles Robbins?'

'He'd be surprised,' said Anna, 'since it's been altered. That is, assuming he was telling me the truth when he promised to keep the original accusation out of it. But he would still believe I was guilty of the security breach, and that I deserved to be fired.'

'You're wrong,' Marsh corrected. 'If I showed him this, he'd see the malice immediately, and you'd have your job back in five minutes.'

'I wouldn't want it,' Anna said bitterly. 'The conditions at N.T.E.L. would still be the same. As a matter of fact, I suspect that Charles Robbins believed me in the first place. He knew I was a trustworthy employee. But it didn't matter. It was just as the other man said: regardless of whether I was believed, I would lose my job.'

'First you say Robbins didn't believe you, and then you say he did believe you.' Alert intelligence was combined with obvious distrust in Marsh's sharp eyes.

'Because it doesn't matter one way or the other,' Anna sighed. 'He told me it's company policy to fire anyone who is even accused of being a security risk. Besides,' she added, 'the person who…did this to me is in a position of responsibility. He's more important to the company than I ever was. My word could carry no weight against his, regardless of where the truth lay. That's why they can keep their job, as far as I'm concerned.'

'Your sour grapes aren't very convincing,' said Marsh. 'You claim you don't care that an injustice has been done you, and that your chosen career has been destroyed. You just want to leave it all behind you, as you say. In favour of what, Anna? Of marriage to a man you refused to invest a little trust in, but who happens to be well enough fixed to take care of your sister? Is that it?'

'Now you sound like a prosecutor,' Anna reproached him. 'I'm your wife, not a felon.'

'Not according to that,' he said, pointing to the file.

'So you don't believe me.' Anger welled up in Anna's frayed nerves, banishing her fears.

'There's no reason to,' he replied evenly. 'You have no credibility. You married me under false pretences; you made no attempt to defend yourself legally against what you claim was an injustice; at every turn you've covered up the truth instead of revealing it. That, Anna, is what a lawyer would say. From a husband's point of view it's much simpler. You have refused me your trust, so I see no reason to extend you my own.'

A bitter laugh escaped Anna's lips as she contemplated the enormity of her predicament.

'This is amazing,' she said. 'I've committed the unpardonable crime of being a victim. I've lost my job and my career. And now my own husband, after going behind my back to investigate my misfortunes, doesn't believe that I'm innocent. Have it your own way, then, Marsh. I've had enough.'

He had stood up.

'So have I,' he said. 'I don't think you deserve it, but I'll give you one last chance to tell me the name of this shadowy character you say is behind all this.'

'Why should I expect you to believe that?' asked Anna, infuriated by his imperious behaviour.

'You have a point there,' he agreed bitterly.

'Marsh,' she said suddenly as the terrible import of their quarrel came home to her. 'I love you. I couldn't tell you about this whole mess—it was too horrible. It was all happening just as I met you, and I wanted to put it behind me. But you must believe me. I intended to tell you everything once some time had gone by…'

'You mean once you were safely married and your bills were paid,' he interrupted.

Agonised by his cruel words, she made a last effort to convince him he was wrong. 'I wasn't keeping silent to protect myself,' she said.

'Then why?' he asked. 'To protect me? I hardly think so, Anna. I'm sorry, for you—for both of us.'

Marsh had thrown open the closet door and seized a jacket. He opened the door to the corridor and stood in silence. An invisible force, powered by all the hopes accompanying her newfound love for him, struggled to turn her to him, to make her plead with him to come back. But something else, born of his obvious lack of trust and her own hurt, made her hesitate and turn in upon herself. And in that split second he must have sensed the inner conflict that kept her from him, for he closed the door abruptly and was gone.

Hours later Anna lay silently in his bed, having long ago given up her tossing and turning, for she was sure that sleep would not come this night.

After throwing away her uneaten dinner and doing the dishes, she had contemplated the apartment. The traces of her arrival were still sparse enough that she could erase them all by leaving now, tonight. It was simply a matter of packing her bags, re-packing the large box with books and personal effects, and calling a cab. She would sleep tonight in her own bed, miles away, and when he returned he would know she had accepted his assessment of their marriage. If he wanted his freedom back, let him have it.

On the other hand, he might return at any moment. It would be embarrassing to be caught in the process of packing her things. He might be angry. He might try to stop her.

Besides, what if his anger drove him to do something foolish? What if he drank too much, or got into some kind of trouble? She should be here in case he needed her.

But most of all, she could not bring herself to abandon him, even though it was he who had walked out on her. She prayed he would return, that he would not despair of their relationship so quickly. If he had a change of heart, she wanted to be here, so he would know she had waited. She herself could not give up so soon on this marriage that had seemed so wonderful only twenty-four hours ago. Perhaps Marsh would remember the happiness they had known these past days. Perhaps he would reconsider. In spite of her impulse to seize what remained of her independence, to go home alone, she could not deny that she needed him.

Sleep, held back by the state of her nerves, but abetted by her emotional exhaustion, crept stealthily over her, and her pained thoughts became tinged with dream fantasies. The blue surface of Crystal Lake hovered before her mind's eye, reflecting multitudes of bright autumn leaves, and rippled by the crisp breeze of Indian summer. She was back in the hotel room. Marsh was smiling again, touching her gently, intimately, as he had the night of their arrival. In his tall, taut presence, so vital and strong in his windbreaker, his jeans, he was so handsome. And he smiled. He was not angry…

She did not hear the quiet click of the outer door, or the muted sounds of him taking off his clothes. The settling of his weight on the bed brought an unconscious purr of satisfaction from her, as she sensed his approach from within her dream. Even the quiet touch of his hand to her cheek, her hair, did not wake her, but stole through the confused levels of her consciousness to her senses, which reacted immediately to him.

For a long, sweet moment, her sleeping mind joined her aroused body in believing that the clock had truly been turned back. The hushed rustle of leaves persisted dreamily in the background of her growing desire. The darkness was that of the hotel room, plunged into daytime obscurity by his sudden closing of the curtains. The daunting warmth of his flesh closing over her own was again the penetrating intimacy it had been in the middle of that rapt afternoon.

Over and over again, in the confusion of her dream, Marsh's hands loosened her jeans, her shirt, her bra. Again and again the fabrics came loose, hung in a disarray produced by passion, slipped softly to the floor. Once more his hand crept to her breast and closed over the poised nipple which clamoured for his touch. Again she was naked, naked as though for the first time, her skin flicked tempestuously by the still, warm air of the silent room. And the hardness of his body grazed her soft curves, so magnetic, so powerful even in the most ethereal pressure. Her own sleek flesh, moving instinctively in its strange, rhythmic way, rubbed and touched him, kissed and released him, slipped luxuriantly over him, making of this contact a weird, teasing magic as old and irresistible as life itself.

Again and again, in this sensual dream fuelled silently by a reality of which she was not yet aware, his lips and hands drove her to a frenzy of wanting as the comforter slid beneath her. She was gripping him, running her slender fingers through his hair, returning his kisses with an abandon that stunned her senses. Closer he came, his touch penetrating even deeper into the heady obscurity of her mind and soul, and she accepted him happily. The tickling, the teasing which had taunted her senses into an agony of desire were already expanding into that enormous fire of fulfilment, of ecstasy, in which he knew her utterly.

Slowly, in little dreamlike fits and starts, she came to herself in his bed. But in this awakening she was coming to him, losing herself in him, and finding herself once again through the passion he inspired in her. Aware now of the terror that had gripped her tonight, she clung to him desperately as his desire grew stronger. All at once the novelty of her surroundings struck her, adding its lush unfamiliarity to the wild probing of his touch. Before she could quite fathom what was happening, her passion was growing, preparing to spend itself here in the darkness with him. With a strength born of desire and fearful love, she grasped him, held him to her breast, as though to convince him that whatever had come between them, this intimacy will remain to bind them together, to provide some small hope that the damage might be undone, the clock turned back, the future saved.

The paroxysm had ended. Quietly Marsh receded from her embrace, and she felt sleep close over her like a soft coverlet. He was still beside her, warm and close, breathing deeply. Aware that he had come back to her despite the gulf between them, she clung to the hope promised by his physical presence, and slipped into an exhausted sleep by his side. When she awoke, he was gone. After a day of restless activity in the apartment, she heard his key turn in the lock once more. His anger seemed gone now. In its place was a strange, disturbing aloofness. Unfailingly courteous and even attentive in his behaviour towards her, Marsh remained politely distant as he answered her questions, spoke in casual phrases of his work, and enquired about her own day.

Clearly he believed the burden was on Anna to prove her innocence and to justify her disastrous concealment of the facts concerning the loss of her job. Unable to forgive her for withholding so crucial a confidence, Marsh hid his feelings behind a façade of cool civility. Even in his occasional laughter over one or the other of the inconsequential events which amused him, he remained quietly unapproachable. Without trust, he seemed to be saying, she could hardly expect more from him than the pleasant, reserved stranger who confronted her now.

His message was not lost on Anna, who would have preferred a thousand angry quarrels to this hollow mood of deferential calm. But as the days passed she discovered in spite of herself that she too could be proud, and stubborn, and demanding. Reflecting that she had nothing to blame herself for beyond being the victim of a malicious plot against which she could not be expected to defend herself, she reproached Marsh for his blunt disbelief. Not only had he gone behind her back to discover the false charge against her, but he gave them his credence over her own word.

The damning personnel file remained on the coffee table

where he had thrown it in his anger. Her glance returned obstinately to it as she paced the apartment. 'What does he expect of me?' she wondered in exasperation. If he believed she was guilty of the crimes alleged in the file, and of marrying him without love, she could hardly expect to convince him he was wrong. Having abandoned his trust in her, he would believe what he chose regardless of whatever action she might take.

But again the thought of her vulnerable friends at N.T.E.L. forced Anna to an effort in which she invested little hope. She put the hated file in an envelope addressed to Charles Robbins, accompanied by a letter explaining that its contents proved there was malice behind her dismissal. Although indifferent to the prospect of regaining her old position, she wrote, she implored Charles to investigate the situation with a view to exposing Peter Deman and protecting his potential victims.

She reasoned that her action must implicitly satisfy Marsh by proving that she did not shrink from defending herself against charges she knew were false. In the improbable event that the company acted upon her request, her name would be cleared. And if, as she bitterly expected, nothing was done, Marsh would have to accept her claim that self-defence was futile against the corporation's inertia and indifference.

But she decided not to tell him of her action until she knew its results. And when her letter went unanswered she shrugged sadly and put it out of her thoughts. What was the point, she wondered, of belabouring a point that was already lost? She had no interest in recapturing the job she had lost, but only in regaining her angry husband's trust. On the other hand, she refused to beg for a confidence she felt she already deserved. Let Marsh himself re-examine his hasty conclusions, she decided resentfully. If she had acted wrongly in hiding her dilemma from him, he had been only too quick to withdraw his support from her. Having rejected her so brutally, he owed her a sign of trust, or even of apology, before expecting her to justify herself anew.

So the stand-off persisted, a marriage between strangers punctuated by bits of insignificant conversation which quickly dissipated into uncomfortable silence. But in the night's quietest hours, as though under cover of a darkness that obscured mistrust and resentment, he came to her, renewing through his caresses a secret contact which persisted underneath the cold civility of the new day.

And thus a pattern was established. Polite strangers by day, Marsh and Anna were impassioned lovers by night. Each time they were intimate, and the heat of his touch stoked daunting fires inside her, she cherished the hope that this closeness promised an end to the discord that troubled their days.

But nothing changed. No matter how early she awoke, he seemed somehow to have arisen and disappeared, as though making a furtive escape from her. His nightly return was hardly an occasion for joyous renewal, since the empty affability of their conversations made her feel lonelier than ever in his company. The evenings passed painfully for Anna, and she went to bed torn by the conflict between her increasing desperation and her secret knowledge that, in the dark of night, she would be his again.

As the days and weeks passed, his lovemaking seemed to take on an infinite variety of meanings. In the absence of real conversation, it was as though all the private feelings which succeed one another during the first weeks of a new marriage were expressing themselves wordlessly through the subtle modulations of his caress, his kiss, the feel of his body.

Sometimes he made love to her with a deliberate violence which seemed to reproach and punish, even as it left her faint with pleasure. At other times his touch was gentle, tender, as though he wished to point out regretfully the bond that still linked him to her, and to strengthen it somehow. Now and then there was a perverse, mocking intimacy in his kisses, a delight in sexual arousal which bypassed trust as it inflamed her shamelessly to him.

And in her own responses to his lovemaking there were a thousand different answers to his unspoken messages. A moan of pleasure on her lips, she would clutch him tightly, and try to pull him closer yet, as though to banish the separation that haunted her. Each time his affection seemed to express a continuing hope for their relationship, she would respond mutely, begging him by her caresses and the little sounds she made to stay with her, not to give up on her.

The entire responsibility for preserving their marriage as a living entity fell on their lovemaking, and never had Anna dreamed that sensual excitement could be so multiple, so marvellous a thing. Yet the passion that bound her to Marsh was not powerful enough to break the silence that tormented her. Each night she knew him a little better, and had a new intuition of what motivated him, hurt him, pleased him. But each day he receded anew into a reserve that her love could not annul.

One morning she found a note on the kitchen table that informed her that Marsh had contacted the University and taken care of Sally's tuition payments for the balance of the year. 'I'll be late tonight,' he added. 'A case.'

His implication was all too clear. He had never relinquished the belief that she had married him for Sally's sake. Well, he would pay, all right, as long as Anna remained home to accept him in her bed at night. He required no real communication beyond that contact. And in order to pay, he must work. She had no right to complain if his case work kept him away until all hours. He was keeping his part of the bargain, wasn't he? Had she not forfeited her rights as a wife when she refused him his right to her confidence?

All too often he called during the day to tell her in blithe tones not to make him a dinner, not to wait up for him. As the weeks passed her loneliness grew more intense, and her own stubborn pride assumed an ever greater place in her thoughts. She could not go on indefinitely in this humiliating position, she told herself. A working woman by inclination, she had no intention of playing the submissive wife for a husband who refused her his respect and attention.

Eventually, she reflected resignedly, this frail skeleton of a marriage must end in separation and divorce. The thought was infinitely saddening, and yet unavoidable. What, then, must be done? Anna's pride told her she must find work. Not only would it obviously be necessary to earn her own living again, at some future date, but she was unwilling to accept this loveless bargain concerning Sally. Let Marsh pay the tuition, then, while there was no alternative. But Anna would somehow find work, without taking the bitter chance of citing N.T.E.L. as a reference, and would eventually pay him back. When it was all over, and she was alone once more, she would look back on this thwarted marriage in terms of expediency. Sally would have been provided for, at the cost of considerable pain and loneliness.

So be it, she decided darkly. Let Marsh's suspicion of her motives become a reality. No longer daring to hope that her relationship with him might be saved, Anna took to the want ads once more, and began looking for work.

CHAPTER EIGHT

'ANNA, *ma chérie*, are you still on nine?' René Lyotard puffed urgently on his strong-smelling French cigarette as he peered between the swinging kitchen doors to the dining room. 'Why don't they leave, for heaven's sake? They got here at six-thirty, and it's almost ten. Oh *les bougres*, finish your wine and go home!'

'Relax, René,' Anna laughed. 'They'll leave. They're enjoying their coffee.'

'You're too understanding, *ma chérie*,' René scowled. 'You were born a saint. But I know you must go home to your husband. And I myself have business tonight. I expect the French to sit up until all hours sipping their brandy, but this is Chicago, *non mais*!'

Anna smiled. René was perpetually excoriating the customers from the safe distance of the kitchen. But as soon as he passed through those swinging doors, he was transformed into the essence of decorous Gallic gallantry.

'Messieurs, dames,' he would greet the guests with an easy flourish, 'I welcome you to Ariel. Something to drink before dinner?' Only as he passed Anna on his way to the bar or kitchen would his professional smile fade into a shrug of exasperation.

'Les gueux!' he would fume. 'Ariel is the most expensive French restaurant in the city, and our clients are a bunch of peasants who wouldn't know a Camembert from a fireplug. I cannot imitate your natural sweetness, Anna. How you stand them I will never know. It is your superhuman

forbearance that gets you such fabulous tips. Not that I begrudge you your success. You deserve it for all you put up with.'

At last the customers stood up to leave. Anna bade them a pleasant good evening and began helping the bus-boy clear the table.

'Anna,' came a stentorian voice from the bar, 'leave that to Henri. May I speak to you for a moment?' Jacques Radier held out his arms lovingly.

'The end of another long day, is it not so, my dear?' he sighed. 'The restaurant business is a demanding one. Now I suppose you will be off to join your lonely husband.'

Anna smiled. 'Actually, I have to meet an old girl friend for a drink, *monsieur*.'

'Oh, *ça alors!*' he threw up his hands. 'Your poor husband must be desperate. Since you agreed to work the dinner hours, the poor man must feel like a bachelor.'

'He's all right,' Anna smiled a trifle ruefully.

'I just wanted to tell you before you leave, Anna, how pleased I am with your work. It is not easy to be the only female *garçon* in a profession dominated by men. But you are doing wonderfully. Even Monsieur Foucault thinks so, and he and I have never agreed on anything in our lives.' He shrugged as he thought of the business partner he could not do without. 'Actually, it is at his suggestion that I wish to ask you something. Your presence has set a sort of tone here at Ariel which seems to be good for business. Roland and I have been thinking that in the role of *hôtesse* you might be even more effective. Not that you are not brilliant at taking care of the tables. What do you think, my dear?'

Anna pursed her lips uncertainly.

'Ah, I know what you are thinking,' he interjected. 'No tips, eh? Well, I can assure you that Roland and I are thinking in terms of a most substantial salary, worthy of any well-schooled *maître d'hôtel*. And, of course, your days of lifting plates of food would be over.'

'You are very kind, *monsieur*,' Anna smiled. 'I'll be happy to work in any way you think best.'

'Good,' he beamed. 'Now, you run along, and we'll talk more of this tomorrow night. A *demain, mon petit.*'

As she said goodnight to her colleagues and prepared to walk out into the freezing November wind, Anna reflected that Monsieur Radier's proposal might be a good idea. Perhaps a job as hostess would be less exhausting.

Anna had grown to love her work at Ariel since the day Messrs. Foucault and Radier had decided, not without reservations, to hire her in spite of her inexperience. She had given no references, claiming that economic hard times were forcing her to go to work to supplement her husband's income. She had not held a job, she said, since before her college education.

Her new employers had shrugged indifferently at her explanation, for they were concerned only with restaurant experience, of which she had none, and preferred to train her themselves in any case. Despite their irascible treatment of each other, both were fond of Anna, and made every effort to make her first weeks of work as easy as possible.

To their surprise and delight, Anna seemed to have been born with the instinctive tact and delicacy required of a highly trained waiter. The aura of quiet friendliness she brought to Ariel seemed to make the customers happy, and she found herself greeted warmly by increasingly familiar faces as the weeks went by. Her slim good looks were not without their favourable effect as well, and more than once she caught a glimpse of a happy client pointing her out with words of praise to one or the other of her bosses.

The pleasure of doing a job well after the idleness enforced by the collapse of her first career was encouraging. And the banter she enjoyed with René and the other waiters made Anna feel she belonged to a hardworking, if somewhat excitable, team of professionals linked by common needs and ambitions. Her busy nights at Ariel took her mind off the continuing estrangement that troubled her marriage to Marsh. She returned home each night with a welcome sense of accomplishment that took the edge off the feelings of failure which haunted her personal life.

Marsh, for his part, had initially said little in response to the news of her new job. Apparently indifferent to the use to which she put her time when she was not with him, he continued devoting long hours to his own work. Although Anna thought she sensed a touch of pride in her energy and initiative on his part, the intuition was soon eclipsed by the pained silence which hung over so many of her hours with him. And so she clung to the excitement of her work as the only bright light in what was sure to be her future life alone.

But marriage to Marsh Hamilton, she discovered, was never as predictable as it might seem, regardless of the mutual stubbornness which seemed to poison her relationship with him. For with studied casualness, during the moments of fleeting reconciliation or mere relaxation which overtook them both, he drew her out gently on her thoughts about the rigours of her new profession and the personalities of her surprisingly accommodating bosses.

'Who runs the cash register at Ariel?' he enquired one evening.

'Madame Foucault,' Anna replied. 'Why do you ask?'

'I wondered whether it was a woman,' he said. 'In France, no matter how fancy the establishment, the *caissière* will always be a woman. The men are trusted to handle the tables, charm the clients and cook the food, but when it comes to the francs the woman is boss.'

'Come to think of it,' Anna laughed, 'Madame Foucault does act the part. Her husband is quite the tyrant when she's not around, but he turns into a puppydog when she comes into view.'

'Perhaps the French have a point,' said Marsh. 'A lot of the businessmen I come into contact with have mucked up their books so badly that they have to pay their accountants more than their creditors.'

'If that's the way you feel about it,' Anna smiled with a touch of complacency, 'you'll be happy to know that when Madame Foucault is indisposed, her job falls to yours truly.'

'You're kidding,' he said, quirking an eyebrow in surprise.

'And not only that,' she added, 'I'm the one who takes Ariel's receipts to the bank in the afternoon.'

'Well, aren't you the unpredictable one,' he smiled. 'So much responsibility already. Aren't you afraid a mugger will assault you for the money, even in that fancy neighbourhood?'

'If that happened,' Anna bristled, 'I'd simply hit him with the bank's money sack—it weighs a ton.'

'I believe you would,' he nodded. 'With that stubborn streak of yours, you'd be a dangerous enemy when roused.'

And he fell silent, his evocation of the independence he had admired in Anna before their marriage no doubt warring with his continuing distrust. For her part Anna could not help feeling satisfied to report her employers' implicit confidence in her to the man who so rigidly withheld his own. At the same time she was aware that through his casual questions, so bland in appearance, he was subtly learning more about her in spite of the silent gulf that persisted between them. Uncomfortably she asked herself whether his inquisitiveness bespoke a remnant of commitment to her. Perhaps, in his grudging way, he still considered himself her husband, and wished to express his support through friendly conversation.

On the other hand, she wondered bitterly, perhaps his occasional interest was born of morbid curiosity about the private life he thought she wished to conceal from him. Perhaps he was interrogating her with an eye to preventing further unbidden revelations about her activities from strangers. The inscrutable silence which so often reigned in his demeanour hardly betokened trust or affection.

Let him think what he liked, Anna decided with a shrug. She herself knew how trustworthy she was, and the steady progress of her new career came as no surprise to her. When the time came her initiative would see her through, notwithstanding Marsh's feelings about her.

The cocktail lounge where Debby Johnson awaited was only two and a half blocks away, but Anna could not suppress a sigh of fatigue as she hurried through Ariel's front door. She felt unusually tired today. Last night was her night off from work, and she had had to accompany Marsh to a party at the District Attorney's house, and had not slept until after one o'clock in the morning. Apparently embarrassed at Anna's invisibility to his colleagues since their marriage, Marsh had wanted her to put in an appearance, since his partners and friends were bringing their spouses. Perhaps, Anna wondered, there might be talk about the wife Marsh left alone during the late hours he worked. She had agreed to go along, in spite of the alienation she felt from her husband and his world. Her job had gone a long way towards assuaging her loneliness and restoring her sense of independence, and she was beginning to face the eventuality of a separation from Marsh with some courage.

'Why don't you wear my favourite dress?' he had asked as she stood in her bathrobe before the limited array of garments in her closet.

'Marsh, no!' she had protested, her eyes darting to the silken contours of the dress on its hanger. Sinuously low-cut in pearl white with slender shoulder straps, it was the most daringly feminine of her evening dresses. 'It's too...'

'Sexy?' he asked with a grin.

'Well, yes,' she admitted. 'I don't think the occasion is right for it.'

'I do,' he said. 'I want to show you off.'

'You're kidding,' she said ruefully. 'That sounds funny coming from you.'

'I don't see why you say that,' he commented.

'I haven't had the impression that you were exactly bursting with pride in me,' she returned.

'Ah-hah,' he drawled, his long arms encircling her from behind. 'You're breaking the lawyer's first law: never assume. Never try to read someone's mind without knowing the facts beforehand. Remember?'

Anna made no response, for the warm touch of his hard body against her back, so intoxicating in its sheer virility, made it difficult for her to concentrate on his teasing words.

'I have many reasons for pride in you,' Marsh murmured against her earlobe. 'Not the least of which is the sight of those long legs in a clinging dress. Why shouldn't I share the pleasure with my overworked colleagues? I won't be jealous.'

'Mmm,' she sighed, too bewitched by his exploring lips and by the hands that had slipped to the curve of her thighs to regret that his compliment was so insubstantial. If he was sincere about having pride in her, he would surely have better reasons than the mere shape of her body.

'I wonder if the D.A. would notice our arriving late,' he whispered seductively into her ear. 'I'm no longer thinking of the dress, but of what goes into it. We don't have to leave yet.'

'Yes, we do,' she sighed. 'We're expected. You owe him the courtesy after all your years with him.'

'When he gets a look at you, he'll understand why I was late.'

'Thanks,' she said, extricating herself from his embrace with a difficulty made greater by her own reluctance. 'But no, thanks. I don't want to cause you embarrassment in front of your friends.'

'No danger of that,' said Marsh, his appraising eyes taking in the contours of her slender limbs under the bathrobe.

And yet embarrassed indifference seemed exactly his attitude after their arrival at the party, for he seemed eager to shun Anna from the moment his onetime boss ushered them into his enormous living room. The faces of the lawyers and judges were unfamiliar, and Anna found it difficult to make conversation with them. They all seemed so tall, so confident, so successful... And they talked endlessly about subjects Anna was virtually ignorant of.

Marsh was anything but helpful in the circumstances. After hurriedly introducing her to a host of strangers whose names she forgot in spite of herself, he disappeared into a den where some close friends from his days as a prosecutor were engaged in jocular conversation about the city's current political struggles. It soon became clear to Anna that he had no intention of emerging, so she did her best to keep up her end of one casual exchange after another as the evening dragged by.

More than a few guests had already left, their overcoats securely buttoned in anticipation of the frigid wind outside, when Anna at last decided to seek Marsh out.

Already tired, she gently suggested that it was time to go home. But Marsh would not hear of it. His levity among his friends seemed to underscore his alienation from Anna, for she had not heard him laugh so heartily since her honeymoon with him.

He was seated on a couch surrounded by young lawyers. Among them was a stunningly beautiful blonde woman whom Anna heard addressed as May. Dressed in a clinging skirt and blouse which accentuated her healthy, sleek curves, May was astonishingly attractive. Her long hair bore the traces of the summer sun's bleaching, and her limpid blue eyes darted intelligently from one young lawyer to another. She seemed quite at home among her male colleagues, and laughed easily at their jokes. At the same time, Anna had the impression that May was quite aware her beauty made her the centre of attraction wherever she went, and frankly enjoyed the attention.

For a long moment, Marsh did not look up to see that his wife had come into the room. Someone was making a joke, and Marsh added a clever rejoinder which made everyone laugh. With a touch of discomfort Anna saw May place her slender hand on Marsh's arm in a gesture of camaraderie which seemed to conceal a grain of possessiveness.

Marsh introduced her as May Reynolds.

'She's beautiful,' Anna observed later, as they drove home.

'May? Yes, I guess so,' he agreed absently. 'She's a damned good lawyer, very aggressive. She'll be a D.A. herself one day, I'll bet.'

Aggressive in more ways than one, Anna thought, but resisted the temptation to mention that May had been flirting with Marsh. Seeing his preoccupied face behind the wheel of the car, she realised he had withdrawn from her once more. With an inner sigh, she reflected that it made little difference to her marriage if other women courted Marsh's attentions. There was not much affection left in him to be alienated, and the marriage itself would not last long.

Tonight Marsh would be late, as usual, so Anna had accepted Debby's invitation to have a drink after work and talk over old times. The two women had not seen each

other since Anna's marriage, and neither wanted to stay out
of touch too long, since the friendship they had developed
at N.T.E.L. was important to both.

'Anna!' Debby exclaimed as the door closed on the night
wind. 'How are you, kid? Gosh, it's been a long time!'

'I'm frozen at the moment, to tell you the truth,' said
Anna.

'Come on, then,' Debby smiled. 'Let's get ourselves a
hot buttered rum or something.'

'How's Barbara?' asked Anna as they sat in a booth towards the rear of the lounge.

'Oh, you know,' Debby sighed. 'The same.'

'Really?' Anna asked miserably. 'Oh, no!' As the waiter
took their order, she thought with quiet horror of the situation at N.T.E.L.

'Debby,' she said at length, 'I feel like such a coward.
To think that Barbara is still suffering from that…'

'Never mind, Anna,' said Debby. 'You did all you could,
and it didn't do any good. There's nothing to blame yourself for.'

'Yes, there is,' Anna insisted, thinking ruefully of
Marsh's legal estimation of the situation. 'I should never
have let the whole sordid mess run its course behind closed
doors. If I'd taken legal action in my own behalf, the spotlight would have been on Deman. As it is, he goes along
with impunity… It's infuriating!'

'Don't blame yourself, Anna. You had to get on with
your own life. Don't forget, you were the victim, not the
criminal.'

Anna had to suppress a wry smile at her friend's words.
In recent weeks she had so accustomed herself to feelings
of guilt over her misfortune that it was difficult to recall
her innocence.

'I don't know if you knew,' Debby interjected, 'that Barbara tried to help you. She went to see Robbins when you were fired. Obviously it didn't make any difference.'

Anna shook her head, contemplating the extent of the damage Porter Deman had done in her life—damage of which Debby could have no inkling, ignorant as she was of the existence of the damning personnel file and Marsh's discovery of it.

'Well,' Debby concluded with an ironic smile, 'at least Deman hasn't got around to me. If he does, he'll get a surprise, I can promise you! I may get fired, but I'll leave him something to remember me by. Maybe a split lip or a bloody nose.'

She fell silent for a moment as steaming glasses of hot rum were placed on the table between them.

'As a matter of fact,' she went on when the waiter had gone, 'we haven't been seeing much of him recently. There's a new girl there now. She's probably getting all his attentions.'

As the glow faded from Anna's cheeks in the warm air, Debby looked concernedly at her.

'You look pale, Anna. Have you been ill?' she asked.

'No,' Anna replied. 'A little tired, I suppose. My job keeps me hopping.'

'How is marriage agreeing with you?' Debby pursued, obviously concealing her concern.

'All right,' Anna answered evasively.

'I still can't believe it. I got a look at Marsh when he was at N.T.E.L. How handsome can a man get!' Debby exclaimed. 'I'm so happy for you, kid. You deserve someone like him. And I guess he came along at the right time.'

'Yes,' Anna agreed, inwardly weighing the absurdity of her words, 'I suppose he did.' She dared not reveal to her friend that her troubles at N.T.E.L. had managed to compromise what had seemed an ideal marriage. If Marsh had entered her life at any other time, her relationship with him would have eluded the rocks on which it was foundering now. Instead, she had met him in the very corridors of N.T.E.L.

'If you don't mind my saying so,' said Debby, her brow furrowed in concern, 'you look downright unhappy, Anna. Are you sure you're all right?'

'Yes,' Anna sighed. 'I'm okay. Don't worry about me, Deb. I'm just trying to get myself straightened out. The last two months have been…well, hectic.'

'Marriage is quite a step, I guess,' Debby observed. 'Of course,' she smirked, 'I wouldn't know, since I haven't been proposed to lately. Or even propositioned.'

With a grateful smile Anna contemplated her friend's accustomed humour. It's self-denigrating aspect never troubled Debby's close friends, for they knew her relative lack of sex appeal was more than compensated for by her irrepressible personality. The dignity and self-respect underlying her jokes at her own expense were never out of sight, and she herself seemed confident that she was not destined for a spinster's life.

'I imagine,' she probed diffidently, 'that a big strong guy like Marsh can be stubborn about what he wants.'

Anna nodded, uncomfortably aware that the other girl's guess was close to the truth.

'So can I,' she smiled. After all, she had her own rigidity to blame as much as that of her wilful husband for her current problems.

'My mother always used to say that one has to let a man have his own way—or at least let him think he does,' Debby laughed. 'Otherwise his pride will make him impossible to live with. Be patient, she'd say, and bide your time until he comes around to your way of thinking. Of course, she was talking over her head, because my father was always impossible, and still is.'

'Maybe he would have been more impossible,' Anna smiled, 'if she hadn't been diplomatic.'

'You could be right about that.' Debby's sparkling eyes were fixed affectionately on her friend. 'But I could never be as passive as she was. When and if I ever get married, I'll probably bring all kinds of trouble down on myself by opening my big mouth when I should be keeping it shut.'

'Nonsense,' said Anna. 'You'll be perfect.' Uncomfortably she reflected that her case was the opposite. It was her silence that Marsh could not forgive.

'Now that you're on the other side of the line,' Debby said in a confidential tone, 'can you tell an amateur like me what it's like? I mean, is it hard to get used to living with a man?'

'Now look who's being diplomatic!' Anna laughed. 'I'll be honest with you, Deb. Marsh is a wonderful man, and I love him. Nevertheless, we're having problems. Sometimes I think it's all my own fault, and sometimes I'm just not sure of anything.'

'That's not possible,' Debby remonstrated. 'I know you, Anna. You're not the type to ruin a good thing.'

'That's what I would have thought,' Anna sighed, 'until this whole…this trouble started. The terrible part is that it hardly has anything to do with us—I mean, with our real relationship. I think I belong with Marsh, but we just can't seem to…to…' She shook her head. 'I'm talking in circles, aren't I? I suppose I just can't bear to go into the details.'

'Don't, then,' Debby smiled. 'I didn't mean to pry. I mean,' she added with a laugh, 'I did mean to pry, but it's none of my business. But look at it this way, Anna: you're still together, aren't you? You're both still committed to each other.'

For how long? Anna wondered miserably while doing her best to return her friend's optimistic smile.

'I know I shouldn't talk,' Debby went on, 'but give it

time, Anna. It will work itself out eventually. Just don't give up prematurely. I saw the way Marsh looked at you at N.T.E.L. If a man ever looked at me that way, I'd drop dead of surprise. I know he feels deeply for you.'

Grateful for Debby's well-meaning support, Anna squeezed her hand. She only wished she could take her encouraging words to heart. But there was no forgetting the fragile state of her imperilled marriage.

'I hope you're right,' she said. 'Perhaps somehow things will work out.'

'Just remember, Anna: if you ever need anything, any help or anything, you know where to come. Okay?'

'Okay,' agreed Anna, allowing herself to hope that there was a grain of truth in Debby's assessment of her situation. After all, she reasoned uncertainly, she and Marsh were not separated yet. Despite the bitter gulf between them, they remained married. Perhaps that fact counted for something…

Debby's smile disappeared suddenly as she peered behind Anna to the entrance to the lounge.

'Listen,' she whispered. 'Don't turn around. I think I just saw Marsh come in.'

Anna turned paler than before. 'Is he…?'

'He's with someone. That's funny…' Debby's brow furrowed in perplexity.

Anna could not suppress her curiosity a second longer. Turning in her seat, she saw Marsh helping a woman off with her coat by a booth near the door. His companion's back was turned, but her lovely blonde hair left little doubt as to her identity. A glance in the mirror behind the bar confirmed Anna's suspicion. Marsh was with May Reynolds.

Possessed suddenly of a strange alertness, Anna scanned the walls behind Debby. There was a back entrance.

'I'm going to have to go,' she said quickly, pulling on her coat.

'Anna…' Debby's eyes glowed with pained sympathy.

'It's all right,' said Anna, squeezing her hand. 'It's not what it seems. He works with her. But I really don't want to see them right now. Keep in touch, all right?'

Debby smiled, although her features were still clouded by a perplexity which Anna was in too great a hurry to notice.

'Take care,' she said. 'Call me.'

The night wind bit savagely through her coat as she hurried towards the subway. Although Marsh's apartment building was only a pleasant walk away from Ariel in warm weather, the winter wind forced Anna to take the one-stop subway ride home.

She stood on the warm platform in an agony of chagrin and conflicting thoughts. Poor Debby! She would certainly arrive at a conclusion less innocent than Anna's assurances indicated. How embarrassing it all was! Certainly, Marsh did work with May Reynolds in an indirect way, and there was nothing so terrible in buying her a drink before saying goodnight. But the look in May's eyes at the District Attorney's party had indicated anything but indifference towards Marsh.

May might well be perfectly aware that Marsh worked long hours and spent little time with his wife. She might suspect that his marriage was in trouble, and have an interest in being as friendly as possible, in anticipation of the day when he would be free again.

To think that, if it had not been for that rear entrance, Anna might have been forced to greet them, to introduce Debby, to converse with them. The embarrassment would have been too much to bear. Everyone would have seen her confusion…

The train roared deafeningly through the tunnel and

screeched to a stop. Anna boarded it and sat down, although
she knew she would have to stand up in thirty seconds and
prepare to mount the long flight of stairs to the street.

There was no denying it—May Reynolds was a very
sexy and attractive young woman. Anna recalled the alert
cleverness in May's eyes last might. She was obviously
intelligent. And right now she was sitting in a cosy booth
with Marsh, chatting about work, perhaps about some mutual interest. Anna had felt May's gaze scan her critically
at the party. How uncomfortable it would have felt, she
thought, to be appraised competitively by those pretty blue
eyes tonight, if she had not made her escape through the
back door.

'Made my escape,' Anna thought with an angry shudder
as she rushed headlong through the wind towards home.
She could not bear the passivity enforced upon her by the
predicament that had begun at N.T.E.L. Although she had
acted with courageous directness in her responses to Porter
Deman, to Charles Robbins, and even to Marsh, she somehow kept finding herself in the position of a furtive, shame-
faced victim. She had had quite enough of concealing embarrassing truths, avoiding confrontations, and fearing the
actions of others.

Somehow she must regain her independence, however
lonely that prospect was.

She had saved most of the money she had earned at
Ariel. Before long she would be in a position to strike out
on her own. Her new career put the N.T.E.L. disaster behind her. If she continued to save scrupulously, she would
be able to pay Marsh back for Sally's tuition. Then there
would be only the future to consider. A future without en-
tanglements, without guilt… Without love, perhaps, but a
person could become used to living without a lot of things.

Anna had just stepped out of a hot, bracing shower and was
combing her wet hair before the bathroom mirror when she

heard Marsh's key in the door. As she stood in the steamy air, regarding her own unhappy face in the mirror, the quiet sounds of his habitual night-time activity filtered into the room. The closet door opened and closed; ice clinked in a glass; a rustle came from the bedroom as he changed his clothes. The phonograph in the living room was turned on as he picked out one of the quiet classical records he used as tranquillisers after a hard day's work. As usual, he didn't bother to greet her.

The pathos of standing alone in the bathroom while her estranged husband went about his solitary business only a few feet away seemed suddenly unbearable to Anna.

'This has got to stop,' she thought. The scene she had witnessed in the cocktail lounge, while perhaps not so significant in itself, was the last straw for this troubled marriage. She could no longer bear the expression of intense pain that clouded the green eyes in the mirror. Deciding not to bother blow-drying her hair, she moved deliberately towards the living room.

Marsh was sitting in a chair, wearing jeans and the white shirt he had worn to work. His eyes were closed. The muted strains of a string quartet filled the room with polite restraint. She sat down uncomfortably on the couch opposite him.

'Can I talk to you?' she asked.

'Oh, hi,' he said, with an amiability that seemed feigned. His eyes remained closed. 'I thought you might have gone to bed.'

Anna remained silent for a moment, reflecting bitterly that he would not even have said hello had she not spoken to him first.

At last he opened his eyes and regarded her quizzically. 'What's on your mind?' he asked.

'Us,' she said simply.

'What do you mean, ''us''?'

'I mean the fact that there isn't any more us,' she said.

'I don't get it,' he sighed irritably, closing his eyes again.

'I think you'd better open your eyes, Marsh,' she said angrily.

'All right, all right,' he sighed, misunderstanding her. 'What is it you want, Anna? I'm tired.'

'So am I. Tired of this whole mess we're in.'

A long silence ensued as they both considered the import of her words. For nearly two months this day had been approaching, and had weighed upon their routine of silent co-existence.

'What do you propose?' he asked with studied calm.

She took a deep breath. 'Divorce,' she said. 'Right away.'

Again Marsh was silent. Although Anna was glad her thought was out in the open, the sound of the word terrified her. These last unhappy weeks had convinced her that her marriage was failing, but had also made it painfully clear that its definitive end would leave indelible scars.

'Is there someone else?' he asked, opening his eyes.

His egotism dumbfounded her. Had he assumed his love-making was so bewitching that she would live in total silence with him until another man came along? With an effort she ignored his question and searched for words which would describe her thoughts dispassionately.

'I mean,' he went on cruelly, 'who would take care of your sister? Without me in the picture?'

'I'll take care of Sally myself, thank you,' she began. 'And as for there being someone else, Marsh, I don't think people who live in glass houses should throw stones.'

'What's that supposed to mean?'

'There's no one else in *my* life,' she said, her voice trembling with anger. 'Can you say the same?'

He stared at her in perplexity. 'I'd like to know what the hell you're talking about,' he said darkly.

'I'm talking about the woman I saw you with tonight,' she said.

His face clouded with growing anger.

'Don't try to deny it,' she added, struggling to suppress the fear his look inspired in her.

A dry, menacing smile curled his lip.

'Have you been spying on me, love?' he asked.

'Not at all,' she answered. 'If I'd wanted to spy on you, I probably would have found out unpleasant things a long time ago. I met Debby Johnson for a drink tonight, and there you were.'

Marsh frowned. 'I really don't understand you,' he said. 'Are you talking about May?'

'Who do you think I'm talking about?'

He smiled ironically. 'I think that job of yours, or something, I don't know what, is going to your head, Anna. There's nothing between me and May Reynolds. We're working together. That's all there is to it.'

'That may be your idea of the relationship, but I doubt that she shares it. If, that is, you're telling me the truth.'

'Don't talk to me about truth, Anna,' he growled. 'You wouldn't know it if you tripped over it.'

'Don't try to evade the question!' she snapped.

'My God,' he laughed bitterly. 'You're really full of surprises. One never knows what to expect from you. I never thought you were the jealous type.'

Anna lapsed into frustrated silence. Why, after all, should she be disturbed about Marsh's relationship with May Reynolds? The failure of their marriage had nothing to do with infidelity. In some corner of her mind, Anna herself must be harbouring an involuntary grain of possessiveness towards the man with whom she lived in such torment.

'Well,' he went on blithely, 'I suppose I can indulge your

mania, since it means nothing to me. The fact is that we're involved with the D.A. on a difficult and rather exciting case at the moment, and my work brings me into contact with May. I buy her a drink sometimes, at the end of the day, or she buys me one. The lounge where you saw us is near my office and her field location. We're regulars there.'

'What difference does that make?' asked Anna.

'I see,' he said, the same sardonic smile curling his lip. 'I forgot my vocation. Every lawyer knows that the jealous mind will put a negative construction on anything at all. You know, Anna, jealousy is a real sickness. It can be treated.'

'Don't talk down to me!' she shot back. 'I've seen the way she looks at you!'

A short, sarcastic laugh escaped him. 'Women,' he said.

'I wouldn't attribute my point of view to my sex, if I were you,' warned Anna, feeling herself flush angrily at his condescension. 'At least I haven't ordered her personnel file from the District Attorney in order to investigate her past!'

He shrugged. 'You're hopeless!' he sighed. 'What difference should it make to you, anyway? I like having a drink with May. She's cute, and fairly witty. Besides, I'm lonely. You're never at home, since you're always working nights. Why shouldn't I have a little amusement?'

'That sounds funny coming from you,' Anna said bitterly. 'You're the one who's never home. My work is the only distraction I get.'

'And speaking of personnel files,' he added, ignoring her words, 'I think an investigation such as the one you suggest would show that our May has nothing to hide. I'll say one thing for her: she's a very straightforward woman.'

'Good for her,' Anna retorted. 'She sounds well suited to you. Perhaps you can take a more permanent interest in her after we separate.'

'I doubt it,' he drawled. 'May has a good head on her shoulders, but she's a bit too candid. Never holds anything back. Wears her heart on her sleeve. No, Anna, she's just not my type. I like a woman with a little mystery.'

'You're fooling yourself, Marsh,' Anna snapped, her growing anger fueled by weeks of resentment. 'Any mystery you might have attached to me has been of your own imagining. I told you the truth about myself long ago. If you want to see a mind that gets pleasure out of putting suspicious constructions on everything, just look in the mirror.'

'I don't think so,' he contradicted her blithely. 'It seems to me that everyone who comes in contact with you has some inkling of your aversion to the truth. For instance, your current employers at the restaurant—are they aware that you used to work at N.T.E.L.? How about your old friend Debby? Does she know why you're working outside your old career? And, of course, there's always me. Why, if I weren't a lawyer, and trained to put two and two together, I wouldn't even realise you sent your famous personnel file back to your old Vice-President.'

'So,' Anna fumed, 'you haven't changed your ways. You're still spying on me.'

'Not at all,' he said mockingly. 'Just using the things I already know to speculate on what's going on behind my back. After all, I'm not in the habit of expecting you to keep me informed.'

'Why should I?' she rejoined. 'Whatever I might say would be greeted with disbelief.'

'You have a point there.'

Anna avoided his mocking gaze, her eyes scanning the cityscape outside the windows. Struck dumb by his cruel words, she fought to control her emotions.

'In all these weeks,' she said at length, 'you've never

forgiven me for something that wasn't even my fault. You have no pity, Marsh.'

'I wouldn't say that,' Marsh shook his head with infuriating suavity. 'I do pity you, Anna. I simply live with you in the only reasonable manner. In a way, I'm the perfect husband for you. A good lawyer is trained to take what people tell him with a grain of salt. He proceeds on the assumption that everyone has something to hide. Since you're a person of whom that is true to an exaggerated degree, I can relate to you quite well by simply assuming that whatever you tell me conceals something unspoken.'

'Wonderful,' Anna snapped. 'I'm glad I'm good for something, even if only for sharpening your professional instincts.'

'The day I proposed to you,' Marsh went on, 'I said you were a woman who needed watching. I had no idea how right I was.'

'I don't think I'll be needing your surveillance any longer, Marsh. To be quite frank, I've had enough of you and your reproaches and your silence. Once you're free, you're welcome to seek out another mysterious woman, if that's what gives you a thrill. Personally, I don't care what you do.'

'I'm grateful for your blessing,' he mocked. 'But I won't hear any talk of divorce. Not now, anyway.'

'Why not?' she asked. 'You yourself admit that our marriage isn't working, that it's a mistake.'

'Not working, I'll agree,' he said. 'A mistake? I'm not sure. Time will tell. There may be residual benefits to a life without trust. You've forfeited your right to any confidence I might have in you, but there's always this, my love.' He rose abruptly from his chair. 'You're still my type.'

A mischievous grin curled his lips as he advanced towards her. Suddenly Anna realised she was dressed only in her robe. Before she could move to defend herself, he had crossed the carpet in one lithe stride and curled his arm around her back.

'You're good-looking,' he said harshly into her ear. 'You're very sexy, in your own way.' His powerful arms held her like an iron vice, and he pressed himself brutally to her.

'Why consider a divorce?' he said, his hands beginning to caress her back, her hips. 'We have a good time together in bed, don't we? And your sister is taken care of, isn't she? And I only ask one thing of you, don't I?' His questions were like little contemptuous slaps which wounded her pride, even as his hands and lips quickened her pulse with tiny spasms of growing desire.

'Your part of the bargain isn't all that bad, is it?' he whispered, his lips caressing the tender hollow of her neck. 'You've got your job, your independence, your privacy. And when the witching hour arrives,' he added, his muscular chest grazing the taut tips of her breasts, 'I give you a pretty good time.'

Anna wanted to cry out, to push him away, and never to forgive him for the humiliation he was inflicting upon her. But already her treacherous body, tingling with insidious sensations, responded to his seductive touch with a shudder he was all too quick to interpret correctly. Glorying in his ability to arouse her against her own better judgment, Marsh laughed against her flesh.

'A bargain is a bargain, my love,' he murmured. 'Why not let yourself go, and enjoy the benefits?'

From the depths of her memory the echo of Porter Deman's cruel words resonated forth to join those of Marsh. It was the same cruelty, the same joy in prostituting her, in coveting her body at the expense of her self-respect. *'Why don't you let yourself go...?'*

With an athletic quickness that took him by surprise she whirled in his grasp and slapped his face with all her might.

For an instant his black eyes gleamed dangerously down at her. Then, with amused admiration for her aggressiveness, he grasped her more firmly.

His lips claimed her own with brutal intimacy, and she heard herself gasp in consternation at her own excitement. His hands had stolen expertly under the fabric of her robe to explore her nakedness, their subtle, knowing movements driving her to fearsome heights of desire. Slowly, with powerful expertise, his arms manipulated the weight of her body, shifting its centre of gravity, now supporting, now letting go, so that she was lowered naked to the carpet, as vulnerable as an insect around which a spider spins its imprisoning web. And all the while Marsh's deep, probing kiss held her in rapt immobility as he stripped off the last shreds of fabric separating her from him.

In a trice he had slipped out of his own clothes, without releasing her from the intoxicating, stunning contact of his body. She felt sullied to her depths, mocked by his arrogant sensuality, degraded by the disrespect with which he had stripped her, pulled her to the floor. What made it all worse was that in his perverse triumph over her unavailing resistance, he felt and knew the strength of the tie that still bound her to him.

She could feel an invisible smirk of victory in the very movements of his limbs as her lips returned his kiss, her flesh burned against his own, and a little groan of helpless pleasure stirred in her throat.

Without haste he prepared to come to her, for her body's shuddering responses made it clear she was ready to accept him, right here on the carpet, in the warm, still air. A hand rested confidently on her breast, the palm a mocking touch against the poised hardness of the nipple. He brushed the sleek flesh of her stomach with a kiss that sent a great shiver of yielding through her. His hand closed over her shoulder, pinning her to the floor like a living, breathing doll, an inanimate object brought to sensual life by his touch.

As she felt the hardness of his body settle luxuriantly over her, she decided to let him have his way without a struggle. She would oppose her passive resistance to his selfish pleasure, spoiling through her pliant coldness the intimacy he sought. But it was no use, for already her nerves tingled with involuntary delight at the warm, sliding touch of his skin on her own.

So she gave up all resistance, and accepted her role as his prostitute, the plaything of his desire. A perverse little voice whose echo stole over her throbbing flesh told her to enjoy herself, to sink into this sensual mire of humiliation, to allow herself to be titillated by the novelty of this experience, by this delight in sex without love. And perhaps her very acquiescence would punish him, she thought vaguely, for he would know that she also could take pleasure in his hard body without asking or receiving any human tenderness from him.

But her resentful thoughts were brushed away like gossamer in the wind by the tumult of involuntary ecstasy which overcame her. The last remnants of her self-respect seemed borne into oblivion as Marsh held her tighter, closer, as her traitorous body arched shamelessly and pressed itself against him, languid, delighting—and all gave way suddenly, all burst and relaxed into a wave of overwhelming passion. He had had his way, for he knew her too intimately to be checked by her defences.

And even now, lying faint in his arms, her eyes closed, Anna looked inside herself for the unforgiving woman who must live without him forever, and it was his black eyes that seemed to look out at her, holding her imperiously with their penetrating gaze.

She stood before the mirror, combing the tangles of sensual rapture out of her hair, having washed the traces of Marsh's assault from her body. He was in bed, reading. The eyes in the glass were tormented, exhausted. Her reserves of initiative seemed at a low ebb, and she felt defeat in every corner of her soul. There had been no love in his touch tonight. He had somehow extinguished it through the cold force of his resentment. And her will had reached its final paralysis, for her senses had actually delighted in being sullied by him.

In her cheeks she saw the pallor that Debby had noticed. Anna alone had suspected the real reason for the changes her body had undergone recently. Tomorrow or the next day she would know the results of the tests. If it was true, she was lost. Pregnancy would mean the end of life as she had known it, and the beginning of a time whose perils she could not even imagine. Married without trust, a mother without a real husband...

But why worry about the future? It would only be more of the same. Time seemed to have ground to a halt, stopping in one hollow instant which spread and expanded, consuming past and future alike. Only this awful unhappiness remained, diffusing itself like a gas, filling up the world, leaving no air to breathe. To think of repairing the damage caused by these weeks of angry silence was a futile thing now. She herself no longer trusted the husband whose confidence she had lost long ago.

There was nothing left but to go on, to endure. Let him enjoy her body, then. If it pleased him, let him have his way. She might as well enjoy him, too.

Or leave him, she thought as her mind jumped from one extreme to another. Go back to living alone, and working at Ariel. Raising her...her baby. Could it be? She was to telephone the doctor's nurse tomorrow. Her mind burned with an anticipation from which all joy and courage had been banished.

The pale face in the mirror swung and disappeared as she turned towards the bedroom.

CHAPTER NINE

'MRS HAMILTON, IS IT?'

'That's right.'

'Can you hold the line a moment? I believe we have the test result.'

Anna sat in anxious silence in the empty living room, her eyes darting sightlessly across the urban horizon outside the window. No sound came across the line; the nurse must have put her on an electronic hold.

With a shudder she glanced at the space of carpet beside the couch. Only last night Marsh had taken her there, brutally, abruptly, without affection. And now she was to find out whether she carried a new life in her body. The strain of the contradiction between the pain of her marriage and the joy of childbearing seemed intolerable. How could she presume to bring a new baby into the world, when her own life was in chaos? A child needs security, and that can only come from a strong relationship between its parents. Without that bond of understanding between mother and father, the infant would be little better than an orphan.

There was only one way out. A single parent would be better than two parents who were at each other's throats...

'Hello? Mrs Hamilton?'

'Yes.'

'Well, we have the result, and it's positive.'

There was a silence as Anna tried to cope with the reality announced by the voice on the line.

'Are you happy with the result, I hope?' The nurse's voice was hesitant, friendly.

'Oh…yes,' Anna assured her, 'of course, I am. Thank you very much.'

Placing the receiver gingerly on the phone, as if afraid to upset some invisible balance of nature at this critical moment, she closed her eyes and took a few deep breaths.

A child! She was to be a mother. For a brief, wonderful moment the thought of the gentle, tiny life within her body banished all other ideas. Whatever the tribulations she had endured these past months and years, only a few months now separated her from the miracle of bringing into the world a tiny boy or girl destined to grow into a real person. A separate personality, possessed of its own unknowable destiny, and yet bearing the wonderful and mysterious traces of the parents who created it. Whom would it resemble? Would it be a boy or a girl? What would be the sound of its little voice as it grew? What would be its interests? Anna's mind was thronged by all the joyful thoughts that come with a first pregnancy.

She stood up and walked the apartment aimlessly. As the couch, the bedroom passed before her eyes, her happiness began to give way to the desperate thoughts brought on by last night's scene with Marsh. Clearly he had lost what remained of his respect for her. He had treated her like a sexual slave. She shuddered anew as she recalled the echo of Porter Deman's cruel, manipulative words on Marsh's own lips. Never had she dreamed him capable of such arrogant cruelty.

She had endured these many weeks of silence in the waning hope that the resentment poisoning her marriage would dissipate with the passage of time. But it had obviously grown worse. Marsh left no doubt that he neither expected nor intended to give real love to his future relationship with Anna. As far as he was concerned, his worst suspicions of her own motives in marrying him had become the only reality of their life together. It was a marriage of convenience, cemented only by mutual self-interest. The blitheness with which he welcomed this existence without affection or trust had been the final blow to Anna's hopes.

It had been one thing to contemplate a divorce for the simple reason that life with Marsh was unhappy. It was quite another to imagine this loveless arrangement as a basis for bringing up a vulnerable child. Marsh's arrogant refusal to consider a separation could no longer be taken seriously. Anna's pregnancy lent a new urgency to the situation.

She must leave him, and soon. Her first step must be to effect the separation she knew to be inevitable. At some point, depending on the extent of Marsh's recalcitrance, a divorce would follow. In the meantime Anna would muster the courage she had left, and start a new life for herself—and for her baby.

For a brief, pained instant she pondered the tragic fate of the marriage which had once promised such a happy future. Deep within her remained a bond with Marsh which would never be severed. Whatever the bitterness that had overtaken her feelings for him, she would never be able to forget those first days of heady excitement in his company, of boundless confidence in him. It was nearly unbearable to think that her prideful silence about her personal problems had had such catastrophic consequences.

But it had happened. The clock could not be turned back. Marsh's faith in her must indeed have been frail from the outset, if he was able to abandon it so quickly. And perhaps her own pride, which would not allow her to beg him to reconsider his mistrust, indicated a secret lack of commitment on her own part.

In any case, there was no point in lingering over the complexities of it all. They had failed to make a life with each other; it was as simple as that. In future Anna would retain one precious link to her stormy tryst with Marsh Hamilton: the baby she now carried. Nothing could take that away from her.

Or could it?

A great fear blossomed within her, and was answered by the fierce protectiveness of motherhood. She would need money to bring up the child. What about her job at Ariel? How long would it be before her pregnancy forced her to quit? Would Mr Radier allow her to take time off to have the baby, and then return to work? Wouldn't Mr Foucault be confirmed in his suspicions of female employees, and insist on letting Anna go?

How would she find another job? She dared not cite N.T.E.L. as a reference; that career was over. Her current bosses might give her a reference, but would she be able to earn enough to support a child?

And what about Sally? If Anna left Marsh, she would have to take on Sally's tuition payments again. How could she possibly earn enough for both Sally and her baby?

Unless she accepted alimony and child support payments from Marsh. Money to pay for her child. *His* child.

An angry chill shot through her body as she contemplated the ultimate danger. If there was a divorce, wouldn't Marsh demand custody of his child? A child not yet born…Marsh was himself a lawyer. Wouldn't he claim that Anna was not capable of supporting the child adequately?

A welter of confused fears threatened to take possession of her. Wouldn't Marsh cite the false pretences under which she had married him, and characterise her as an unfit mother? A scheming, mercenary woman who had married him for money while hiding the truth about herself…

Losing control of her thoughts, she imagined him supporting his claims by producing the damning N.T.E.L. personnel file in a divorce court. She saw herself vainly trying to protest her innocence before a judge, after already having failed to convince her own husband of it. She saw herself attempting to explain why she had never acted to disprove the file's charges, to regain her job, to clear her name… Was she not a security risk? A woman who had tried to use her sexual favours in order to avoid prosecution for her crime?

'For heaven's sake,' she stopped herself with an exasperated laugh, 'get control of yourself! These are nightmares, not real possibilities. It will all work out somehow.'

But in her momentary panic she had began removing some of her clothes from the closet, as though in preparation for a hasty escape from Marsh. And now, as she contemplated the dresses and shirts that hung in his closet, the idea of leaving this apartment did not seem unreasonable. After last night's cruel quarrel and this morning's dramatic news, she needed time to think. Marsh's bitter, scowling presence was hardly conducive to dispassionate reflection.

And Marsh himself could certainly benefit from some well-deserved solitude after his lamentable behaviour towards her. Let him think things over as well, she thought. When they had both had time to cool off, she would tell him about her pregnancy, and firmly insist on an equitable solution to their mutual problem.

Her overnight bag was already filled. Her winter coat lay on the bed beside it. She had moved with a sort of nervous automatism in her preparations to leave. After briefly considering calling Sally, she decided against the idea. Better to stick to her policy of leaving Sally's untroubled college life free of her older sister's complex problems.

After a moment's hesitation she dialled her office number at N.T.E.L.

'Debby Johnson, please,' she said into the receiver.

'Just a moment.'

A loud click jangled in Anna's ear.

'Research 4-A.'

'Call for Debby Johnson.'

'This is Debby.'

'Hi,' Anna began uncertainly. 'This is me.'

'Anna! How are you?'

'Fine. Listen, Deb, would it be terribly inconvenient for you if I stayed at your place for a couple of nights? Or even just for tonight?'

'Not at all,' Debby answered brightly. 'I'd love to have you. But are you all right, Anna? You sound upset.'

'I'm fine,' said Anna, a trifle shocked to realise that her anxiety was so palpable. 'I just need to get away for a little while. Marsh and I…well, things are not going well. I have to do some thinking, and I can't do it here.'

'All right,' Debby said authoritatively. 'Just relax, Anna. Let me see…I'll tell you what. Do you want to meet me down here after work, or would you rather go over to my place right now?'

'Perhaps I should go straight to your apartment,' said Anna, feeling loath to set foot on N.T.E.L.'s premises.

'Okay, why don't you just head right over, and I'll call the superintendent—he'll let you in. But do me a favour, Anna. Don't go back out once you get there. You sound a little nervous, and my neighbourhood isn't the greatest. Just wait for me to get there, all right?'

'All right,' laughed Anna, touched by her friend's excessive concern. 'I'll see you later. And thanks a million, Debby.'

After what seemed an eternity of stops and starts in the inner city's crowded traffic, Anna's taxi came to a halt before Debby's ancient brick apartment building. The West Side location was a complex bus ride away from the Loop, so Anna had hailed a cab after stopping at her bank to withdraw sufficient funds for a few days on her own. A

maze of unfamiliar streets had passed before her tired eyes
during the long ride, and to her surprise she found herself
nearly lulled to sleep despite the cab's bumpy progress.

Debby's superintendent was waiting for Anna, and even
insisted on carrying her bags upstairs. Apparently grateful
for someone to talk to, he managed to air his opinions on
the city's political and economic woes in the two minutes
it took to reach the apartment. Mustering a smile, Anna
thanked him for his help and gratefully closed the door.

Now she sat, her emotions drained, among the furnishings she recognised from occasional visits to Debby during
her years at N.T.E.L. Debby's knitting basket was on the
couch across from the television. Pictures of her parents
and brothers stood on a table. A few of the myriad detective
novels she devoured each month were scattered here and
there. In the middle of the carpet, like a foreign creature
standing at sixes and sevens in the midst of all this do-
mesticity, was Anna's overnight bag, draped by her coat.

Listlessly Anna tried to recall the episodes in her past
which had been accompanied by the strange, bereft feelings
she now experienced in this lonely silence. There was the
time she and Sally had gone to stay with an aunt while
their parents attended the funeral of a grandparent. There
was Anna's first day at summer camp, when she was eleven
years old. And her first day at college, in the unfamiliarity
of the dorm. Above all she recalled the first day she had
sat at the kitchen table in her family's home, knowing that
the place would soon be sold and disappear from her life,
for now her parents were both dead. How strange the things
of the world seem, she reflected, when one's life is at a
crossroads. How unfriendly and foreign the carpets, the
windows, the furniture.

Yet somehow, with the passage of time, she had always
managed to make a place for herself among people and
things which gradually took on the warm supportive glow

of the familiar. But she could not help wondering whether such accommodation were to be hers again soon. For months now she had seen the few secure reference points in her life shaken by circumstances, and then finally destroyed. What flat, what furnished room lay ahead for her once her inevitable separation from Marsh became a reality? What future home awaited her new baby next summer? At what hospital would she have the baby? Where would she buy its clothes?

Exhaustedly she gave up thinking of practical things. Moving Debby's knitting basket to the floor, she reclined on the couch and stared mutely at the ceiling. One thing was sure: wherever she ended up, she would not be alone. Her baby would be with her. And no matter what struggles lay ahead, she would soon find herself feeding the child, buying it toys, playing with it, in a room somewhere…

Boy or girl? she wondered dreamily. The little hands would wave and grasp at her hair, her face, during the first months. The child would coo with pleasure between the crying spells which would be its only way to communicate its needs. She would carry it around the room, rocking it in her arms to soothe its tears away. She would go to a department store to shop for its first winter jacket, a tiny garment made of quilted, shiny material…

She had sunk into sleepy reverie when a gentle knock came at the door. Sitting up with a start, she wondered who it could be. Had Debby come home early? Had she lost her key?

Recalling Debby's warnings about the neighbourhood outside, Anna tentatively turned the knob and opened the door enough to see into the hallway. Dark eyes were staring into her own. A shock of wavy hair, tossed by the wintry wind outside, hung over the strong brow. Concern was in the ebony eyes, along with an enigmatic gentleness she could not fathom.

She stepped back in involuntary trepidation. In a trice Marsh had entered the room and closed the door behind him.

Still retreating despite herself, Anna moved towards the couch. The anger and suspicion she felt at his sudden appearance were outweighed by the visceral fear his powerful form evoked.

He was advancing calmly, a curiously friendly and even mischievous look in his eye.

'You're not running away from me, are you?' he smiled.

'No,' she answered shortly, unsure of his meaning. 'How did you know I was here? Why aren't you working?'

'I am working,' he said. 'I've just finished a job, and I'm touching bases with the people directly concerned with it.'

'I don't understand,' she said, giving him a wide berth as he sat down. 'How could you know I was here?'

'That was a piece of luck,' he said. 'I happened to be standing right next to Debby when your call came. You know, Anna, it's funny. You've never had anything but bad luck from N.T.E.L., but I seem to get my best breaks there. First I bump into a beautiful woman who becomes my wife, and then I'm lucky enough to be standing there when she calls up in search of a place to stay.'

'Debby shouldn't have told you,' Anna frowned. 'I wanted...I want some time alone, Marsh.'

'Of course you do,' he said. 'What woman wouldn't want some time away from a husband who didn't have sense enough to put his faith in her? Especially after the poor fool spent weeks making life a hell for her, because of his stupid, stubborn pride?'

'Marsh, what are you saying?' Unnerved by the tenderness of his demeanour, Anna could not suppress the reflexive suspicion produced by her many angry days with him. 'I don't understand you.'

'What I'm trying to say,' he smiled, 'is that since the

day I met you, Anna, I've been the luckiest man in the world, and too damned stubborn to appreciate the fact. If you're willing to listen to me, I hope I can convince you that I'm not all bad.'

'If you're talking about last night,' Anna said coldly, 'you might as well save your breath, Marsh. What happened wasn't the end of the world. I didn't leave home today because of one quarrel, but because…'

'I know,' he interrupted, 'I know, Anna. Maybe you should have walked out on me weeks ago. I'm just happy you hung on as long as you did. It shows that you had something left for me inside you. If it isn't too late, perhaps you'll be willing to take a chance on me—on us—one more time.'

'Nothing has changed,' she protested, determined to find out what was behind his apparent change of heart.

'That's where you're wrong,' he corrected. 'Everything has changed. I've changed, Anna. Why, you'd be amazed at how many things can change in one morning. For instance,' he said with a wry grin, 'there's a fellow over at N.T.E.L. named Porter Deman who's out of a job today. I'm sure that was the last thing in the world he expected to happen.'

Anna started involuntarily at his mention of the name she thought he had never heard.

'Porter Deman?' she repeated confusedly. 'How did you…'

'And,' he smiled with the complacency of the cat who had eaten the canary, 'you have an unlikely friend to thank for getting Mr Deman his walking papers. Can you guess who?'

She shook her head, dumbfounded by his revelations.

'A lady named May Reynolds,' he grinned.

Anna stared at him with a perplexity in which a first tiny hint of confidence glimmered.

'May?' she said. 'What do you mean? What happened? What are you saying?'

'Before I go on,' he laughed, taking her hand, 'I want to know if you're going to sit here quietly and listen to me, and not jump up and run away without hearing the facts. If you don't mind a small reproach, Anna, I think your trouble all along has been your tendency to go off alone with your problems, instead of asking yourself who your real friends are. Now, will you trust me long enough to listen?'

She nodded uncertainly, feeling a stir of renewed faith under the chaos of her emotions.

'Actually, Anna,' Marsh began, 'I can't blame you all that much for the secretiveness that's brought on your troubles. I'm not an ogre, you know—though I may have acted like one all this time. I can understand what sexual harassment can do to a person. Of course the shock would be terrible, and you would want to forget it at all costs. But hiding the truth from those you love has its own high price, you know.'

'What have you done?' she asked. 'How did you find out…?'

'Well,' he said, 'I certainly didn't get the help I needed from you, did I? It took me a while to get my sanity back, after seeing that damned file, and since you wouldn't tell me Deman's name I had to find out for myself. Now that I look back on it all, I can see that you were afraid of what I'd do to that worm if you told me. I have to admit you were right. I was so angry at him—whoever he was—and what he'd done to you, that I let my anger spill over on to you. I should have realised that you would tell me the story in your own time but instead I blamed you for not trusting me with it from the beginning. I was wrong, Anna, and I apologise.'

As he spoke, the firm lines of his face softened, and Anna

began to recognise in him the brightly introspective man she had found so irresistible during the first days of their relationship.

'And,' he sighed, 'the whole story was so outrageous that I'll confess I had my doubts about your complete innocence. There's no point in apologising for that, because it's unforgivable. I had my nerve to doubt you, when I was so outraged that you didn't trust *me* enough to tell me the truth in the first place.'

'It wasn't a question of trust,' Anna explained. 'It was…shame, and embarrassment, and I don't know what else. I should have told you, Marsh. But at the time, I didn't know what was in that file. I just knew that he'd done something…'

'I know,' he said. 'I understand, Anna—although I didn't at first. Being as stubborn as you are, I had to figure things out in my own way and in my own time.

'After our quarrel about the file,' he went on, 'I couldn't forget your reasons for not suing N.T.E.L. to get your job back. The only way to do justice to you, on the assumption that you were innocent, was to get the guy who framed you. In order to do that I first had to know who he was. So I made a call to the lady whose apartment we're now sitting in. She told me the whole story: Porter Deman, you, Barbara what's-her-name, Charles Robbins. She didn't know the details about the classified file you were supposed to have pulled from the computer, but she damned well knew the real reason they fired you.'

He smiled, his large hand grazing Anna's cheek.

'I had a lot of male instincts to keep under control,' he confessed, 'and it wasn't easy. But I've had some experience in this kind of thing, so I came up with a plan to get at the truth behind your file. It was pretty simple—the oldest trick in the book, as a matter of fact. Good old May Reynolds, who, as I told you, doesn't happen to be my type—but who is a crackerjack professional and a good-looking woman—went over to N.T.E.L. and got herself a job in your department. This was after I had a little interview with the head of Personnel, Mr Robbins, who had already been contacted by me, and was only too happy to oblige me.'

Placing a finger under her chin, Marsh tilted Anna's face towards his own and grinned with rueful humour.

'Poor Anna,' he said. 'You really haven't had much luck with me recently. Chuck Robbins is a nice guy, and he was terribly guilty about letting you go. He'd suspected there was something in your story, but hadn't bothered to investigate it thoroughly. When I had his secretary print out your personnel file, he nearly had a heart attack. Of course he could see the malice behind it, so he knew he'd made a big mistake.'

'Was all this the reason why he didn't answer me when I sent him the copy you'd ordered?' asked Anna. 'I never forgave him for that, you know.'

'For that, you can forgive him,' Marsh nodded. 'He was protecting our operation, which had to be secret. For the rest, Anna—for not believing you in the first place, and for not investigating Deman himself—you can forgive him if you have a charitable heart. He was scared to rock the boat, I suppose. Of course, once he'd seen the doctored personnel file and talked to me, he had no choice but to go along with us.

'So,' Marsh continued with a deep breath, 'May, under an assumed name, and dressed in her sexiest outfit, went to work at N.T.E.L. Before a few days had passed, the inevitable happened. Deman cornered her in a back room and told her she'd better have dinner with him, or else. She refused, politely. The next day it was the same thing, only he put the screws to her a little more—dinner with me, or you're fired. Fearfully, May accepted the invitation. At dinner, he put his cards on the table. A good personal relationship is the key to a good working relationship. And so on. Does that ring a bell?'

Anna nodded, flushing anew under the memory of what she had suffered at the hands of Porter Deman.

'Well, we couldn't stop there,' Marsh went on. 'Heroically, courageously, Miss Karff—that was May's alias—resisted Deman's threats. It went on for several weeks—weeks during which, across town, you and I, both as stubborn as ever, were giving each other the silent treatment.' He paused. 'I'll get around to apologising properly for that later. And to making it up to you somehow, Anna. I acted like a pig, and I'll never forgive myself.'

'Marsh, if only I'd known that you were trying to help me all along,' Anna sighed. 'Why didn't you tell me? Why did we have to go on the way we did?'

'Several reasons,' he sighed. 'There was May's cover to consider, and we still didn't have definitive proof of your innocence. After all, there were no traces of Deman's own hand on the computer, either with the classified file or with your doctored personnel file. But most of all, Anna, I'm afraid it was because our quarrel had escalated itself out of all proportion to the situation. I was still mad about the way you'd hidden things from me, and I was in no mood to let you off the hook until I had the goods on Deman. When you sent that file back to Robbins without telling me, it seemed that you were determined to go on keeping your secrets. And last but not least,' he frowned, 'was your new job at Ariel. I couldn't help thinking you were planning to walk out on me as soon as you'd made enough money. Was I wrong, Anna?'

She shook her head in chagrin. 'I'm afraid not,' she admitted. In retrospect she realised she had given Marsh ample reason to fear that her commitment to him was fragile indeed. And now she recalled the probing intimacy of his lovemaking during these unhappy weeks. Her own tormented emotions had blinded her to the wellsprings of affection and commitment his touch had communicated, in spite of his anger.

'Well,' he returned to his story, 'Deman used all his wiles to try to cajole and threaten young Miss Karff into giving him what he wanted. He's really an eloquent man, in a grotesque sort of way—a born blackmailer. What he didn't realise was that every one of his finely turned phrases was going right through the mike in May's bra and into a tape machine at an office across the street.' He laughed. 'Some of those nights when I was working late were quite entertaining. Well, Miss Karff refused and refused, taking pains not to be too alluring in her demeanour, so that no one could accuse her—us—of entrapment. Finally, Deman resorted to the tactics he had used against you. "You've had it, Miss Karff, you're finished at N.T.E.L. I'll get you fired and no one will believe you," and so on. That was this week.'

He shook his head. 'The man is certainly clever,' he admitted. 'He didn't want to frame her in the same way he'd done it to you—too obvious. So he went for the simplest solution. He decided that Miss Karff had stolen a letter from his files.

'Today was the red letter day,' he concluded. 'Deman showed up in Chuck Robbins' office, the so-called stolen letter in his hand. He said he'd found it in Miss Karff's desk. Without a word, Chuck handed him his resignation. He told me later this morning that the look on Deman's face was worth writing home about. Naturally he demanded an explanation. Chuck pulled out a cassette, turned on the tape recorder, and there was good old Porter Deman, explaining to poor Miss Karff that since she hadn't seen fit to let him have his way with her, he would see she lost her job.'

Marsh laughed contemptuously. 'Deman, of course, claimed the girl was a misfit, a scheming seductress who'd entrapped him. Chuck told him who she really was, and then pulled out a deposition made by Barbara what's-her-name—Moore, isn't it?— testifying to what Deman had done to her. Then, for the *coup de grâce*, he simply handed Deman a copy of your doctored personnel file. Well, that did it. Porter signed the resignation. Of course, there's a law against sexual harassment, and the indictment has already been handed down.'

'I can't believe it,' sighed Anna.

'That we got him?' Marsh asked.

'I thought he'd never be stopped.'

'All things are possible,' Marsh smiled, 'when people work together, Anna. When they trust each other. I guess you and I both had to learn that the hard way.'

'Marsh, I don't know what to say,' said Anna. 'When I told Mr Robbins the truth in the first place, and lost my job anyway, I thought the battle was lost. If I'd told you everything then…'

'But you hardly knew me, remember?' He grinned, shaking his head. 'I've had a lot of time to think this over, Anna, and it seems to me you weren't at fault. You had plenty of evidence that the system didn't work for victims like yourself. Why fight a losing battle? Even May and I, as lawyers, had to force the corporation to recognise its mistakes. And you're not a lawyer. Your discouragement was perfectly justified.

'But,' he added, his powerful hand resting gently on her shoulder, 'I have my lucky stars to thank for the fact that you felt you knew me well enough to marry me. Although I imagine you've had more than one occasion to think that was a mistake, too.'

Anna shook her head. 'No,' she said. 'I regretted what

was happening, and I did think we would have to separate, but I never felt it was a mistake from the beginning.'

'I had a feeling you still had some faith in me,' he smiled, 'since you didn't walk out on me when you had ample reason to. Until today, that is.'

Anna pondered the new light thrown on the past by his revelations. Clearly, the slender thread of commitment binding her to Marsh had weathered many a storm without breaking.

'I wasn't leaving you for ever when I came here today,' she said. 'I needed time to think, Marsh.'

'I don't blame you,' he agreed. 'There was a lot to think about. I hope you don't blame Debby too much for telling me you'd be here. And by the way,' he added, 'she explained to me about last night's comedy of errors. You were apparently so upset at seeing me in that lounge with May that you didn't notice that Debby was even more flabbergasted. After all, she only knew May as Miss Karff from N.T.E.L., and she was wondering how in hell I knew the girl. But Debby is a smart woman. She had an inkling of the truth right away.'

Anna sighed deeply. 'This is all too much,' she said. 'Too good to be true.'

'But it is true,' he murmured, taking her gently in his strong arms. 'It's all over, Anna. You've had a tough time, you've been abused and insulted. And, I'm sorry to say, you didn't have the benefit of the support I could have given you.'

He kissed her forehead, her hair, with a delicate tenderness whose tinge of regret underlined the sincerity of his words.

'I was so crazy about you,' he said, 'from the first moment you bumped into me outside those elevators, that I must have been scared of my own feelings. I was used to handling life on my own, and I suddenly realised that from that day on I couldn't live without you. I've tried to hide from it, but it's as true today as it was then, Anna. I love you.'

At last, after weeks and months of increasing despair, Anna began to feel the familiar warmth she had nearly forgotten. Was it possible? Could she be at home at last in his arms?

'I'm glad you didn't give up on me,' she sighed.

'The feeling is mutual,' he smiled. 'Although I must say I was a little worried today.'

Suddenly Anna recalled the emotions that had driven her from his apartment this morning.

'Anyway,' Marsh was saying, 'it's all in the past now, and I dare to hope that we'll finally be able to invest some confidence in each other. Porter Deman is out of a job, and Charles Robbins is waiting for you to call. He wants you to come back and take over the department, and he's hoping against hope that you'll accept his apologies. Think you're interested?'

Anna squirmed to her knees on the couch and looked into his eyes with the same glimmering happiness that had bewitched him during their honeymoon.

'I'd need maternity leave,' she smiled.

Marsh gazed at her in shock until the meaning of her words came through to him.

'You mean...?'

She nodded. 'There'll be another little person in the Hamilton family before too long. And probably every bit as stubborn as his parents!'

'When did you find out?' he asked.

'Today,' she answered. 'That's why I left. I was at my wits' end, and didn't know what to do. But now I know what to do.'

She kissed him tenderly. His arms encircled her with the special gentleness she thought she had lost for ever.

'Anna,' he whispered, 'let's go home. I could sit here for ever, just telling you how much I love you, but you've had a hard day, and you should rest.'

'Yes, let's go home,' she smiled, her arms resting comfortably around him. 'But I don't feel like resting.'

She felt his lips touch her own. His kiss seemed a promise, charged with the call of a lifetime of happy hours, beckoning from a sunlit future. Her senses yielded willingly to him, for she knew that the past could no longer trouble this intimate beginning.

The future was now.

NUMBER ONE

PROLOGUE

MANY months later, when it was all over and behind her, she would be grateful for life itself.

With a shudder she would recall that her very existence had been at stake that bright morning when the struggle began.

How silently our nightmares steal upon us, she would muse. On shafts of gay spring sunshine their first dark threads creep forward, coiling around us with furtive stealth even as we breathe in the cool air of day, a carefree smile on our lips.

Indeed, death itself had been at her elbow that first morning.

But she had not died. Instead she had awakened to a new world of searing pain and numb oblivion, and sudden ecstasies too enchanting to describe or to forget.

Once begun it had seemed endless, that infinity of joys and sorrows rearing before her all at once like a strange, foreign fate. Yet it was hers. How could she say no to it, when its sinuous paths opened within her own breast?

And when she pondered its unseen approach, a single instant hung hard and luminous before her memory. It was the last instant of a placid, ordered life whose time had run out.

There was a face in the mirror. But it was not her own face.

Then everything shattered as the future closed in.

CHAPTER ONE

THE tumult of stunned applause had died abruptly, and a hush of almost unbearable anticipation hung in the air above Pine Trail Golf Club's hallowed eighteenth green. A gallery of over five thousand, joined by millions of television viewers, fixed its eyes on a tiny dimpled ball which lay on the close-cut, rolling slope not twelve feet from the hole.

The television image magnified the little white sphere to huge proportions. Behind it Bermuda grass glowed like jade in the shade of the huge old oaks whose presence offered the sweltering spectators some relief from the unseasonable heat of this last Sunday in May. In the distance, the ranks of North Carolina long-leaf pines lining the fairway shone only as an out-of-focus background, dark and rather foreboding.

The camera's enormous blow-up of the ball was not as absurd as it seemed, for this was the last hole of the final round of the prestigious Southern Invitation tournament—certainly the most important event on the L.P.G.A. tour at this time of year—and the result of this ball's movement towards the hole would determine the outcome of the championship.

'It's all up to Joanna now,' the network commentator announced dramatically from his position high in the TV tower behind the green. 'After seventeen holes in the deadlock for the lead at eight under par, with no other players even close, she appeared to have the tournament in her pocket only two minutes ago. Peggy Byrne had put her ball in the bunker and seemed sure to make bogey. But as you can see in the replay,' he said as the image divided into a split-screen, 'true to her reputation as a clutch player, Peggy made the amazing happen.'

On the left side of the screen Peggy Byrne, the venerable holder of forty-seven tour titles and a great favourite among fans, was shown in slow motion, blasting her half-buried ball out of the bunker in a high arc that landed it on the slope above the hole. Zooming quickly to watch the ball trickle down the incline, closer and closer to the flagstick, the camera caught the magic and improbable moment when hundreds of hands raised skyward in shock and delight among the cardboard periscopes in the gallery to salute its disappearance into the cup.

Through her miracle shot Peggy had turned a sure bogey into a birdie, and thus put all the pressure on her opponent.

The replay image stopped in freeze frame as Peggy's plump, athletic figure was shown climbing out of the bunker. With her patented cheerful grin she waved to the astounded crowd.

On the right side of the screen a pair of tanned legs had moved into position beside the motionless ball on the green. In a patch of sunlight their shapely ankles and slender calves glowed golden brown above white golf shoes. Before them hung the stainless steel shaft of a putter whose offset aluminium head was now poised behind the ball.

'A few moments ago,' the commentator went on as Peggy's frozen smile receded and disappeared, 'it looked as though a par would win the tournament for Joanna. Now she must make this twelve-foot birdie putt to force a play-off, or Peggy will win the championship outright.'

The putter head stirred imperceptibly as the fascinated camera moved slowly upward along the shaft, past the soft curve of willowing female thighs to a pale lavender skirt and a pair of slender hands curled with almost surgical delicacy around the club's rubber grip.

The image slid higher to reveal two brown arms and bare shoulders emerging from a white cotton tank top whose fabric hugged the gentle swell of rounded breasts underneath. The camera's languorous ascent heightened the impression of lithe tensile strength almost coyly concealed behind the sweet, lissome contours of this already famous figure.

A ponytail held flowing blonde hair, bleached already by the sun of the spring tour, away from gold-flecked green eyes that darted calmly from the ball beneath them to the target twelve feet away. They were quiet eyes, reflective and even vulnerable under fine arched brows. Yet in their depths glimmered iron discipline and total concentration.

Thin but sensual lips, pursed slightly in this tense moment, and a creamy complexion burnished by long days spent in the sun, completed the unique and much-admired image of Joanna Lake.

Though a long shot of her stance at address would have identified her instantly to a knowledgeable observer, the networks' director, always aware of the fans' fascination with her unusual beauty and unmarried status, could never resist caressing her visually whenever she was the focus of drama, as today.

'I'm sure none of us would like to be in Joanna's shoes right now,' the announcer's murmuring voice continued. 'She's played a brilliant tournament, as always, but this time she must have been sure that victory just couldn't slip away. Yet that's what will happen unless the consistency she's famous for gets her through this putt.'

The tension in his voice echoed the torn emotions of the gallery and of the millions of viewers listening to him. Peggy Byrne, the courageous veteran who had survived a life-threatening kidney ailment ten years ago and gone on to win great victories, was on the way to her personal goal of fifty tour titles, and everyone wanted her to reach it before injury or passing time forced her to retire.

But Joanna Lake, famed for the perfection of her swing and her disciplined approach to her profession, was no less a heroine to legions of fans. She had entered the tour seven years ago at the tender age of twenty-one, not long after the break-up of a precocious, unsuccessful marriage whose only legacy was her infant daughter. As time passed her fiercely independent personality and dedication to her child became well-known aspects of her public persona.

No less celebrated was the mystery of her performance on the L.P.G.A. tour. In seven years she had won the Vare Trophy for lowest stroke average three times, and had been leading money winner twice. Yet, incredibly, she had won only three tour events in her entire career, and none in decisive fashion. Though she was considered one of the top women pros in ratings and in earnings, victory always seemed to elude her.

The conundrum that was Joanna Lake's golf game only seemed to underline the appeal of her natural, unpretentious beauty, for it added a tinge of vulnerability to her reputation as perhaps the most dependable competitive player on the entire tour.

Her marriage, ancient history now, had left her a lovely and vibrant young mother, supremely eligible and proudly self-sufficient. Sports publications, their editors regretful that her lack of tour victories prevented them from presenting her on their covers more often, seized whatever occasions they could to publish articles about her as 'the L.P.G.A.'s best-kept secret' or 'golf's quietest sex symbol'.

Thus a groundswell of excitement had erupted only minutes ago when it seemed that Joanna was at last to break through in her first important championship. Perhaps, it was hoped, her always fine efforts would begin to be crowned with victory.

But again she was in danger of losing.

If any of these thoughts were in her mind as she stood over her ball, they were not visible in the calm, motionless features of her face. So deep was her concentration that she was unaware of the millions of eyes fixed admiringly to her slender form, and of the myriad hopes and fears that made her the focus of so much attention.

Nor was she consciously aware that a single pair of eyes, indifferent to the crowd's expectations, was focused upon her with particular intensity.

Slowly the putter head moved back from the ball.

'Whatever the outcome,' the commentator was saying, 'this round will certainly go down as the most thrilling closing round in the history of this championship, and as the most exciting finish we've broadcast this year.'

As he spoke a camera high in the tower showed Joanna bent over the ball. Twelve feet from her the flagstick swayed in the warm breeze. Then the close-up returned. The putter's head was moving forward now, suspended with perfect tempo over the bent grass carpet, striking the ball firmly in its passage.

Now the camera beyond the hole watched the ball roll as unseen hands removed the pin, watched Joanna's eyes follow the roll as thousands of hearts leapt in the huge, silent gallery.

She had struck the putt flawlessly. The ball moved a bit to the right to make up for the break caused by the slope. Then it began to curve back, back into the line leading into the cup's dark depth.

But the hot sun had baked the bent grass more than Joanna or her caddy had anticipated over the course of the afternoon. The green was a trifle faster than it had been all week.

Her ball, moving a shade too fast, lipped the cup, began to fall, was forced upward by its own momentum, and spun off to the right as the stunned crowd, sure it was going to go in, roared its collective split-second convulsion from joy to disappointment.

Waves of impotent sympathy seemed to flow from the gallery towards Joanna's fragile figure. But respectful and even delighted cheers for Peggy Byrne were already beginning to be heard, for her victory was something to celebrate.

Minutes later, having congratulated Peggy and accepted her winnings with a smile as dozens of cameras clicked their attention to her photogenic beauty, Joanna was on her way to the locker room, her mind absorbed by a single thought.

She could hardly wait to call Tina.

A determined group of reporters stopped her before she could reach the clubhouse. Though she knew what their questions would be, and had answered them a thousand times before at dozens of other tournaments, she was cheerful and even humorous in reply.

'Joanna,' a well-known sports writer said, 'you seem to have continued your tradition of brilliant second-place finishes here today. Are you disappointed to have come so close without winning?'

'Not at all,' Joanna shook her head. 'When Peggy makes a shot like the one she played out of that bunker, there's nothing you can do but take your hat off to her and be glad you were there to see it. She has her own way with a sand wedge, and I don't think anyone else could have made that shot in quite that manner.'

'Your putt came awfully close,' another man said. 'Are you sorry it didn't drop and get you into a play-off?'

'I gave it a good roll,' she replied, 'so I'm not disappointed. Besides,' she laughed, 'the way Peggy was playing today, I can't help thinking she would have come up with something else to win, even in sudden death! I needed everything I had just to stay with her as long as I did. She deserves the win.'

Though the questions were polite, their undercurrent was obvious, and it was Ron Lieber, the least friendly of the journalists she knew, who characteristically put it into blunt words.

'A lot of people,' he said without smiling, 'wonder whether you choke in tough situations. That last putt, for instance, seemed makeable enough in the circumstances. Did you choke?'

'No,' she answered, hiding the sign of exasperation she felt rising within her. 'I thought I stroked that putt pretty well. I wish it had gone in, but it didn't. Still, it was one of my better efforts today.'

'Nevertheless,' he pursued grimly, 'we notice a pattern in your career. You've only won three championships, and in all three cases the front-runners collapsed at the last minute to leave you in the lead. It's being said that you can't win except by default.'

Joanna shook her head with a patient smile. *Anything to get him out of my hair*, she thought privately.

'Don't count me out yet,' she said aloud. 'I've won before and I'll win again—if I play well. But I don't choke. I'm proud of my concentration and my consistency. I'll admit that it's pretty hard to win when one or another of our great players is out there having an extra special day— but that's golf for you.'

Smiles touched their knowing faces as they saw how deftly she had parried the aggressive question. Another reporter, anxious perhaps to help extricate her from Lieber's sour clutches, began asking about Pine Trail's layout and the strategy needed to play the course well. Joanna was considered the most analytical and knowledgeable of all women pros where the subtleties of golf courses were concerned, and her opinions were always eagerly sought.

The tiring interviews went on for twenty minutes before she excused herself with an apologetic smile and hurried towards the locker room. She knew Tina was waiting in Sarasota for her mother's habitual post-tournament phone call, and she intended to make it even before undressing.

She knew the room would be nearly empty, for her threesome had been the last and most of the professionals would be gone already. None of the club members had played the course today, since it was reserved for the tournament, so only an isolated tennis player might still be there, showering and changing before going up to the terrace lounge for a cocktail.

She had passed through a long corridor lined with portrait photos of the club's wealthy members, and was nearly to the locker room's heavy oak door, when a man loomed suddenly before her.

'Great tournament, Miss Lake,' he said, towering over her in the small hallway as he blocked her way. 'Sorry about the result.'

'Thank you,' said Joanna through a pained smile, moving to sidestep him. But without seeming importunate he managed to cut her off.

'I wonder if I might have a very brief word with you,' he said.

'I really must…' she said tiredly. 'I'm sorry, I'm in a kind of a hurry. Perhaps if you called my secretary…'

Perturbed by his sudden presence, she glanced quickly into his dark eyes and to the door behind him.

'I'm a great fan of yours,' he said, smiling down at her from his tall frame, 'but I'm here in a business capacity. I'm sure it will interest you. My name is Reid Armstrong.'

He extended a large hand, and reluctantly she took it.

'I'm happy to meet you,' she said, 'but as I say, I really must go now. If you'll call my...'

'I understand,' he said. 'But before you go, perhaps you could help me with a question—a historical question about golf. Since you're an expert on the subject, perhaps you'll know the answer.'

Joanna pursed her lips, trying to hide her irritation. *If it will make him go away*, she thought.

'How many of the championship golf courses in this country were designed by women?' he asked.

'That's easy,' Joanna laughed. 'None. All the architects were and are men. No woman has designed a tournament layout, Mr—'

'Call me Reid,' he interrupted. 'How would you like to be the first?'

Taken aback by his words, she darted a perplexed glance to his tall body and handsome face. Beneath careless waves of dark hair tinged with premature, sandy grey which gave him an oddly roguish sort of halo, he was smiling with sensual lips, his intelligent eyes riveted to her uncomfortable self. The strong lines of his tanned face suggested that he was in the prime of his thirties, all confidence and puckish humour, and quite sure of his ability to get whatever he wanted out of her.

But the irises under his dark, incisive brows were sharp and probing, and for an instant she recalled her strange impression that someone beyond the gallery and TV cameras had been watching her intently as she putted out on eighteen today.

'I don't understand,' she said, shrugging off the thought.

'I represent a group of investors who need an architect for a new course in South Carolina,' he told her. 'Beaufort County, near Hilton Head. You know the area.'

She certainly did. It was perhaps the richest single region

for championship golf courses in the entire nation, and the tour had brought her there many times.

'It's simple,' he concluded bluntly. 'They want an architect. Someone excellent, someone with imagination—because they want to compete with Harbour Town and the other great courses nearby. I'm the finder they've hired, and frankly, I think you're the person for the job.'

'I...Mr Armstrong, I don't...'

'Reid,' he corrected with his inscrutable smile.

'I have no experience as an architect,' protested Joanna, unable to prevent her gaze from straying past him towards the locker room. 'I've never designed a golf hole in my life.'

'But you've thought about it, haven't you?' he said, apparently taking pleasure in hemming her in physically as well as conversationally.

She hesitated. 'Perhaps I have,' she admitted at last. 'But not in a serious, business sort of way.'

'Miss Lake,' he said, 'you shouldn't be overly modest about your abilities—or your ambitions. I'm here because I know your reputation as an analyst of golf courses, and of the game in general. I'd like you to have a look at the layout in question. It's an ocean-view situation, plenty of acreage, good soil, and lots of natural hazards. If you find it interesting, we'll talk about a commission.'

He had wasted no time in coming to the point, and he looked down at her now, his brow arched appraisingly.

'You seem to have more confidence in me than I do in myself,' she protested, glancing at her watch.

'That may well be true,' he said significantly, his gaze touched by teasing humour and by a curious, caressing glint of sympathy.

'May I ask what you mean?' she returned, irked by the impertinence of his manner.

'Look at it this way,' he said. 'If you accepted the job

of architect for my people—and please understand that they fully intend to attract major championships for both men and women once the course is built—that would be an awfully ambitious project. It would make quite a name for you. It would make history, in fact. Now, unless I miss my guess, you're not the sort of woman who's comfortable with that kind of notoriety.'

'I'm not?' she repeated, bristling at his presumption.

'I think you prefer a low profile,' he explained. 'Of course, that attitude can stand in the way of legitimate ambitions, if you let it go too far. It can even prevent the development of an important talent.' His tone was cajoling.

'For a person who's never met me,' Joanna said impatiently, 'you seem to think you understand me pretty well.'

'In some ways,' he replied, 'the TV image doesn't lie. I've watched you many times. As I said, I'm a fan of yours.'

'So you did say,' she nodded, fully aware that he would not hesitate to use flattery to get what he wanted, if he thought it necessary.

'I think you're a nice person, Miss Lake,' he told her. 'Perhaps too nice. Your game is an aesthetic one. You adjust it to the specific qualities of the course you're playing. That makes you a pleasure to watch, and earns you a lot of fans. But,' he added, 'you're not the killer type, who goes out to defeat other people, and to send them home disappointed while you take the spotlight for yourself. Have I misinterpreted your screen image?'

For an instant she regarded him curiously, fascinated despite herself by the straight, hard line of his jaw and the muscular contours of his neck and shoulders. He was not only a devilishly handsome man, but appeared to be an athlete of some sort.

'Aren't you getting off the subject a bit?' she asked at length.

'Was I?' he asked, raising an eyebrow mockingly.

'Mr Armstrong,' she sighed, her patience at an end, 'I'm sorry, but I absolutely must go. Don't you think you'd better…'

'I'll tell you what I think,' he said more seriously. 'I think that if you took a look at the layout I have in mind, you'd find it intriguing. You'd consent to work on a tentative design for that area, and once you got started on it, you wouldn't want to stop—your natural curiosity wouldn't let you. You'd finish the design, and it would be brilliant—like everything you do in your profession. My committee would jump at the chance to build it. And the whole business would be a great step forward for women in golf.' He shrugged. 'Someone has to take that step. Why not you? You're respected and you have the ability.'

Unsettled by his unceremonious demeanour and bold proposal, Joanna returned his steady gaze with difficulty.

'And,' he added blandly, 'to be quite frank with you, the very fact that you're a woman, combined with your inexperience, will allow me to get you for this job cheaper than I could get a name male architect. That's a consideration.'

'So it's a bargain you're looking for, is it?' asked Joanna with a wry smile. 'Can't you afford a man?'

'To answer your question,' he said, 'getting you would be a great bargain indeed, Miss Lake.'

His crossed arms made the fabric of his sports coat cling to his powerful back and shoulders as he looked down at her through dark irises in which a gleam of blue seemed to wink laughingly. She could see not only an intention to tease and to manipulate in those sharp eyes, but also a fugitive caress of genuine respect and—the thought was perplexing—pride in her.

'Correct me if I'm wrong,' she said, banishing the wave of restful warmth that had emanated from him to enfold her so suddenly. 'I imagine your investors are mostly men, and quite traditional in their outlook, like all country club people. Would it be safe to say they don't yet realise you've approached a woman with your proposition?'

He grinned. 'Your intelligence comes highly recommended,' he said. 'Yes, you're right. But I think I can guarantee you that if your work is up to your usual standards, I will be in a position to see that they accept it.'

She nodded, loath to take him at his word and yet half-convinced that he could make good on his promises.

'So you see,' he concluded triumphantly, 'with you having taken the first step, other women will follow. Less talented women, perhaps. But you'll have broken the ice.'

Joanna sighed. 'If what you say is true,' she said, 'your offer would certainly interest most of the top women pros. It might interest me. But I have to go now, Mr Armstrong…'

'Reid.'

'I have to go now,' she insisted, stubbornly refusing to call the stranger by a first name, 'and call my daughter.'

'Tina,' he said simply. 'She's a beautiful child—I've seen pictures of you together. She must be about to finish third grade.'

'Yes,' allowed Joanna, unnerved to hear information about her private life roll off his tongue so easily, 'she is.'

'Well,' he changed the subject with brusque assurance, 'how about dinner tonight? I'll lay out all the details for you.'

She shook her head. 'There's a dinner for Peggy tonight. I have to be there.'

'Lunch tomorrow, then?'

Again she shook her head, not quite daring to edge around him for fear that he would actually move to block her way. 'I'm driving back to Sarasota tomorrow morning,' she said. 'The next day I have to go to Orlando for another tournament. It's the beginning of the summer tour, you see…'

'All right, then,' he said. 'Breakfast tomorrow will be perfect. I'll meet you at your hotel. Will eight o'clock do?'

Joanna sighed, defeated. Obviously he wouldn't take no for an answer. 'Seven-thirty would be better,' she said. 'And right here on the club terrace. I'll have some last-minute business to attend to.'

'That's fine,' he smiled, extending a large tanned hand. 'You won't regret it. See you at seven-thirty, Miss Lake.'

She shook the warm, dry hand, seeing her own slender palm disappear into its caressing depths. For an instant she wondered in involuntary panic whether he would let her go. The very touch of him seemed to confirm that in his mind all obstacles must yield to his initiative, his power.

But he broke the spell with a grin. A moment later he was gone, having stood aside with a matador's grace to let her through to the locker room. Yet something of him remained around her, persistent as the smile of a Cheshire Cat, still teasing, still plying her with inscrutable charms as she hurried towards the phone.

That night Joanna spent her accustomed half-hour in the oil-scented bath which calmed her tired nerves while softening her sun-dried skin. She made it a habit to end each day of competition this way, replaying with closed eyes the eighteen holes she had faced earlier, analysing her club selections and the mechanics of her swing.

But her concentration was ceaselessly troubled by her painful knowledge that with the summer tour at its height she would see little or nothing of Tina in the two months to come. Even the sound of the little girl's bright telephone voice, already shorn of the hesitations it had borne only a year ago, made her feel lonely and anxious to hurry home tomorrow for a precious Monday together.

Her one real regret about professional golf was the gruelling summer schedule that kept her from watching the dynamic growth of Tina's tender limbs and unique personality. Karen, her long-time secretary and friend, cheerfully assumed the role of guardian in her absence, but Joanna was acutely aware that the responsibility took her away from her private life and budding career as a freelance writer.

Joanna had followed her call home with an equally traditional long-distance consultation with her college coach and mentor, Carl Jaeger.

'Jojo,' he had said, 'your round was a beauty. I'm sorry the network only covered the last five holes.'

In his gentle way he was pointing out a truth whose importance Joanna clearly saw in retrospect. She had not lost the tournament on the eighteenth hole, but much earlier, when she had inexcusably missed short putts for easy birdie opportunities on the seven and tenth holes. She resolved to get in several hours of practice on the putting green before Thursday's opening round.

Now that Pine Trail's eighteen difficult and picturesque holes were behind her for another year, Joanna found herself dreamily picturing their borders of dogwood and azalea and rhododendron shrubs, and the sycamores and black willows intentionally planted by the architect thirty years ago to compete with the triumphant stands of pine. He had had to plan the entire course around the creek which wound its way through marsh and pasture land, creating water hazards on seven of the holes...

She opened her eyes suddenly, feeling the warm water wash around her naked limbs as she started in her surprise. She had ceased thinking as a player and was second-guessing Pine Trail's architect.

'It's because of that man,' she told herself irritably. 'That Armstrong man. Reid...'

And all at once she seemed to see his rugged, handsome face smiling down at her, goading her, tempting her…

Despite his impertinence, she told herself in all honesty, he had managed to prick her interest. If only for the sake of women's progress in a sports world dominated by men, a commission as architect would be something to think about.

But she had not been deaf to the sardonic humour in his voice. He wanted to paint a picture of her as a woman who was afraid of her own ambition, and for that reason alone she longed to bring him up short somehow. If not by refusing his unlikely offer out of hand—since she was already saddled with more than enough obligations—then perhaps by accepting it, just to show him she could not be so easily psychoanalysed.

The complacency in his sharp eyes came back to taunt her. Their gaze had seemed to strip her naked, she mused, while ironically promising only to look, and not to touch.

Sleep did not come easily that night, and Joanna had to force herself to forget the nerve-racking aspects of the profession she loved.

'I've got to get home,' she thought before drifting off at last.

The next morning Reid Armstrong was as hard to handle as he had been in the corridor outside the locker room. Joanna arrived on the terrace to find him lounging comfortably over coffee in a pair of tight-fitting jeans which hugged his slim hips and flat stomach, and a cotton shirt open at the neck, revealing the crisp tangle of hair on his deep chest. He was the very image of lithe male confidence languid in repose.

In the morning light she noticed once more the flecks of emerald and cobalt blue which gave his dark eyes their laughing cast, and the sandy tinge lurking among the careless strands of his black hair. His long arms, uncovered on this warm morning, were obviously extremely strong.

There was something complex and multiple about his colours and his smiles, as though he was not content to remain within a single identity, like other men, but was prepared to be all things for all people. That curious ambiguity only added to his buoyant charm, for he was vibrantly compelling in his erect physical presence nevertheless.

Joanna supposed he must be an enormous success with her sex, although his mysterious, blithely knowing gaze made her conclude that he was far from her type of man. He lacked the candour and seriousness she saw as necessary attributes of the unknown man she might meet and belong to some day.

Over breakfast he repeated not only his convincing arguments in favour of her doing the course design, but also his importunate probings of her personality. He seemed to admire her precisely for the boundless ambition he thought he saw in her, and to find nothing to criticise her for except her failure to unchain that ambition entirely.

She could not recognise herself in the portrait sketched by his comments, for she considered discipline and consistency to be her best and most salient qualities. By the time they rose to leave she felt their conversation was at a stalemate in every respect.

'Let me ask you something,' she sighed as they made their way among the tables towards the fragrant lawns leading to the parking lot. 'Why haven't you approached one of the big tour winners, like a Wright or a Whitworth—or a Peggy Byrne—with this proposal? Surely their names are more prestigious than mine. Wouldn't your committee find one of them a more credible choice?'

'In the first place,' he told her, 'I couldn't care less what they think. I want to find the best possible person for the job. But,' he added with his teasing look, 'before you get a swelled head, I'll tell you something else. The big winners in any sport are often not the most cerebral types. They play by instinct, and since they win, they don't spend a lot of time analysing the subtleties of their game.'

Joanna stopped short, darting him an angry gaze. 'You mean,' she asked, 'you want me because…'

'Because you're a loser?' he smiled. 'If the shoe fits, Miss Lake…'

'Thanks a lot,' she said with an incredulous shrug.

'For instance,' he explained, ignoring her pique, 'I don't imagine it's easy to beat a legend like Peggy Byrne in a big tournament like the Southern Invitation. Mentally, I mean.'

'I don't understand.'

'Well,' he went on dryly, 'she's the great popular favourite, the winner over her illness, and she's shooting for her fiftieth win this year, isn't she? She can't very well get it if someone like you stands in her way, can she? Think how disappointed she'd be if she had to retire without reaching her goal.'

'You're very presumptuous,' observed Joanna. 'If you think I, or any other pro, would give less than a hundred per cent…'

'Not consciously, no,' he allowed. 'But I understand ambition, Miss Lake. Every professional athlete must have a lot of it. And he or she must be able to cope with it mentally. Ambition requires that we make other people lose, that we take the spotlight for ourselves, and refuse to share it. That's not a comfortable position for certain types of athletes.'

'And you think I'm one.' Gratefully Joanna saw her small station wagon come into view in a nearby row of cars parked on the already baking blacktop. She could hardly wait to put this arrogant man behind her.

'I'll tell you what I think,' he said, taking her bare arm in his large hand as he scanned the driveway. 'I think you're the best shotmaker in women's golf. And I think you have the best brain in the sport. However,' he went on, studying her hair and eyes with his appraising gaze, 'I suspect you need some mental training—training to win, I mean, as opposed to mere preparation for competition. Few people realise how important that is.'

'Thanks for the advice,' she cut him off, controlling her temper with an effort. 'Here's my car.'

'To get back to the business at hand,' he said, holding the door for her, 'when can I expect you in Beaufort? You'll want to see the layout.'

'I have tournaments to play,' she replied shortly. 'Perhaps after the season... But I'm sure you'll find someone else before then.'

'You have a break two weeks from now,' Reid pointed out calmly. 'Between the Jacksonville Pro-Am and the Eastern. You could fly down to Beaufort County at our expense and look things over. If you like what you see, you can start work next fall when the tour is over.'

'I intended to spend that week...' she stammered, taken aback by his foreknowledge of her schedule.

'With your daughter,' he interrupted. 'Fine. She'll be out of school by then, so you can bring her along. There are lots of fun things for kids near me—and I'm sure she could use some adult male companionship.'

He had struck a nerve, and she had to fight to keep it from showing in her face.

'You don't like to take no for an answer, do you?' she asked, looking up at him from the hot driver's seat.

'No need to,' he grinned, 'when a proposal is to everyone's advantage. When will I hear from you?'

Joanna shook her head. 'I honestly don't know. Why

don't you send me some sort of map of the layout, perhaps a description…'

'It's already in the mail,' he said. 'Probably waiting for you in Sarasota.'

She raised an eyebrow. 'You're very efficient,' she commented.

'I'm paid to be,' he replied with his unflappable smile.

'And you assume an awful lot.'

'I don't think so,' he said. 'This is an opportunity—for you and for me. The job is tailor-made for you—you'll see.'

'Goodbye, then,' she said, shifting into reverse as welcome waves of cool air flowed over her bare legs from the air conditioner.

'For now,' he corrected, reaching to shake her hand. His palm was dry and protective, even in the hot morning air, and the trace of its touch remained as she turned away to grasp the wheel.

Clearly her first impression of him had not been far off, she mused as she backed the car gingerly out of its space and set off between the rows of parked vehicles. He was like the Cheshire Cat; not quite there, since one could not make him out, and yet refusing persistently to go away, his smile lingering in the air around…

The TV network's sound trucks, a clumsy fixture in the parking lot all week, were already gone, as were many of the cars belonging to players and journalists. The station wagon purred smoothly as its interior cooled.

Once she was on the open road the trip would be pleasant. She enjoyed driving to southern tournaments held not too far from home, for the restful ribbon of road and lovely scenery helped her to clear her mind in preparation for the next competition. Besides, the car seemed closer to Tina than the impersonal cabins of jet airliners.

At last the parking lot gave way to the smooth, tree-lined

road, and Joanna pressed the accelerator. With surprising alacrity the compact wagon leapt forward.

She glanced in the rear-view mirror at the clubhouse behind which the eighteenth green, scene of her latest near-win, awaited today's round of members. Stolid as ever, the Tudor building presided over one of the most challenging courses in the South.

Before she could return her gaze to the road, a sight on the wide veranda of the clubhouse caught her eye. Outlined against the morning sky, a tall man stood alone, his arms crossed over his chest, staring straight in her direction.

It was Reid Armstrong, she realised in that split second. Even across this considerable distance which widened at every instant, he was watching her, scrutinising her, his alert gaze seeming to take in her every reaction.

He'll never give up, Joanna thought with sudden trepidation. Even in her own car, speeding homeward, she felt oddly caged, vulnerable as a fleeing prey before the quick talons of the predator.

That was the last conscious thought she was to experience for many hours.

A flash of blue seemed to overtake her from the direction of the road ahead. There was an oddly remote crunch of metal, and then a sudden twisting that gripped the car mercilessly, growing in power until it wrenched at the road, mutilated the trees and sky, tore at the sunlight, and engulfed the whole world.

Then nothing.

CHAPTER TWO

IN her dream an eclipse of the sun had taken place. Night had covered everything. Blinded, she had to make believe she could see the walls and corridors of her father's house.

Dad was with her. He was pointing out a famous masterpiece hung on a wall. It was the pride of his collection. Her eyes made useless for seeing by the eclipse, Joanna began to cry. But he seemed not to notice.

How strange, she thought, that he should be blind to her blindness. But she must admit it. She must confess her shame.

Daddy, I can't see.

Meanwhile the enemy soldiers were already coming in, breaking down doors, shouting orders to each other, streaming in dark ranks around Joanna like stampeding bulls who miraculously spare the victim in their path.

Since it was wartime, all normal rules were suspended. Everything must be burnt, broken into pieces, used against the enemy or blown to smithereens before the enemy could make use of it.

Her father was nowhere to be seen now. And how terrible it was to be dressed only in her pyjamas, a pathetic little figure alone on the landing, while the troops overran everything with their fearsome shouts! In mute terror she watched, her eyes too young to show their panic.

'*Come on, little lady,*' the enemy leader said, scooping her into his arms as he beamed an amused smile down upon her. '*Show me the way.*'

His sword rattled horribly against his belt, a snakelike thing alive in its sheath. But his smile was protective, almost paternal.

'There now,' he laughed in triumph, swooping her higher and higher as the roar of cannon and hooves grew louder and louder, unbearably urgent and hurried, rising to a horrid peak…

She awoke with a wail of terror heard only as a muffled moan by the special nurse.

'Do you need something for the pain?'

At first the words sounded as foreign as the walls surrounding Joanna. Still dazed by the intensity of her nightmare, she fought to understand where she was.

The sheets were cool and comfortable. But she barely felt them, for the roar of noise inside her mind had become a climax of physical pain unlike anything she had ever experienced. Indescribably sharp and cruel, it nevertheless grew worse.

And worse.

She caught a glimpse of her leg in traction. To her right she saw the shadowy figure of a doctor hurrying into the room. Then, with all the odd naturalness of a hiccup or a sigh, something happened for the first time since her forgotten childhood. Joanna cried out aloud.

'All right, all right,' the nurse was saying. A hand patted her shoulder impotently.

'Get me a tray, Bev,' came the physician's voice. 'Let's give her a hundred milligrams of Demerol intra-muscular. She has a lot of raw pain.'

Time was standing still, paralysed by unbelievable suffering, as firm hands gripped her and a tiny stab, laughably insignificant, broke the skin of her shoulder. With a strange lucidity she felt the liquid spurt from the needle's point into her flesh.

Then an enormous cottony dullness began to cover everything, muffled and slack, suffocating and yet welcome, for it overcame everything and banished this nocturnal world of agony and helpful, ineffectual human voices.

Am I dying? she wondered vaguely, floating into indifference. The thought would have been almost comforting in comparison with this hideous, unending victimisation that had engulfed her—had she not finally remembered who she was.

'Tina,' she moaned, unheard by the forms moving in the darkness.

Then she was asleep.

When she came to herself again a bright bar of sunlight hung across the ceiling. Its image seemed to pierce her pitilessly, fuelling what she now realised was a splitting headache behind her eyes.

Before she could close them a nurse and two doctors, alerted by the sound she must have made in awakening to her pain, converged around her.

'Joanna?' a soft voice emerged from one of the faces, soothing her with its North Carolina drawl. 'How are you feeling this afternoon? A little groggy?'

Her grimace must have told him the truth, for she saw the flash of concern in his eyes.

'Tina,' she murmured.

'Don't worry,' he said, articulating his words with exaggerated clarity, as though she were deaf. 'We're going to give you something for that pain in just a minute here. Your daughter and Karen are right outside in the corridor with Mr Armstrong. You're going to be fine. Do you understand?'

She nodded, satisfied that Tina was here. Waves of sharp pain flowed and throbbed through all her limbs, deep under her skin, as though unseen hands had cruelly toyed with her very insides during her sleep.

So I'm alive, she thought with a little pang of irony. *I can see and hear and think and feel. The better to suffer with.*

But she was grateful for life if it would allow her to be with Tina. And in her excitement she made her first mistake. She tried to move.

'No, no, no, no,' the doctor smiled indulgently as a shock of unspeakable agony smote her. 'Don't try to move. Just lie quietly and listen. Okay?'

For an answer she looked pleadingly into his grey eyes.

'My name is Dr Morrison,' he said. 'And this is Dr Diehl, from South Carolina. He's your doctor, too. You had an accident yesterday morning on the country club road. Do you remember, Joanna?'

Again she saw the mirror, the dashboard, the flash of blue against the overhanging canopy of trees, and her eyes darting an instant too late through the windshield. She nodded numbly.

'Good,' he said. 'You're a lucky young lady, Joanna. You were hit almost head-on by a fellow in a pick-up whose steering line broke. He had no control over his vehicle at all. Luckily, he's going to be all right, too.'

He had taken her hand gently. Though his touch sent new waves of pain through her, she squeezed the hand.

'All things considered,' he said, 'I think you're doing pretty well. You have a lot of bad sprains, a couple of hairline fractures in your ribs and right arm, and possibly some concussion.'

Even as he spoke the circulation of her pain began to centralise itself, and she realised what he was saving for last. The upraised knee was the focus from which her agony radiated.

The simple knowledge of it nearly made her cry out. She reached towards it stupidly, for it was in a heavy brace.

'Yes,' he nodded, stopping her hand with his own. 'You see, now, that's why we wanted to talk to you before giving you any more pain medication. The knee hurts a lot, does it?'

Joanna nodded, her lips pursed in consternation. 'Quite a lot,' she gasped, her eyes belying her measured words.

'Okay,' he said. 'That's what we need to know.' He glanced at his colleague, a younger man with greying fair hair and a droopy moustache.

'Hello, Joanna,' the man smiled, moving closer beside her. 'Can you tell me a little about the location of that pain?' He gestured without touching the knee. 'What would you say? On the outside of the knee, or the inside?'

She nodded, then shook her head in confusion.

'I...' she stammered. 'Inside.'

'Towards the middle, you mean. Towards the space between the legs.'

Again she shook her head, infuriated by her inability to explain herself.

'Or do you mean inside the knee itself?' he asked helpfully.

She nodded with a grateful smile.

'But not in the back of the knee,' he probed, his finger tracing an outline in the air. 'How about right behind the kneecap?'

Again she nodded, nearly terrified to hear the location of that horrid pain pinpointed so cruelly.

'All right,' he nodded. 'We're going to have to do something about that. But right now Dr Morrison will order you some medication.' Smiling under his moustache, he retreated from her field of vision, and Dr Morrison's careworn, fatherly face returned.

'Well, young lady,' he said, 'today we're going to try

you on something a little more human than that Demerol.
Your pain won't go away completely, but you'll be aware
of what's going on around here. How does that sound?'

'Thank you, Doctor,' she said hollowly, clinging anew
to the hand he proffered.

'You're going to be tired again,' he warned. 'You can
see your visitors while this injection is taking effect, and
then you'll have another nap—though not for thirty hours
this time, I hope.'

'Is that how long…?' She tried to touch her perspiring
forehead and saw heavy tape around her right arm.

'Partially because of the Demerol,' he smiled. 'But you
took quite a beating in that car of yours. Your knee hit the
dash, and probably the steering column as well. The X-rays
of it are clear, so we know that the problem inside is with
cartilage or ligaments. I called Dr Diehl at the suggestion
of Mr Armstrong—he told me he witnessed the accident.'

'Reid…' murmured Joanna, reproaching herself too late
for calling the man she barely knew by his first name.

'He's quite concerned about you,' the doctor told her.
'He's hardly left the hospital since you got here. Actually,
he already knows Bob Diehl, who is, as you may know, a
specialist in orthopaedics and sports medicine, and sort of
got us together on this. He's a very determined man, your
Mr Armstrong.' He laughed. 'I think he's even got your
convalescence all planned out, as you'll soon discover.'

She nodded vaguely.

'And,' he added, 'he's been very good for Tina since she
got here, if I may say so. Would you like to see her now?'

Suddenly Joanna glanced in panic at her taped limbs and
bruised hands.

'What about the rest of me?' she asked. 'What do
I…look like?'

'Like what you are,' he replied seriously. 'An accident
victim, Joanna. You have multiple contusions and abra-

sions, you're black and blue all over—but you'll be fine in time. Don't worry about Tina, she's seen you already. Children tend to accept things well. My goodness, but she's a bright little girl. The nurses have all fallen…'

'Can I see her now?' pleaded Joanna, unable to wait another moment.

'Sure thing,' he laughed.

A moment later Karen's freckled face and curly hair came into view. At her side was Tina, the worry in her wide eyes masked by tactful cheer.

'Mommy?' she said, patting Joanna's black-and-blue arm with a small hand. 'Mr Armstrong is going to teach me how to ride a horse!'

'Good,' Joanna sighed, too overjoyed by the sight of her daughter's face to pay much attention to her words. 'I'm sorry if I worried you,' she said, stroking the round little cheek beside which a pigtail hung fastened with rubber bands. 'Silly old Mommy managed to crack up poor Louisa.'

Tina shrugged generously at the sound of the station wagon's pet name. 'Oh, that's all right,' she said. 'Karen says we'll get a cousin of Louisa to take us around.' Behind her Karen pointed a thumb down with a grimace to indicate that the car was damaged beyond repair.

Joanna held jealously to Tina's hand as she looked at Karen. 'Is everything all right otherwise?' she asked.

'No problem,' said Karen. 'Your friend Reid is quite a guy. He's made fast friends with this one,' she glanced at Tina, 'and kept the nurses hopping! He acts like your guardian angel.'

She leaned closer as Tina watched the nurse prepare a syringe. 'It's funny,' she said, 'you'd almost think he feels responsible in some way. Anyhow, you're lucky he's been around. He called me in Florida, and helped me decide what business to do before we left, and what to bring for you. Where did you meet him?' The glimmer in her eyes bespoke her admiration for Reid's obvious charms and her assumption about the nature of his relationship with Joanna.

'Oh,' Joanna sighed, confused, 'at the club. I don't know.' Despite her concentration on Tina, the pain in her knee was becoming unbearable again, its intensity sapping her mental energies. Gratefully she felt her new injection being given.

An iridescent emptiness descended upon everything as the pain began to recede. For a long moment she kept her eyes on Tina and tried to be lucid. Surprisingly, the effort was not uncomfortable. She slipped from thought to thought as down a gentle slope leading into a propitious future.

'I'm alive,' she told herself. 'I'm still able to think, to plan, to act. I'll be able to walk out of here soon and go back to taking care of Tina.'

Then she realised with a start what had been missing in the news she had received these last few minutes.

No one had promised her that she would walk again—let alone play professional golf.

Without relinquishing her daughter's hand she let her eyes close. Instinct directed her away from panic and towards last resorts. Tina was still here, healthy and loving as always. Karen was here.

And outside somewhere, in the corridors of this hospital whose name and location she had not even thought to ask, Reid Armstrong waited.

It was called Holy Family Hospital, Joanna found out when she awoke again and began making the nurses' acquaintance. She was in Fayetteville, North Carolina, not far from Pine Trail's rustic location. Thanks to Reid's presence and quick action at the scene of her accident, she had arrived in the emergency room only twenty-five minutes after the collision.

Karen, true to form, had carefully made all the necessary arrangements both here and in Sarasota after hearing from Reid. The insurance company had been informed and the car taken to its final resting place, Joanna's twisted golf clubs and battered suitcase having been rescued from its interior. Tina's school was notified that she would be away for a couple of days. Even Joanna's winnings from the Southern Invitation had been sent to her Florida bank.

Dr Diehl was all business when he returned without his older colleague.

'I'll need you to sign this release for surgery,' he told her, placing a form on the rolling table which bore Joanna's untouched liquid breakfast. 'I want to go into that knee of yours this afternoon and see if I can't do something about your pain.'

This afternoon, she thought with a pang of dread.

'How…how serious is it?' she asked.

'I won't know that until I get a good look,' he said, holding out a small instrument that vaguely resembled a ballpoint pen. 'This is what I'll use, Joanna. It's called an arthroscope, and I'll be operating "through it", as we say. The incision will be small—only a couple of stitches afterwards. I won't bore you with all the anatomical details,' he smiled.

Painfully she lifted herself to her elbows so that her eyes would be somewhat on a level with his own. She was tired of being stared down at.

'I think you'd better bore me,' she said through teeth clenched by discomfort. 'My body is crucial to my profession.'

'Of course,' he said, easing her back down on the sheets. 'Your immediate problem is what we call a traumatic chondromalacia. Your kneecap took a hard, direct blow, and I suspect that the cartilage behind the kneecap is roughened as a result—possibly with a few loose chips floating around. This is causing that intense pain. Now, I'm going to clean up that situation with a special tool that shaves the inside of the kneecap. It cuts off the fragments and sucks them in, just like an electric shaver. Meanwhile, we'll flush your knee joint with a lot of fluid, to make sure that we get all the loose fragments out. Although we're not scientifically positive of this, we suspect that those little chips contain an enzyme that can damage cartilage, so they have to go.'

He smiled encouragingly. 'That's the end of it. I think I can promise you some good relief from the pain.'

'Will I be…normal, then?' asked Joanna, determined to know the whole truth.

'Well,' he frowned, 'the chondromalacia is definite, but I'd be less than honest if I didn't tell you that it's probably not all you have to worry about. Your X-rays don't show anything broken, but you may have other problems which could be quite serious.'

'Such as?' asked Joanna, trying to hide her worry.

'Your collateral knee ligaments are probably bruised or torn, on the inside or the outside part of the joint,' he said, his finger pointing out the area without touching it. 'And your lateral meniscus—that's the cartilage that acts as a shock absorber when you work the knee—may be damaged. If it is, it will never heal, because cartilage happens to be about the only part of the body that has no blood supply. We'd have to do something about that.'

He sighed, apparently convinced that his recitation could only bore and frighten her simultaneously, while sounding like gibberish.

'Also,' he went on, 'you may have lost a chip or two out of the end of the femur—the thigh bone—when the force of the accident crushed your tibia into it. We call that an osteo chondritis dissecans. Then again, you might have a tear in one of the inner knee ligaments, right in the centre of the joint, between the leg bones. That's called the anterior cruciate ligament, and repairing it is no simple job. I'm going to be checking for all these things today, because none of them show up on an ordinary X-ray.'

Having absorbed this complicated vocabulary with difficulty through waves of pain, Joanna forced herself to ask the question that had tormented her for hours.

'Will I play again?'

Dr Diehl looked directly into her eyes.

'I don't know, Joanna,' he said. 'I don't know if you'll walk normally again, or run normally, or climb stairs normally, or end up with a trick knee that gives out once in a while, or a knee that hurts when it rains. There's no way to tell until we test you thoroughly. And we can't begin to do that until we get rid of that pain.'

'I see,' she said quietly. 'This afternoon…'

'The anaesthesia will be general,' he nodded. 'The surgery will take about forty-five minutes. I wouldn't worry about it if I were you,' he glanced at the release she had sighed. 'It's not dangerous surgery in any way. But I think you should be aware that, whatever happens, you're going to need some follow-up and a lot of physical therapy. I'll need to see you at my clinic in Charleston starting Friday at the latest.'

He smiled. 'That's where Reid Armstrong comes in. He lives not thirty miles from our clinic, and he tells me he's all set to put you up, and Tina as well when she finishes school, while you convalesce. Personally, I think it's a good idea. The clinic is basically an out-patient operation, and it would be very boring for you to stay there.'

Struggling to take all these facts in, Joanna looked up at him.

'Reid Armstrong?' she queried. 'I barely…'

'Another advantage he'll offer you,' he went on, 'is that he knows my methods. I helped him out once, years ago, when he was injured playing college football. You're going to need a whirlpool and some Nautilus equipment, and he's already arranged to have it installed, I believe. A friend in need, as they say...'

Joanna could only nod helpless acquiescence. Unnerved by the thought that she might be irreparably damaged in some way, she could not deal with his bewildering revelations.

Surgery.

The word terrified her. She had never been in a hospital as a patient in her life. She had never injured herself in a sports career that already spanned more than a decade. A bad attack of 'flu was the worst ailment she had ever suffered.

She could not force from her mind the stories she had heard about the dangers of anaesthesia. That, no doubt, was the chief concern behind the release Dr Diehl had made her sign.

Silly, she reproached herself. *That's about as likely as getting hit by a...*

Then she remembered. She *had* been hit by a truck, when she least expected it. The unlikely could and did happen.

She sighed in consternation. Normal life seemed so remote now, exiled by this artificial reality of pain, fear, and drugged apathy. And Dr Diehl steadfastly refused to promise that one day she might be herself again.

The five hours before surgery would have been unbearable had it not been for Reid and Tina, who entered the room not long after Dr Diehl's departure. His large hand on the little girl's shoulder, Reid dwarfed her strikingly. Yet she seemed at home in the shadow of his huge, smiling form, and sat in his lap complacently when she was not wandering the room or holding Joanna's hand.

'You're big news already,' he said, showing her the latest issue of *Sports Illustrated*, whose editors had managed to include a small note about her accident after their account of her loss to Peggy at Pine Trail.

'Karen has all the newspapers,' he added. 'Your face is all over the sports pages. Looks like injury is better publicity for you than winning!'

'Very funny,' sighed Joanna, grateful for his levity even though she could not for the life of her understand what he was doing here.

'Tell me,' he asked Tina, 'what do you think of your mom today?'

'Mm-m,' the child hesitated, twisting on his lap, 'same as always, I guess. She's a little black and blue, of course, but that's to be expected in the circumstances.'

Joanna had to smile at Tina's precocious language. Reid merely nodded in silent agreement, neither patronising her nor hiding his amusement.

'Which is worse?' he asked. 'Her contusions or her confusion?'

'What are you talking about?' Joanna erupted from her bed. 'Drugs or no drugs, I've never been more clear-headed in my life!'

'Good,' he drawled. 'That means you can start making plans for your convalescence at my place.'

Joanna shook her head, too emotionally exhausted to start a lengthy argument with him. It was impossible to comprehend that this total stranger had somehow managed to choose her doctor, to determine the site of her recovery, and even to befriend her daughter. Yet it was Reid who had called the ambulance for her, Reid who had called Karen—and now Joanna could even recall having read or heard from other athletes about Robert Diehl's fame as a sports specialist.

Everywhere she looked in her jumbled life, it seemed, Reid had suddenly managed to leave his mark. From the moment he had loomed up in front of her in the portrait-lined corridor at Pine Trail, it had been impossible to get rid of him. Circumstances had added themselves to his natural persistence, so that now he had become a virtual fixture in her existence, at once indispensable and unfamiliar.

Who could tell, she wondered, what others must think of her relationship with him, since he had been haunting these hospital corridors so loyally? What must Dr Diehl think? And Tina...

And, if the truth be known, she reflected uncomfortably, Reid had even played a part in causing the accident itself. Of course, she would never be able to admit that embarrassing fact to anyone—much less to Reid himself. But she could not wipe it from her memory. Even as the small figure in her rear-view mirror, Reid had managed to fascinate her sufficiently to distract her from the road ahead.

And, as luck would have it, that single instant had been the crucial one.

No, she thought ashamedly. No one must ever know of her foolishness or her chagrin.

And yet Reid seemed to know or suspect the truth of the situation. Even Karen had felt his sense of responsibility in his overwhelmingly scrupulous presence here, his protectiveness as Joanna's 'guardian angel'...

She blushed to think that she and Reid shared this most intimate secret, despite the fact that they were still perfect strangers. A secret that they could never confide to anyone else—or to each other.

It was all too much, she thought resignedly. Some day, when this mess was behind her, she would be on her own and self-determining again. But for the moment she was helpless and frightened, and she could not disdain the confident humour with which Reid kept her from dwelling on the surgery to come.

And he was unfailingly cheerful, teasing her unmercifully as he watched Tina's peregrinations about the room or held her in his lap.

'When you think of it,' he said blandly, 'things always have a bright side. While you're at my place there won't be much to amuse you, so you'll have time on your hands. I'll show you the Black Woods layout and maps, and you can give some serious thought to the design, maybe even plan a few holes right away. I know you'll fall in love with the place. And, if you're as lucid as you say you are, I won't hesitate to expect great things from you.'

Joanna had forgotten all about the proposal which was at the source of her misfortune.

'Honestly,' she groaned, 'you are the most presumptuous man I've ever met in my life! You've got me up to my neck in your own plans, and I don't even know if...'

He looked over Tina's shoulder at Joanna, his dark eyes alert as those of a jungle cat. The child, absorbed in the book she had brought, did not see the intensity that quickened his irises.

'If you'll walk out of here?' he asked, reading Joanna's fears easily. 'I'll tell you something, Miss Lake. You'll not only walk out of here—on crutches at first, I'll admit—but you'll play golf again, and you'll win. I intend to see to it. And I don't like to take no for an answer.'

His gaze softened. 'And,' he added, 'you're going to be the first woman to design a top-twenty championship course. I want it to be a difficult test, you know, so that when you play it on the tour you won't have an unfair advantage as the architect.'

'For heaven's sake,' she sighed, hiding her gratitude for his confidence, 'you might as well call me Joanna.'

'All right,' he said, patting Tina's shoulders. 'And you can call me any names you like—as soon as you're back in top shape.'

As the minutes stretched languidly into hours, Joanna watched the interplay between Reid and Tina from her propped-up position in bed. It was more than obvious that he had easily won the child's friendship and trust—probably during the nocturnal hours when his reassurance and distracting presence prevented her from worrying that her mother would die from the accident.

Yes, Joanna mused as she watched their quiet laughter and conversation. They had the air of two people who have been through something painful together. Something that has brought them closer.

Yet all the while she could not help noticing his enormous male vitality, coiled in that small chair across the room, sending its waves of silent urgency in her direction, unbeknownst to her oblivious daughter.

Or were the drugs and the pain playing tricks on her again? She could not tell. In his gentle humour and unflappable confidence there was a virility that charged the air around him, forcing her into acute awareness of him as a man at every instant. Despite herself she blushed to think he was seeing her in her battered condition.

Even as she reflected on these ideas, the medication for her pain was wearing off in preparation for the general anaesthesia which must come this afternoon. As the hour drew nearer for fearsome oblivion, her thoughts became more coloured by her nagging discomfort, and it seemed that her emotions were in as bad a mess as her body.

She was angry at Reid for his brusque, manipulative invasion of her private life—and grateful to him for his help. His irritating certainty that she would eventually do his bidding seemed unforgivable; yet there was nothing so unreasonable about what he had asked.

Fate seemed to conspire with him at every turn. In his arrogance he had promised Tina he would teach her how to ride a horse. Yet, in all likelihood, he had calculated the probabilities beforehand and knew he would be in a position to make good on his promise.

With a pang she thought how quickly Tina had attached herself to the first truly male figure she had been close to in her young life.

'Well,' she sighed inwardly, 'I suppose it's better to have him on my side than against me. At least he's more encouraging than Dr Diehl!'

Now the pain was radiating in a weird symphony from her knee to all the corners of her body. Clear thinking was no longer possible. She was almost grateful when the nurse came with a tray for her preparatory injection.

Let's get it over with, she thought grimly as the needle punctured her. Let Dr Diehl use all his skill and heroism if necessary. Anything to deaden this awful, angry pain!

'You'll feel a little sleepy now,' said the nurse in a hurried but amiable voice. 'The orderlies will bring a table in a moment to take you to the operating room.'

Sleepy? Joanna thought. *Dopey is more like it.* The words were taking on an antic absurdity as the powerful drug overwhelmed her senses.

Sleepy, Dopey, Grumpy, Bashful...

She thought she was laughing at the silliness of everything around and inside her. But already she was being wheeled under the corridor's painted ceiling, doing her best to respond to the orderly's pleasant question about golf. But the simplest words would not come. She found herself unable to make her mouth move properly.

Then there were doctors around her. She heard Robert Diehl's voice, harsher and more authoritative now. The anaesthesiologist, a kindly, bespectacled man, forced a needle into her vein and sat beside her, his smile vanishing as he said, 'She's ready, Doctor.'

Horrified to be capable of thought just as her body was to be invaded by foreign instruments, Joanna fought to help her mind wander away.

In time she would see to everything, she resolved. She would make decisions, take command of things, take care of Tina. When she was on her feet again. She was accustomed to being in charge of her little family, and nothing would change that—Reid Armstrong notwithstanding.

But for now she must withdraw from this reality of pain and dread.

So she let herself slip into the past, numbed by the brutal anaesthetic. She saw herself seated as Tina had been, comfortable and complacent, on the secure and unmoving lap of a man as steadfast as an edifice, on a hot summer evening in a small Southern town, on a porch beside a quiet street, long ago, long before the busy, hurried years that had led to this moment of truth.

CHAPTER THREE

'*Scoot over an inch, honey—these old legs of mine are going to fall asleep in another minute.*'

Paul Lake's voice, its lilting drawl as rhythmic as the swaying old couch on which he sat in the shadows, was the sleepy destination of each sunlit day, and its sweetest moment for Joanna.

She could feel him nod approval as she recounted her doings at school or at play in the neighbourhood. Absently he patted her shoulder, acknowledging her childish words with little murmured responses, alert to the muted sounds from inside the house where Ellen was seeing to Chris, and yet all grave attention to Joanna.

She was eight years old, and if she had a care in the world, it was always banished by this lulling, whispered hour in the cradle of her father's arms. The sound and touch of him were as permanent and warmly dependable as the crickets under the porch, the katydids falling silent in the trees, and the neighbours who passed by on Grandview Street with a wave and a smile.

So secure was that nightly moment, stretching before her in its lazy perfection, that she tried her best to make it last. But it was, after all, the end of the day, as Paul always seemed to know before she did.

'Upsy-Daisy,' he would croon as he raised her to his own great height, the front lawn wheeling past her half-closed eyes as the screen door swung open. 'That's my girl!'

And she would be asleep before he placed her softly on

her bed—and only half-wakened when Ellen came up to kiss her.

So that, in a way, the languid moment on the porch had never ended, but had gently closed her eyes to what came after.

She had been born in Atlanta, where the steel and granite towers Paul helped build with his construction crews stood as shining symbols of the New South.

But she had spent her first years in the tiny town of Crane, twenty-five miles away. And it was there that she put down her emotional roots, her ears filled with names like Macon, Albany and Savannah, her field of adventure encompassing all the dark corners of the venerable but rickety house that Paul had bought for his new family.

Like the porch's swinging couch, whose occasional whines of old age lent the still night air some of its charm, the house came to bear innumerable traces of Paul's patient, stubborn repairs. Piqued in his engineer's mind by the challenge of outwitting inevitable decay, he liked to amuse himself by fixing the most unsteady of its ancient trappings, rather than to replace them with something more seemly.

Having long since learned to cease protesting his heroic labours in the name of common sense, Ellen would watch him with lips pursed in a half-smile of resignation, and then turn back to her own housework, tossing her curly hair over a tired shoulder as the smile's ghost lingered in her busy eyes.

Paul's aura of quiet calm, incarnated for Joanna in the warm lap and long arms whose embrace was firm and comforting as the ground under one's feet, seemed to be his particular and irreplaceable essence. It pervaded even the moments when he had to discipline her or Chris, the vibrant little sister born three years after her. Though Joanna could not understand at the time, it was also a crucial balance in his loving marriage to Ellen, a far more volatile personality than he.

Everyone said that little Joanna, with her grave eyes and thoughtful demeanour, took after Paul, while bustling, excitable Chris was her mother's daughter. And even that familiar pronouncement, spoken now by a red-faced uncle, now by a smiling grandparent, seemed a faithful friend, a pleasant landmark of life on peaceful Grandview Street.

Joanna felt privileged to be likened to the tall, reflective man whose inner serenity seemed obscurely linked to his power over objects. It was Paul who restored things and made them permanent, no matter what the damage wrought by accident or the passage of time. Thanks to Paul, what was old could also be what lasted.

Years later, when she realised how deeply she had come to love her South for the endurance with which it hid and protected its gentle roots even as harsh decades of change overtook it, her wistful thoughts would turn to Paul.

For in her life he had been the slow and comforting passage of days, each one as perfect and familiar as the last, their stately rhythm providing a wide-eyed little girl with the sense of security her growth required, while exposing her unfortunately and inevitably to the lulling illusion that some things are permanent.

One day she came home from third grade to find a police car parked in front of the old house. Inside, two officers sat uncomfortably on the living room couch, their black uniforms sending cold tendrils of strangeness into all the corners. Ellen was seated as far from them as possible, five-year-old Chris on her lap. She seemed to have recoiled from them in panic, as from their news. Her tear-stained eyes shot to Joanna with an odd look, angry and pleading and perhaps resigned, which passed unnoticed by the others.

Joanna knew before she had to be told. Paul was dead.

He had been killed in a scaffold accident high above the
site on which his men were working. His last breaths were
drawn in the emergency room of an Atlanta hospital, far
from his home and family. There had not been time to
inform Ellen until he was already gone.

With the quick adaptability of childhood Joanna survived
her loss. In her mind Paul was a shadow now, a presence
in every warm Georgia night. In fact, he was as much part
of the night's quiet essence as of the old house's dignity.
So convinced was she of his continuing influence over her
life that she viewed Ellen's cold grief with puzzlement.

She never forgot that brittle, pleading look that Ellen had
flashed her in the presence of the officers. Whether it carried a weight of responsibility or not, somewhere inside her
child's heart Joanna decided that she must serve as a living
link not only between Paul and his widow, but between
Ellen and little Chris, who risked growing up without ever
experiencing the warm security Joanna herself had taken
for granted.

Joanna was the lucky one, the first-born child for whom
Paul had lived too intensely to be eliminated by death.
Therefore, she reasoned, she must help those who had lost
him.

So it was that, when Ellen found full-time work, Joanna
became adept at helping to prepare dinner and clean the
house. Before long she was attending Chris's school plays,
walking with her to the dentist or paediatrician on Main
Street, reading her school reports and the childish stories
she wrote, and generally assuming a maternal role which
the three-year gap between the sisters would never have
justified otherwise.

A year after Paul's death Ellen sold the house and moved
her family to a comfortable but nondescript apartment. Unseen and unfelt by anyone, Paul Lake took up a position

deeper inside Joanna's soul, secure and invisible to outsiders, now that his beloved house was gone.

And life went on as grade school gave way to junior high. Ellen worked hard, with a stolid, somewhat harsh gaiety, while slim, reflective Joanna devoted herself to Chris, who grew more spunky and vital each year.

Joanna found herself inexplicably popular at school. She was in the chorus, on the debating team, and was voted Most Intelligent in her class. Everyone admired her and came to her when in need of advice. It was assumed she would go to college and become a professor or lawyer or doctor.

She alone never questioned her certainty that she would one day become an engineer.

But again the gentle sequence of days passing one like another showed its fragility.

On a windswept day in March, when she was in eighth grade, Joanna was asked by a classmate to join her for a round of golf.

The girl was Sissy Macomber, the daughter of an extremely rich and respected family. Having set her sights on making friends with her popular classmate, Sissy cheerfully showed Joanna around the Country Club's fabulous oak hallways lined with studio portraits of the prosperous men who were its members.

The girls sneaked into a huge lounge filled with overstuffed chairs, and purloined a few delicious-looking peanuts from wooden bowls in the empty bar. After their round of golf they ate hamburgers in the dining room and bowled a game in the small alley beneath the members' steam rooms and squash courts.

Joanna decided she had not had so carefree and amusing a day in a long while. A trifle jealous of Sissy's heedless enjoyment of such money and luxury, she went home to prepare dinner as usual.

But her frail fourteen-year-old presence had made its impression at Fairhaven Golf and Country Club.

Juan, the caddy who accompanied the girls on their somewhat giggly eighteen-hole outing, saw Joanna miss the ball completely on her first swing. The patient pro shop assistant explained to her the virtues of keeping one's eye on the ball, and on her next swing Joanna obediently hit a vicious slice that screamed far out of bounds.

But Juan noticed with his practised eye that the ball had flown at least one-hundred and seventy-five yards in the air.

By the end of the round he could hardly wait to tell his fellow caddies what he had seen. Correcting her mistakes with uncanny instinct, Sissy's young guest had improved dramatically with each hole she played, and had actually finished the back nine in fifty strokes. Such a performance from a pure novice was unheard-of.

Word soon reached Ralph Kohler, the club professional, who related it to Mrs Macomber. That lady, determined to cement her daughter's new friendship, spoke with Ellen Lake on the phone before inviting Joanna to join Sissy for another round.

A week later Ellen informed Joanna that she might play golf every day throughout the summer, since an arrangement had been made with some neighbours to watch out for eleven-year-old Chris.

Somehow Joanna never thought to ask why her golfing friendship with Sissy had become so time-consuming, or why she found herself receiving regular lessons from Ralph Kohler. She contented herself with the dozens of Cokes, bags of potato chips, hamburgers, and conversations about boys that made up her days with the gregarious Sissy.

Ralph Kohler realised that in Joanna he had found a

once-in-a-lifetime pupil. Thanks to her perfect instinctive concentration and natural inclination towards neatness and correctness, she could play a casual round punctuated by laughing byplay with Sissy—and all the while refine her talent, perfect her swing, choose her shots with ever-increasing intelligence and foresight.

By summer's end the club teemed with whispers about Ralph's prodigy. Joanna was still only five feet tall and weighed eighty-seven pounds, but the gentle curves of her shoulders and thighs concealed fine muscles, and her every move was so filled with fluid rhythm that she already seemed a young champion. Her game was approaching competitive quality with a rapidity that left witnesses breathless.

But Ralph bided his time. He knew that golf was just a game to Joanna, so he treated it as such. He rewarded her progress with sodas and ice cream cones, kept Sissy near her, and made her play catch with the caddies, watching her carefree animal grace in admiration from a distance. When he met Ellen he tried to imagine the tricks of heredity that had produced a young miracle like Joanna. But Ellen was not particularly athletic—and the girl's father was dead.

Golf became a fact of life for Joanna. She never gave a thought to what she was doing, even when her training extended through most of the winter, taking up more hours each day, even when she had to learn to budget her time in order to finish her schoolwork.

Sometimes she would return home to find Ellen reading to Chris or teaching her to sew. And now Chris was old enough to help with dinner. Grateful for each smile she saw them exchange, Joanna felt both relieved that they got along so well together, and a trifle jealous of this closeness from which she was so often excluded nowadays.

* * *

The next summer Ralph entered Joanna in the Western Junior Girls' Championship, which she won easily, defeating competitors who had been brought along for seven to ten years by their own club pros or hired teachers. Her performance passed as a fluke among the alert observers who knew how little experience she had.

But when she won the U.S.G.A. Girls' Junior Championship the same summer, her anonymity became a thing of the past, as did the playful aspect of her golfing experience. Besieged by eager reporters who asked her everything from the mechanics of her game to her opinion on world events, she could only answer in abashed, graceless monosyllables. Yet her innate seriousness as an individual charmed the press, and the seeds of her future popularity were sown.

By the time she won the Georgia Amateur Championship at the age of sixteen, Joanna was finding golf a burden. The subtle pressure she felt from all sides to continue time-consuming competition made her feel cramped and conspicuous at school. Though a confident champion on the golf course, she remained a gangly, frightened adolescent inside her emotions. Golf was tearing at her and losing its appeal.

She solved this problem by playing each round, each tournament in a sort of controlled trance. Her mind far away in reveries about the handsomest boy in the junior class, she let her body solve its own problems on the course. Ignoring her competition, she let herself float among the girlish fantasies that came naturally to her.

Without realising it Joanna had discovered a secret known only to the greatest of athletes. By keeping her inner mind off the demands of her game, she freed the secret mentality of her nerves and muscles to function without stress. She played her best through the simple fact of not forcing her shots. By taking the pressure off herself she became a pure athlete.

By the middle of her junior year she had won amateur championships all over the south. Admiring articles about her flawless swing, shotmaking imagination and amazing consistency had appeared in all the golf magazines.

Yet now her thoughts were further from golf than ever. It was time to think about college. But Ellen's hard-earned savings were laughably inadequate for such an idea.

And only now Joanna began to speculate uncomfortably on how much Ellen might have spent on her three years of golf training and competition. She cursed the distracting hobby that had blinded her to her responsibility to her family, even as it had made her miss so many happy, ordinary days with Ellen and Chris these past years. Days that were as remote now as her chances of becoming an engineer.

But all at once the silver lining of those bumpy adolescent years showed itself, as the colleges and universities from all over the United States offered Joanna complete golf scholarships.

Infinitely relieved not to have to be a burden on Ellen, Joanna at last saw some usefulness in her talent for golf. She accepted the offer from the University of Georgia in Athens—not only because of its warm southern location, propitious for golf in winter, but also because it was in her beloved state and near her mother and sister.

At first the university was unfamiliar and scary. The dorms were filled with strange, confident young women who seemed not to share Joanna's fear of the abrupt and demanding professors. But Joanna applied herself, forcing back her feelings of distress, and made good grades.

The intercollegiate golf competitions she participated in seemed at once to separate her from her peers and to swallow up her free time. Were it not for Carl Jaeger, her coach at Georgia and a champion as a professional three decades earlier, Joanna would have grown to hate the game that was now a necessity for her scholarship.

Carl became a virtual father to her during their first season together. Having taken an immediate liking to the quiet, serious girl who could beat his best male players, he set out to refine her natural ability while making her feel more comfortable on the course.

Pricking her instinctive engineer's wit and curiosity, Carl taught Joanna to appreciate the intellectual challenge of golf's chesslike complexity, and to perfect clever shots which other players lacked the imagination to conceive.

Astonished by his pupil's uncanny grasp of subtleties it had taken him twenty years to learn, Carl began to believe that with proper training she might find a place for herself in the amateur record books, and his conviction was hardly shaken when, in her first year with him, Joanna won the Women's Southern Amateur, placed second in the Women's South Atlantic Golf Tournament, and helped her team to victory in the Women's World Amateur Team Championships.

At eighteen Joanna was not only an intercollegiate celebrity, but was one of the most highly regarded amateur players in the world. But unbeknown to her legions of unseen fans, she was one of the loneliest college sophomores in the country.

She could not seem to get used to life without Chris and Ellen. Her golfing journeys to unfamiliar places only exaggerated her sense of exile in a coldly competitive world which must soon separate her for ever from the home she loved. Though her engineering major stimulated and distracted her, she knew that it, also, was leading inevitably into a solitary future. Each time she went home on vacation she felt like a stranger in the apartment whose daily routine she no longer shared.

Her adolescent shape had given way to a lithe, willowy

figure which attracted the opposite sex perhaps more than she would have liked. Yet the college men she met seemed immature and flighty. And she suspected that they feared her somehow—not only because she was an athlete, and a famous one to boot, but also because there was a fundamental seriousness about her, inherited from Paul, that harmonised badly with their impulsive ways.

Tormented now by guilt over the expense of her amateur career, she longed to graduate and find work as an engineer. But two more years of school stood between her and a field whose storied opportunities were already being diminished by the near-collapse of the space programme. Meanwhile, she knew it was time for Chris to begin thinking about college, and for Ellen to wonder where her younger daughter's tuition money must come from.

Joanna was at sixes and sevens. An unbearably depressing emptiness had descended over her life, and she could not see a way into the future.

She met Jack Templeton when she was in this painful state. And Jack seemed tailor-made to pluck her out of it.

He belonged to an old-established family whose ancestors included two Civil War generals, and whose enormous wealth was traceable not only to the Old South's confluence of cotton and tobacco farming, but also, it was rumoured, to the exploits of the arrogant buccaneers who had once plundered its coastal waters.

Joanna had met him, predictably enough, on the golf course. An avid golfer, like generations of his family's men before him, he played a scratch game and had been on the golf team for two semesters before his studies and fraternity obligations forced him to quit.

When Jack found that he could not beat Joanna, despite his superior strength off the tee, he applauded her excellence without a trace of ill-humour and immediately placed her on a pedestal for her bright personality as well as her athletic skill.

For her own part, Joanna could not be blind to her new friend's extraordinary charms. A tall, lean man in his senior year, Jack glowed with the easy confidence Joanna lacked so sorely. With his curly black hair and aquiline nose, his square shoulders and long, striding legs, he cut a dashing figure. Though one sensed generations of breeding in his gentility and impeccable manners, he bore his ancestry with carefree negligence.

His intense and even hawklike look, dark eyes flashing with quick wit and intelligence, fascinated Joanna most of all. He intended to seek a career in government service after completing his political science degree, and he made no secret of his healthy contempt for his family's reactionary attitudes. Yet in his very independence of mind, so roguish and devil-may-care, he seemed outlined against the colourful background of his adventurous forebears.

Soon he invited Joanna to dinner, to the movies, and to do her studies with him. He asked her to join him with his parents when they visited Athens, and squired her through the rather uncomfortable occasion without a false step, keeping his dour father at bay with sparkling humour while showering his mother, a quiet and seemingly defenceless little woman, with a son's easy affection.

Jack made no secret of his admiration for Joanna, or, as time went on, his desire for her. The touch of his warm hands on her shoulders gave way at last to caressing embraces, his friendly kisses to more passionate, probing ones. And Joanna realised all at once that she was seriously involved with him.

Her thought must have communicated itself in the gravity of her limpid green irises, for he smiled, took her hand and, as easily as he had so often carried her golf bag or held a car door open for her, proposed marriage.

'In the first place,' he said, 'I can't live without you, Joanna. In the second place, my family is afraid of you. And in the third place, you're the only girl I've ever met who can destroy me on the golf course. I see a lifetime of defeats ahead of me. Won't you make it a reality?'

In the laughing glitter of his dark eyes there was respect, deference, and the vulnerability of a young man in search of his own future—as well as the fugitive trace of the romantic buccaneer who swears undying allegiance to his lady. He was an exalted lineage made solid and handsomely human—and he wanted Joanna.

Suddenly it seemed that her continuing education, her uncertain career, his own future struggles, and her sense of responsibility to Ellen and Chris, must all yield to the great sigh of relief brought by that simple, infinitely welcome fact. He wanted her.

With one word she could put an end to her floundering solitude. Life as Joanna Templeton spread before her, a sane, regular vista, just as in her childhood she had imagined the stately world of adults to be.

She said yes.

She was to recognise her error an instant too late.

The wedding was held the day after Jack's graduation in a small church near Ellen's apartment in Crane. Jack's parents were there alone, without the hundreds of Templeton relatives who undoubtedly had expected to attend. Jack had had his way in ensuring Joanna the quiet wedding he knew she wanted.

But the look in Ellen's hazel eyes was worried that day. Catching a glimpse of it in a mirror from across the room, Joanna thought she recognised it. Ellen was responding uncomfortably to the Templetons' small talk, her arm curled tightly around Chris's shoulder, as though to hold her close and protect her from a fate still unseen by anyone but Ellen herself.

All at once Joanna remembered. It was that secret look, filled with harsh resignation, that Ellen had shot her way in the presence of the two policemen the day of Paul's death. But now it was a private shadow in Ellen's features, hidden from Joanna herself.

As usual, Ellen's simple, acute intelligence was clairvoyant. Within days after her marriage Joanna began to suspect that something was wrong.

Jack decided to go to work for his father's investment firm after all, now that he had graduated, and to postpone his career in public service until he was settled and had made some contacts around the state. He and Joanna moved into an attractive Savannah apartment, with the unspoken understanding that after a suitable interval they would start looking for an appropriate house.

Jack's accustomed smiles grew less and less frequent when he returned from work. Joanna began to notice a look of stubborn recalcitrance under his dark brows when a subject came up that challenged certain ideas he held dear— ideas to which he had been happily indifferent only weeks or months before.

His sense of humour seemed more brittle, more sardonic now, and was turned with surprising venom on people and things he had fancied in earlier times. And it was never, never directed at himself or his family, as it had been when she first knew him.

Puzzled by the surprising change that had come over him almost overnight, Joanna supposed the sudden pressure of marriage and a necessary livelihood were taking their toll on his nerves. But when her tender solicitude only succeeded in making him more sullen and moody, she suspected a deeper trouble.

Jack simply was not himself any more. A dour heaviness

seemed to have overtaken him, banishing his youthful vivacity. She noticed not only his family resemblance to his staid father Charles, but also an almost unwitting style of carriage, a way of picking up a cup of coffee or entering a room, a turn of phrase, which imitated the older man disturbingly.

Peering intently at herself in the mirror, Joanna wondered whether she was suffering from some sort of hallucination. The kind young man she had married was gone, and in his place was a stranger who behaved as though he had been hurt or cheated in some way, and who obviously blamed Joanna for being unwilling or unable to make things right. To make his reproach crystal clear he rejected her attempts at affectionate reconciliation with harsh, dismissing words.

When she finally bristled at the thankless nursemaid role he expected her to play, he became abusive, accusing her of slights and betrayals so subtle that it was impossible to be sure from his twisted smile whether he was serious or, in some sick way, joking.

For weeks she was amazed and tied up in knots by the strange guilt he seemed bent on attributing to her. Then all at once she realised the truth.

Jack's whole courtship had been a charade. He had never intended pursuing an independent life with Joanna. His marriage meant the opposite to him; it signified his coming of age and inevitable surrender to his family's domination. That was why he had brought his new wife straight to Savannah and gone to work for his father. He would never seek appointive or elective political office unless it was under the aegis of his family or their friends.

Jack had chosen a life of dependence in which he could never compete as a man with the father he feared. And he blamed Joanna for his own weakness—and always would.

The revelation was so stunning in Joanna's mind that she could not believe it at first. But it made so much sense, and explained so much that she had seen and heard in the Templeton family, that she could doubt it no longer.

She contemplated silent, helpless Flora Templeton, who had spent a lifetime fluttering about the rooms of her wilful husband's huge old house, and was now incapable of a single independent thought or act.

Is that what I have to look forward to? Joanna wondered, seeing herself mirrored in Jack's grim, reproachful eyes—and she already knew she was not going to wait around to find out.

She was on the point of broaching the subject of separation when, three months after her wedding, she was told she was pregnant.

It was a pivotal moment for Joanna. Though tempted to cling to her painful marriage in order to ensure some sort of security for her unborn child, she knew that a childhood in Jack's family could be nothing but madly insecure. The fearful thoughts about Ellen and Chris that had haunted her before her marriage were forgotten now. Sanity and happiness were too valuable to be sacrificed to mere financial survival.

She decided to renounce her personal failure before the child was born, and leave Jack to the life he had chosen for himself.

To her surprise, Jack docilely agreed. Apparently aware that Joanna was his match in will and stubbornness, he was more than willing to seek a more pliant mate elsewhere.

Their divorce was made final a week before Joanna completed her solitary junior year at Georgia—and a month before Christina Lake, named for Joanna's own sister, was born.

Taking a deep breath, Joanna resolved not to accept child support from the Templetons; she did not want Jack to feel either an obligation or a parental privilege towards the child he had sired almost by accident.

She applied for a renewal of her golf scholarship effective after her baby's birth, but was told that all athletic scholarships were expressly forbidden to women who became pregnant. So she took out a university loan for tuition, bravely borrowed money from Ellen for books, found a furnished room in Athens for herself and her baby, and brushed up on her already speedy typing. She would type dissertations and course papers to support herself until she graduated.

On a hot June morning she entered the County Hospital near Crane and had her baby. Her labour seemed short and almost painless, but when it was over she was surprised to hear Ellen say it had lasted nine hours.

She could not take her eyes off the baby. A creature of indescribable beauty, Tina was utterly individual. She resembled neither Joanna nor Jack, nor any of the Templetons or Lakes; she was her own unique little person.

On her return to Athens Joanna saw an item in the social column announcing the engagement of Jack Templeton to the youngest daughter of a Savannah family nearly as wealthy as his own. The two families were joined by financial ties going back for generations.

Joanna laughed and danced around her furnished room with Tina in her arms. She was truly free at last from the marriage that had threatened to ruin her life. Jack was safe in his own future, and in her arms she held the greatest gift he could have left her.

Her marriage had lasted less than a year. Now she was out in the real world, and glad to be there. Its fresh air more than compensated for its dangers and challenges.

Oddly enough, Joanna thought with a rueful smile, Jack had never made good his promise. Not once after their marriage had he joined her on the golf course. Though he did not ask her to give up her golf—reasoning, no doubt, that her fame distinguished him in his family while falling nicely into the category of amateur talents for females, such as piano playing or landscape painting—he had played exclusively with his old fraternity brothers or newfound business associates.

But her smile was forced, for her own days as a golfer were over. Golf could no longer help her through school. Engineering must now absorb her thoughts.

Thanks to her midnight struggles with quantum mechanics and high-energy physics during Tina's sleep, Joanna made the Dean's List midway through her senior year.

Two months before the graduation for which she had worked so hard, she was interviewed by visiting recruiters from corporations representing the spectrum of engineering opportunities nationwide. To a man they looked askance at her divorce and the fact that she was the sole support of her daughter.

'If we hire a man,' she was told, 'he'll stick with us, and go where we tell him to go. But what if you remarry, Miss Lake? What if you have a second child? What if your next husband gets transferred? All the time and money we'll have spent in training you would be wasted. If times were easier, things would be different…'

To her horror Joanna saw her engineering diploma for what it was: a frail piece of paper barely adequate to assure her the lowest-paying of jobs.

For Ellen's sake she went through her bitter graduation ceremony, returned her cap and gown and put her diploma in the closet of her furnished room in Athens. Her four years of college were all but useless to her. She had no earning power, and a child to support.

For the third time in her life Joanna was totally at sea.

Karen Gillespie, the vivacious and hardheaded former college room-mate Joanna had hired to babysit for Tina when classes kept her away from the room, came to her rescue with a careless shrug.

'Turn pro,' she advised. 'Go on the L.P.G.A. tour.'

Thunderstruck, Joanna objected that she had not touched a golf club in over a year.

'Look, Joanna,' said Karen, 'you were a great amateur champion. I know you as well as I know myself. You've got good nerves and you don't get discouraged when things don't go your way—unless I miss my guess, those are exactly the qualities a professional athlete needs.'

Carl Jaeger disagreed vehemently when Joanna went to see him. The women's tour, he said, was just as gruelling as the men's, but with even lower financial rewards for all but the top five players in any tournament.

'It's not a living, Jojo,' he shook his head. 'Most of the women who don't quit after a year or so on the tour have their own money, through marriage or family. No one breaks even through actual winnings, except for a very few. Take my advice: just relax and be calm. You'll find a job if you keep looking. You'll get married again—no man in his right mind would let you get away! You have a beautiful daughter to take care of—and you'll have more children. If you want to pursue a brilliant amateur career, I'm behind you all the way. But not the pro tour.'

Karen shook her head when she saw Joanna return home crestfallen.

'Carl's old-fashioned,' she laughed, wrinkling her freckled nose. 'He played the tour when big tournaments paid the winner five hundred dollars. He doesn't believe you'll rise to the top. I do.'

She insisted she would take care of Tina while Joanna competed in the L.P.G.A. Qualifying School. 'I've just finished a degree in English,' she joked. 'What does that qualify me for, if not babysitting? Go get 'em, Joanna!'

After two weeks of desperate training Joanna filled out her application, took the train to Greensboro with her clubs, and played the seventy-two hole tournament that was the Qualifying School. She placed second with a five-under-par two hundred and eighty-three and was given an amount of prize money which barely sufficed to pay her caddy.

But she had accomplished her purpose. On the basis of her second-place finish she was granted L.P.G.A. playing privileges—provided she paid her dues and insurance.

Taking a deep breath, she entered the Winston-Salem Classic the next week. She survived the cut after thirty-six holes, finished in a tie for tenth place, and returned to her Athens room with a check for two thousand three hundred dollars.

Joanna was on her way.

From every mistake she made, she learned. As the rounds and tournaments followed one another, the seasoned professionals she played with did their best to encourage her, and gradually the butterflies left her stomach.

She approached her profession with dedication, refining her strokes on the practice tee and putting green, training herself carefully and devising a high-energy diet which kept her slim and strong.

No longer the distracted schoolgirl who had played golf in a haze of fantasies, Joanna executed her shots with complete concentration now. She analysed her effort on each hole, comparing her performance to the result she had planned.

Her hard work paid off. Before long her tempo and mechanics had reached a point of subtle perfection which amazed those who saw her play. Experts compared her fluid swing to that of the legendary Joyce Wethered, and her fairway woods and long irons were declared to be the most uncannily accurate in the history of women's golf.

And her winnings reflected her skill and consistency. After two seasons on the tour she made a down-payment on the house outside Sarasota, whose proximity to so many courses in the warm Florida winter would facilitate her practice. Karen, overjoyed at having sold a novelette to a national magazine, came along 'for the ride'.

By her fourth year on the tour Joanna was an international star, visible to the public not only during competition but also through endorsements and in the press, where she was eagerly sought as an articulate spokesperson for women in golf and a penetrating analyst of the game itself.

Affiliated as touring professional with Nakoma Springs Golf Club, near her new home, Joanna was a respected member of the community, and gave her time to charitable causes whenever possible.

She was a happy young woman—but a realist. Her disastrous marriage had left her scarred and brittle. She was in no mood to let her yearnings to feel wanted lead her into calamity again. Deep inside she wondered whether she would ever be happy in love.

'Maybe I'm accident-prone where men are concerned,' she shrugged, tempted to stop believing that the man she might some day long to give herself to would want to have her.

But she had Tina. Nothing could take that away from her.

Her only worry was that the child had no father. Tina was growing more unique, more special every day. She was so tactful, so serious and sweet, never complaining about being a child of divorce, or about Joanna's long absences in the spring and summer... Sometimes it seemed as though this wise little daughter was comforting her mother for having uncorrectable failings.

But Joanna pushed these thoughts to the back of her mind, reasoning that no one's life is perfect, and that a woman could not ask more of herself than to do her best for those she loved.

Chris had grown into a lovely young woman, married a hard-working local man in Crane and had two children on whom Ellen doted. Protesting that the money Joanna sent her was always too much, Ellen remained in her old apartment and continued to work at her old job. The family seemed happy.

As one year followed another Joanna's fame increased. Her lovely face and figure captivated millions of fans who saw behind them her struggles, her strength, and her courage—as well as her vulnerability.

For her mystique as the 'winner-loser' of women's golf was now a firmly established facet of her public image. Brilliant and even incomparable though her golf game might be, something kept her from winning.

Something.

She had become almost an expert at deflecting the question of her failure to win as she was at striking a fairway shot or lining up a putt. But it would not go away, and she knew it.

Thus life went on until the day Reid Armstrong appeared.

CHAPTER FOUR

'WAKE up, Joanna—wake up, now! That's right…'

It was not like being awake, she decided as the recovery room nurse's hurried features smiled down at her. She struggled to answer, but moving her lips was like walking over a mountain of cotton balls.

Satisfied, the nurse disappeared.

Joanna drifted into oblivion, her eyes open like those of a wounded animal.

When next she woke she was in her room. Black night loomed beyond the window blinds. The T.V. hung on the wall like a haggard, prying eye.

Joanna rang for the nurse, and after many minutes an unfamiliar young woman entered and told her to rest. Dr Diehl would be in tomorrow morning.

Joanna's knee was heavily bandaged and elevated. She could no longer feel the intense pain behind the kneecap. But she could not feel anything else, either, except the dullness and apathy and confusion and nagging inner ache that seemed the essence of life in this hospital. The stab behind the kneecap had simply settled into the general throb of her battered body.

Am I cured? she dared to hope for an instant. But the effort was too much, and emotionally exhausted, she closed her eyes.

The elevated knee would not allow her to toss and turn. She lay immobile, straying half asleep from one sinister dream landscape to another, as the night's darkest hours passed her by.

The next morning Dr Diehl appeared at last—and Joanna knew instantly what the forced smile on his thin lips meant.

'The news is good,' he said unconvincingly. 'You're going to be fine, Joanna. You'll need a lot of physical therapy, and you'll come out of this with some residual weakness in that knee, but you'll be able to live normally.'

He began discussing aspects of the surgery and her convalescence as the nurse busied herself behind him. Joanna could see he was in a hurry to leave her; the pleading looks she could not help sending in his direction did not seem to slow him down.

'What about…my golf?' she asked at last, feeling as though she were breaching a taboo subject.

He shook his head with a pained frown.

'Joanna,' he said argumentatively, 'you have multiple sprains, very serious ones, in your knee ligaments, both lateral and medial. I suspect some microscopic tears in your cartilage, and I know for sure that your patella tendon has been torn. Now, your knee is going to recover, but it's going to be on the weak side—weak enough to hurt your confidence in it, and that's going to hurt your golf game. You may still play, but not at a championship level. I hate to have to tell you this, but you may as well know it right now. I don't want you holding on to false hopes.'

He smiled patronisingly. 'Try and look on the bright side,' he urged. 'You've had a brilliant career in golf, but all athletic careers have to end some time. Now, you're a beautiful, desirable young woman; you're sure to get married again one of these days soon. You have a lovely young daughter. Life doesn't end without professional golf.'

If I were a man, Joanna mused bitterly, *he would sing a different tune*.

But anger availed little against the terror inside her.

I will play again, she thought desperately. *I must play again*. No one had warned her about post-operative depression. She felt a curious letting-go in all her nerves, a desire to lie down and stop trying to cope with the brutal exhaustion of each new thought, each impression.

And now, with the whole world hammering nightmarishly at her last reserves of strength, she realised that she must greet Tina and say goodbye to her in a single moment. It was Joanna herself who had insisted that Karen take Tina back to Sarasota today. The child had already missed three days of school on her account, and the school year was at its end. Now that the surgery was over and pronounced successful, there was no reason for her to be here.

'Mommy, is your knee feeling better?' the little girl asked hesitantly after Karen had brought her in.

'Much better, honey,' said Joanna, forcing a happy smile. 'Be good to Karen, now. And you and Suzanne behave yourselves with Miss Ward. And don't forget to give her the flowers on your last day.'

'I won't,' Tina promised, still holding her mother's hand as she popped from the bedside to the floor.

Screwing up her courage, Joanna planted a brisk goodbye kiss on her daughter's cheek and patted her shoulder with a black-and-blue hand.

'And save your papers!' she called after her, stricken to think that she would not see Tina's last two weeks of third-grade work until long after it was done.

A moment later they were gone, Karen having affectionately steered her vibrant little charge through the door with a hand on each pigtail.

Apparently having decided not to leave Joanna time for morbid thoughts, Reid appeared almost instantly, his teasing grin lighting up the room as he placed a colourful flower arrangement by the window.

'Well, Joanna,' he announced blithely, 'looks like it's just you and me.'

Joanna burst into tears.

For what seemed a long time Reid sat on the edge of her bed, the gentle touch of his hand on her own doing little to assuage her grief.

'I can't say that's the most delighted reception I've ever had,' he joked when her tear-stained eyes finally turned to him.

'It wasn't you,' she sighed her disapproval of his humour. 'It's just…just…' Renewed sobs of consternation choked her.

'Take it easy, now,' he murmured, touching a finger to her cheek. 'Just relax. You're going to be fine.'

She shook her head in impotent dissent. 'The doctor,' she stammered. 'He says…'

'I know what he says,' nodded Reid. 'And I'll tell you something, just between you and me. Bob Diehl is an expert at what he does—the best, in fact. But athletes are machines to him. He doesn't understand desire. I know, Joanna. He treated me for a lumbar disc problem when I was a sophomore in college. He told me I'd have to quit football altogether. But during the next two years I caught fifty passes and scored more points than anybody except the kicker.'

Joanna struggled to weigh his words coherently. Life seemed so utterly black that she had hardly the energy even to meet his gaze.

'Listen,' he went on. 'I've seen your chart, Joanna. You've got some sprains and some possible cartilage damage. I've known dozens of athletes who have played out their careers with similar problems.' He laughed. 'I'll bet you didn't know that among the entire outfield of the New York Yankees last year there wasn't a single intact knee cartilage.'

He grew more serious. 'And,' he said, 'to tell the honest truth, Bob is a little old-fashioned where women are concerned. When he looks at a shapely leg like yours, he doesn't think of grinding out months on the pro golf tour. He thinks of a happy home and lots of children.'

There was softness behind his probing eyes as he smiled down at her.

'So you see,' he concluded, 'Bob doesn't see what you're made of under that pretty face of yours. I do. You'll come out of this good as new—if you want to.'

Joanna nodded exhaustedly.

'More than that,' he added, 'you're coming out of this *better* than new. I intend to see to it.' He grinned. 'You're a fine athlete, but you need someone to watch out for you. You've been going it alone for too long.'

Against her better judgment Joanna let her tired hand rest in his. She hated to hear him speak of her dependence. He was all health and handsome strength, while she felt beaten to a pulp, black and blue all over and perhaps damaged beyond repair. In his boundless confidence he seemed so foreign, so alien—yet he alone offered her the encouragement she so desperately needed.

Though her depression told her he should leave her to her dark despair and go about his sunny business, she wanted him to stay. Manipulative and arrogant he might be—but he was on her side. He believed in her.

But what if he's wrong?

She banished the awful thought and, with a sigh of uncertain gratitude, let her half-closed eyes linger on his tanned face.

Two days later Joanna was allowed to leave the hospital. She barely slept a wink the night before her departure, so great was her eagerness to get on with her unknowable future.

'Are you really sure about this arrangement?' she had asked Reid during visiting hours. 'I feel a little funny about coming to your house. I'm…imposing,' she concluded, her liberated ideas not allowing her to give voice to her scruples.

'Not at all,' he shrugged. 'It's a business arrangement. That's what my house is for, more than anything. I'm a middle-man, Joanna; I bring people there all the time on business visits. Besides, Tina and Karen are coming soon. And,' he added with a wry smile, 'if you're worried about the proprieties, Mrs Hughes, my housekeeper, will be moving in for the duration of your stay. She'll chaperone us, if you feel you can't trust yourself.'

'Very funny!' Joanna reproved him, her lips pursed in irritation.

At eight a.m. he wheeled her through the hospital's sliding doors and into a hot North Carolina morning. The air was thick with humidity, but to Joanna it smelled fresh as spring after the hospital's antiseptic coldness.

At her insistence Reid left the air-conditioning off in the large sedan he had brought. Joanna's plush seat reclined deliciously, and the soft breeze coming through the vent caressed her legs and arms with lulling sweetness.

'We'll go straight down 95 to Beaufort County,' Reid decided. 'Not the most picturesque route in the world, but it's the fastest way. I imagine you've driven it a hundred times on your way to tournaments.'

With a glance to his right he smiled. Joanna was fast asleep.

She awoke at the shudder of the engine being turned off. Reid was leaning back in his seat, his smile glimmering beneath a quirked brow. She could smell the ocean.

'Where are we?' she asked, rubbing her eyes sleepily.

'Beaufort,' he said. 'You're a lady who knows how to sleep—you've been out the whole way.'

Joanna looked out the window to see a magnificent seascape framed by green hills that led gently down to beaches and marshland lush with long grass and elders. Beneath the stands of pines she could make out palmetto and magnolia trees. Were it not for the pastures in the hills the scene would have looked totally wild. It was a fantastic display of natural beauty, uniting all the elements that made this part of the country famous.

'Why have we stopped here?' she asked. 'It's beautiful.'

'Glad you think so,' nodded Reid. 'The big pine forest down the beach gave it its name. This is it, Joanna: Black Woods.'

Joanna stared at the landscape, trying to imagine it as the setting for a championship golf layout. Gulls and terns wheeled in the air over the gently washing surf. In the distance a heron stood alone, desultorily preening its feathers. She saw a sandpiper on the rocky beach. The ocean breeze was heavy, balmy. It would blow a driven golf ball steadily inland, off course.

The marshes were the habitat of many of these birds and animals. Who would imagine what effect bulldozers and artificial water systems might have on their lives? Would some of the sea-birds be driven away to quieter waters if changes in the shore foliage affected the fish swimming here?

Seeing two creeks snake their way down the hills toward the ocean, Joanna recalled Reid's description of the layout as being rich in natural water hazards.

'Quite a showplace, isn't it?' he asked.

'Yes,' she said, fascinated by the delicately ordered ecology that made the place unique.

'Worried about keeping it that way?' he asked, guessing her thoughts.

Sleepy and irritable, she glanced at him. 'Someone should be,' she said.

'Good,' he smiled. 'Perhaps you'd better think about taking on this job. Otherwise I may have to settle for an architect who will mutilate the whole landscape just to get a course out of it.'

'Don't make it my responsibility,' Joanna protested. 'I haven't agreed to anything yet.'

'As a professional,' he said, 'you must have played some awful layouts along with the good ones, so I'm sure you'll want to see that a site like this was served well.'

'How do I know women will even be allowed to play this course?' asked Joanna on a querulous impulse. 'How do I know the country club they put here would even accept me as a member? It may interest you to know, if you didn't already, that ninety per cent of the clubs in this country will not accept single women members.'

Reid raised an eyebrow. 'That's news to me,' he said. 'But, come to think of it, the golf world is pretty old-fashioned, isn't it?'

'That's the understatement of the year,' sighed Joanna. 'There are only a handful of women club pros in the country, and they have to live with constant harassment. Most of the championship courses are designed only with men in mind. The women's tees are ill-kept and sloppily placed, so that our skills aren't fairly tested at all when we play. And I can think of some country clubs where men play big tournaments, and women are not allowed to play at all.'

His nod of assent was touched by teasing humour, as though he were more amused than anything else by her resentment.

'I don't see what's so funny about it,' she said crossly. 'Women have had an uphill battle in golf, and still do. I don't mind telling you I wonder whether your investors will seriously consider any design done by a woman.' She folded her arms in frustration.

There was sympathy in his laughing eyes.

'That knee has you pretty worried, doesn't it?' he asked, his penetration shocking her.

'Who said I was worried?' she fumed, irked to see her thoughts divined so easily by a virtual stranger. 'Perhaps I was. Perhaps I am.'

'Life is full of obstacles, Joanna,' he said through his smile. 'Unfair ones, to boot, and for both sexes. Sometimes there's nothing to be done about them. But it is important that you learn not to be your own worst enemy.'

'What's that supposed to mean?' she asked, angered to hear him trivialise her complaints.

'Maybe this golf club will be as stodgy as any other,' he said. 'But you can make sure the course is well designed. You have that power. And when and if you play it as a competitor, you have the power to win. Nobody can beat you—except yourself.'

His look was suddenly intense. Unable to make him out, Joanna glanced uncertainly into his dark irises.

'But you're not going to win anything,' he smiled, 'until we get you a cup of hot tea and some aspirin, and something to eat. Shall we go home?'

As he threw the car into gear she reflected that once again he had hit the nail on the head. Underneath her vexation was a wave of pain which had gained in intensity during her long sleep.

Home, as it turned out, was an extraordinarily beautiful two-storey house whose white clapboard was broken by large picture windows. From inside Joanna realised what their purpose was. Since the house stood on a hill overlooking Saint Helena Sound, superb views of sky and ocean were framed by those windows—views cleverly taken up by glass breakfronts and bookcases inside the house's brightly lit rooms.

Some of the paintings on the walls even had glass frames

intentionally arranged to superimpose reflected seascapes over the pictures underneath. The result was that the whole place had an oceanic look, inside and out.

Hobbled by her unfamiliar crutches, Joanna went into the spacious kitchen and was greeted by Mrs Hughes, the housekeeper who doubled as live-in cook when Reid had guests. Her soft Southern drawl ringing with particular charm against the image of her greying hair and bright eyes, she extended a hand.

'I'm delighted to meet you,' she said. 'You won't remember, Miss Lake, but my daughter Katie sent you a fan letter once, and you wrote her the nicest response. She absolutely idolises you. I may have been presumptuous, but since we live right down the road I told her she might be able to meet you, and your daughter when she arrives. Katie would be happy to show her around these parts.'

Helping her down the stairs with a strong arm around her waist, Reid showed Joanna the basement. On the padded floor were benches and weights, Nautilus and Cybex machines for leg lifts and presses, and a padded table for other exercises.

'We're all ready for you,' he said, 'thanks to Virginia. In a week or so we'll get to work on your hamstrings and quadriceps, and of course both knees.' He smiled complacently. 'Yes, you're going to have a lot of fun here, Joanna. Bicycling, walking, swimming, jogging on the beach.. Why, I'll have you running up and down those stairs in no time!'

'Makes me tired just to think of it,' she sighed. But her athlete's eye told her the elaborate machinery he had assembled aimed at more than mere physical therapy in the wake of an accident. In this room was all the wherewithal to train her for competition.

'This place,' she said when they were upstairs once

more. 'It's lovely, but, if you don't mind my saying so, it doesn't seem…'

'Lived-in?' Reid laughed. 'I'm afraid you're right. I bought it three years ago because I thought it would be a good investment. I came here on business, saw this place at a bargain price, and bought it on an impulse. Then those ocean views began to get to me, so I stayed here and kept my apartment in Atlanta as well. I never got around to selling the house. So I'm of two minds—I can't get rid of it, and I can't make a home out of it.' He smiled. 'Just having you here brightens it up. When Tina gets here it will really seem human.'

He saw the reaction in her tired eyes.

'Missing her?' he asked.

Joanna nodded.

'Well,' he said, 'I'm sure Miss Ward is taking good care of her. And Abbas and Allie and Lynn and Suzanne will keep her company until the end of school.'

'How did you know all that?' asked Joanna amazed to hear him reel off the names of Tina's friends so blandly.

'Tina told me herself,' he laughed, 'while you were in your Demerol trance at the hospital. Friends and school seemed the logical thing to ask a little girl about on the first meeting. Especially a girl who might be scared about her mom and be able to use some distraction. Why, I know all about Miss Ward. I know she used to be a stewardess, and she took a trip to Hawaii last summer and got caught in a hurricane, and she can be rough about math but is nice about reading. I even know about the Embarrass-Kings.'

Joanna smiled to hear the girls' name for the intimidating fourth and fifth graders on his lips. Obviously he had been good for Tina during long hours that must have been quite frightening to her. Perhaps his promises about horseback riding and swimming had not been so irresponsible after all.

'Tina says she's very beautiful,' he was saying.

'Who?'

'Miss Ward.'

'Oh,' said Joanna. 'Yes, she's very attractive, for your information. If you're interested,' she added wryly, 'I'm sure Tina would be happy to introduce you if you're ever in our area.'

Reid made a hands-off gesture. 'I have more than enough women in my life, thank you,' he said. 'What with you here, and Tina on her way as soon as school is out…'

'I'll just bet you keep busy,' Joanna laughed. 'I hope we won't be in the way.' Indeed, she thought, the curiously impersonal furnishings of the house, beautiful as they were, seemed to suggest the lifestyle of a handsome, busy bachelor who enjoyed seeing many women while committing himself to none.

'Come on,' he said, seeing the fatigue in her eyes. 'I'll show you your bedroom. After you've had a nice nap you can call home to tell them you got here safe. Then we'll think about dinner.'

Joanna hardly saw the beautiful bedroom whose pastel curtains were closed against the waning sunlight. She sank gratefully on to the large bed as Reid placed a quilted comforter over her, his large hand touching her bandaged knee with delicate concern.

She looked up at him from her helpless position on the spread. Pain and exhaustion had conspired to put her in a susceptible mood. How handsomely erect he was in his dauntless confidence as he stood over her in the shadows of this foreign place! Here in his own home, he was prepared to repair her damaged body at all costs, to palpate it and work it with his knowing hands until it was strong enough to suit him, no matter what her doctor thought about her condition…

Since the moment he had entered her life, it seemed, the

world she knew had flown from her, replaced all at once by strange new vistas at whose centre he loomed, tall and powerful and maddeningly indispensable.

He closed the door behind him, his smile shining down upon her for a last second. Then he disappeared into the unseen corridors of this odd, anonymous house which was to be the site of her doubts and sufferings, her hoped-for rehabilitation, the sleepless nights of her worry about the future—and perhaps unforeseen temptations.

'If only Tina were here,' she thought as dreams overtook her.

CHAPTER FIVE

'LIFT. Good...again. Does that hurt?'

'...'

'All right, wait a minute. Good. Lift again. Does that hurt?'

The infuriating voice of command was deep and relaxed. Joanna shook her head, too breathless to articulate an answer.

The pain in her thigh was unbearable, yet she knew that somehow she had enough strength left for the last two repetitions. Reid never chose too much weight; just enough to make life an agony.

'Good. Two more.' A dry finger touched the sweaty flesh of her leg, testing the sinews above the left knee.

'Does that hurt?' the maddening voice asked for what seemed the thousandth time.

'Yes!' she gasped, beside herself with frustration as she lifted her leg against the padded bar for the last time. Her back arched and straining, she was held into the machine by the safety belt about her waist. Reid seemed as much a part of this crazy bondage as the machine itself. 'What do you take me for?' she asked angrily, her halting breaths coming in little jerks. 'Some kind of masochist?'

'No,' he smiled without taking his eyes from her knee. 'Just a feminist.'

'Very funny,' she sighed, feeling drops of perspiration flow down her exhausted back and along the thigh whose quadriceps muscle was in a constant state of trauma from the exercises he made her do.

Upstairs Tina was probably chatting with Virginia or reading one of the favourite books she had brought. Later she would go riding or swimming with Reid while Joanna rested and exercised on her own.

It had been three weeks since the day Joanna had come here from the hospital, and nearly six days since the long-awaited morning of Tina's arrival. Already a new routine had set in, admittedly necessary but far from what Joanna would have desired.

She saw Tina in the morning and at noon, unless an outing with Reid or Katie Hughes kept her away for lunch. At dinnertime the child would bring her tired mother up to date on her day's activities, eating savoury dishes cooked by Virginia while Joanna made do with bland low-calorie meals.

In the evenings Joanna relaxed in an orthopaedic easy chair and looked on as Tina sat in Reid's lap, read him passages from her books, or watched the classic movies offered by his television subscription service.

Whenever Joanna saw Tina, it seemed, she saw new evidence of her easy closeness with Reid. His deep voice and ready humour clearly delighted the little girl no less than the powerful arms that swept her up for hugs or piggyback rides, or merely to hold her out for admiration by his dark eyes. She held his hand happily when they walked together, her energetic little frame dwarfed by his long limbs.

'She takes after you,' he confided in Joanna. 'She's very precise and methodical about her books and her dolls. But there's a strong creative imagination underneath all those brains.' He darted his teasing glance to her reflective features. 'Of course,' he added, 'she's a lot more trusting than you.'

'She's had less experience,' Joanna returned.

'I guess you could say that,' Reid allowed. 'But sometimes I wonder whether it wouldn't be better to be surprised by trouble than to expect it all the time.'

'Oh, I don't know,' said Joanna. 'I've had more than my share of surprises lately.'

'I suppose you have,' he nodded, his inscrutable smile caressing the face and slender body which still bore black-and-blue areas under a sallow complexion.

After three relaxed days spent bringing Joanna up on all her news and ogling the furnishings in Reid's rooms, Karen had left for Sarasota. She intended to oversee the house and whatever business came up—including the buying of a new car—and at the same time to finish the mystery novel she had been working on for many months. Joanna felt a pang of guilt at the life that kept Karen from her own work, and was glad to see her leave for a few weeks of welcome solitude.

Her crutches gone now, Joanna limped around the house in futile search of amusements to pass the time when she was not working out or resting. Having set up a handsome design table in the study, complete with fluorescent lamp, blueprint paper, and maps of the Black Woods layout's elevations, draining and soil content, Reid made a point of not offering her any interesting books or magazines to read, so that her curiosity would be drawn ever closer to the prospective design.

He drove her to the layout, showed her how to take his jeep there when he was not available, and discussed golf course architecture with her, his studied casualness belying his obvious hope that she would get to work in earnest before long.

But in her private thoughts about the beautiful landscape she had hit a snag. As a player she complained for years about the unfair placement of women's tees on championship golf courses. Now she realised it would be virtually impossible to design a single hole whose dimensions would not be unfair either to the longer-hitting male player or the weaker female.

One sex or the other must suffer, it seemed, unless separate courses were designed for each. No wonder, she mused bitterly, that country clubs exclusively for women had sprung up over the years to match those reserved for men.

Her intellectual quandary became truly paralysing when added to her acute awareness that she had absolutely no experience as an architect. She could not imagine herself giving the order that would transform the Black Woods' virgin perfection into something man-made and perhaps environmentally disastrous.

So she hesitated, distracted from her scruples by lingering pain and the exhaustion brought on by her spartan training regimen. The monotony of her days, combined with traces of post-operative depression which overtook her when she contemplated her damaged body in the bedroom mirror, sapped her energy.

It was one thing to jealously covet the cheeseburgers and pizzas Tina enjoyed so blithely with Reid, while Joanna suffered with her lean broiled meats and cottage cheese. It was quite another to recall that underneath these temporary deprivations lurked the very real possibility that her career was over for ever.

She had visited Dr Diehl in Charleston often enough to know that he considered her future in golf a lost cause. The pressure of secretly hoping for a result of which her own physician had long since despaired threatened to reduce her to listless melancholy.

That was where Reid came in. Acutely aware of the obstacles Joanna faced, he knew how to keep her on edge mentally and physically, even if it meant needling her to ever greater progress through irritating manipulations. Now cajoling, now humiliating, now psychoanalysing her until she flushed with anger, he forced her to press forward with a programme whose ultimate goal was their unspoken secret.

Frustrated, Joanna remarked on the pain her exercises were producing in her uninjured leg.

'That's natural,' he told her. 'We can't neglect the good leg, or it will weaken. Besides, when we build the reflexes and muscle tone in the uninjured knee, the damaged one benefits from that biological information. It's called cross-education.'

'Can it work both ways?' asked Joanna dryly. 'Because my right leg is beginning to feel as though it's had an accident, too!'

She grew to hate the number twelve, because it was the invariable number of repetitions Reid required for each progressive-resistance exercise. As her strength increased he simply added more weight to the pulley system behind her back, making her feel all the weaker.

'You would have made a great coach,' she gasped one day after her twelfth knee lift. 'Your players would have murdered you in your sleep!'

'That's why I have you,' he drawled. 'You're too careful to commit murder. On the other hand, a little of the killer instinct is in every champion. Maybe we're moving you in the right direction.'

Joanna's back ached constantly from her workouts. Her thighs and calves were tight with pain when she walked up or down the basement stairs, jogging and bicycling were distressing ordeals in her condition. But her battered limbs were growing stronger, and she knew it. Their very discomfort was a positive sign. And as her body repaired itself she felt strange new longings in her woman's senses, flowerings of unforeseen awareness which disconcerted her—for they grew in intensity with each passing day.

*   *   *

'One more, now. Press. Is that hurting?'

With a final lunge, her back and legs in agony, her bandaged forearm pushing down on the seat beneath her, Joanna extended her knees for the twelfth and last time. The suspended weights clanged behind her back as she let the pedals fly towards her once more.

'Ouch!' she cried as a sharp stab of pain shot above her knee.

'Did you hurt yourself?' asked Reid, reaching a large hand to touch her throbbing thigh.

Too exhausted to answer, she shook her head. A lock of her blonde hair had escaped the sweatband over her forehead, and managed to fall across her cheek in her exertions. She pushed it away as his fingers ran delicately around her knee.

'Where does it hurt?' he asked coolly, his hands moving to compare the taped knee with its uninjured partner.

'Never mind,' she started to say. 'It was just...'

A gasp shook her before she could finish. As his dry fingers slipped over the soft skin behind the knees, a daunting surge of feeling had flashed through her, making speech impossible as it left her breathless with involuntary excitement.

'Are you sure?' he asked, palpating her more carefully now, his hands in search of swellings or suspicious areas of weakness. Hoping against hope that he was blind to the tumultuous response of female sinews under his unwitting caress, Joanna cursed the audible sign that had nearly given away what she had spent days and weeks trying to hide.

'Yes,' she said, catching her breath, 'I'm sure. If you'd just let me get out of this thing,' she added briskly, 'I'll be fine.'

Reid reached to undo the seatbelt around her waist as she sat panting before him, and his appraising eyes watched her knees work as she slipped out of the machine.

'Wait,' he placed a hand on her shoulder before she could move towards the stairs. 'Sit a second while I look at you.'

Placing his hands under her arms, he lifted her on to the large padded table. Her flesh tingled to feel itself held by him, if only for a charged instant.

'Good,' he said, flexing and extending her knee slowly as she watched. 'No extra fluid. You're in better shape than I thought.' His fingers grazed the damp skin under her thigh, sending unseen thrills of pleasure up her spine, and she had to suppress the sigh that was on her lips. Her gaze lingered on the tanned skin of his face, the flecked blackness of his eyes under careless waves of tawny hair. The T-shirt he wore clung to powerful chest muscles and broad shoulders. He carried his athlete's body with graceful negligence, his movements lithe and easy.

From the first hours she had spent in this house Joanna had told herself he was not her type, and could not possibly attract her. But the passing days had brought unbidden revelations about her own instincts as well as the unsuspected depth of his virile charms.

Before long she had been forced to admit the truth to herself. She had been too long alone, too long without a man. The wildfires in her senses when Reid was near were too dizzying to deny.

Whether it was his odd amalgam of hard male attractiveness, puckish humour and demanding discipline that fascinated her, or merely an upsurge of sensual awareness due to her weakened condition, the result was the same: she was anything but indifferent to him.

And what was worse, the agony of wondering whether he suspected the guilty delight his touch kindled in her only seemed to make it the more insidiously captivating. As he watched her workouts with calm, evaluative eyes, his complacent supervision maddening her, she suffered the more to feel her treacherous body arch shamelessly before him, its exertions veering constantly towards more sinister rhythms.

Even her gasps of pain and exhaustion, as she sat strapped in the seat only inches from his probing eyes and hard man's limbs, were embarrassingly indistinguishable from the sounds of love.

She cursed the impudent caprice that leapt from inside her aching flesh to reveal itself, seeking to tempt him while bypassing her better judgment. Yet, try as she might, she could not quiet it.

'You're all right,' said Reid now, placing his hands around her waist to help her down from the table. In her eyes there must have been a trace of her bewilderment, for he met their sidelong gaze with a smile as he patted her hips in approval. And for a terrible, wonderful instant Joanna wondered whether the ferment inside her had somehow touched him after all. How odd it would be to see that handsome face draw close to her own, here in this cool underground room, under these harsh, strange lights which had come to signify their physical time together and the secret they shared. How indescribable to feel those dry, sensual lips touch her own, graze her cheek, her neck, and gently close her eyes...

'*Boo!*' The small, sharp voice sent a shock wave down her spine.

'Who's there?' Reid made a pretence of jumping back in fear.

Tina popped out from under the table and stood, hands on hips, in the centre of the room.

'What are you doing down here?' asked Joanna, suppressing her gasp of surprise.

'You're late,' said Tina through her mischievous smile. 'It's time for lunch.'

Reid was standing with his arms folded, as though at a

safe distance. 'I thought you were a spook,' he said seriously.

'She can be when she wants to,' Joanna laughed.

'Well, that's fine,' he said. 'I told Mrs Hughes this house didn't have any spooks, and that I was thinking of getting rid of it in favour of more spooky accommodations. Now I can rest easy.'

A moment later they were ascending the narrow stairs, Reid coming last as Tina rushed ahead. Doubly embarrassed at having run the risk of being discovered in her disarray by her daughter as well as the man whose potent charms were playing such cruel tricks on her emotions, Joanna listened to the halting rhythm of her own breaths. Others must surely attribute it to the residual stress of her workout, she decided hopefully.

She alone must live with the knowledge of its true cause.

That night she helped Virginia prepare dinner and watched an old Bette Davis movie on television with Tina until fatigue overtook them both.

'I'm going out,' Reid told her after she had kissed Tina goodnight. 'I have an appointment to keep.' He looked at his Rolex watch, and back at Joanna sternly. 'It's about time for you to be in bed,' he said.

'Yes, Master,' she yawned. 'It will be a pleasure.'

Despite herself she wondered if he was keeping a date with one of the many women he must know. His attire, casual and roguishly handsome as always, gave no hint of his destination. It was possible, she knew, that he conducted serious business during his nocturnal outings so as to be free to spend time with her and Tina in the daytime. But he revealed nothing of his own doings.

As she started down the corridor to her room she could hear the surf washing quietly in the distance. Its balmy fragrance suffused the house, joining soft echoes to the delicious fatigue in her limbs.

She passed the study, with its maps and design tools shrouded in darkness. On an impulse she entered the room and turned on the fluorescent lamp craned over the table.

'Silly,' she thought, grasping a fine pencil with languorous fingers and pushing open the large sketch pad. 'Just a...'

Just a thought, she wanted to say to herself. But she had pulled back the chair and sat down, her hair flowing over her terrycloth robe, without realising what she was doing.

Her engineer's education came back to her as the sketch of a golf hole took shape under her pencil. Many was the time in college when she had agonised for hours over a problem in mathematics or physics, only to see it solve itself with striking ease when a single preconception was stripped away.

But she did not wait for thought to catch up with the force gathering inside her. Already the hole was nearly complete, with its bunkers and rough, the men's tee on the right, high up in the woods, the women's tee a hundred yards distant, behind the creek...

She pushed the design aside and began another. When that was finished she began another.

Briefly she reflected that the light was still on beside her bed, and that she should turn it out. She realised she was thirsty, and then forgot to get a glass of water. She did not hear Virginia go to bed.

The designs she was creating made sense, and yet they were not golf holes as anyone else understood them to be. But she did not wait to ponder their practicality. She continued drawing, afraid that this odd train of thought would pop out of her mind as quickly as it had popped in unless she followed it now.

She knew Reid would be angry with her if he found out

she had stayed up so late. She resolved to turn out the light at the sound of his car—and then forgot her resolution.

The digital clock beside her showed three forty-five a.m. when a hand touched her shoulder, sending a shock through the naked limbs under her robe.

'You're up late.' Reid's voice was a pleasant murmur in her ear. She felt his long arms extend to the desk top before her as the warmth of his deep chest grazed her billowed hair.

In silence she watched him turn the pages of the sketch pad. Five golf holes, complete with estimated yardage, hazards, tees for men and women, and notated wind direction, passed before her eyes. His tanned fingers held the pages furled under the bright light as he studied the designs.

'Explain something to me,' he said, pointing to the first sketch. 'Isn't the women's tee even farther from the green than the men's? That seems strange.'

'Not at all,' Joanna replied, pointing to the page. 'You see, from the woman's angle the hole is a three hundred and forty-five-yard par four. Her tee shot is against the wind, so she has to lay up short of the water hazard, and then she has a difficult short iron to the green.'

'But the man's tee is so much closer,' Reid pointed out. 'Can't he reach the green in one?'

'Of course he can,' said Joanna. 'That's why, for him, the hole is par three.'

'You're kidding,' he shook his head. 'Different pars…'

'They're equalized later on,' Joanna explained. 'But the point is that the challenge is entirely different for each sex on each hole.'

For a long moment he turned the pages in silence. 'The male and female players,' he said at length, 'will hardly see each other, except on the greens.'

'Isn't that the case on a conventional course?' she asked,

looking up at him. 'On this layout, at least, the challenge will be fair for both.'

In silence he evaluated her words.

'What do you think?' she asked at last.

'I think,' he smiled, raising her gently to her feet and brushing a strand of hair from her cheek, 'that you're a tired lady who needs some sleep.'

Joanna frowned at his noncommittal words.

'I also think you're a genius,' he went on, his dark eyes glittering in the shadows. 'I told you the Black Woods would make history with you as architect, and one of these days I'm going to congratulate myself for being so right.' His large hands rested warmly on her tired shoulders. 'And,' he added, drawing her to him, 'I think you're even prettier in person than you are on television.'

His embrace was easy and amiable, welcome as his confidence in her. But the Black Woods had flown from her consciousness, their expanse as limitless as her wonderings about where he had been tonight, and with whom.

Only the mad tremors under her skin remained, along with her fear that he might feel them, and her forlorn certainty that it was only as a friend that Reid held her thus.

CHAPTER SIX

'LET'S go, little one,' Reid's deep voice echoed down the hallway.

'Coming,' came Tina's murmur as she put down her book and skipped out of her room.

Reid stood with Virginia in the kitchen, putting the finishing touches to a large wicker picnic basket and beach bag. Both were dressed lightly, for the July morning outside was so hot that only the ocean breeze made normal activity bearable.

'Sure you'll be all right here alone?' Reid asked Joanna. 'You can come along, you know. A day at the beach won't hurt you. As a matter of fact, you look too pale. You're spending too much of your time in the basement.'

'Then you'd better put a sun lamp down there,' Joanna joked, 'because you know you'll never let me out long enough to get any sun.' She shook her head. 'No, you all go on. I'll keep the home fires burning while I do my own work.'

Reid stopped to check the tape on her knee. He had wrapped it with extra care this morning, as he knew she would be doing her exercises alone.

'If anything comes up,' he said, 'give my answering service a call. They may know where we end up. Otherwise tell anyone who calls that I'm gone for the day.'

Thirteen-year-old Katie appeared at the door, her freckled face aglow with her pleasure over the day's outing.

'I guess we're all here,' said Reid, his eyes resting on Tina as she hugged her mother.

'Have a good time,' said Joanna, kissing the little girl's cheek. 'And don't swim out too far. Stay with Mr Armstrong or Katie.'

A moment later they had all left, bound for a long day in the sun on Hilton Head Island. After watching the car crawl down the hill Joanna turned back to the kitchen.

Downstairs the machines waited, along with the weighted boot Joanna used for her quadriceps and knee exercises. In the refrigerator were the lean meat and hard-boiled eggs reserved for her solitary lunch.

In the study down the hall waited the Black Woods design. All eighteen holes were in place now, each one like an embryo whose final features are not yet evident, but whose destiny is planned in advance. Only a few short weeks had passed since her nocturnal breakthrough, and yet Joanna had seen the entire layout come to life in her imagination with miraculous rapidity.

The experience was as fearsome as it was fulfilling. Almost overnight, it seemed, she had found herself attempting something of which she had never dreamed herself capable. And now the process was growing inside her and on the pages she sketched, real and beautiful and unspeakably exhausting.

All that was required for the Black Woods to come into being as an inspired, aesthetically revolutionary test of golf was that its architect remain at a fever pitch of mental energy until its birth pangs were over.

The task seemed impossibly big for one inexperienced woman. Yet it was being accomplished, one day at a time, under Joanna's pencil. Somehow she knew she would hang on until the last idea, the final touch, had come to her.

But today she was not going to work on the Black

Woods design. Nor was she going to touch the exercise machines downstairs.

Joanna had another plan. And now that the others were gone, certain to be miles away all day long, she intended to put it into action.

She prowled the house one last time before leaving. Though she expected to be back by early afternoon, she felt a furtive impulse to make sure everything was in order.

A friendly letter from Carl Jaeger lay on the desk beside the design table. On an odd whim Joanna had decided not to tell Carl that she had agreed to undertake the design. Though he had long supported her in whatever she chose to do professionally, she somehow could not bring herself to tell him she had taken on so ambitious a project. In the wake of her immediate physical problems, her sally into architecture seemed premature.

Indeed, she thought as she passed the kitchen bulletin board, to the golf world at large her playing days appeared over. Reid had pinned up a morosely triumphant article by Ron Lieber announcing Joanna's imminent retirement, based on supposed confidential information from sources at Holy Family Hospital.

'I'll be the one to announce my retirement, Ron,' Joanna had told him angrily when she called to protest his report, 'not an unnamed source who sat in on my surgery.'

'Suit yourself,' he had shrugged. 'I have newspapers to sell, Miss Lake.'

Alongside the article Reid had affixed a wire service photo of Joanna jogging on the beach. It had been published in sports sections under the headline, *Can She Come Back?*

Reid found the media's efforts to make hay out of Joanna's plight amusing. 'Wait until you actually return to competition,' he laughed. 'The publicity will be unbelievable. They have you dead and buried now, the better to resurrect you when you show them you can play. It's all dollars and cents to them,' he added with his cheerful cynicism, 'and it will probably net you some new endorsements when you're back.'

Also on the cork board was a colour snapshot of Joanna and Reid and Tina on a Beaufort street. It had been taken during their first week together, when Joanna still bore all the overt marks of her accident.

She smiled now to recall her embarrassment at being seen in public in her bruised and bandaged condition. Since she was in the company of a man and a child, she feared she gave the impression of a battered wife whose scars bespoke raging quarrels with her spouse. Indeed, when a strange man approached, his features clouded by concern, she wondered in alarm whether he wanted to offer her his protection.

'I beg your pardon,' he asked, 'but aren't you Joanna Lake?'

Suppressing a laugh at her own silly imaginings, Joanna nodded. The man, a tourist staying on Hilton Head with his family, asked to be permitted to take a picture of her for his daughters, who would be heartbroken to have missed her. Apparently impressed by the threesome she made with Reid and Tina, he insisted on snapping them together. Two weeks later the snapshot came in the mail along with a letter of thanks.

Joanna contemplated it now, a trifle disconcerted by its penetrating revelation of the pattern that had emerged in the weeks after it was taken. Tina stood comfortably between the two adults, her hand nestling in Reid's large palm with candid trust and confidence. With her sandy hair and dark eyes she could easily pass for his daughter, and Joanna for his wife. Indeed, under the softening influence of Tina's warm feelings for him, Joanna herself seemed to smile a sidelong glance of reluctant affection his way, even as her eyes looked directly into the camera.

And in her gold-flecked irises there was a curious, palpable mixture of discomfort in the wake of her operation, dread over her uncertain future, and visible, elfin expectancy, as though she knew a secret she was hiding even from herself.

She turned away, unnerved by the photo's prescient capturing of so many intimate feelings. From her first meeting with Reid she had decided that he was an alien creature, a self-interested wheeler-dealer worlds apart from what she admired in a man. Yet a wilful little part of her, charmed by his humour, his understanding, and his closeness with Tina, reached out persistently to him.

'He's not my type,' she told herself, frightened by sensual stirrings which seemed to beckon her to perverse and merely physical enjoyment of his handsome body. But even that scruple, she realised, was insufficient, for her dangerous impulses went beyond the aching need his nearness created in her woman's flesh. It was as though that prohibited little corner of her had made up its mind that he was, after all, her type—that she felt and wanted to feel married to him, there on the public street where all could see, and that, were it not for the absence of one delicious pleasure that all husbands and wives enjoy together, they would indeed have made the perfect family with the little girl who stood so naturally and gracefully between them...

Confused, she thought how odd it was that Tina, whose obvious attachment to Reid was magnetising her own relationship with him, simultaneously acted along with Virginia as chaperone in this beautiful, quiet house where temptation might at last have overwhelmed Joanna's resistance had she been alone with Reid.

And even that daunting notion was mere wishful thinking, she decided with a shrug. Reid's very blitheness in his dealings with her made clear that her femininity was the least of his concerns. When he complimented her on her good looks he did so with deliberate indifference, as though he were assessing her professional attributes. It was as a businessman that he calculated her talents and sought to prick her ambition.

He wanted his course design, she realised. His sense of responsibility about her accident decreed that he see to her convalescence. For the moment he was pleased to enjoy the female companionship she afforded him, and to give free rein to his natural affinity with Tina.

But it went no further. The very elegance of this house, so cool and impersonal, was clear evidence that Reid kept his private self far removed from the guests he received there.

In confidence Virginia had told her a story related by a business acquaintance who had stayed for a weekend during her first year with Reid.

'He told me Reid came from a wealthy old family,' she said, 'but broke with his parents in a pretty scandalous way. They had him engaged to a girl from an even richer family. Why he went along with it as long as he did, no one knew—though the girl was apparently mad about him. He broke the engagement all at once, practically leaving her at the altar. When his father threatened to disinherit him—an idle threat made in anger, so the story goes—Reid jumped at the chance, as though it was an offer he couldn't refuse. He finished school on his football scholarship, went into business—strictly as a middle-man, without ever working for anybody or owning a firm himself—and became a great success.

'I've been his housekeeper three years now, and I don't claim to understand him,' Virginia admitted, 'but I get the feeling he can't bear to be manipulated by others. So he goes his own way and does the manipulating himself. He's very careful, and very private.'

Virginia did not amplify on the social life of which she must surely know something, but Joanna took for granted that Reid's many conquests with the opposite sex had taken him no nearer to marriage. Clearly he preferred his unhampered bachelorhood to a husband's entangling obligations.

With a sigh she darted a last glance at the writing desk beneath the bulletin board. A letter from her insurance company lay where she had left it yesterday, accompanied by a settlement cheque many hundreds of dollars below the price of her new station wagon, which was still in Sarasota with Karen. Joanna had insisted on a model with heavy duty suspension and a powerful engine regardless of the expense, for she liked a responsive vehicle and a safe one.

Tina had named the new car Michael, sight unseen. Her choice of a masculine name in the wake of Louisa's violent end was not lost on her mother.

Most of all Joanna was acutely aware that she would earn nothing as a player this summer. Endorsement offers would be hard to come by if she did not return to the tour soon. Her affiliation with Nakoma Springs must eventually dissolve unless her competitive career was restored. Indeed, years of hardship like those she had known as a girl might lie in wait for her and Tina unless she found a way to prove Robert Diehl's dour prognosis wrong.

That was why she could wait no longer to test the strength of her knee. Reid's painfully disciplined training programme had done its work, and Joanna could lift her weighted boot or push at a Nautilus bar with alacrity. But she had no way of knowing whether the tendons and ligaments could stand the strain of a good, hard golf swing and brisk follow-through, repeated over and over again as competitive play required.

Today she would know the answer.

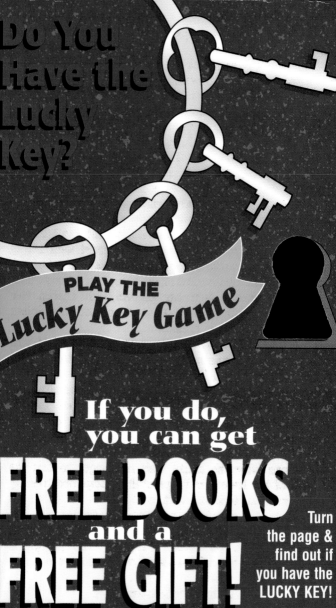

PLAY THE
Lucky Key Game
and get

HOW TO PLAY:

1. With a coin, carefully scratch off gold area at the right. Then check the claim chart to see what we have for you — **FREE BOOKS** and a **FREE GIFT** — **ALL YOURS FREE!**

2. Send back this card and you'll receive brand-new Harlequin Presents® novels. These books have a cover price of $3.75 each, but they are yours to keep absolutely free.

3. There's no catch. You're under no obligation to buy anything. We charge nothing — ZERO — for your first shipment. And you don't have to make any minimum number of purchases — not even one!

4. The fact is thousands of readers enjoy receiving books by mail from the Harlequin Reader Service® months before they're available in stores. They like the convenience of home delivery and they love our discount prices!

5. We hope that after receiving your free books you'll want to remain a subscriber. But the choice is yours — to continue or cancel, any time at all! So why not take us up on our invitation, with no risk of any kind. You'll be glad you did!

YOURS FREE!
A SURPRISE MYSTERY GIFT

We can't tell you what it is...but we're sure you'll like it! A
FREE GIFT—
just for playing the **LUCKY KEY** game!

FREE GIFTS!

NO COST! NO OBLIGATION TO BUY!
NO PURCHASE NECESSARY!

The Harlequin Reader Service™ — Here's how it works:

Accepting free books places you under no obligation to buy anything. You may keep the books and gift and return the shipping statement marked "cancel." If you do not cancel, about a month later we'll send you 6 additional novels and bill you just $3.12 each, plus 25¢ delivery per book and applicable sales tax, if any.* That's the complete price — and compared to cover prices of $3.75 each — quite a bargain! You may cancel at any time, but if you choose to continue, every month we'll send you 6 more books, which you may either purchase at the discount price...or return to us and cancel your subscription.

*Terms and prices subject to change without notice. Sales tax applicable in N.Y.

If offer card is missing write to: Harlequin Reader Service, 3010 Walden Ave., P.O. Box 1867, Buffalo NY 14240-1867

BUSINESS REPLY MAIL
FIRST-CLASS MAIL   PERMIT NO. 717   BUFFALO, NY

POSTAGE WILL BE PAID BY ADDRESSEE

HARLEQUIN READER SERVICE
3010 WALDEN AVE
PO BOX 1867
BUFFALO NY 14240-9952

NO POSTAGE
NECESSARY
IF MAILED
IN THE
UNITED STATES

dealings with her made clear that her femininity was the least of his concerns. When he complimented her on her good looks he did so with deliberate indifference, as though he were assessing her professional attributes. It was as a businessman that he calculated her talents and sought to prick her ambition.

He wanted his course design, she realised. His sense of responsibility about her accident decreed that he see to her convalescence. For the moment he was pleased to enjoy the female companionship she afforded him, and to give free rein to his natural affinity with Tina.

But it went no further. The very elegance of this house, so cool and impersonal, was clear evidence that Reid kept his private self far removed from the guests he received there.

In confidence Virginia had told her a story related by a business acquaintance who had stayed for a weekend during her first year with Reid.

'He told me Reid came from a wealthy old family,' she said, 'but broke with his parents in a pretty scandalous way. They had him engaged to a girl from an even richer family. Why he went along with it as long as he did, no one knew—though the girl was apparently mad about him. He broke the engagement all at once, practically leaving her at the altar. When his father threatened to disinherit him—an idle threat made in anger, so the story goes—Reid jumped at the chance, as though it was an offer he couldn't refuse. He finished school on his football scholarship, went into business—strictly as a middle-man, without ever working for anybody or owning a firm himself—and became a great success.

'I've been his housekeeper three years now, and I don't claim to understand him,' Virginia admitted, 'but I get the feeling he can't bear to be manipulated by others. So he goes his own way and does the manipulating himself. He's very careful, and very private.'

Virginia did not amplify on the social life of which she must surely know something, but Joanna took for granted that Reid's many conquests with the opposite sex had taken him no nearer to marriage. Clearly he preferred his unhampered bachelorhood to a husband's entangling obligations.

With a sigh she darted a last glance at the writing desk beneath the bulletin board. A letter from her insurance company lay where she had left it yesterday, accompanied by a settlement cheque many hundreds of dollars below the price of her new station wagon, which was still in Sarasota with Karen. Joanna had insisted on a model with heavy duty suspension and a powerful engine regardless of the expense, for she liked a responsive vehicle and a safe one.

Tina had named the new car Michael, sight unseen. Her choice of a masculine name in the wake of Louisa's violent end was not lost on her mother.

Most of all Joanna was acutely aware that she would earn nothing as a player this summer. Endorsement offers would be hard to come by if she did not return to the tour soon. Her affiliation with Nakoma Springs must eventually dissolve unless her competitive career was restored. Indeed, years of hardship like those she had known as a girl might lie in wait for her and Tina unless she found a way to prove Robert Diehl's dour prognosis wrong.

That was why she could wait no longer to test the strength of her knee. Reid's painfully disciplined training programme had done its work, and Joanna could lift her weighted boot or push at a Nautilus bar with alacrity. But she had no way of knowing whether the tendons and ligaments could stand the strain of a good, hard golf swing and brisk follow-through, repeated over and over again as competitive play required.

Today she would know the answer.

She did not like to imagine Reid's wrath if he found out what she intended. *He won't find out*, she decided with a grim glance into the study. Reid assumed she would be working on the design today. If he returned to find the jeep gone, he would think she had taken it to the Black Woods.

But she would be home long before he returned.

She drove along the coast road to the spot she had passed several times before. She knew what she was looking for.

It was a golf centre, including a driving range, miniature golf course for tourists and their children, and par three layout. She had never bothered to notice its name.

She parked the jeep in the gravel lot and walked through the enormous morning heat past the Coke machines beside which young boys stood munching potato chips out of bags they had bought inside. The driving range was nearly empty. In the distance the ball collector drove slowly back and forth, picking up the red-striped practice balls as its driver sat behind his heavy mesh screen.

The range proprietor looked at Joanna without expression as he took her money and handed over an ancient, battered women's driver and a bucket of balls. The heat seemed to have ruined his business for the day. He stared forlornly over his tattooed arms at the television in the corner, knowing he would sell no more than a few miniature golf rounds and bags of potato chips or popcorn until twilight. Only young boys were out in this fainting heat.

Joanna walked quickly to a cubicle, poured the painted balls into the dispenser, and used the club head to pull down the chute which deposited the first ball on the rubber tee.

She stood at address, rocking back and forth to test her balance, aware of the tightness of her left knee, and perhaps of a fugitive weakness she had never felt there before.

Never mind, she told herself, pursing her lips in concentration. *Just hit it.*

Before she could begin her backswing a sight beyond the concession stand made her shrink with furtive suddenness behind the cubicle's screened partition. On the first hole of the miniature golf course a tall man was standing with a little girl. Bending over her slender body, he was showing her how to hold a putter.

For a panicky second Joanna had thought that, incredibly, they were Reid and Tina, and she smiled ruefully at her error. But all at once it occurred to her that she might be recognised here. Her ponytail and taped knee would give away her identity to anyone familiar with her recent career. She even wore the tank top whose stretch knit and pastel look were her trademarks.

But she reasoned that no one was here except a few small boys, come on their bikes from nearby neighbourhoods for a Coke and some chips or candy. It was a weekday morning. She had picked the perfect time. No one would notice her.

Again she addressed the ball. After a moment's concentration she struck it. It sailed over two hundred yards, lofting handsomely before drifting to the weedy grass of the driving range.

In her legs Joanna felt nothing unusual. Her twisting follow-through, though an inevitable strain on her collateral knee ligaments, had not been painful.

Encouraged, she struck a second ball, then a third, a fourth. With each swing she forced herself to put full weight on her convalescent knee. On her sixth shot she went for length. The ball, hit with perfect tempo, sailed over two hundred and sixty yards.

Then she began to guide the ball, fading it intentionally, then drawing it, and finally aiming right for the two hundred-yard marker. With satisfaction she heard her balls whack the wooden planks of the pockmarked sign, far across the littered field.

Directing her attention away from her knee, she hit the entire bucket of balls, then bought another. The tremendous heat of the morning seemed to loosen her. The broken-down old club, whose grip had been taped and re-taped like her own sprained limbs, was poorly balanced, but she knew how to compensate instantly for its deficiencies, and before long it had become an extension of her arms, her back and legs, and she knew precisely where each swing would send the ball.

For the first time in two months she felt in her limbs the coolly professional self-assurance she had taken for granted before her accident, and thrilled to recognise her own talent as it came to life after so long a sleep.

Midway through the second bucket of balls she began to hook her shots. She realised her left knee felt languorous.

Testing the leg, she walked back and forth in the cubicle. The knee was weak and tired.

Wisely, she turned to leave, then stopped in her tracks.

A group of boys in shorts and dungarees was standing behind the cubicle, the smallest and most raggedy-looking gallery she had ever had.

'Lady,' said a red-haired boy whose T-shirt bore stains Joanna recognised as grape juice, 'you hit the ball just like Jack Nicklaus. Are you a pro?'

Joanna smiled at his candid admiration. 'Thanks for the compliment,' she said. 'But, you see, I'm tired already. Would any of you gentlemen like to finish this bucket of balls for me?'

Eagerly they took the club from her and began taking turns striking the balls with ungainly swings. They all waved happily as she got in the baking jeep and drove away.

The knee was swollen and painful by the time she entered the air-conditioned house. Sighing gratefully in the cool air, she cursed herself for having pushed herself a shade too far when the evidence of strain was already palpable.

Perhaps, she thought dully, she never should have gone out in the first place. But it was too late to turn back the clock.

Reid would be back this afternoon. How could she hide what she had done from his sharp eye?

She thought of the athlete's bible slogan, R.I.C.E.—Rest, ice, compression, elevation. She took two aspirins and gave herself a lengthy ice massage. Then she lay on her bed with the throbbing knee taped and elevated. She prayed it would improve before Reid got home.

After two hours in bed she tried to walk to the kitchen. She could only limp painfully. She tried to eat a snack, but her discomfort and chagrin took away her appetite.

Seeking to pass the time by working on the Black Woods design, she found herself unable to concentrate. The holes danced confusedly before her eyes.

Feeling like a guilty child, she limped ashamedly about the house. At last she slunk down to the basement and sat on the table, as though her proximity to the tools of rehabilitation could somehow strengthen the knee she had managed to harm. Still dressed in her skirt and tank top, she made a pathetic figure in the mirror.

At last she heard the garage door open, heard the girls rush into the kitchen above as Reid and Virginia brought up the rear, and a moment later Tina came down the stairs.

'Mom!' she exclaimed. 'I learned how to do a somersault under the water. Katie can do it twice. Wait till I show you!'

'Good for you, honey. Did you have a nice picnic?'

As the child answered Joanna saw Reid come into view. His brow furrowed in concern and then disapproval as he stared from her knee to her guilty eyes.

'Why don't you see if Mrs Hughes needs anything?' he said to Tina. 'I want to talk to your mother.'

He approached, touched the knee, flexed and extended it gently, and saw Joanna wince.

'What have you done?' he asked, all business even in his anger. 'Where did you go? The jeep was still warm.'

She looked at him with half-hearted defiance.

'The driving range.'

He shook his head, bitterly amused by her foolishness.

'What did you hit?' he asked. 'A driver?'

She nodded, grimacing anew as he moved the knee through some of the one hundred and fifty degrees of which it should have been capable.

'How many balls?'

'I don't know,' she sighed. 'A bucket and a half...maybe fifty or sixty. I don't know.'

'And you quit when you got tired?'

She nodded.

'Did you give it some ice?' he asked.

'Yes.'

Softly his finger traced the skin over the knee cartilage and ligaments, moved the kneecap back and forth, and checked for fluid accumulation as he extended her leg.

'You little idiot,' he grated when he had finished. 'What do you think we've been doing all these weeks? Strengthening this knee so that you can ruin it for ever in one morning? Do you want to go to the U.S. Open again, or do you want to leave your career at a cheap driving range?'

'I'm sorry.' Joanna dared not meet his reproachful gaze.

'Don't apologise to me,' he said. 'It's your career. Look in the mirror and apologise to yourself—or to that little girl upstairs. But not to me.'

Hot tears quickened in her eyes as the pain in her knee joined her guilt over what she had done. But she fought them back, too proud to weep shamefacedly before him.

'I thought I had Joanna Lake here,' Reid went on, 'the consummate professional, the queen of consistency and good sense—not some impetuous child who would jeopardise her own training just because she's in a hurry to play again.'

All at once anger came to Joanna's rescue under his stinging words. She had been under his sway long enough, she decided as she glanced into his hard eyes.

'You're right about one thing,' she said firmly. 'It is my career—not yours. You can break my back all day with your exercise programme, Reid, but when it comes to swinging a golf club on the pro tour, I have to do that myself. No one can do it for me.'

She hesitated, unsure of her own meaning.

'I had to know,' she concluded.

'And now you've found out,' he prodded derisively, 'that you can't drive sixty balls without straining your ligaments and possibly setting your convalescence back by a month or more. Does that satisfy you?'

'Perhaps it does,' she insisted, putting a reluctant arm around his shoulder as he helped her up the stairs. 'But I had to know if I can still hit the ball. I may have been wrong in going this soon or in staying so long, but at least I did something on my own. And I have only myself to answer to.'

They reached the landing and started past the kitchen towards her bedroom. As luck would have it Virginia and the girls were nowhere in sight.

'It's easy for you to talk,' Joanna went on, limping angrily beside him as he supported her with a long arm. 'You're not the one who has to worry about my future—I am.' She glanced warily around her, alert to her daughter's whereabouts. 'Dr Diehl thinks I'm only good to push a shopping cart for the rest of my life. It's I who have to wonder what's going to become of Tina.'

'Tina won't be better off,' he replied implacably, 'if her mother behaves like a child instead of an adult. A responsible athlete knows how to take things a step at a time—I would have thought you knew that.'

The soft pastel hues of her bedroom came into view as afternoon clouds flashed by in the glass of the painting on the wall.

'I've said it before, and I'll say it again,' Reid concluded with deliberate complacency, 'you need someone to watch out for you.'

'Don't tell me that!' cried Joanna, infuriated by his proprietorial manner. 'I don't need anyb…'

'Don't need anybody?' he mocked. 'How would you have gotten up those stairs and down this hallway without me?'

'I'd have managed,' she insisted as he deposited her unceremoniously on the bed. 'I haven't needed you or anyone else all these years, you know. I got where I am on my own.'

Reid stared sardonically down at her swollen knee. 'Yes, I can see that,' he said.

'What's that supposed to mean?' she asked, though his implication was maddeningly clear.

'I wasn't the one behind the wheel the day you got yourself into this, was I?' he asked, his handsome face bent over her in the still air.

Pushed beyond her limit, she stared daggers at him.

I was doing fine until I met you. The words had almost popped out before she could manage to suppress them. She knew how much they would have hurt, for she had no doubt he was aware of the part he had played in causing her accident. But she also knew she had only herself to blame in the final analysis. Provoked though she might be by his arrogance, she could not bring herself to use the truth against him after all he had done for her.

'You treat me like a slave,' she changed the subject irritably. 'It's as though my body belonged to you. I have no rights and no freedom around here. I'm at your beck and call all the time, and when I'm not following your orders I sit around with nothing to do. You leave your instructions and then you breeze out until all hours, doing God knows…'

'So,' he grinned down at her, his eyes flashing mockery in the shadows, 'you're jealous, are you? Now I'm really beginning to understand you.'

'Don't you dare say that!' she shot back, beside herself with frustration. 'You think you're the centre of the world…'

'All right,' he interrupted, his palms raised in a hands-off gesture as his probing irises rested upon her, and Joanna recognised the odd look that seemed to strip her to the buff while teasing her with the promise not to come too near. But now there was an unaccustomed gentleness in it that disconcerted her. Suddenly she felt too aware of her own shame to be as angry with him as she would have liked.

'You're as stubborn as they come, Joanna,' he told her, 'and as independent. You'll do exactly as you please, right or wrong. And for that, believe me, I admire you.'

He touched her knee for a last time. 'As far as I can tell,' he said, 'nothing is sprained. The swelling will go down soon enough. But from now on I want you to do what *I* say, and not what that strong will of yours dictates. Is that clear?'

Catching the shade of lingering anger in her gold-flecked eyes, he shook his head admiringly.

'Damn,' he muttered, 'you are a lovely woman. But your looks alone won't make you a living.'

Before she could decide what his words meant he had drawn her to him and kissed her cheek. He held her closer, patted her back with a protective hand and, on an apparent impulse, brushed her lips softly with his own.

'Now,' he said, helping her to lie back while he placed cushions under her left knee, 'get some rest. I'll be back after a while.'

A moment later he had closed the door behind him. The shadows of hot afternoon glowed through the curtains.

The pain in Joanna's knee was deep and exhausting. But she did not feel it. Her lips had come dizzyingly alive, their thrill coursing far beneath her skin.

She lay stunned with wanting in the darkness, her body on fire, her mind in an agony of indecision.

CHAPTER SEVEN

To Reid's surprise and Joanna's delight, the fateful day at the driving range had been a first step upward rather than a disaster.

The knee felt stronger the next morning, and stronger still the following day. It seemed that one good workout at her actual golf swing, with its graceful follow-through and fluid tempo, had reminded her injured sinews of what their job was. In good order they responded.

Joanna felt surer of herself when jogging and bicycling, when doing quad sets and leg lifts with her weighted boot, and when negotiating her endless Nautilus exercises under Reid's direction. She could sense the end of her convalescence drawing nearer. She was less depressed and irritable now that the day for flying on her own wings seemed a real eventuality.

Her nerves tingled with new strength and vigour as July reached its torrid end. But unbeknown to anyone else, the mad ferment in her senses, stoked to a fever pitch by the sweet brush of Reid's lips the night of her transgression, went on apace. She tried to blunt its urgency by reminding herself that he had only intended to cheer her up in the wake of his own harsh words.

And indeed, since that moment he had been his old self, upbraiding her pitilessly for her occasional failure to comply with his orders, prodding her constantly with the sharp edges of his humour, and bantering easily about her foibles with an amused Tina. He apparently thought she had got off too easily at the driving range, and deserved to be taken down a peg. Yet he was easy and affectionate even in his authoritarian moments.

The little signs of his admiration, from his tender handling of her knee to the regard in his sharp eyes when he discussed the Black Woods design with her, were unmistakable and meant a lot. But part of her longed to draw conclusions from his respect that the rest of her knew to be unjustified—and so she continued to suffer quiet agonies alone.

Her sidelong glances, hooded and abashed, caught the hard lines of his shoulders, the crisp tangle of hair on the deep chest under the open collars of his shirts, the roguish, sensual curve of his lips. She found herself so close to him that she became expertly familiar with his clean, tangy male scent, the tiny changes flashing across his complex eyes and through his voice to suit his mood. The shape of his hands and fingers was intimate knowledge to her, as were the muscled contours of his thighs and hips.

In guilty solitude she coveted the male energy behind his laughter, and the fascinating variety of his smiles. In his dauntless cheer she no longer saw the superficiality she had once attributed to him, but an almost aesthetic depth of character. There was hard, cold courage behind those blithe smiles and jokes, and a powerful intellect and awesome virility which had perhaps won many uphill battles in life.

It was impossible to be indifferent to him. Small matter if he didn't know she was alive, if his levity covered over whatever awareness he might have of her shameless impulses, and if Tina stood as the crucial chaperone between them, Joanna's senses were full of him at every instant of the day, and his handsome form stalked her dreams at night, caressing and enfolding her as she slept.

She could not get him out of her mind. His intervention in her life, begun with the accident, was now complete.

When she looked inside herself to wonder who she really
was, and what was becoming of her, it was his black eyes
that seemed to look out at her, holding her in the thrall of
their knowing gaze.

Yet it was not as a secret lover, a charmed prince, that Reid
spoke to her over breakfast a week after her ill-advised day
at the driving range. It was as her appraising coach.

'I'll tell you what,' he said. 'Tina is spending the afternoon with Virginia and Katie. Why don't we hang around
until they go, and then get in a quick round of golf?'

Joanna's face lit up.

'Reid, do you mean it? Really?'

'We'll go to Bayside Links.' He frowned a warning. 'But
we'll play the back nine only. You'll ride in a cart, and at
the first sign of weakness in that knee, we're coming
straight home. Is that clear?'

She nodded obediently, too overjoyed at her good fortune to ask questions.

Joanna's clubs were still in Florida, so Reid rented her a
set at the Bayside Links pro shop. Like so many of Beaufort's genteel inhabitants, the club pro said nothing to
Joanna, though his decorous nod signified that he knew not
only her identity but also the probable importance of the
occasion.

Reid drove the cart to the tenth tee, and they were off.
Joanna played her first shots gingerly, and then began to
stroke the ball with greater confidence. Her putting felt
even more rusty than the rest of her game, but it too improved.

Despite her concentration on her swing she found herself
scanning the fine old course's fairways with an architect's
eye. It was easy to see that the Black Woods layout, according to her design, would offer women a far more subtle

test of golf than Bayside, while assuring male players a championship challenge as well.

Reid, for his part, seemed more intent on Joanna's game than his own, though he drove the ball long distances without apparent effort. He studied every movement of her body, every facial expression that might connote pain or fatigue, and he was alert to the level of concentration with which she attacked the course.

By the time they reached the fifteenth tee he must have been satisfied that she was in reasonably good condition for he began to put pressure on her.

'The winner gets to skip Nautilus tonight,' he said teasingly.

'You're on,' she nodded, determination quickening under her smile.

They had halved their first five holes at par. Thanks to his natural ability and superior strength off the tee, Reid was able to stay even as Joanna went for birdie after birdie on the closing holes. When they came to the eighteenth green they were still tied. Joanna had uncorked a fairway wood worthy of her international reputation, and her ball lay only ten feet from the cup. Reid gave his own ball a fine roll from thirty feet, and it missed by inches.

'This is your chance,' he told her. 'Make that ten-footer and you're the winner.'

'I'm aware of that,' Joanna murmured as she lined up her putt.

'Good,' he prodded annoyingly. 'Because if I were a professional I'd hate to think I couldn't beat an amateur.'

'May I have a little silence?' she asked in irritation.

'On the other hand,' he drawled, 'I am a man. I suppose that makes a difference.'

Infuriated by his words, Joanna needed an effort of will to turn her anger into disciplined concentration. With deliberate calm she stroked her ball straight into the cup.

Before she could reproach him for his snide behaviour the sound of enthusiastic applause broke out behind them on the stretch of lawn leading to the clubhouse. A small, informal gallery had formed after Joanna was recognised on the fairway, and was calling out its appreciation of her putt and its encouragement for her eventual comeback.

'Go get 'em, Joanna!' She heard the friendly shouts, charged with humour and genuine warmth. Though Karen had forwarded hundreds of fan letters to her through the summer, the sight of that small group of boosters touched her, for she realised that her struggle for rehabilitation was not lost on them. Despite the widespread reports that her career was at an end, they continued to believe in her.

With a smile and a wave she bent to retrieve her ball, then shook Reid's outstretched hand. At that instant she heard the click of a shutter, and a photographer came forward from the apron.

'Mind if I use it, Miss Lake?' he asked with a glance at Reid. 'Local folks know you're here, and it would give them a thrill to see you on the sports page.'

She looked at Reid. Smiling, he shrugged.

'All right,' she said. 'You're welcome to it, if you want it.'

'Thanks a whole lot, Miss Lake.' And the man was gone in the dispersing gallery.

'You played a nice back nine,' said Reid. 'That was a good-looking birdie putt just now.'

'Thank you,' she said. 'You weren't much help.'

'Really?' he quirked a mocking eyebrow. 'I thought I gave you the little spark of anger you needed. If you can stay mad at the women on the tour the way you do with me, you'll win everything in sight.'

Joanna shook her head as he helped her into the cart. She could not help pondering the secret understanding that had bound her to him in the wake of her accident. Though he loved to exasperate her, he was her strongest ally; he alone believed in her utterly.

'I can't,' she murmured.

'Can't what?' he asked, his eyes scanning her face.

'Stay mad at you,' she admitted with a rueful smile.

They returned home to find a note from Virginia, who had decided to gratify Tina's wish by taking her to the drive-in movies with Katie. Since it would be late when the show ended, Tina would be allowed to complete her dream evening by sleeping in Katie's upper bunk.

'They have a nerve, to leave us to our own devices,' Reid frowned. 'Well, we'll show them. How about dinner out? Can you use a break from your lean hamburger and cottage cheese?'

'Now you're talking!' smiled Joanna.

After a whirlpool bath to rest her knee, she chose a soft, clinging shift whose simple lines accentuated the femininity she feared she had lost over these painful weeks. It felt wonderful to look at her shapely legs without the cumbersome tape, her slender arms without their black and blue marks and bandages. She saw in the bedroom mirror that her face was truly clear now, and vibrantly healthy. The green eyes looking out at her in the dusky light bore an almost impish look of anticipation that disconcerted her.

Reid met her in the corridor, tanned and handsome in his light slacks and sports coat, his hair still damp from his shower, the clean aroma of him suffusing her delightfully.

'Now,' he took her arm familiarly, 'where's that photographer when we need him? You look like a million, Miss Lake. I'm proud to be seen with you.'

Joanna turned to see herself in the hall mirror, standing beside him in the warm golden glow of sunset. Her breath nearly caught in her throat, for, dressed as they were for a festive dinner out after their round of golf, they looked startlingly like man and wife. Fiddling with an earring to hide her emotion, she realised she had never felt closer to him than tonight.

Reid must have sensed the drift in her thoughts, for he spoke with wistful humour. 'What am I going to do,' he asked, 'when you and Tina go back home and leave me all alone here? Life is going to be mighty dull.' He shrugged unhappily.

'I'm sure you'll get along as you always have,' she smiled, imagining the many women he must know.

'Well,' he sighed, touching her sleek hair with fingers that caressed her neck lullingly, 'a fellow simply has to adjust. I'll make do, but it won't be easy.'

Gently he turned her towards the foyer. The ocean wheeled in the glass frame of an abstract painting on the wall. It was time to go.

And all at once Joanna felt as though they both knew something they had never known before. Yes, she mused as he held the door for her. As though they had come to the last unspoken agreement, their final secret pact.

So it was that the first vodka Martini she had tasted in two months sent shivers of quiet excitement through her limbs. Reid had chosen a beautiful seafood restaurant whose delicious smells harmonised bewitchingly with its subtle décor and massive windows overlooking the shore.

They spoke little as the friendly waiter brought savoury mussels and clams, crab and shrimps and lobster in a magnificent array before fading into the muted background where local people and a few lucky tourists conversed in relaxed tones.

When he returned to refill their wine glasses with chilled white Bordeaux, Reid was watching with satisfaction as his hungry guest enjoyed her unaccustomed feast.

'And how is the Catch of the Day?' came the waiter's caressing South Carolina drawl.

'She seems to be doing very well,' joked Reid without taking his eyes from Joanna.

She could only blush at his humour, for a mood of sweet acquiescence had fallen over them both. Tired but happy, Joanna matched him smile for smile, never daring to look in the face of her own inner feelings, or to hope that she was not alone in feeling them.

They drove home along the coast road in the gathering darkness. The hushed boom of the surf echoed in Joanna's ears, a warm counterpoint to the breeze furling the boughs of the trees in the scented air.

The house seemed familiar and domestic, and not at all its huge, impersonal self, as Reid pulled the car into the garage and led her through the inner door.

She took off her shoes and stood barefoot in the kitchen as he excused himself, and a moment later she heard the low tones of his voice as he spoke on a faraway phone. He must be calling his answering service.

It occurred to her that he might be leaving soon, going out as he did so often to unknown destinations while she stayed home. But tonight Tina and Virginia were gone as well.

Suddenly Joanna felt atrociously vulnerable and even embarrassed, at sixes and sevens alone in the kitchen. She longed for Reid to return, for him to say something, anything by way of setting a tone for the rest of the evening— even if it were only to send her unceremoniously to bed.

At last he returned. He must have thrown his coat somewhere, for he stood tall and strong in the slacks that hugged his powerful legs, his shirt open at the neck, the very picture of triumphant masculinity at ease with itself.

'Well now,' he appraised her from across the empty room, 'what have we here?'

Pursing her lips in answer to his teasing look, Joanna drummed a finger on her folded arms.

'It seems to me,' he observed, 'that certain people have had a very long day, and should be thinking about a warm bath and a long sleep.'

She stood before him, her weight on her right leg. His acute eyes noticed her posture immediately.

'Now look,' he said. 'She's favouring her weak knee again.' Striding forward quickly, he swept her up by her waist and deposited her on the kitchen counter. The sheer fabric of her shift slid upward along her thigh, baring the knee whose scar was now faded to a tiny speck.

Reid leaned over her, his large fingers closing delicately around the skin he had taped so many times.

'I hope you're not hiding any pain from me,' he said, flexing and extending the knee gently as his eyes followed its movements. 'Because I'm responsible for this little outing, you know. It would be my fault.'

Joanna blushed despite herself as he touched her, his hand so large that it could nearly close around her slender thigh. What she was hiding, she knew, was far more guilty than mere pain. And as he stood before her, his perfect man's body sending its waves of thrilling warmth through her senses, she knew she was perilously close to being unable to hide it an instant longer.

'Does that hurt?' he asked, turning the knee slightly.

Dying inside, she looked up at him, and her heart leapt within her breast as with a great inner sigh she risked everything.

'No, silly,' she smiled, 'it doesn't hurt.'

Her fingers had strayed hesitantly to his hair, languorous but sure, in their way, and caressed its careless waves, felt its fine fragrant expanse for the first time before her hands clasped around his neck. She did not flinch when he looked into her eyes, his gaze sharp with surprise and perhaps disapproval.

She merely smiled, prepared now to stake everything on him, to let herself be torn and ruined if he refused her. The subtle pressure in the cool fingers around his neck told him what she wanted as she pulled him to her with soft entreaty.

And all at once she was in his arms, her body lifted from the counter and pulled full length against his own in one fluid motion. She had no leisure to tell herself how delightful it was to run her fingers through that black hair, to caress those shoulders, to feel the myriad tiny shudders of her femininity against his hard limbs—for already his kiss was upon her, unbearably penetrating and delicious, and she was limp and helpless in his embrace, her courage spent.

Now Reid knew the secret that had tormented her all these weeks. The next move was his, for she had bared everything. It was within his power to take her brutally to her room, to make her his slave there or put her to sleep like a naughty, forward child.

So she clung to him, languid and luxuriant, her senses quickening madly under his touch. Her hands had slipped to his broad back, stroking the muscled flesh with little shocks of delight, slipping down to his waist as her face turned up to his. Again he kissed her, cradling her soft body with a long arm while he furled and caressed her billowed hair. His lips joined her own with exquisite gentleness.

A wild joy took possession of her, for she could feel the acquiescence in his warm hands, his willingness to accept what was about to happen, and even to protect her, as he always had, from her own doubts.

The dark night wheeled before her half-closed eyes as he bore her through the shadows to her room. He deposited her with ethereal delicacy on the silken spread. There was moonlight in the window, and the walls shone silver and

iridescent around her. It seemed there was a hushed, secret
sigh of compliance in the darkness itself, a conspiracy of
yielding that opened her senses to him.

Stunned, she lay that way until his kiss made her sit up
and strain towards him. She felt knowing palms slide over
the body whose injured sinews they had comforted for so
long. Dry and calm and concerned, they caressed her. But
now she trembled in her very centre at the hot ferment they
stoked under her skin, the shudders of ecstasy their passage
coaxed from her.

Already her shift had slipped away somehow, and in the
quiet rhythm of Reid's touch her underclothes were coming
off, stripped away with all the grace of petals in the breeze.

Naked, she watched as he stood up in the penumbra.
Outlined against the glimmering walls, he removed his
clothes and stood in his stately nudity, huge and straight
and handsome as she had always imagined he would be.
Joanna held out her arms to him.

Enthralled to feel him cover her, his hard bands of muscle melded flawlessly to her woman's curves, she realised
in breathless excitement that she had never wanted a man
so terribly, never dreamed of a pitch of desire so feverish
as this.

Reid seemed to sense the transport that shook her, for he
was kind and tender as he gathered her to him. Her hips
and thighs and stomach awoke to the touch of his hard
flesh, her breasts to the lithe stroke of his lips and tongue.
And she knew now that this unearthly pleasure was all new,
blissfully unfamiliar, for she had never been made love to
like this, never known so sweetly and perfectly.

She felt the surge of his enormous heat, and was un-
ashamed to feed and excite it, for she had nothing to fear
now, and was certain of it. She touched him and led him,
delighted to feel him respond to her with his aroused power
as her soft limbs surrounded him. Hard and potent, he gave

himself to her as surely as he had given her his smiles, his teasing looks, his harsh commands and encouraging words all these weeks.

Now the great swell of his need upraised her, thrust her higher and higher, and she gave him all of herself gladly, her hands in his hair and upon his broad back and on the taut thighs beneath his waist. Her sighs and murmurs enfolded him, and she heard the low groan of passion stir in his throat as he kissed her and held her, closer and closer, his hard essence joined to her in hot bursts of pleasure unimaginably intense, unspeakably intimate.

Then all was poised and breathless on the edge of peace while their passion spent itself in the shadows. Reid cradled her and did not let her go as her gasps softened to little sighs and shudders in his arms. The hands and lips that stroked her cheek, her breast, so sweet and gentle, told her something she felt she could hold on to for ever, no matter what the future held.

She knew now that he was perfect for her, had understood her utterly and given himself just as she wanted him, in that wondrous, charged moment. He had come from nowhere to enter her life, to change her and make her perfect for him, so that in this silent darkness she might experience the thrill of being known so beautifully.

And if he had come to her thus, only to recede into his own destiny, then so be it, she thought with a little spasm of defiance. Let time take him away, and humiliation descend upon her. He was hers tonight.

And perhaps he felt her wild opening to him, her heedless willingness to confront fate that way. For, a warm and steadfast partner, he joined her in her defiance, he stayed with her all night long. They lay somnolent in each other's arms, charmed by the moonlight, caressing each other softly until passion rose to draw them together once more. Both knew that this lovely tryst might be their first and last,

and so they discovered each other again and again, in surprise and delight and rapture.

How many times she belonged to him that night Joanna
would never know. Each intimacy she shared with him was
stunningly unique, too beautiful to ever recapture or forget.
The varieties of his tenderness were indescribable.

And when at last sleep came to bind them, in the night's
darkest hour, after the moon had set, she knew she was a
changed woman, and would never be the same again. But
she could welcome the awful vulnerability inside her, the
fearsome yielding helplessness, because he had stayed with
her, and even now held her in his arms. Surely the magic
of that embrace would give her strength to go on alone
when he was gone.

One perfect night to hold off the entire future.

Joanna had known equations more improbable.

CHAPTER EIGHT

SUMMER was ending.

There was no denying it, despite the blazing August heat
that kept tourists and residents at the beach or indoors. The
calendar did not lie. Soon the migratory birds would depart
with the human visitors, leaving the graceful herons and
egrets to their year-round home. The famous golf courses,
booked up now for tee-off times, would return to their
placid off-season tempo.

It seemed that a great pressure had been lifted from
Joanna's life—at least for the moment. By dint of innumerable knee lifts, quad sets, and stretching exercises for
her back, hamstrings, hands and arms, all under Reid's
stern aegis, she had restored her body to the strong, supple
condition she had taken for granted before her accident.

Since their historic first round together, she had played
golf with Reid when he was available, and alone or with
young Katie Hughes when he was not. Gradually abandon-
ing the use of electric golf carts, she now tramped eighteen
holes of fairway with vibrant confidence in her stamina.

Having pronounced her latest examination in Charleston
the last, Robert Diehl considered Joanna to be entirely rehabilitated, though unfit for professional competition in the
sport she now pursued as a hobby.

Joanna alone knew that she could play the game of golf
from tee to green as well as she ever had. She found she
could compensate for the predicted residual weakness in
her left knee through judicious use of tape to restrict excess

motion, along with a minor adjustment of her swing. The great test of competition in exhausting four-day tournaments against top pros would have to wait, of course, until next spring.

That left a long fall and winter of conditioning and mental preparation. Though impatient to play again, Joanna was resigned and philosophical about the months ahead. One season, after all, was not too much to sacrifice to convalescence in the wake of so serious an injury.

The Black Woods design, meanwhile, had reached its final, strikingly original form. All eighteen holes were finished and clearly sketched in their definitive positions relative to the ocean and hills around the layout.

'What happens now?' Joanna had asked the night she presented Reid with the finished product.

'I'll submit it officially,' he told her. 'There will be meetings. You may be called in to explain a few things. These people will need to be reassured that this is a championship layout, and not just a crazy idea.' He shrugged. 'But I'll do whatever arm-twisting is necessary, even though it may take time. You've done your part. The design is perfect, unbeatable. When it's all over, there'll be a contract, and of course a fee—which will make up for some of the tournaments you've missed this summer. Then you'll relax until you get your next commission.'

His dark eyes bore the look of intent, brooding concentration she had often noticed when he scanned the design or talked about it. She realised that his own contribution to its future might involve subtleties of business acumen, perhaps of persuasion and compromise, whose importance he preferred not to mention.

Joanna's eventful and challenging summer in Beaufort had served its productive purpose. After the trauma of the accident, which left her feeling broken and hopeless, the process of healing had joined the joy of creative inspiration in repairing her physically and mentally.

Clearly the moment was at hand for a confident return to Sarasota, where school would soon begin for Tina and a variety of business obligations awaited her mother. There were dealings with her agent, her insurance company, and the staff at Nakoma Springs to take care of, along with taxes and correspondence and a score of other duties which had kept Karen Gillespie from her novels and her boyfriend far too long.

The shimmering summer seascape of Beaufort County, with its Golden Islands and cloudless skies, must now take its place among the many images in Joanna's crowded memory. There was no reason to stay here any longer.

She should have been delighted to get on with her independent future after so lengthy a hiatus, but instead she was torn by emotions more painful than anything she had experienced in the darkest hours after her accident.

It seemed that she and Tina had barely had time to accustom themselves to the routine of life in Reid's house before it was hurtling towards its end. And a peaceful, sweet routine it had been, its daily rhythm punctuated by Joanna's spartan exercise and Tina's outings with Katie when Reid was away on business. The two girls walked the nearby lawns and pastures together or swam at the beach within sight of Virginia's kitchen window. Occasionally Joanna would look beyond the bridle path at the end of the lawn and see them crabbing together in the sand, their pails by their sides.

As luck would have it, Tina was sufficiently precocious to relate easily to her older playmate, though Katie's maternal instincts, without an outlet at home, might well have cemented the friendship in any case. Her father having died years ago, it fell to Katie to send her older brothers off to their summer jobs and close the house before coming 'the back way' to Reid's kitchen door. Joanna soon discovered herself to be high in the pantheon of the young girl's adored heroines, and had to nudge her gently into accepting her as Tina's mother and a merely human adult.

The hot summer days had passed in gentle uniformity, their customary schedules broken occasionally by special events which hung pleasantly in Joanna's memory. There was the night Reid took everyone to see a revival showing of *Gone with the Wind*, which he knew to be Tina's favourite movie. And there was the day Joanna had taken her bicycle to meet Reid and Tina for a picnic lunch at one of the crossroads linking the bike trail and bridle paths. The three had eaten their sandwiches under the bored eyes of the tethered horses, much to Tina's delight.

But most of all there was the warm familiarity of life together. Reid, more than ever a figure of almost paternal dependability in Tina's eyes, presided over the background of her adventurous world while not hesitating to discipline her on the rare occasions when her little transgressions merited it.

He read with her every night, and came to know the entire range of authors who absorbed her imagination. He was privy to her observations about her teachers and friends, and knew her intention to become an author of children's books when she grew up.

When Joanna watched them together she felt the trust and mutual respect that underlay the interplay of their personalities. Tina's implicit confidence in Reid shone in her manifest contentment as she sat on his lap, held his hands or toyed with the buttons on his shirt.

But it was impossible for Joanna to contemplate their closeness dispassionately, as though she herself were not involved in it. For her fantasy of life as a family with Reid, which had so tantalised and disturbed her when their summer together was just beginning, now seemed a reality that was all the more magical for remaining unseen by the outside world.

Indeed, if Tina experienced a daughter's secure sense of belonging with Reid, then Joanna herself possessed the precious essence of life as his wife.

Their opportunities for privacy were rare—a stolen afternoon in Charleston, an evening in Atlanta after Joanna had consulted a sports kinesiologist there—but somehow they sufficed, along with the occasional moment at home when she could let her feelings show in the green eyes that rested on Reid's face or in the hand that touched his own.

Denied a wife's free access to her husband's caresses, denied even the little hugs and casual kisses which are the public signs of a young couple's affection, Joanna nevertheless felt joined to Reid by a bond whose mysterious power exceeded anything she had imagined possible in her wildest dreams about marriage.

Perhaps, she mused, it was the very difficulty of this shadowed communion with Reid that made its accomplishment so special. When they were together in Tina's company, or with Katie and Virginia, they bestowed their tenderness on each other in a language so covert, so indecipherable to anyone but themselves, that Joanna felt its subtle essence, light as a whisper, like a charm that penetrated with almost occult difficulty to her heart.

She already knew Reid's perfect male limbs, the variety of his scent, the salty taste of him on her lips. Now she knew the complex eloquence of his silence, and the gentle support he communicated through the most offhand of words and glances.

In his palpations of her knee, a scarcely necessary precaution nowadays, there was a calm memory of the intimacy he had shared with her silken skin. His way of holding a chair for her, or of brushing a windblown strand of

hair from her cheek, was no less redolent of the quiet
knowledge they could not but hide from those around them.

For her part, Joanna found herself shaken by a thousand
inner thrills when she reflected that the hands that grazed
her hair, her shoulders or her knee in these everyday moments, knew every inch of her, and had set her every sinew
aflame in their passage, not so long ago.

She could still see herself, naked and suffused with desire, reflected in the tawny eyes that smiled down upon her
now. And she saw Reid's body in a new light, as flesh
dedicated to her own and united with it—for underneath
his open collar she knew the clean hard line of his pecto-
rals, the lean descent of muscle under his chest to his stomach, where crisp hair descended in a little whirlwind shape
towards the lithe sinews beneath his waist.

Without shame she had known those beautiful contours
of pure virility, caressed and coveted them as though they
belonged to her. And Reid, who knew where she was damaged and hurt and vulnerable, who had seen her at her
worst, Reid had accepted her and wanted her. As he gave
her ecstasies of unbelievable fulfilment, his embrace was
tender and knowing, as though she were indeed his, had
always been and would always be his own.

So it was with private exultation that she felt herself
enfolded by a warmth which was all around her every day,
as though she were truly married. Alone in her bed at night,
she seemed to nestle still in Reid's arms.

It was bewitching, that private tryst conceived in silence
and yet so real, consummated in plain sight and yet unseen
by anyone. But Joanna could know its joys only at the price
of its inevitable pain. For neither she nor Reid had spoken
of love, or even of the future. The understanding they
shared was in another dimension—intimate, no doubt, romantic and even heroic, but necessarily doomed.

Acutely aware that she had made the first move towards

him when she could cope with her desire no longer, Joanna could not bring herself to lay the slightest claim to Reid. He was a man who had already conquered his freedom at a cost and a risk known only to himself, and she knew his life was his own.

Joanna was both a harsh realist and a dreamer. She was no stranger to impermanence and insecurity, and could accept them as facts of life. Her struggles in an often unfair world had accustomed her to coping with disappointments, losing illusions, and standing on her own two feet. But she also retained traces of belief in the gentility and propriety handed down from her Southern forebears by Paul and Ellen Lake.

In her mind, love and marriage did not overtake one in the dizzy manner of her affair with Reid Armstrong. Women did not throw themselves at men the way she had done. No, love and marriage had a more stately and traditional tempo and mood, which included hesitant probings, sincere statements of frank admiration, promises made and kept.

Reid was the opposite of these things. He respected no tradition and accepted no status quo. He lived without strings, and believed in nothing but his own initiative.

'I'm a businessman,' he had told her often enough. 'I pursue my own advantage. If it dovetails with someone else's, we both come out ahead.'

From the beginning he had made clear that his relationship with Joanna was a business association based on mutual self-interest. His obvious respect and esteem for her did not change that fact.

And now, consenting adults, they had indulged in a physical involvement which had no meaning and no importance. Having initiated it herself, Joanna could hardly harbour any illusions about it.

Reid was far from the marrying kind. Having accepted

him thus, she knew both the peace and the despair of her intimacy with him. She welcomed what she had of him—his humour, his friendship, and her memories—and forced herself to see in his calm silence not only the obvious understanding that their relationship involved no commitment and no permanence, but also his awareness that she considered him free and made no claim on him.

And perhaps, she told herself, perhaps the quiet tenderness in his dark eyes bespoke his gratitude for her renunciation.

She hoped so. She wanted to be strong for him, and to justify his confidence in her. Thus he would never know what her courage would never reveal: that he had changed her life for good in this brief summer. His smiling image had penetrated to the most private corners of her past and future, and could no more be dislodged than her soul could be torn from her body.

She loved Reid, and she would always love him.

Now, at last, he had lost his Cheshire Cat ambiguity and coincided with himself—in her woman's heart, where he belonged and would forever remain. And Joanna, true to his promise and his commitment, had healed and grown vibrant and supple again—but her new persona was like a vine twined around his hard limbs. It was through him that she had come to herself, healthy and strong and exultantly full of her need for him.

And now, because she must use that precious strength to let him go, to give up the one support that made her feel like a whole woman again—now, suddenly, she did not feel whole.

With a shrug that concealed a breaking heart, she resolved to do what was necessary and inevitable.

School would begin in Sarasota during the last week of August. In the reluctant way that visitors and vacationers have, Joanna and Tina scanned the calendar and chose a date for their departure. From that moment on life could no longer go on as before. It was sadder and less carefree, for it was under the shadow of its end. One felt one was going through the motions of an existence that had seemed so real and solid only days before. The beaches, trees and pastures, and even the horses, had a halo of impermanence about them.

Now they must leave this beautiful, impersonal house where Reid had come to rest in the midst of his life's peregrinations three years ago, this house he hardly considered his own. And a terrible thought told Joanna that he, too, might be leaving it soon, selling it when it ceased to amuse or profit him, and moving forward into a future as inscrutable as his past, a future far from this time and place.

So that the house, handsomely anonymous, would be like those holiday cottages and resorts whose empty rooms contained the ghosts of people who had met and shared romance there during the charmed days of a long-ago summer that had seemed endless until it had been inevitably cut short by time.

And here she would leave a part of herself that she could never regain.

In the last days before their departure Reid was bright and humorous as ever, whether through bravery or simple tact Joanna could not tell.

'Just think,' he told Tina, 'you'll be a fourth-grader now. The younger kids will be scared to death of you. How do you reconcile yourself to being an Embarrass-King yourself?'

'Oh, I can reconcile myself,' said Tina, snapping up the adult word with ease. 'Because Suzanne will be with me, and if Suzanne can be a fourth-grader, anyone can.'

'What about Lynn and Allie and Abbas?' he asked.

'Well, they'll be there, too. But I'm just sure that Suzanne will be in the same class and reading group with me,' she explained, articulating her fond hope as though it were a certainty.

Joanna's heart was breaking as she watched them together. Tina had never had a father. The only male presence in her life had been Carl Jaeger, a distant grandfatherly figure who sent her birthday cards and spoke to her on the phone at Christmas. With uncomplaining courage she had lived as a child of divorce. Joanna had suffered to see her spend afternoons and nights with friends who had fathers, and had even taken miserable comfort from the fact that, with the divorce rate as high as it was, Tina knew more than a few children in the same predicament as she, and so could feel less alone.

But Tina had taken to Reid so naturally and beautifully, planting her roots in the rich soil of his friendship. And now this gift that had been held out was to be taken away. It was a cruel thing for her little heart to bear.

They must both leave the tall, vital man who had presided over their summer with such blithe assurance. And each, in her own way, must go on living as though he had never crossed her path. But there was no turning back the clock, no sewing the heart shut, no erasing the memory of him from the mind and soul.

The morning of their departure dawned bright and still. Over a quiet breakfast Reid spread his cheerful humour.

'Here,' he said, placing wrapped packages in front of both of them. 'I want you two to have something to remember me by.'

Tina unwrapped her box to find a cuddly teddy bear whose golden fur would set it apart from any other in the collection Reid had often heard her describe.

'I think I'll call her Sandy,' she said, instantly taming the new acquisition and determining its sex.

'Go on,' Reid pointed to the small box before Joanna.

Inside it was a tiny gold charm on a chain, in the shape of the slogan '#1'.

'Thank you, Reid,' she said, barely able to return his wry gaze.

'Remember, now,' he said, 'this is part of our agreement. I told you I'd see to it you came out of this mess better than new—and I always mean what I say. You won't really be through with me until you're a winner on that L.P.G.A. tour. Unless you get out there and bring home the first-place money you deserve, you'll have me to answer to. Is that understood?'

With the kindest smile she had ever seen, he put the charm around her neck. Fighting back her tears of joy and anguish, she nodded her obedience to his warning. She knew she would happily lose a thousand tournaments if it meant he would come back to her.

But he would not come back. The goodbye in his eyes was real, and there was no point in pretending she had not seen it.

So she clung to the little charm as a final sign of his admiration, forcing herself to banish the forlorn hope that it might mean something more. As his warm hands brushed her shoulders she resolved for the last time to accept what she had of him, even if her sacrifice meant permanent exile from her very self.

Moments later they were outside in the driveway beside the new car Karen had left for them to bring home. In the back were Joanna's clubs, their suitcases, and a large bag containing the books Tina had brought with her or acquired this summer.

'You'll take care of your mom for me, won't you?' asked Reid, sweeping Tina high in his arms for a last hug before he put her down. Nodding her yes, she kissed his cheek.

Then it was Joanna's turn. His arms encircled her back

with quick, friendly warmth. Hesitantly she returned his embrace, not daring to show her emotions in front of Tina. Her slender hands lingered for a split second on the hard flesh beneath his shoulders, alive with a message too frail to reach its destination, for time had run out.

Torn by the impotence of wanting to tell him so much, and knowing she could not, must not, she met his eyes with a last smile, then turned away.

The new station wagon purred softly as she edged it along the drive leading down to the road. The distant beach lay vacant beyond the bridle paths at the base of the lawn. A hushed repose seemed to have descended upon the sea and sky.

A sudden impulse made Joanna look into the rear-view mirror before turning on to the roadway. She saw Reid standing before the house, his arms at his sides, watching her recede from him perhaps for ever.

Unable to bear the sight for more than an instant, she looked quickly back to the empty road spreading before her. But as she did so she caught a glimpse of Tina crying quietly into the fur of her new teddy bear.

Pridefully the little girl turned away to look out the side window, wiping at her eyes with a small hand as she avoided her mother's gaze.

with her about the baby. When, if ever, he had promised to call? While there was news, she reflected, but even the most scrupulously busy of writers and lecturers would have dinner together, or some activities.

She cut off her speculations. The vanity of imputation.

Any thought she might possibly direct at Reid would only make things worse, it inevitably would not help her. Forcing to regularly expect that his futile attempts

CHAPTER NINE

As September approached it seemed that survival from day to day was all that counted. The fragile ray of hope which persisted under the banality of the hours was mentioned neither by Joanna nor Tina.

Their attractive but modest ranch home on its quiet street seemed singularly dull after Reid's palatial oceanview house. But its familiarity was comforting.

Tina went about her business with the mute endurance of childhood. The only sign that something was wrong was her failure to call Suzanne. Apparently unconcerned to anticipate fourth grade under her new teacher, she closeted herself with her dolls and books, or moped sluggishly about the house. Joanna could only hope that the natural resiliency of her age would see her through.

But they were both changed; there was no denying it. Joanna could not suppress the feeling that her time with Reid had been a strange dream, begun by the brutal accident and ended in the bitter-sweet confusion of summer's end.

But if it was a dream, she reflected, it had left more than its share of palpable scars in its wake. For so many years she had taken pains to depend only on herself. Now she knew the awful strangeness of needing and wanting a person who was no longer there. The void inside her could not be filled or ignored, and she knew it was haunting Tina as well.

She still had her knowledge that Reid would be in touch

with her about the Black Woods design. He had promised to call or write when there was news. One day soon she might actually see him, if only on business. Perhaps they would have dinner together, or spend an evening...

She cut off her girlish hopes with a shrug of impatience. Any illusions she might harbour about Reid Armstrong could only make things worse at this already difficult time in her life. Forcibly reminding herself that his gentle goodbye in Beaufort had signified nothing more than a friend's affection, and perhaps the discomfiture of a sometime lover who feared her dependence on him, she put him firmly behind her.

There was nothing to do now but get Tina ready for school and endure the winter. Joanna enrolled at a nearby Nautilus centre, began practising her golf, and did her best to take an interest in her agent's suggestions for her immediate future.

She knew she must wait until next spring to find out whether she had a future at all in her profession.

So long to wait for news that might be bad...

One day she was in Sarasota shopping with Tina for school clothes. In a half-hearted effort to cheer the child up she had brought her to a favourite fast food restaurant for lunch. They were ready to leave when an oddly familiar voice addressed her.

'Hello, Joanna.'

Though she knew the face looking down at her, she could not place it at first. Its elegant lines were a bit harder than she recalled. Harder and heavier...

Then it hit her.

It was Jack—Jack Templeton.

She nearly laughed to think she had not recognised him. He was her ex-husband and the father of the child who now sat beside her, toying with an uneaten French fry.

The child who had never known him.

'Tina,' she said, fumbling in her purse, 'would you take these quarters and see if you can win something for yourself back there?'

With a curious glance at the stranger Tina took the coins and moved towards the video arcade adjacent to the dining room.

'Sit down,' invited Joanna, clearing away the loose wrappers on the table top. 'I'm sorry it's such a mess.'

'Just for a minute,' he smiled. 'I'm on my way to a meeting, but I noticed you and thought I'd say hello.' There was something unpleasant in his demeanour as he sat down before her. In his hand was a rolled-up magazine. 'I'd heard about your injury, but I saw a picture of you on the golf course in the sports pages the other day. I hope you're feeling better.'

She nodded vague assent.

'Did you meet Reid on the golf course?' he asked abruptly.

Taken aback, she recalled that the photo of her with Reid on the eighteenth green at Bayside Links had been sold to a wire service, and had appeared in newspapers all over the country. If Jack had recognised Reid, that could only mean he knew him already—as his casual first-name reference to him certainly suggested.

'Not exactly,' she said. 'I met him before my accident. We had a business deal together—some golf architecture.'

'Black Woods,' he nodded, leaning his heavy frame against the moulded plastic booth. 'Sorry about the way it turned out.'

Thunderstruck at his words, Joanna allowed her gaze to stray over the lines of his face and body. He wore an impeccably tailored suit, light and handsome, the jacket thrown over his arm in the noon heat. She could see that he had gained some weight around the middle, which accentuated the aura of prosperity about him. She had forgotten how tanned he was.

Though he still seemed powerfully muscled, her athlete's instinct told her he was out of condition. There was a trace of dissipation in him, but she lacked the practiced eye which might have linked it to alcohol.

'How did you know about that?' she asked, unable to conceal the candid vulnerability of her words.

'I'm on the board that's financing that club,' he explained. 'And on the course committee, in fact.' He twisted a bit uncomfortably on the narrow seat. 'Naturally I was disappointed for you, but I'm afraid the result wasn't unexpected.'

A sinking feeling came over her as she fought to return his gaze without flinching. She knew now that this meeting was no accident. Jack had come here in search of her. He intended to hurt her. Deep underneath her present fear she even thought she knew why. She recalled having heard somewhere that his second marriage had ended in divorce several years ago, without providing him with the son he must have desperately wanted.

In his slightly twisted features she saw the weak, angry man she had divorced. He must be lonely, and frustrated by his failure to give his father a grandson. He had seen Joanna's photo with Reid.

And now he had seen her with his own daughter, whom he had never met.

But these thoughts were a mere flash at the back of her mind, pushed aside by her certainty that he possessed a weapon capable of hurting her seriously. The triumph in his dark eyes left no doubt of it.

'I don't understand,' she said, screwing up her courage.

'Well,' he said, pretending to hesitate before discussing an unpleasant topic, 'I mean the committee's decision. Naturally, I voted for you, being prejudiced.' He laughed sheepishly. 'But it was all a pro forma exercise. You couldn't get such a revolutionary design past a bunch of fogies like that even if it was done by Jack Nicklaus—much less by a woman.'

He raised an eyebrow in feigned perplexity. 'Funny,' he added.

'What do you mean?' she asked.

'Well,' he said, 'when that vote took place—and of course the result was a foregone conclusion—I couldn't help wondering why Reid would encourage you to do such a crazy thing. After all, as the finder he knew what sort of group he was working for. That's pretty conservative golf country—I've been on several boards of directors in that area over the years, and I know.'

Joanna recalled that Jack's only real profession was inheriting his father's financial responsibilities. Jack was the custodian of the family name on various boards of directors, and as such oversaw the progress of his father's investments. It came down to the role of an enormously wealthy errand boy.

'The whole thing didn't make sense,' he concluded, avoiding her eyes. 'Unless...'

'Unless what?' she asked, anxious for him to show whatever weapon he possessed.

'Well,' he said uncomfortably, 'this is a bit embarrassing, Joanna. How well do you know Reid?'

'Not well,' she said, reminded by the chill of dread inside her that this lie had more than its grain of truth. In fact she did not know Reid well at all.

'He's a bit of a ladies' man,' said Jack, his smile of distaste distancing the observation from himself.

'I'm not sure I follow you,' she returned.

'Forgive me,' he went on implacably, 'but you're considered one of the beauties of the ladies' tour. Deservedly so, of course,' he smiled. 'If Reid took a liking to you, he wouldn't want to take no for an answer. I know him. He stops at nothing when he takes a shine to a girl. He'd take advantage of his finder's position to offer you that commission, even if he knew there was no chance in hell of your proposed design being accepted.'

'You're presuming a lot,' Joanna said tonelessly.

'It does sound crazy,' he drawled. 'I couldn't understand why you'd undertake such a hopeless thing. I thought I knew you to be levelheaded to a fault. But I told myself that Reid is after all a handsome devil. He can put quite a rush on a female.'

He glanced at her knee, which was lightly taped for the long shopping walk.

'Of course, I didn't consider your injury. It happened just about then, didn't it?'

His probing enraged her, for she alone knew the role Reid had played in controlling her convalescence after the accident he had had a share in causing. But she contented herself with a noncommittal nod.

'Well, it doesn't matter,' Jack sighed complacently. 'I do hope that, at the right time and in the right place, you can make a name for yourself as an architect. I suppose it was good experience, even though it seems cruel of Reid to have let you go through with finishing the whole damned thing.' He shrugged. 'Maybe he just wanted to be able to tell you he had submitted it, and to blame the result on the committee. Or,' he quirked an eyebrow, 'perhaps he thinks he can sell it somewhere else. He's not the sort of man to throw away an advantage. He'll kill two birds with one stone if he gets the chance.'

He was reaching into the inside pocket of his suit jacket.

'This might interest you,' he said, handing over a letter in a business envelope.

'What is it?' she asked.

'Just to show you how cheap these committee members

can be,' he shook his head in disapproval. 'They hired an expert to evaluate your design. But it was a hatchet job from the beginning. They picked a fellow who could be counted on to assassinate the design, once he knew it came from a woman.'

Joanna had to force back the tears welling up in her eyes as the curt letter opened before her.

'Clever, innovative,' the words flashed up at her, typed in large pica figures. 'Unfortunately,' the letter went on, 'the plan shows both inexperience and self-indulgence.'

'An unfair test of golf for both sexes,' she read at the bottom of the page.

The letter was signed by Carl Jaeger.

'Funny,' Jack was saying, 'I thought Carl was so high on you. But I guess some things are even bigger than friendship. Too bad,' he pursed his lips sadly.

Joanna could neither speak nor look at him. She fought to regain her composure.

'Well,' he went on, 'with Avery Follett as architect the course will be what they want: old-fashioned as they come.' He touched the magazine he had with him. 'It's already in the Announcements,' he said. 'I suppose Avery can't hurt the land too much.'

Avery Follett was a well-known golf course architect whose designs were predictable in their workmanlike, unimaginative contours. Joanna recalled bitterly that his courses were uniformly unfair to women players.

'When did all this take place?' she asked, cursing herself for revealing her ignorance. 'This meeting…'

'Oh,' he rolled his eyes towards the ceiling, 'it must be a couple of weeks now.'

Joanna stared straight at him. Though deeply hurt by his blows, she had recovered her sense of perspective.

'You came a long way to tell me all this,' she said. 'Have you said all you wanted to say?'

It was his turn to avoid her eyes. 'I thought someone should warn you,' he shrugged.

She took a deep breath.

'How are your family?' she asked.

'Oh, fine,' he replied uneasily. 'Mother and Dad are after me to get married again, but I tell them three strikes and you're out.'

A small hand on Joanna's wrist tore her intelligent eyes from his face. Tina was standing beside her.

'Mom,' came her decorous whisper, 'I'm bored. I don't like those games. Can I take my book outside and read?'

'No, honey,' Joanna smiled. 'We have to leave.' Unceremoniously she rose and took Tina's hand.

'Give your parents my best,' she said to Jack. 'Nice of you to say hello.'

She saw him turn away in sour triumph as she left the restaurant.

An hour later Joanna found herself alone on the beach looking out over Siesta Key to the Gulf of Mexico. On the sand beside her was a copy of *Golf Journal*, whose Announcements column indeed bore news of Avery Follett's nomination as course architect for the Black Woods Country Club in Beaufort, South Carolina.

Beside the magazine was a cardboard mailing tube. Inside it was Joanna's copy of the Black Woods design. She had addressed the label to Reid Armstrong before leaving home. Karen, seeing the look in her eyes, had quickly agreed to take care of Tina until her return.

She had stopped here to think before going on to the post office. But rational thought would not come. Isolated midday beachcombers and sailboats passed unseen before her eyes. Only anger and hurt swirled inside her head.

Like all cowards, Jack Templeton had waited to strike

until he knew his victim had no defence against his weapons.

'Perhaps it was good experience,' he had said in his triumph.

She shook her head bitterly. After all she had learned, all the joyful inspiration and imagination and excited effort she had poured into that design, she knew now it had never had a chance. Her strange and beautiful agony of self-discovery had been for nothing.

Her work had been done in a void created by Reid's treachery. And it had all happened because her accident immobilised her, taking her away from the summer tour and making her vulnerable to a proposal she would never have had the time or inclination to accept otherwise.

All because of the accident, which itself had resulted from Reid's arrogant invasion of her life, and from her own stupidity...

And now her life, so calm and controlled only three months ago, was in jagged pieces she would never be able to put together again.

Thanks to Reid.

'All for nothing,' she thought.

Rendered violently alert by pain and humiliation, her mind darted past all the scenes of her summer-long relationship with Reid, and focused without pity on damning images whose significance she had never questioned before.

I'm a great fan of yours, he had said that first afternoon after her loss to Peggy Byrne at Pine Trail. *But I'm here in a business capacity.*

The cleverest of liars, he had used his salesman's aggressiveness to get his foot in the door with her.

I'd like to ask you a historical question. How many of the championship golf courses in this country were designed by women?

She recalled the mocking way he had stood aside to let

her pass in the corridor beside the Pine Trail locker room, and his irritating claims that she was afraid of her own ambitions.

How would you like to be the first?

It would be a great step forward for women.

The tones of his cajolery haunted her, alternatively provocative and lulling.

I think you're even prettier in person that you are on television.

'My God,' she thought, reddening with shame, 'what a fool I was!'

Reid had tried every trick in the arsenal of a handsome, seductive man. He had appealed to her vanity, to her personal ambition, her creativity, her social consciousness as a representative of women in golf—and even to her anger. Where his other blandishments failed, his psychologising remarks about her loser's mentality had succeeded in getting under her skin.

And she had been attracted to him from the very beginning. Why deny it now? She could still remember her solitary bath the night after the Pine Trail tournament. His face, so devilishly handsome, had haunted her thoughts no less than his tempting proposal.

And he must have sensed her response. He must have known he had a chance with her. He was probably calculating the next move when the providential accident occurred, landing her in his clutches for an indefinite period. From that moment on he must have realised he had only to stay close to her, flatter her, keep her busy and, in his own subtle way, play hard to get. Prolonged contact with his physical charms would do the rest...

One advantage remained to make his ascendancy over her complete: the affection of her fatherless daughter. He had quickly covered that ground while Joanna lay unconscious in her hospital bed. By the time she had awakened to her pain and helplessness, Reid had made all his arrangements for her convalescence, and made his promises to Tina...

And now, three months later, that innocent little girl was preparing to enter fourth grade with a painful void inside her little heart. Thanks to Reid.

As though she had not suffered enough already in her young life.

Cold fury overtook Joanna now as the image of the exploiter crystallised around Reid in her mind. Perhaps Jack was right, she thought. Having set out to seduce her for his own amusement and satisfaction, Reid might well have been impressed by her talent as an architect, and might even now have vague plans to sell the design, or its principle, elsewhere.

He would kill two birds with one stone if the opportunity arose. That was his nature.

Now she understood the brooding look that had come over him whenever he studied the design. It was a look of calculation and cunning. Always aware of its inevitable rejection, he had to plan his own actions with that fact in mind.

When he could avoid submitting the design no longer, he had done so. It had been refused, of course. He had instinctively avoided telling her the truth about its fate until he could think of a way to let her down easily, to convince her that he was not responsible for the committee's decision, that all was not lost...

So that he could keep her on a string, keep her happy, and perhaps condescend to dally with her when his business took him to Florida or when he felt bored or lonely...

For he certainly did not have to worry about her attachment to him. Had she not thrown herself at him shamelessly the night he took her out to dinner after their round of golf? The mad pitch of desire in her soft limbs must have been pathetically obvious to him. As was the girlish, romantic cast in her eyes as her sidelong glances betrayed her dependence during those last weeks of the summer.

And at this very moment he was probably busy somewhere with someone else, his thoughts turning occasionally to Joanna Lake with musing concern. He must take care of her somehow, and keep her available while making sure that her starry-eyed possessiveness did not become a problem.

I'm a businessman. I always pursue my own advantage.

Yet, as she touched the gold charm around her neck, her eyes on the mailing tube beside her, it was not Reid that she blamed for the cloud of misery that had descended on her life. It was herself.

Thanks to her own flawed instincts where the opposite sex was concerned, her beautiful daughter had been born of a doomed, futile marriage, and scarred by a fatherless childhood. And now the child had been hurt yet again, her hopes raised and dashed, thanks to her mother's irresponsible and idiotic behaviour.

With a deep breath Joanna brought her thoughts under control. What mattered now was not Reid. He was out of her life. She must decide what to do.

She would earn nothing from the design she had spent the summer working on—that was obvious. She had won no money this season, after the Southern Invitation. She had bills to pay, and precious little income to pay them with. Should she sit on her hands, dry her tears, and count her pennies all winter while waiting for the uncertainty about her profession to be ended when next year's tour began? Should she try for the hundredth time to put her manifold failures behind her, and look prayerfully to the future for better luck?

The answer came to her as she stood up, dusting the sand from her skirt. She hurried to the post office. After a moment's thought she took the '#1' charm from around her neck, threw it in the tube with the design, and mailed it.

Then she went to the nearest pay phone, gave the long-distance operator her credit card number and her caddie's phone number in Arkansas.

'Robbie,' she said, grateful to hear the mountain twang of his familiar voice, 'are you working for anyone next week?'

'No, Joanna. Just building a porch with my brother.'

'Can you meet me in Ithaca on Sunday?' she asked. 'The Tournament of Champions will be held there next week, and I'm eligible to play without qualifying. Take your motorcycle, or a plane if you want. We're going to play that tournament.'

Hiding whatever perplexity he might feel, Robbie agreed without comment, and Joanna hung up the phone with a deep sigh.

In her present mood the sole course of action open to her was obvious. She had made an irremediable mess out of her personal life, and could expect no one to come to her rescue. The future depended on her own initiative, which had been reduced to practically nothing by events she could not control and people she had naïvely thought she could trust.

But she could still swing a golf club. No one could do that for her, or stop her from doing it if she chose to.

The odds were against her, and she knew it. But fourteen years of training and experience would guide her when she faced this most difficult of tests.

Determinedly she walked towards the lot where her car was parked. She was alone now, and ready to act alone on her own behalf. Her solitude would have been almost comforting had it not been for one persistent thought which hammered underneath her resolve, though she dared not put it into words.

If Reid had lied about the Black Woods design, perhaps he had also lied when he said she would play golf again.

CHAPTER TEN

SHE was not surprised when the doorbell rang the night before her flight to Syracuse.

She had just put Tina to bed. After a glance into her room she went through the kitchen and opened the side door.

In the moonlight Reid stood before her.

'What are you doing here?' she asked, unafraid to unlatch the door so she could see him clearly. The involuntary tremor in her stomach irked her, for she would not allow herself to be afraid of him. She was ready for him, and had been for hours and days.

'I think you know that,' he said. 'You haven't answered my calls, and I'm sick of talking to Karen when it's you I want. So I came.' His eyes gleamed in the moonlight. 'I got your little package,' he added.

After a moment's hesitation Joanna slipped through the door and closed it behind her. She intended to handle him out here and get rid of him. Tina would never know he had been here.

The half-moon spread silvery light over the lawn and flower beds. Crickets added their thrum to the soft stirring of leaves in the breeze.

'Well,' he said, 'I'm waiting. What happened to make you send me the design that way?'

For an angry instant she contemplated him. His severity was clearly a ruse designed to keep her attention. He was a salesman, a wheeler-dealer who hated to take no for an answer. He would do anything in his power to retain some sort of influence over her. The only sure way to defeat him was the strategy one used with all salesmen: to simply refuse to argue with him.

'Reid,' she said, mastering her emotion with difficulty, 'listen to me. When I've finished you can say whatever you wish to say, and then I want you out of here. I know the design was rejected. I know the commission has gone to Avery Follett. I know what you did in Beaufort, and,' she sighed, 'I know why. As far as I'm concerned, our business together is finished. If you have any sense of pride, you'll walk away from here.' She thought for a moment. 'That's all,' she concluded.

Despite herself she recoiled an inch as the shadow of his tall form covered her in the moonlight. His eyes seemed to bore into her, aroused and flashing.

'You saw that little item in the *Journal* about Follett, didn't you?' he asked. 'What did you do? Put two and two together?'

She shook her head, not wanting to join in the dialogue he wanted to initiate. She knew he would argue anything, deny anything, say anything, just to keep her talking.

'The details aren't important,' she said curtly.

'You never learn,' he sighed. 'I've told you and told you to leave the business end of this whole deal to me. I'm a professional at this, as you are on the golf course. I don't know who's been putting ideas into your head...'

'Reid,' she cut him off, 'why do you go on? Why don't you just leave? Why don't you leave me alone?'

'Because,' he said, staring down at her from his terrible height, 'for one reason, I want to peel the scales from your eyes. And for another, I have a business relationship with you that is too valuable to drop.'

'No,' she nodded, revolted to think of the male needs he undoubtedly had in mind along with his financial plans,

'I'm sure you don't want to drop it.' She folded her arms. 'But my word is final. Keep the design. Do whatever you want with it. Throw it in your garbage can in Beaufort if you want. Paper your bathroom with it—I won't have anything more to do with it!'

There was perplexity in his gaze, as well as suspicion— or the pretence of it. Joanna told herself she must take none of his words or gestures at face value. In two minutes Reid would be gone, having feigned anger or hurt or who knew what before he finally gave up. She must merely survive those two minutes.

'Listen to me,' he said, 'before you jump to conclusions. I didn't tell you about the Follett business for two reasons. In the first place, it wasn't important. In the second place, I didn't want to worry you about it when you had other things on your mind.'

'Not important!' cried Joanna despite her resolve. 'It seems to me it was a yes or no situation. The answer was no. Someone else got the job, Reid. What else is there to say? Have you no honesty?'

'Your job,' he persisted, 'was to conceive the design. Mine was to see it through with the committee. Why don't you let me do it?'

His words amazed her. He would say anything to cloud the issue.

'Do with it what you wish,' she said. 'But leave me. Please. Now.'

'Don't turn away from me,' he warned, his large hand closing around her arm in a grip which was not without its hesitancy, as though he were afraid to jerk her backward for fear of hurting her injured body.

Yet there was infinite urgency under that softness, and she was shocked to feel sensual flares of responses quickening inside her as he held her motionless in the cool night air.

'I need to know,' came his deep murmur, 'that you're all right.'

'That's wonderful!' She whirled in his grasp, wrenching her arm. 'Well, don't worry your head about it, Reid. You put me up, helped me train, and kept me busy all summer—in more ways than one. I owe you a debt of gratitude. But all good things must come to an end.'

'What's that supposed to mean?' he asked.

'You only did what came naturally to you.' The cruel words sprang from her lips with a harsh eloquence that surprised her. 'You did what your instincts told you to do. Well, that can cut both ways!'

He stared at her, genuine surprise vying with the anger in his eyes.

'You're fond of calling yourself a businessman,' she told him, seeing that she had hurt him. 'You got what you wanted. And I'm back on my feet now. Our relationship was mutually beneficial, and now it's over. Why beat a dead horse with your lies?'

'Lies?' Reid's hands closed around her arms. 'So you don't believe me.'

Her flowing blonde hair outlined by the moon, she shook her head, refusing to look at him.

'I wonder when I've ever given you occasion to doubt my word,' he said. 'I'm not going to let you get away with this.'

'That's rich!' she said bitterly. 'How can a person who's nothing to me decide that he's not going to let me get away with something? You're out of my life. The next time you see me, if ever, will be on television.'

'And you'll have me to thank for that, in part,' he said.

'I have you to thank for the fact that I was injured in the first place!' Joanna spat back, losing control of herself. 'You knew it all along—you practically said it yourself.

It's thanks to you that I may never compete again. Thanks to you, Reid. Now haven't you done enough?'

She knew her cruel shaft had struck home. An enormous rage seemed to seize him, more at himself for having armed her thus against him, than at her for plunging the dagger.

'So that's how it is, then,' he grated. His voice was low, menacing.

'Yes,' she said, beside herself with anger and guilt. 'Unless you'd like to get Tina out here and see what she has to say. She might be willing to take your side. She doesn't know you, after all, as I do. You've done a great job of winning her confidence. She has no reason to think badly of you, does she?'

Joanna felt a horrid escalation of emotion in the soft night air between them, more and more violent, and she had the awful presentiment that everything was about to come out, including the feeling she could not banish in herself whatever her pain, the feeling that continued to fuel and spark her very cruelty, binding her to him despite herself, making her want to hurt him as he had hurt her, so that he could not forgive her or forget her, ever, ever.

And Reid must have sensed what was truly behind her slashing, furious words, for he silenced her with a kiss so intimate, so brutal and penetrating that she felt her whole body tense in an unforeseen spasm of excitement against the maddening hardness, the electric virility of him.

Pinioned by his mouth no less than by the iron grip of his long arms, she gasped in ecstatic consternation to feel her squirming, twisting limbs forced closer and closer to him. Already their struggles were alive with a lithe and slippery animal pleasure she could not quell. He was coaxing it from her, that soft rhythm of female yielding, and she could not think how to stop him.

A mad paroxysm of anger and delight shook her all at

once, deep and uncontrollable, and she could only shudder in his arms, limp and defenceless and unforgiving.

At last he released her, gentle in his triumph.

'So,' he said, 'we both had our fun. Is that it? We passed the time together. And that was all it meant to you.' His low voice was cruel, painful in its intensity.

'Yes,' she said, to silence him, to banish him. 'Yes, that's what it meant.'

A moment later she found herself alone in the shadows. The half-moon was rising fast, spreading pale rays across the sky. She heard the distant throb of a motor, the thump of a big car leaping into gear.

Then nothing.

Nothing. The word was fearsome, sending creeping tendrils of emptiness through all the most vulnerable corners of her soul.

A first sob shook her in her solitude. A pang of weakness shot over her knee as she sank to the cool grass. She knelt there, her tears flowing unchecked, in the darkness outside the house where her daughter slept.

And now it seemed that the whole world had receded from her, leaving her alone here in the darkness and the silence, with no companion other than the ironic, romantic moon, rearing above her like a mocking symbol of her final failure in love.

For what seemed an eternity she sat alone, her hurt leg extended beside her. Her hands touched the tender grass under the magnolia tree. She contemplated the sweet indifference of the balmy night, hovering over her like an old acquaintance, a mute witness.

She knew Reid would not return. She had pushed him too far, hurt him as he richly deserved to be hurt. Now he was gone, having no doubt understood in his cold heart that she was not buying what he was selling. He had turned tail and gone, his sharp eye in search of greener pastures.

And taken her heart with him.

With a sigh Joanna raised herself to her feet and moved through the night towards the screen door. It closed quietly upon her slender form.

CHAPTER ELEVEN

CHAPTER ELEVEN

'LADIES and gentlemen, your attention, please.' The announcer's voice resounded among the gallery massed around the first tee at Maple Hills Golf Course. 'Our next threesome will include Sandra Noble, from Rochester, New York…'

Appreciative applause greeted the attractive young professional, who had won her first tournament only two weeks ago, and thus qualified for today's event.

'Yvonne Shelby, from Canton, Ohio…'

The popular veteran of ten successful pro seasons smiled her acknowledgment of the crowd's applause.

'And Joanna Lake, from Sarasota, Florida.'

A small ovation erupted, tight with suppressed emotion, as Joanna tipped her cap to the gallery. The TV cameras zoomed pitilessly to her left knee, which had been taped by Robbie this morning.

'This is a dramatic and touching moment for Joanna's many fans,' the network commentator murmured. 'Some observers have questioned her decision to play this week. She has not, of course, won a tour event this year. But the official rules of the Tournament of Champions allow the holder of the previous year's Vare Trophy to compete regardless of whether she has won in the last twelve months. Joanna holds that trophy, as she has tree times in the last seven years, and so she has decided to play. But the primary concern here today is her physical condition. We may be seeing the last hurrah in a great career, and there's the risk of permanent injury if that left knee is subjected to too much stress. There are those who think Joanna should have retired immediately after her tragic accident. But here she is.'

No one gave Joanna a chance in the tournament, and she knew it. Her participation was a human interest story, spiced by the familiarity of her lovely face and figure and the visible signs of her injury. The press was already making hay out of what it saw as her mad eleventh-hour attempt to salvage a wrecked career.

'What makes you think the knee is ready?' one of the reporters had asked after her practice round on Monday.

'I think it's ready,' she had replied simply.

Then it had been Ron Lieber's turn.

'How do you expect to beat a field like this, all tournament winners, coming off an injury like yours?' Clearly he was irritated to see her competing at all, since he had announced her retirement in his column a month before.

'I'll do my best,' Joanna smiled noncommittally.

Charlie Sullivan, the oldest and most respected member of the group, added his question.

'Since her victory over you at Pine Trail, Peggy Byrne has won the Salem Classic and finished second three times. She seems to be at the top of her game right now, and this event undoubtedly represents her last chance this season to win her fiftieth tournament. I think it would be safe to say she wants this one badly. It will be awfully hard to beat her, won't it?'

'You're telling me,' nodded Joanna, her candour bringing appreciative laughter from the journalists.

Oddly enough, it was Peggy herself who had offered something more than the wanly sympathetic words of encouragement Joanna had been hearing from fans and fellow professionals all week.

'Don't let them get you down, Jo,' she had said in the

locker room, her plump hands on Joanna's shoulders. 'They had me dead and buried when my kidneys gave out, but I didn't give up. And you won't either. I know what you're made of. You're no loser, and you're no quitter.'

The sincerity in the older woman's sparkling eyes was as real as Joanna's certainty that she would give no quarter on the golf course. Peggy was a battler and a great sportswoman.

But her encouragement could not wipe out Joanna's fear that she was indeed taking a desperate chance by playing this week instead of resting through the winter. She felt tender and wounded inside. There was no guarantee that the stress of a four-day tournament in the company of the tour's very best players would not force her to push herself too hard.

Even the choice of golf course was anything but propitious, she reflected. Maple Hills had always been bad luck for her. She had been in contention in at least half a dozen tournaments here over the years, and had been defeated each time by the course's great length, its famous, unpredictable wind, or her own poor play in crucial situations.

Somehow she always found herself plagued by nagging little injuries such as backaches, sore wrists or cramped legs when she played here. Once she had even come close to being struck by lightning when a sudden storm interrupted her round.

Maple Hills was not Joanna's favourite course. Yet its long fairways, lined by tall trees in the hills high above Cayuga Lake, were handsome to look at and made an intriguing challenge. She enjoyed passing Cornell University's beautiful campus on the way from her hotel, and found the changeable summer weather of western New York a bracing background for competition.

Her three practice rounds with Robbie confirmed that the course was as straightforwardly difficult as ever. Only drives and fairway shots of extreme accuracy could produce birdie possibilities on its long par fours. The even longer par fives and short, heavily wooded par threes were less difficult, but if the dreaded wind became a factor, as it always seemed to at least one day of every tournament here, every hole became a formidable enigma.

The brisk walk over the hilly terrain had tired Joanna's knee considerably, and she had had to rest it in an elevated position every night. She had shown Robbie how to tape it so as to offer her a modicum of support during play, but she felt compelled to give it copious ice massages after every round.

Meanwhile she did elaborate stretching exercises for her back, legs, neck, wrists and fingers. She ate lean meats and fish, baked potatoes and vegetables without butter, apples and melons, and drank only skim milk and fruit juice, eschewing the black coffee she adored. Her mental exercises were as disciplined as her physical efforts. She worked on her concentration and prepared herself for the inevitable ordeal of managing her game and the golf course under stressful conditions.

There was weakness in her knee—of that there could be no possible doubt. The trauma to her collateral ligaments and cartilage had left its mark. It could not incapacitate her, but, in Dr Diehl's baleful phrase, it threatened to damage her confidence in the knee, and thus to take the competitive edge off her play.

If she let it.

That was the challenge, she decided as she played her practice rounds and worked out on the driving range and putting green. She must compensate for the weakness in her knee. But at the same time she must put her trust in it, and believe that it would support her.

Thus she must avoid hitting down at the ball, trying to scoop it off the ground or guide it upward. She must swing away smoothly, her natural rhythm unhampered by fear or pain. But at the instant of follow-through, when her body's turn twisted the left knee outward, she must make a minimal adjustment in her mechanics so as to take some of the pressure off the injured joint.

If she succeeded she would hit straight and play effectively, although she would lose a small amount of distance on her drives and fairway woods.

If she failed, her journey here would have been for nothing, and the premature end of her career would be staring her in the face.

She knew the odds were against her, for she had not had time to refine the thousand little subtleties of tempo, timing and equilibrium that made up her deservedly famous style as an athlete. Her body was not in optimum condition, and she lacked the sharp competitive instincts her rivals had honed over the long season which was now reaching its peak.

But inside her a cold concentration, born of anger and loneliness and hurt, told her she would not give in. She was alone and vulnerable, but darkly determined to use every trick she had learned as a professional.

Initiative was hers. No one could take that away from her. Permanently scarred she might be by injury and by her own mistakes, but now she was where she belonged: on her own and in charge of her destiny.

The threesome in the fairway had moved out of range. The gallery on the first tee watched in silence as Sandra Noble teed up her ball and stood at address. Applause followed her compact, efficient swing.

The butterflies in Joanna's stomach were uncontrollable as Yvonne Shelby took her turn. The quiet veteran sent a picture-perfect drive down the fairway and picked up her tee with a nod to her fans.

Joanna's moment had come. She could feel the affection of her many supporters filter through the massed galleries, the press and the network cameras. But even more, as she swung her driver in a soft arc over the grass, shifting her weight gently from one leg to the other, she could feel resignation and incredulity in the millions of eyes focused on her.

She was not the woman whose consistency had amazed the golf world for seven years. They all knew it. Tina and Karen knew it, too, though they had accepted Joanna's decision without protest.

She was not whole, and everyone could see it.

And somewhere the man who had had a hand in the event that had crushed her body might well be watching her. The man she would never see again, but who had taken a piece of her heart with him when he abandoned her to her solitary fate.

She would never be whole again.

But she would do one thing. She would play this round of golf today; nothing and no one could stop her.

A thrill of excitement pumped her up as she addressed the ball. Oblivious to the hush of the concern that had descended over the gallery, she glanced quickly down the green corridor of fairway between the trees.

Pain be damned, she thought as she raised the driver high in the air. *I'm as ready as I'll ever be.*

She brought the clubhead down.

But in that split second she had favoured her weak knee. The ball hooked left, out of bounds, as the gallery sighed its disappointment. Observers looked at each other significantly as Joanna Lake took a double bogey six on the par-four opening hole at Maple Hills.

After the first two rounds the Tournament of Champions was deadlocked. The hungry field of top pros was playing well in perfect weather conditions. Four women were tied for the lead at four under par, and six others were within two strokes.

The eyes of the golf world were on Peggy Byrne, who had followed her brilliant opening sixty-nine with a lacklustre seventy-three, and stood within striking distance of the lead. Everyone expected her to make a move during Saturday's round and be in contention for the championship on Sunday.

Joanna Lake, having played the first round in a shaky seventy-five after two double bogeys on the front nine, and the second round in seventy-five as well, was written off as well out of the hunt, for the leaders were in ten strokes ahead of her.

Peggy Byrne did not disappoint her millions of supporters. Loose and confident in the crisp, still air of Saturday afternoon, she shot a stirring sixty-eight which tied her for the lead at six under.

A brief shot at the beginning of Saturday's network broadcast showed Joanna in the warm sun with her patented tank top and wrap-around skirt. Her ponytail identified her instantly to the audience, as did the taped knee which was now an unwelcome feature of her screen persona. The commentator made sympathetic comments about her mediocre but courageous performance, and intimated that she might well be playing her last televised tournament.

Their commercial instincts piqued by the human interest potential of Joanna's losing battle against a crippling injury, the network executives ordered their director to give her more air time. With her soft features, her shapely legs mutilated by the tape, and her eyes showing a touch of pain, she projected an almost ethereal beauty that hypnotised the galleries watching her.

Thus it was that the attentive cameras focused admiringly on her tanned limbs as she putted out on the eighteenth green in the shadows of late afternoon.

Yet that final putt, to everyone's surprise, was for a four-under-par sixty-eight and a brilliant third round.

Unbeknown to anyone, Joanna had made a desperate, last-ditch adjustment in her game after a long, meditative bath in her hotel room on Friday night. Her tempo on backswing and follow-through had been rushed as a result of her insecurity over her injury. By slowing her swing and distracting herself intentionally from the tired feeling in her knee, she thought she could correct her mistake.

She ran the risk of tiring the knee further, and perhaps re-injuring it. But her pride would not allow her to play ineffectually before millions of viewers. The long winter of inactivity yawned before her. Beyond it, perhaps, lay a future without golf. She must perform well this weekend.

The strategy had worked, for her sixty-eight on Saturday was impressive and solidly executed, though she remained far behind the leaders.

'If only I could have played three rounds of sixty-eight!' she cursed herself aloud that night.

That's always what a loser says, she mused suddenly, her eyes riveted to the tired face in the mirror.

Sunday morning dawned cold and windy in the hills above Ithaca. Cayuga Lake sat slate grey like a huge puddle in the valley below. As Joanna ate her solitary breakfast, the network director and commentators were planning a series of inserts throughout the day's broadcast to show highlights of her distinguished career. Having seen the effect of her image on viewers during the third round, they wanted to add drama and ratings to the tournament's closing holes by speculating loudly that this heroic fourth round might be Joanna's last championship effort.

Despite her slacks and windbreaker Joanna could feel the

bite of a chilly breeze on the first tee. A scheduling mix-up had put her in a threesome with Peggy Byrne and her co-leader, Linda Sherwood. Though she felt out of place with two players who were doing so much better than she, there was nothing for it but to play her best.

After calculating the strength of the wind she addressed her ball and swung.

'We may not see her again,' the commentator whispered, 'but no one will forget the sight of that wonderful, fluid swing over so many courses these past seven years. And the courage she has displayed this week certainly goes beyond winning and losing.'

The ball sailed two hundred and twenty-five yards and floated to the ground in the centre of the fairway. Robbie took her driver from her as she stood back to watch her partners hit.

'Sixty-four will win it,' she heard him murmur. He looked away as she turned towards him in surprise. In six years she had never heard Robbie say a word on the course except to announce her precise distance from the pin.

He thinks I can win, she mused, amazed by his confidence.

Moments later they had started down the fairway. Too late, an urgent message was handed to one of the marshals on the tee. It was passed along from marshal to marshal throughout the day, but in the confusion of the final round somehow never reached Joanna.

The gusts that shook Maple Hills were even worse than anyone had anticipated. They blew perfect drives into fairway rough and bunkers. They blew accurate approach shots off the greens, and almost immediately the entire field began to lose strokes to par.

Only Peggy Byrne seemed able to stand up to the ravages of the wind and cold, thanks to her natural strength and shotmaking ability. She kept her ball within bounds, made difficult putts, and finished the front nine at even par for the day. She was already alone in the lead, for her competitors had been unable to keep up with her pace in the inclement weather.

A curious sidelight of the broadcast was the outstanding performance of Joanna Lake, whose image was seen often since she was paired with Peggy. Not only was she striking the ball with surprising authority, the commentator noted in his sympathetic voice, but she had managed to set up several easy putts for birdie through fairway shots of uncanny accuracy.

At the end of nine holes she had actually gained four strokes on par, while everyone else was struggling just to stay even.

Of course, that did not mean she was in contention. She remained four strokes off Peggy Byrne's pace, and the back nine at Maple Hills was known to be even more difficult in the wind than the front nine. Nevertheless, it was said, she deserved credit for her improbably fine play.

At the tenth tee Robbie took a can of fruit juice from Joanna's bag and watched her drink it while he massaged her knee. His rough hands were gentle and hesitant on her soft flesh as he murmured words of encouragement in his Arkansas drawl. She knew he had seen the slight limp she had developed over the last few holes; she had noticed it herself on the fifth.

Too early, she thought.

But already her mind was far away from the present moment. Eyes closed, she was sailing over the tenth hole, the eleventh, and the entire back nine, floating mentally over the fairways and on to the greens in the gusting wind, making shots she knew she had to make.

She knew that angry wind; it had beaten her here before. In her mind she contemplated it now with respect. It was a rippling, excitable sort of creature that hovered above the trees, slapping at anything that invaded its element, including golf balls.

One must not fight it, she decided. One could only lose, as she had done so many times before. Instead, one must collaborate with it, acknowledging its dominion over this hilly ground. One must offer it one's ball with a certain humility. Thus propitiated, the wind itself would do the rest.

'You've got 'em, Joanna,' Robbie was saying. 'You can't lose!'

She nodded without hearing.

It was all Peggy Byrne could do to salvage par on the tenth hole by one-putting the green after a stupendous pitch-and-run that had the chilled gallery cheering madly.

But before she could make that four-foot putt, Joanna, who was away, sank her sixteen-footer for a birdie. Surprised applause greeted her fine effort.

On the par-three twelfth hole, Peggy could no more hold the green in the whistling wind than anyone else, and had to save par through a brilliant approach chip and ten-foot putt. Joanna, having driven her ball to within eight feet of the pin with a brisk five iron, sank her putt easily for another birdie.

By the thirteenth tee the TV cameras were no longer focusing on Joanna for the hurt knee hidden by her slacks and for the probable end of her career. She was alone in second place now, a respectable contender at two strokes off the lead.

The par-five thirteenth would normally have offered a player of Peggy's strength a tempting birdie opportunity. But today the savage wind made its narrow fairway seem almost non-existent. Forcing her shots from rough to rough,

Peggy again saved par through a clutch putt that broke frighteningly before dropping.

Joanna was on the green in regulation and one-putted from twelve feet for another birdie.

The galleries buzzed with excitement as she passed. Somehow, inexplicably, she seemed to have harnessed her own determination to the caprices of the wind, married her ball to the flowing grass and heaving tree limbs of Maple Hills. Her shots charged through the air above the fairways and floated to the greens as though guided by huge, invisible hands.

Slow as always to appreciate an unseen change in the momentum of a tournament, the commentators realised Joanna was in line for victory only when her ball lay on the sixteenth green, a dozen feet away from a birdie that would tie her for the lead with Peggy.

Joanna slammed the putt straight into the back of the cup.

In sixteen holes of golf on one of the most difficult courses in the Northeast, in the cruel wind that made that course so famous a beast, Joanna had gained eight strokes on par. The leaders who had been so many strokes ahead of her this morning were now far behind.

Even as the stunned gallery at the sixteenth erupted in applause at Joanna's putt, an electric hush seemed to come over spectators and journalists alike. They watched her slender limbs in awed fascination as she picked her ball out of the cup. The change in the cold air was palpable.

She's going to win, they were thinking.

If the wind and the course and her injured knee had not slowed her thus far, nothing could stop her now.

Except Peggy Byrne.

Alone in their tie for the lead, Joanna and Peggy both played the seventeenth hole in par. The network cameras had ceased bothering to cover the play of any other competitors, for it was obvious that one of these two would win.

'One can't help being reminded today of the epic struggle that was joined between these two women only three months ago at Pine Trail,' the commentator said. 'That day it was Peggy Byrne who came out on top, thanks to an amazing bunker shot on the final hole. If she wants to win her fiftieth tournament here today, she may need just such heroics to do it, because Joanna is applying tremendous pressure through her superb play.'

His words struck a chord in a million minds, for Joanna's awesome rush to the lead from a great disadvantage had obscured the one flaw in her game that might offer encouragement to Peggy's many supporters: her reputation as a loser.

If Peggy could not beat her, she might yet beat herself.

The eighteenth hole at Maple Hills is as famous a finishing par five as exists in the United States. Its slowly curving fairway, five hundred and eleven yards long, leads past huge bunkers and a transversal creek to an elevated green protected by a water hazard and thick, encroaching rough.

Joanna's booming drive sailed two hundred and forty yards before landing in perfect position short of the creek. Despite her reputation for great strength off the tee, Peggy could only manage a far shorter effort. Her careful second shot left her a seventy-five yard wedge to the green.

Robbie's hand flirted with the one-iron in Joanna's bag. A conservative and accurate second shot seemed the logical choice for Joanna. But she asked for her three wood.

'It looks as though she's going to go for the green,' the commentator said as her image appeared on the monitor before him. 'It's a gutsy thing to attempt in this wind, but no one is forgetting that Joanna has been considered the premier fairway wood player in the world for years now.'

Before addressing the ball Joanna glanced at Peggy, who was waiting for her caddy. For the first time she noticed the lines in Peggy's face, and realised that the older woman was nearing the end of her great career. The freckles and laughing eyes and frizzy hair beloved of millions of fans could not conceal the onset of middle age.

No wonder Peggy wanted her fiftieth title so badly, Joanna thought. Time was running out for her.

Distracted by the depressing thought, Joanna lost her concentration for the first time. She hooked her powerful three wood into the thick rough rimming the distant bunker which guarded the green. Had it flown straight, her ball would be on the putting surface. As things stood, her ambitious effort might well have done more harm than good.

Cursing her lack of concentration, she watched Peggy seize the advantage by lofting her easy wedge shot in an arc that dropped her ball no more than ten feet from the cup.

'That rough Joanna is in,' said the colour commentator, 'is far worse than the sand itself. She's going to have terrible footing, and the ball will fly. Meanwhile Peggy will be putting for birdie, and if I know Peggy she'll put everything into that stroke.'

Suddenly the unseen flow of emotion in the galleries seemed to have changed direction. Having played with almost inhuman efficiency all day, Joanna had not only silenced the network's doomsayers, but had made Peggy's scrappy wind play appear frail and ineffectual. Only moments ago improbable victory seemed sure to go to the younger woman, for her icy nerves and aggressive shot-making were putting unbearable pressure on the popular veteran.

But now it was Joanna's turn to show the soft, vulnerable face the public had admired for seven seasons.

'It looks as though Peggy will pull out her coveted fiftieth today after all,' the announcer said, 'despite this amazing challenge by Joanna Lake, who seems indeed to be running out of gas now. I don't see how she can stop that ball of hers on the green. As soon as it hits the surface it's going to run all the way to the front edge, and she'll have all of sixty feet coming back.'

Alert to the slight limp that was visible despite her wind-whipped slacks, the camera watched Joanna approach the bunker's edge. Her taped knee twisted painfully as she addressed the ball, one foot in the trap and one foot in the thick grass of the rough. Only the cold wind sighing in the trees broke the silence as the press and gallery contemplated her.

Joanna hesitated, looking from her half-buried ball to the flag-stick forty feet away. She knew she faced an almost impossible shot. Many times as a professional she had found herself in positions like this, had shrugged and made bogey, and hoped for birdie on the next hole, the next round, the next tournament.

But today there was to be no next hole.

She could feel the millions of eyes fixed on her, still tense with anticipation and yet convinced now that she was the loser. They were all waiting for her to overshoot the green, to miss the huge putt or chip coming back, to congratulate Peggy on her birdie and her fiftieth victory.

Her fingers were numb on the grip of her wedge. Her legs and arms were chilled by the wind, and her left knee ached alarmingly. But she felt nothing except that eager waiting, that imminence on the edge of resignation.

The marshal, his demeanour imperial under shiny grey hair, kept the gallery back as Joanna stood poised to swing.

She could feel the force of a collective will urging her to get it over with.

They can't hit it, she thought darkly. *They have to wait for me to do that.*

And suddenly a thought rose and flowered in her mind. She looked down at the ball. It seemed joined by invisible threads of force to the gusting wind and the bent grass of the green. Between her and that impossible sixty-foot putt from the front apron lay the hole itself. She had only to stroke the ball directly into the cup in order to avoid disaster. She had only to execute this one unlikely stroke, the stroke of a lifetime, to beat the only woman who had offered her a bit of true encouragement during this terrible week, the valued friend whose fiftieth tour victory was at stake.

A stroke to defeat her.

Joanna raised her club quickly and struck the ball. It popped crazily into the wind, hesitated for what seemed an eternity, and floated to the green, already a pace beyond the flagstick. But she had somehow managed to stun it with a backspin which jerked it suddenly up the slope, backward against the grain and, with a finality that left the gallery stunned and breathless, into the hole, into the bottom of the shadowed cup.

Even the glib commentators were at a loss for words to describe the reality visible on the monitors. Peggy's birdie putt was irrelevant now. Joanna had won the tournament outright.

Seized by an abrupt wave of weakness, she felt oddly embarrassed by what she had done. Pain and languor made her touch her taped knee as she climbed out of the trap. She wanted to meet Robbie's friendly eyes, to hand him her wedge and stand out of sight somewhere as Peggy holed out before the appreciative crowd.

But Robbie had receded from her and blended into the mass of people who were standing up. Deafening noise confused her, and she turned in disorientation to see if Peggy was going to putt out.

But Peggy was standing in the centre of the green, her putter under her arm, smiling as she joined the thousands of spectators in the standing ovation that had exploded under the cold sky, and that grew now in power and intensity until it seemed to drown all thought under its crashing weight.

Joanna could not believe her eyes and ears. The spectators, marshals, greenskeepers and journalists were all on their feet, applauding and calling out words of praise and affection, their thousands of smiles resting as one on her slender form.

Flushing in her amazement, she started across the apron to take her ball from the cup. She wanted to tip her cap to the cheering multitude of faces, but all at once she was afraid the slightest movement would make her lose her balance. The putting surface reared before her, and she felt faint.

It was Peggy who came to her rescue, supporting her with a strong arm around her shoulder and guiding her to the cup in which her ball nestled against the pin. Men with hand-held cameras hovered near her as she retrieved it and threw it to the gallery.

And now Peggy stepped back a pace, and Joanna stood alone before the public, realising at last that the full force of that exultation was for her. Through eyes clouded by pain and fatigue she smiled her acknowledgment, waving and blowing kisses of thanks for the tide of warmth and sympathy that rose and rose before her.

She saw hundreds of index fingers raised skyward, proclaiming that she was Number One, the very best of the very best, for today at least. And she knew now that countless fans had waited and worried with her as she fought to save her career, and perhaps waited and hoped long years for this moment when the spotlight would belong to her at last.

Joanna Lake, said the unnecessary graphic under her familiar image on television screens in forty countries.

Winner.

CHAPTER TWELVE

JOANNA would remember that day as a chaos of her own making, a maelstrom which must surely engulf her unless she could find its hidden principle in the tangled forces of her whole life.

She came to herself blinking and confused before a welter of lights, cameras and microphones. Peggy's plump arm was around her shoulder once more, for she had putted out and was receiving her second place winnings.

'We're all sorry that either of you great players had to lose,' the commentator was saying.

'Not at all,' Peggy laughed. 'For seven years I've known that Joanna was going to do this to me some day. And now that it's happened, I'm just glad I was here to see the round of golf she played. I lost to the best—and that's a privilege.'

'Joanna,' said the tournament chairman with the inevitable prosaism of those who congratulate winners, 'you played a truly historic round today. How do you feel?'

She tried to think of something light and tactful to say, but the words would not come. She realised her reserves of energy were completely drained.

'I...I guess I'm a little tired,' she said at last, her weak humour sending waves of sympathetic laughter through the crowd. Before she could continue she felt a weakness in her left leg so sudden that she nearly fell down at his feet. Only an enormous effort of will kept her upright, and she had to grasp his arm outside the cameras' view to steady herself.

He must have sensed her extreme weakness, for he resumed with alacrity, 'I'm sure that's no wonder. Coming back from knee surgery the way you have, in one summer, and beating a field as great as this one, on this difficult course in the wind—that's an achievement that won't soon be forgotten. And I want to add my congratulations to everyone else's on one other point, which our viewers may not have heard about yet. I understand that, as well as being the winner of the Tournament of Champions, you've made history in another way today. You've been officially selected as architect for the Black Woods championship course in South Carolina. That's a great step forward for you personally and for women in golf.'

Everything else he said was lost on Joanna. She struggled to mumble responses to his questions while her mind raced ineffectually to comprehend his tidings.

It was not possible, she decided numbly. One cannot live days and weeks of one's life under an assumption based on logic and fact, and then be told that the opposite is true. The clock cannot be turned back. Real events cannot be undone.

They rejected it, she reminded herself, loath to be carried aloft now by a bubble destined to burst. *It never had a chance.*

Unless Jack had lied.

Unless the *Journal* had been mistaken in its announcement of Avery Follett's nomination as architect.

Unless Reid had told the truth.

In a mist of bewilderment she was signing the cheque for her winnings. Robbie was helping her examine her score card before signing it, and repeating the improbable score over and over again, sixty-two, sixty-two, sixty-two. Inside the clubhouse the reporters' familiar faces loomed before her. She saw Ron Lieber, impassive and cold, regarding her with the ghost of a shrug.

'Miss Lake,' he asked, 'to what do you attribute this surprising turnaround…?'

'Ron,' said a laughing colleague whose fingers encircled his arm in a hard grip, 'give up!'

Lieber stepped back to take notes as the others called out questions.

But Joanna was too exhausted to answer.

'Don't worry, Jo,' came a friendly voice, 'we'll cover for you. Shall we say that you're tired but happy?'

It was Charlie Sullivan, his mild features lit by an avuncular smile. Joanna nodded, then touched his hand.

'The Black Woods,' she whispered. 'What happened? I didn't know…'

'They released it to the press this morning,' he told her. 'They accepted your design in a meeting yesterday. I don't know why nobody told you, Jo. Maybe they didn't want to bother you with it during your final round.' He raised an eyebrow. 'Would it have made a difference if you'd known before you went out on the course today?'

Stunned, she looked into his eyes. She would never know the answer to his question, and she was glad she would never know.

Moments later she was in the locker room, her knee stripped of its tape and receiving a desperately needed ice massage. Her fellow pros added their congratulations with quiet little hugs and pats, reminding her softly that she must get some rest. Aware now that she was in a state of physical and mental prostration, she dared not look at herself in the mirror.

In a few minutes she would call Tina. Then she would arrange somehow to get herself back to the hotel for a rest. Much later, after a decent interval of silence and oblivion, she would try to sort out what had happened to her today.

'Joanna?' A voice tore her from her reverie. 'I'm sorry to disturb you…'

She looked up to see the unfamiliar face of an attractive, middle-aged woman. Its features struck a distant chord. She thought she had seen it in a photograph somewhere.

'I'm Bettina Clarke,' the stranger smiled. 'We've met, but you probably don't remember me. It was at an L.P.G.A. meeting last year.'

'Oh,' stammered Joanna, cursing her forgetfulness. 'Of course. How are you?' Bettina Clarke was an L.P.G.A. official known for her work in tournament promotion.

'I know you must be all in,' she said, 'but I just wanted to tell you how delighted we all are over the Black Woods. It's a great step for women. And I want to add my personal word,' she added, brushing a lock of greying sunbleached hair from her brow. 'I saw your design, and it's absolutely the greatest.'

In confusion Joanna smiled. 'You saw it yourself?' she asked. 'How did…?'

'A man named Reid Armstrong showed it to me. He was lobbying everybody he could find in the organisation to have a look at it—on the quiet, so to speak. We all saw it, I think, over a period of days. It's been our best-kept secret ever since.'

At a loss for words, Joanna could only shake her head in perplexity.

'I'm really not clear on this,' she said at last. 'Did he say why…?'

'Oh, yes, he told us in detail. He said he knew there was going to be political trouble with the Black Woods committee if a woman was proposed as architect. He'd been sceptical himself, he said, until he actually saw what you'd conceived for the course. That convinced him, and he saw his job as simply making sure the inevitable happened sooner rather than later.'

Joanna smiled. 'He's such a confident man,' she said. 'It's not easy to say no to him. He wanted us to make a

sort of formal, although confidential statement to the effect
that when and if a course based on your design became a
reality, the L.P.G.A. would endorse and work for a major
tournament to be held on that site.'

Her brown eyes sparkled. 'His reasoning was obvious. If
the Black Woods committee knew that your design would
attract a major L.P.G.A. tournament, they would see important revenues coming in year after year, and a corre-
sponding membership in their club. Well, we could hardly
refuse after we studied the design. It's such a fantastic document, such a brilliant concept. We met last week and
drafted the letter. I guess it did the trick—although I must
say Reid Armstrong might have done without it if he had
had to. I have a funny feeling he's been in contact with a
lot of big-money sponsors already, and applying quiet pressure all over the place.'

Joanna was too tired to hide the truth. 'I thought my
design had been rejected,' she said. 'I was sure of it.'

'You mean the Avery Follett business,' the other woman
nodded. 'That was a political manoeuvre, I understand. It
was engineered by a faction on the committee that was
afraid no one would join the country club if the course was
designed by a woman. They rushed through a vote when
the other members had their backs turned, so to speak. Reid
found out about it, of course, and he stayed in close touch
with all the individuals involved and kept up the pressure.
He even talked to Avery, who was perfectly aware that the
offer they had made him was not firm.'

'I don't know what to say,' stammered Joanna. 'I'm in
a state of shock.'

'I'm awfully sorry,' said Bettina, touching Joanna's
hand. 'I thought you knew more about it all. I just assumed
Reid would be keeping you informed.'

He tried to tell me, Joanna thought, her heart sinking.

'Well, he must have had his reasons,' concluded Bettina.

'Perhaps he didn't want to upset you with the sordid details of it all until he had good news to report. I got the distinct impression he wasn't particularly enamoured of the committee members or their friends. I think he relished the challenge of making them do what they didn't want to do.'

She had stood up to leave, but hesitated, her smile a trifle embarrassed.

'I suppose I should keep my big mouth shut,' she said, 'but my woman's instincts told me that Reid Armstrong has it pretty bad for you, Joanna.' She laughed. 'I'm sure he isn't alone in that, with your looks. But I think you have quite an admirer there. I know how hard he fought for you. The last thing he would want would be for you to be hurt. Anyway, all's well that ends well.'

A moment later she had gone, leaving Joanna alone with the hurtling avalanche of new thoughts which had overtaken her.

An hour ago she had believed she was alone in the world, and must depend entirely on her own initiative. That belief had fuelled each of the carefully calculated strokes that had won her the Tournament of Champions. Solitude, her inescapable fate, had at last seemed to come to her rescue on the golf course.

Now she had lost that most basic of assumptions. The rehabilitated body that had executed those winning shots, she realised, owed its strength and suppleness to Reid Armstrong. And the competitive spirit that had driven her onward, past the brilliant field at Maple Hills and finally past the great Peggy Byrne herself, came in large measure from Reid's impact on her.

Even the cold anger that had guided her strokes in pitiless concentration, forcing fear and pain into distant corners of her consciousness—even that owed its intensity to Reid.

Three months of her life wheeled before her mind's eye like the colours of a kaleidoscope. And there was no denying the pattern their days and nights formed now—the pattern Reid had predicted. She was a winner in competition, and her design for the Black Woods would become a reality.

'He told the truth,' she repeated to herself in amazement as the knee that had known his touch so many times bathed now in its ice.

When have I given you reason to doubt my word? His warning voice came back to her, perplexed and angry. And only now she could hear the hurt in its deep tones.

I don't know who's been putting ideas into your head...

Now the incredible truth was coiled mercilessly around her. Reid had asked her to believe in him for a few days and weeks, after having dedicated months of his life to her and to Tina. And she had turned away from him, investing her credence in the one man on earth most obviously motivated to hurt her: Jack Templeton.

Jack had come armed with tempting grains of truth to support his lies. There was something almost pathetic, in retrospect, about the little exhibits he had flourished in his triumph. Yes, she mused: they were damaging enough. But she should have seen through them when she realised it was not by accident that he had come back to interrupt her life.

Instead she had allowed his spiteful, petty performance to compel her belief, to change the course of her existence—while the little girl who had never met Jack, the child who loved Reid Armstrong, played unwittingly only a room away.

For an instant Joanna almost forgave herself for turning that darkest of corners, as the letter signed by Carl Jaeger flashed across her memory. It had been easy to assume that the ultimate betrayal was possible, the final nightmare, once she had seen that letter.

And Jack must have assumed that in advance. Jack, who

knew where she was most vulnerable. Jack, who had known
Carl since his days as a player on the Georgia golf team—
and who had perhaps solicited the letter himself as a member of the Black Woods committee.

Now the awful significance of Jack's membership in that
hidebound group, thanks to the tentacles of his father's
money, came home to Joanna. Undoubtedly it had caused
him to cross paths with Reid at one time or another, and
to know that Reid had offered the design commission to
Joanna Lake.

But there was more to it than that. Joanna imagined the
unsuspecting affability with which Reid must have lobbied
the fearful committee members to accept her innovative
design. He must have twisted their arms, cajoled and pres-
sured them in his blithe way, without ever realising that
among them was a man who was drawing his private in-
ferences from everything that was said.

Unsuspecting, Reid must have worked for Joanna with
all his skill. Was it possible that a trace of the tenderness
she had seen so often in his tawny eyes might have been
visible when he spoke of her before the committee? If Bettina Clarke had noticed that impalpable shade of emotion
in him, why not the committee members?

I saw the picture of you with Reid on the golf course.

Joanna recalled the opening gambit in Jack's cruel assault on her. He had seen the photo snapped by the Beaufort
journalist the day of her very first round of golf with Reid.
Sold to a wire service, the picture had appeared in newspapers all over the country, showing Joanna shaking Reid's
hand after defeating him with her final putt.

From her soft smile in that photograph Jack must have
drawn the conclusion he had been tempted to draw from
his own suspicions of Reid. And indeed, the picture had
been taken only hours before Joanna had given herself to

Reid, her senses on fire with the joyful knowledge that he wanted her and accepted her.

With halting breaths she sat now on the locker room table, seeing herself trapped in the frame of the photo which was visible to all the world, visible to those who might want to harm her, to harm Reid…

Confused, she thought how difficult it was to escape the clutches of the past. In breaking with his own family Reid had rejected the very society that had produced Jack. A society whose genteel surface was built on greed and venality, a society of cold, empty people who believed in nothing.

But Reid had believed in Joanna. And in committing himself to her so honestly, he had allowed the very forces he had spent a lifetime outwitting to take their revenge— in the form of Jack Templeton.

She shuddered to think that it was her own forgotten past which had come back to coil around her and, in that sinister crossroads, to fool her into turning against the only man who was on her side. Reid's mistake was to have placed his trust in her without arming himself against the dangers surrounding her. Dangers come from her past, which she herself could not see.

How strange to consider Reid's own vulnerability, she mused. Reid, who trusted no one, who could be manipulated by no one…

I don't know who's been putting ideas in your head.

Thunderstruck, Joanna gasped aloud.

'He knew!' she told herself in shock. 'He knew everything!'

Reid was a thorough man. He would research the background of anyone he came in contact with including the committee members. Including Joanna herself!

He must have been aware that Jack Templeton was her ex-husband. And when the letter from Carl Jaeger was used as a pretext for rejecting her design, Reid must have seen it, known about it, and understood its real importance.

But he did not tell her, for obvious reasons.

It wasn't important. I didn't want to worry you about it when you had other things on your mind.

It all fitted. Reid considered himself Joanna's friend and protector. When he found out that the two men who had been closest to her were united against her, he could hardly be inclined to upset her with such terrible news.

Particularly when it was not news that in any way daunted him where her course design was concerned. Convinced as always of his own abilities, he must have simply resolved to see the design accepted, as he had promised— and to shield her from the dirty knowledge he possessed about Jack and Carl.

But then she had banished him cruelly, furiously, her pitiless words striking far deeper than her disappointment over the design could have justified.

Why beat a dead horse with your lies?

Why not get Tina out here? She doesn't know you as I do.

She dared not linger over that awful scene. But she knew now that under the worst of insults Reid's sense of honour had decreed that he not stoop to defend himself by denouncing others. Deeply hurt by Joanna, he would not hurt her back.

And after that night he had continued his efforts on behalf of her design, and had achieved the success he counted on from the beginning.

Wherever he was now, he must be thinking that he had at least proved he had been true to his word. Powerless to oppose Joanna's stupid incredulity through argument, he had done so by bringing about a reality she could not deny.

'What must he think of me now?' she reflected miserably in the solitude of the locker room. 'After all he did...'

Conflicting ideas tormented her as she considered her situation. Her own sense of fairness required that she apologise to Reid. Yet no apology could undo the damage done by her horrid, cruel words the night he had appeared at her house. And no kindly destiny could unravel the dark threads of chaos that had coaxed those words from her lips, sealing her doom as they bound her once more to her unhappy solitude.

But the unspoken thought taking shape in her mind outstripped despair itself as it lifted her from the table and propelled her with irresistible urgency towards the telephone. Indifferent to the pain in her leg, she fumbled in her purse for her credit card. Moving like a sleepwalker, she found coins and a telephone number.

If Bettina Clarke had seen that impalpable light of tenderness in Reid's complex eyes when he spoke of Joanna, it could not be entirely non-existent. If Jack had used his knowledge of it as a weapon in his own intrigues, it must have been real.

And Joanna herself had spent bitter-sweet weeks of ecstasy and heartbreak believing in that light even as she forced herself to renounce it.

How could it have been a mere illusion? People saw it. It had effects in the real world.

'Reservations,' came the voice on the phone. 'Can I help you?'

'I hope so,' said Joanna. 'I have a reservation for tomorrow morning's flight to Sarasota. Could I get on a flight to Savannah tonight? And I'd like to rent a car, please.'

She turned to look at the locker room. It seemed as foreign a landscape as her own life. The centre of gravity of her whole existence was outside her now, exiled in a distant house on a hill overlooking the ocean.

She trembled with anticipation, her fingers crossed desperately, as she waited for the voice to come back on the line.

For she was no stranger to impermanence.

A light may be real, she knew, and still go out.

Hours later, oblivious to the unutterable fatigue her decision had brought upon her, Joanna closed the door of her rented car and stood in the darkness outside Reid's house.

She could hear the hushed boom of the surf on the beach beyond the bridle paths. Under her feet was the driveway on which she had stood when she said goodbye to Reid while Tina watched. She could still feel the impotent message of love and renunciation that had quickened in her fingertips as they touched his hard back that day.

The Southern night was balmy and lit by stars. Before Joanna stood the jeep which had driven her to the Black Woods so often, and been her accomplice the day of her furtive excursion to the driving range. Beside it was the big sedan in which she had slept on the long journey from Fayetteville.

On the distant beach Tina had played with Katie and swum under Reid's watchful eye while her mother jogged or rode her bicycle along the trails that crisscrossed these hills. In the quiet air over the lawn Joanna could still hear the little shout of glee that came from Tina's lips as Reid had swooped her up, a giddy packet of vibrant energy, for a ride on his shoulders.

Behind the shadowed sights and sounds that greeted her under this starry sky were all the invisible threads that had joined together over the stately passage of the days to create her beautiful, painful summer. They were made of laughter and worry and well-kept secrets, those threads—and most of all they were made of hope.

And even now she could feel the million unseen dreams and yearnings that had come from the remotest times of her life to knit themselves into that shimmering fabric of summer, only to be torn away by her cautious hand when she left this place.

She forced herself to look back at the cars. They were both here. That meant he was home. Taking a deep breath, she approached the door.

It began to open before she reached it. Too late she realised the sound of her car must have been heard inside at this silent hour. In a flash she thought of the private life she was about to disturb.

Reid stood before her, framed by the light of the vestibule behind him. He was dressed in jeans and a sports shirt which hugged the muscled contours of his body.

Try as she might, she could not move a step closer to him. For an instant she saw indescribable emotion, quick and intense, in his dark eyes. Then he leaned casually against the door frame, his arms folded, his old humour come to stand between him and his visitor.

'What brings you here?' he asked.

The words that stirred on her lips were not those she had planned to say. Like a mystery they came, foreign things that did not belong to her. Yet she knew she must not hold them back.

'I need someone,' she began unsteadily, meeting his gaze with the last of her courage. 'Someone to watch out for me.'

His smile touched her softly as he looked down upon her. But he was shaking his head.

'No, you don't,' he said. 'You don't need anyone, Joanna. You're a winner.'

Her heart sank within her breast. She could feel his strength arming him to free her.

'Unless,' he said, 'you mean someone to rub your sore knee and see that you get your rest. Someone to make sure you don't jump to conclusions about who your real friends are…'

He had stepped forward, placing gentle hands on her shoulders. 'Someone to be a father to that little girl of yours,' he said. 'Someone to marry you, and love you for ever, so that you'll never, never be alone again…'

She was in his arms, home at last, it seemed, for the first time in her memory. His lips were against her hair, and she heard them murmur truths that warmed her like the tenderest of caresses.

'I was in love with you long before there was a Black Woods golf course to design,' he said. 'I fell in love with you from watching you play golf on television. When I saw the chance to meet you, I jumped at it. How was I to know that my meddling in your life was practically going to get you killed, and ruin your career and leave you scarred and injured?' He shook his head. 'I was happy to see you win today, because it at least meant you were whole again, even if I'd lost you.'

'No,' Joanna whispered. 'Not whole. Not without you.'

He glanced past her at the driveway. 'I hated to let you go this summer,' he said. 'I wanted us to be together, but I didn't dare ask where we stood.'

She nodded against his chest, too overcome to tell him how deeply she had shared his anguish.

'So you didn't mean…?' he asked, his words calling up the most terrible of all the obstacles that had separated them.

'I love you,' she said, clasping him to her with all her strength. 'I've always loved you.' She brushed his lips with her own, her hands in his hair and around his neck, her heart bursting with a reality she could not contain. 'Forgive me.'

'For standing on your own two feet when you knew you had to?' Reid shook his head. 'That's nothing to forgive,

Joanna. And as for being slow to realise that the time for going it alone was past—I'm no stranger to that mistake myself. But it's all behind us now, isn't it?'

She held him closer still, as though to draw courage from him for the last step she knew she must take in order to be his.

'Yes,' she said, 'it's behind us.'

'For ever?'

The future had come alive within her breast, triumphant and infinite as it banished the world to which she had clung with all her might for so long. And the pain of being swept up that way might have torn her apart, had she not felt herself safe and secure in the arms that held her now, their power coursing through her boundlessly.

She saw herself mirrored in his smiling eyes, no longer the solitary woman who had fought so desperately to remain on her own, but eclipsed now by someone new, someone capable of opening herself to him joyfully and completely. And all at once the last step seemed gentle and easy, as though she had known the way from the beginning, but lost it somehow, until this quiet night and these strong arms could show it to her once more.

'For ever,' she said.

A STRANGER TO LOVE

PROLOGUE

THE young woman lay in darkness, her sandy-coloured hair splayed in soft billows across the spread which covered her naked body. The gentle curve of her breasts rose and fell soundlessly as she slept. In repose her fine features bore a childlike innocence, dominated as they were by the long lashes over her closed eyes.

A tiny tremor shook the slender fingers of her resting hand in the silence. The creamy flesh of her brow furrowed in an unconscious frown, and then softened as the dream thought passed.

In her dream she was back home with Mother and Dad. But the house on Everit Street did not resemble itself. The rooms were larger, darker, more melancholy.

A party was going on. The guests were all dressed in white. It was as though they were functionaries of some sort, the bland uniformity of their garb bespeaking the nature of their trade. A host of milkmen, perhaps, or ice-cream men gathered for an occult purpose which Mother and Dad seemed to understand quite well.

Dad introduced Laura around. The men smiled down at her as they held out their tanned hands. Their expressions were sympathetic and yet somehow implacable.

Then she was on a train which roared along gleaming rails past landscapes she had never seen before. Outside the window she could see people going about their business on horseback, or pushing little carts along the dirt paths. They tilled fields where fruits glowed like rich candy under the golden sun. She was lost, and must find her way to a station where she might change trains.

But the train showed no sign of stopping. Instead it gained speed, taking Laura further and further from home. The tunnel was approaching with fearsome urgency, like a predator whose quick jaws would close over its victim, ineluctable and cruel. The car hurtled forward, its violent flight making her dizzy. In a moment she must surely slip from her seat and cling in terror to the hard floor of the careening carriage, as though otherwise she would be flung into space by the sheer force of it all…

Her eyes opened with a start. For a moment the soft obscurity around her seemed to rock and heave with the ghost of the leaping train. Then all was still, and her eyes began to close.

The hushed intimacy of the soft spread against her breasts and thighs told her she was naked. Dreamily she wondered what had become of her nightgown. The grey light of dawn shone pale across a ceiling which was not that of her bedroom in New Haven. The muted city sounds outside were not those that greeted her on weekday mornings when she reached to turn off the alarm moments before it rang.

The rooms of her lifetime wheeled slowly through her imagination, seeking to adjust themselves to the walls she now felt around her. She recalled the bedroom she had occupied as a child on Everit Street, and her dorm room at college. Out of nowhere loomed the cabin she had lived in at summer camp, with its hard wood floor and the scent of pine needles and campfires to which she had awakened on fresh summer mornings.

For a long somnolent moment she watched with pleasure as her familiar rooms paraded before her in a silent panorama.

Then, with a little start of terror, she remembered she was not alone.

Everything came into focus with jarring suddenness. No wonder, she thought, her sleeping mind had tried to transport her to a familiar place. The quiet room hovering around her was indeed strange. She had never seen it before last night. And the city outside had been nothing more than an image in a hundred travel books until yesterday.

No wonder, indeed, that she hesitated to turn her eyes to the sleeping man beside her. She had never shared his bed before.

Holding her body still, she listened for the sound of his breathing. It was barely perceptible, calm and regular.

The taste of his skin was still on her lips. Every corner of her body bore the trace of his touch, and of his clean virile scent. Her senses, dulled by sleep, began to awaken to their own memory of his hard body.

Now he slept peacefully. But a few short hours ago he had been a storm of pleasure around and inside her, unimaginable in its intimacy. The flesh of her breasts quickened anew as images of softly probing lips and hands hung tauntingly before her mind's eye. The naked limbs luxuriating under this warm coverlet tingled still from the caresses which had teased them into a fever of wanting. Delighted to have been known so totally, inflamed to so perfect a height of excitement, her traitorous body slumbered in the glow of its satisfaction, indifferent to the scruples haunting her mind.

She blushed from head to toe in the shadows.

It was all too plain now. The unreal landscape of her dream seemed haggard and pathetic now that wakefulness had shorn it of its fascination.

Well might she resuscitate Mother and Dad in her sleeping mind, she reflected bitterly. They were both dead and gone now. The house on Everit Street was sold. She was alone now, a woman on her own and in charge of her existence.

To the outside world she was Laura Christensen, president and majority stockholder of one of the largest corporations in New England. Only six weeks ago the business press had teemed with speculative items about the responsibility thrust upon her, and about the fate of her company.

They were all watching in curiosity to see what she would do. Investors, executives, journalists, competitors... All eyes were upon Laura, and she could feel their speculation, their scepticism, their indifferent interest. Would Christensen Products retain its precarious position of strength in a recession economy? Or would its young president show herself incapable of steering it on the right course?

The Wall Street Journal had somehow got hold of her college yearbook picture and printed it alongside the brief account of her accession to the presidency of the company. She had cringed to see her youthful image published for all to see. Though four years had passed since the photo was taken, Laura could not deny that the face she saw in the mirror each morning retained its girlish vitality.

Would the *Journal*'s readers—cunning entrepreneurs and bankers, alert investors and brokers—draw the right conclusion from the picture of callow youth displayed on its back page? Would they quickly understand that a major company had fallen into the hands of a silly schoolgirl?

For this morning such was precisely Laura's concept of herself. A silly young girl, well out of her element in the cut-throat business community of the East Coast. An inexperienced junior executive thrust into a limelight she could neither cope with nor escape.

At last she dared to turn her eyes to the sleeping man beside her. His black hair was tousled by his night's repose, but also by the impassioned caress of Laura's own heedless fingers last night. The strong lines of his hard face were softened now by sleep, but when he awoke his ebony irises would scan the world around him with their alert gleam.

Sheepishly Laura glanced at his long, powerful limbs, at the square shoulders above his deep chest. All that had been hers last night. And she had been his.

She barely knew this enigmatic man. Yet, within the dizzy space of six weeks, he had made himself indispensable to her. Underneath his harsh, demanding exterior she had thought she saw the shade of a tenderness for her and a sympathy for her plight. She had clung to that shade without daring to question its reality. After all, was she not the plaything of the storm of events that had engulfed her? Should she not be grateful that he had taken pity on her in her extremity, and agreed to marshal the daunting resources of his intelligence and expertise in her behalf, when his instincts must surely dictate that he leave her to her fate and seek his fortune elsewhere?

Yet she cursed her helpless dependence no less than the insidious desire that had inflamed her towards Frank Jordan. Had he not providentially joined the company only a month before the cataclysm which left it in Laura's unsure hands, disaster might already have resulted. It was thanks to the unflappable confidence behind Frank's penetrating eyes that Christensen Products retained its fighting chance for survival. No one saw his picture in the *Journal*, but it was Frank whose initiative had kept the company afloat until now, and his guile and courage remained the key to its future.

Gratefully Laura had accepted his counsel and followed his recommendations, for she knew she had no choice.

And now she had given herself to him.

A wry smile of dismay curled her lips in the silence, for she knew her shame went deeper yet. For weeks she had awaited the charmed moment when he would catch the signals her woman's body sought to attract him with. And when it had finally happened, here in this alien room in a strange city, she had been his eager partner, her sighs of rapture indicating her delight and relief that, in this way as well, he had taken pity on her.

She was all open to him now, defenceless and dependent. She dared not imagine the thoughts which might lurk behind his inscrutable irises when he awoke to find her here. She must hope against hope that, whatever his contempt for her, he would find it in his heart to go on as before; that his newfound loyalty to the company Sam Christensen had spent a lifetime building would outstrip his scorn for the behaviour of Sam's heedless daughter.

His powerful body stirred beside her, and was still once more. A lock of his dark hair had fallen across the strong brow over the angular contours of his face. Even in sleep he seemed vital, alert as an athlete coiled for action.

In a few moments more his eyes would open. He would remember everything, and know exactly what it all meant—for Frank Jordan always knew where he stood. In six weeks Laura had learned to admire that sharp gaze which scanned the world of men like a clear beacon, calculating, evaluating, knowing. She prayed it would still rest upon her with its spark of friendliness, and lead her through the labyrinth in which her company was mired.

She had cast her lot with him, and must trust him now. For without Frank Jordan she was surely lost.

To think that three months ago he had had no existence for her at all! She had been a bright, cheerful young woman pursuing an orderly career, without a thought for the fragility of her sunlit life.

The rabbit runs free in the fields, she recalled an old parable, *and the hounds play in the courtyard. But the rab-*

bit's fate is already sealed. Thus it had been for Laura as well.

And now the hounds were upon her.

In another minute he would be awake. She must look ahead, imagine what he would say and do. Try to predict whether things would be changed between them, and whether he would still stand between her and the things she could not control.

But it was no use. As she lay numb in her nudity, in these last moments of silence, the future was as unknowable as ever.

She could only recall how it had all started, and wonder again at the twisting whirlwind of happenings that had uprooted her so suddenly from her careless past.

CHAPTER ONE

'LAURA, I want to make you a Vice-President of Christensen as of the first of the year.'

Sam Christensen smiled with a touch of irony at his daughter's pursed lips and furrowed brow. He knew what her response would be.

'Dad,' Laura smiled at last, shaking her head in amused disapproval, 'do we have to start this again? I'm happy just where I am. If you give me more responsibility, you'll turn me into the same sort of workaholic the company has made of you. Is that what you want?'

'That's not what I want, and it's not going to happen,' Sam said, his husky voice bubbling with its accustomed energy. 'I own the company. I have a right to be overprotective about it and to work long hours. Your mother understood that, and so have you. But if you're suggesting that I overwork my executives...'

Ruefully Laura smiled her admiration for Sam's famous talent at argument and cajolery.

'There you go, putting words in my mouth again,' she said. 'I didn't say your high-level people aren't happy. But they will be more than a little annoyed when they see an inexperienced nobody like me elevated to a position on par with their own. They're experts, Dad. I'm only a novice at this business.'

'Well, now,' Sam said with a theatrical gesture of hurt pride. 'First she tells me I'm a slavedriver, and now she claims I don't know better than to hire incompetent executives.'

'Dad!' Laura returned, her patience wearing thin. 'Please don't be this way. If you need more help in Research, why don't you simply find someone truly competent and hire him—or her? There are experienced people all over the country who would love to come to work for you.'

Sam Christensen shook his head slowly as he twirled the empty wine glass in his hand. Even in her exasperation at his stubbornness Laura had to admire his vitality. The small brown eyes looking out from beneath his thick brows were alive with a sparkling urgency from which a touch of humour was never absent. The hint of grey at his temples only served to accentuate the youthful thickness of his sandy-coloured hair. Everyone said Sam looked twenty years younger than his age, and Laura herself was often disconcerted by his energy. After a long day spent in the busy workshops of Christensen Products' research division, she felt so drained that her father's buoyant high spirits seemed nothing short of superhuman.

The company was his life's blood, and had been for the last thirty years. From its first halting steps in the turbulent business world of the East Coast to its present status as a major producer of precision industrial parts and small appliances, Christensen Products had been Sam's vocation and avocation combined. With a zest that daunted his competitors and assured the fidelity of his employees, Sam watched over the company, now expanding its capacities, now cutting back, now pioneering a new product, now struggling with a faltering market. He was the company's mother hen and cheerful master of ceremonies, and his every executive move bespoke more than a mere ambition for growth or success. It was genuine love for his vulnerable, growing creation that motivated him, as each bright young executive he hired soon learned.

Sam's profit-sharing arrangement with his employees was considered revolutionary when he first instituted it over a generation ago. His experiments with four-day work weeks and innovative retirement programmes had the experts in Personnel scratching their heads in befuddlement—until the resulting increases in Christensen's productivity forced them to acknowledge his genius for getting the most out of his workers.

With the passing years Sam had become a legendary figure in the business community. When his wife died as he was approaching retirement age it was assumed that he would finally hand over the reins of his company to one of his trusted lieutenants, and content himself with a place on his own Board of Directors. But Sam surprised everyone, including Laura, by throwing himself into his work with more eagerness than ever.

'I've promised my daughter I'll retire and take it easy,' ran his oft-quoted statement in a New York business magazine's admiring profile, '—as soon as she reaches the age of sixty-five.'

Indeed, only Sam's protective concern for his daughter seemed a more urgent consideration than his own future. After her mother's death he found time for regular visits to the large university where Laura was completing her degree in engineering. Though he kept his own grief in a private corner of his personality, he spoke with touching intuition of the pain such a loss can bring to a young woman starting out in life.

'Death is not a welcome guest, Laura,' she recalled his grave and realistic words. 'You've got to feel bad. Your mother would have expected you to. But she would also want you to bury your loss, keep her in your memory, and start living again. You go back to your work now, and show those professor types what you're made of. One of these mornings you'll wake up feeling good again.'

At the time Laura had accepted her father's kindly support and reassurance without a second thought. Today, when she looked back on those painful times, she could not find words to express her gratitude for the sacrifices Sam had made on her behalf. Though a busy and influential businessman whose company was rapidly becoming a small empire, he would appear on campus to take her to dinner, to a movie or concert, for all the world as though he had no obligations which could compete with his pride in his daughter's academic achievements.

Upon her graduation Sam offered Laura a position in his company.

'We like to interview as many promising young people as we can,' he said with a straight face. 'Of course, with your qualifications, you'll want to consider other possibilities, other companies perhaps. But I think I can promise you an exciting outlet for your talents at Christensen Products. Naturally your own decision will be final, and whatever you choose will be fine with me.'

With new eyes Laura studied the Research Division she had occasionally visited as a curious schoolgirl. Sam Christensen was an inventor at heart, and never shrank from investing time and money in exciting product ideas and the people who refined them—even if the time for such products had not yet come in the uncertain economy of the moment. Laura's college education had equipped her to contribute creatively to product development, and she could see opportunities for a rapid increase in her own knowledge through work at Christensen.

Still, Laura wondered whether she should go to work for her own father. The idea came as a surprise, for Sam had never mentioned it during her high school or college years.

Her decision was made for her when she studied the finely tuned interrelationships of all the divisions at Christensen's New Haven headquarters. While working in research Laura would be able to learn all there was to know about materials, test marketing, design and manufacture. Rather than languish in an isolated corner of the corporation, she could follow each new product from its birth on the design table or computer display to its final role in a modern factory or consumer household.

Finally, Laura was impressed by the camaraderie and high spirits of her father's employees. From the line workers to the highest executives, they admired and trusted Sam Christensen. What was more, they seemed delighted with the prospect of working with Laura, and no one hinted at the slightest resentment of her.

It was too happy and stimulating a situation to refuse. One month after her college graduation Laura came to work in New Haven. With Sam's agreement she found a comfortable apartment at a convenient distance from work. Sam continued to occupy the stately house on Everit Street.

'You'll feel better on your own,' he said. 'You're an independent young woman now, and there's no reason for you to be tied to your old man's house. Besides,' he added with his wry smile, 'the wild parties at my place would keep you from getting your sleep.'

In the four years since that happy beginning, Laura's ideas about her professional future had changed radically. No longer content to pursue her original plan of working exclusively in engineering, she began to look forward to the distant day when she might run her own small business. Perhaps, she reflected, something of Sam's proprietary tenderness for his own products had rubbed off on her. More and more she imagined herself working closely with a team of business professionals to create and market innovative consumer products. One day she would control a modest company of her own, and would be familiar with every detail of its operations. To watch such an enterprise grow under her own care would be a dream come true.

Sam must have sensed this budding ambition in his daughter, for his sparkling eyes rested proudly on her as he answered her eager questions about Christensen Products' complex financial structure during their regular dinners together. But as time passed Laura realised there was an ulterior motive behind his encouragement. Sam shared her dream that she might one day control her own company. But he wanted that company to be Christensen Products. What was more, his timetable for Laura's rise to top-level executive responsibility was far more ambitious than her own.

Today's lighthearted argument was merely the latest skirmish in a quiet battle which had been going on between father and daughter for over two years. Laura was not at all convinced that her relatively limited experience in research qualified her for so challenging a position as Vice-President. Nor was she sure that her sudden rise in rank would please the employees with whom she had worked on such friendly terms. Given the choice, she knew she might well prefer to remain prudently ensconced among her creative, somewhat excitable research colleagues, and to confine her ambition to lobbying Sam for the manufacture of certain new products which remained at the prototype stage. Chief among these was an ingenious portable dust filtration system designed by a Christensen engineer named Randy Powers. The unique sensitivity of the filter Randy had invented permitted the little machine to virtually eliminate dust throughout several rooms of a house or apartment.

Laura's cost analyses had convinced her that the device could be marketed at an affordable price. But Sam insisted that in the depressed economy of the day its immediate production would be too great a risk against projected profits. Through continuing cajolery and thorough marketing projections Laura hoped to change his mind.

Now, as she contemplated Sam's plump body and expectant eyes, Laura had no inkling that her choices were about to run out.

'Dad,' she said, 'you have your own contacts. Why don't you find someone who is truly qualified for this job? Someone who is already respected in his field...like Frank Jordan.'

The name slipped out before Laura could suppress it. Only a month ago Frank Jordan, a top executive in the New York headquarters of the enormous Schell International conglomerate, had delighted Sam by agreeing to join Christensen Products. Jordan's reputation as an expert manager and financial analyst had preceded him and, on the few occasions when she found herself in his presence, Laura had decided that his arrogance more than matched his reputed abilities.

'Frank Jordan?' Sam shrugged. 'He's a special case. He's trained for a bigger pond than Christensen, but he simply got sick and tired of all the red tape in that Schell behemoth. He likes our products, and we're lucky to have him. But he's a troubleshooter rather than a specialist.'

Troublemaker is more like it, Laura thought ruefully. The memory of Jordan's sharp, piercing eyes and roguish demeanor had irked her since their first meeting. Though he stopped short of real condescension towards Sam's executives, Frank seemed sceptical of nearly all the business concepts they took for granted. After listening with an air of calm evaluation to the proposals of others, he would respond with laconic, pitilessly analytical remarks which bespoke a colossal self-confidence to match his highly original business mind. Laura could not help suspecting that Jordan, who was rumoured to have been a trusted confidant of the great Armand Schell himself, considered himself to be slumming in a mid-sized company like Christensen Products.

Her impression was hardly diminished by the ill-concealed mockery of the glances he shot her way. Uncomfortably she wondered whether he was pigeonholing her as the spoiled corporate daughter whose abilities did not justify her position. And she was more than a little daunted by the aggressive and even ruthless view of marketing tactics to which he was implacably committed. To judge by the hard, handsome lines of his tanned face, he was a man in his mid-thirties who had already tasted so much power and success that he was pleased to lower his personal sights for Sam's sake. Yet his demeanour suggested so boundless an ambition that Laura could not understand why he had not sought a company presidency for himself.

'Perhaps Jordan is not the best example,' she admitted. 'But the business world is full of experts, Dad. I'm only a beginner.'

'Laura,' Sam sighed, 'on one point only I'll agree that you are inexperienced. That point is hiring. I've been moving this company along for thirty years now, and I've hired and fired a lot of high management people. I've learned one thing from my experience: you've got to fill your responsible positions with people who care about the company, over and above their ability to do the work. I can spot that quality a mile away, and smell out its absence just as easily. You have the dedication I want and need, Laura. You're not in this business just to buy yourself a house with a swimming pool. You want to learn and to contribute. Now, give your old man credit for some old-fashioned good sense. I want you to take over Research because I know I can count on you to do the job for this company.'

'And if I failed?' Laura asked quietly.

'That's impossible,' he shook his head. 'I know what you're made of, Laura.'

Sam seemed to have tired suddenly. His ruddy cheeks

had gone slack, and he touched his forehead with an unsteady hand.

'Dad, let's not talk about this any more now,' Laura said.

'Where's Mary?' Sam frowned. 'Tell her to get me an aspirin, would you, honey? I've got the damndest headache.'

'I'll get it myself.' Pushing back her chair Laura hurried from the dining room. Sam's one concession to his doctor's orders was the large bottle of aspirins in his upstairs medicine cabinet. He took one tablet per day in accordance with the current theory that the drug's anti-coagulant properties might provide insurance against circulatory troubles.

Laura shook two tablets into her palm and started down the stairs. The twang of a fallen glass against silverware in the dining room below made her hurry her steps.

Sam was staring into space, his expression wan and depressed. Laura had never seen such sad preoccupation in his sparkling eyes. His water glass lay on its side on the tablecloth.

'Dad?' Laura approached him, alarmed by the sudden change in his demeanour.

But before she could place a hand on his shoulder he exhaled sharply, gasped, and fell forward, his face on the table top.

'Dad!' Laura cried in confusion. 'Mary!'

The colour was beginning to leave the unconscious man's cheeks. Laura grasped his wrist, touched his neck, and saw her own tears fall on his shoulder.

'Mary! Call an ambulance. Hurry! I think he's had a heart attack.'

Desperately Laura fought to recall the resuscitation techniques she had learned while a college student. She pulled her father's inert body to the floor. The pupils of his staring eyes were dilated, immobile. To her horror there was no pulse.

Time seemed to curl upon itself and disappear like a fold in a curtain as she pressed at the burly chest beneath her, for in a trice white-shirted men were pulling her away from her father and shouting orders to each other as they worked on his motionless form. Underneath the plastic mask covering his mouth and nose, Sam Christensen seemed even less himself. His blue face was neither sad nor happy. It was adamant, stubborn, empty.

Laura knew then that he was already dead.

She rode with him in the ambulance, banished to a corner of the vehicle by the busy paramedics. Bleakly she followed his stretcher to the emergency room, and stood unseeing as the doctors extended its aluminum legs and moved him to a heavy table.

No one thought to force her to leave as a resident, barking commands to his team, forced a syringe into Sam's chest. Everyone moved so quickly, Laura thought without hope. The body jumped like a marionette attached to unseen strings as the electrodes sent shocks through the gel smeared over its chest.

For what seemed an eternity the struggle to revive Sam continued, punctuated by grunted, irritable words of encouragement and exhortation from the doctors. As their science reached its limits, they called to Dad, importuned him to wake up, pleaded with him.

It had taken ten minutes. Sam Christensen was pronounced Dead on Arrival at Yale-New Haven Hospital at 7:21 p.m., November 9th. The cause of his death, as written on the certificate mailed to Laura three days later, was a massive stroke.

CHAPTER TWO

'I'M afraid we can't help you any longer,' Andrew Dillon said coolly from behind his enormous executive desk. 'First Federal's policies on corporate debt may seem inflexible, but without them we would go bankrupt ourselves. Your company is in arrears on sixty million dollars' worth of short-term debt, Miss Christensen, and most of those notes will come due within the next six to seven months. First Federal simply can't carry Christensen Products on those terms.'

Through the haze of her anxiety Laura noticed Andrew Dillon's coldly efficient demeanor. He was all business—there was no doubt of that. The cup of coffee he had decorously poured for Laura now sat untouched by her side, its steaming warmth having vanished along with her hopes. Still vital in his late middle age, Andrew Dillon looked down upon her through grey eyes under his immaculately tonsured white hair. Behind him the Manhattan skyline gleamed under the bright November sun outside the First Federal Bank's enormous headquarters.

As President of the bank, Andrew Dillon was responsible for every transaction going on in the hundreds of offices throughout this building, and in branches all over New England. Lulled at first by his gentle urbanity, Laura had come to realise that it concealed his banker's interest in his own institution's prosperity—at whatever cost in indifference and even cruelty towards those beholden to him.

'I…I don't understand how this could have happened so suddenly,' Laura stammered. 'I'm sure…'

'I think you'd have to discuss that with your own accounting people,' Mr Dillon interrupted. 'I know your father was perfectly aware that Christensen was on the brink of an urgent financial situation. However, he did not apprise us of his intentions in the matter. With Sam Christensen dead, sad as the situation is, the bank really has no alternative.'

Laura reddened to hear the note of condescension in his voice. Clearly he believed that Christensen Products was an unacceptable risk for his bank since the demise of its dynamic founder.

'What do you suggest?' Laura asked evenly.

'Well.' Andrew Dillon moved slightly in his chair and placed his elbows on the desk before him. Laura thought she sensed a trace of animation in him at last. 'There are of course many options which you'll want to discuss with your own people. Bankruptcy is one.' He pronounced the word without a hint of hesitation or sympathy.

'Bankruptcy?' Laura exclaimed in shock. 'You can't mean that.'

'As I say, it's one option. Bankruptcy would allow you the retention of a fraction of the company's assets while satisfying your creditors. The other major option, of course, is a merger. This is somewhat more problematic, since you'd have to find a corporation large enough to absorb your debt. However, I think there is a chance in this direction.'

'What chance?' Her head spinning, Laura fought to concentrate her attention on his every word.

'First Federal has some minor dealings, for instance, with Schell International's American division. Of my knowledge I am aware that Schell has an interest in some of the markets your father has developed over the years. I don't know if they have any intention of acting on that now, of course. Multinational corporations like Schell are unpredictable. Sometimes they make decisions virtually overnight, and sometimes they take months or even years. Nevertheless, Schell seems to me a good bet for you.'

For years the financial publications Laura read had been full of news of the enormous Schell Corporation. Its subsidiaries spanned the world, and for twenty years its stock had grown steadily in value. Christensen Products, despite its own large size and importance to the economy of the East Coast, was a mere corporate midget compared to the Schell empire.

Yet Laura recalled that the business press rarely spoke of Schell's recent dealings with real admiration. The conglomerate's reputation as an innovative manufacturing and construction entity seemed to have tarnished even as its power increased. Perhaps, Laura wondered, this was the reason Frank Jordan had decided to leave its anonymous ranks in order to work for Sam.

'Such a merger would mean the end of my father's company,' she said quietly.

'Not necessarily,' Andrew Dillon smiled. 'The name might well remain the same. Your product line might not change appreciably. But Schell would, of course, have management responsibility and control of your Board. You yourself, Miss Christensen, would certainly have a place within your company—or, if you preferred, you could of course live quite well on what the merger would bring you.'

Inwardly Laura felt a rush of anger at the implacable calm of the man before her. She knew that absorption by Schell would destroy the independent company her father had slaved thirty years to build. Many of the executives he had trained so carefully would be fired, and the practices he had begun in product development would be superseded by Schell's own ideas. Christensen Products would be no more than a paper company.

'If you like,' Andrew Dillon was saying, 'I can look into the situation myself. A little informal chat with Roy Schell could do no harm. I can simply mention that you might be interested in a merger—at the right price, of course, and on the right terms.'

Laura took a deep breath.

'Let me discuss this with my own people,' she sighed, 'and I'll get back to you.'

A frown replaced Andrew Dillon's mild expression.

'Fine,' he said coolly, rising to usher Laura out. 'Let me know what you think. But remember that time is short. If you want to avoid simple bankruptcy we'll have to move with alacrity. One has to prepare the ground for these things. And one more thing, Miss Christensen: please accept my sympathy over Sam's tragic death.'

'Thank you, Mr. Dillon. I'll be in touch.'

'I'm afraid First Federal is right about one thing, Laura. Sam left the company in a dangerously overextended condition, and we're going to have to do something about it.'

Fearfully Laura looked into the tawny irises fixed upon her. Rob Colwell was seated by her side in the conference room adjacent to Sam Christensen's empty office.

'But closing our factories and laying off our workers,' Laura sighed, 'strikes me as hardly more acceptable than bankruptcy.'

'Don't lose your sense of perspective,' Rob warned. 'We're only talking about three factories. Christensen Products will survive this cutback and come back strong when the economy improves. Remember that, Laura. We're down, but we're a long way from out.'

With an effort Laura returned his smile. Nothing could shake Rob's blunt gallantry. Throughout Sam's funeral on

Sunday he had remained at her side, steadfast and silent while several of Sam's distinguished business colleagues, partners and competitors alike, delivered impassioned eulogies for their lost friend. And now that Sam's passing had been reported and his thirty-year stewardship of his beloved company chronicled in all the business newspapers, Rob remained as Laura's closest link to Sam himself.

Ten years ago Sam had hired Rob as a fresh-faced business school graduate bent on making his fortune. But Rob had soon surprised himself as well as his employer by showing complete indifference to formal advancement within the company's ranks. Business, it turned out, was an entirely intellectual challenge to him. He cared only to understand the corporation in its most intimate workings, and to offer a consultant's advice on the best strategies for improving its sales and productivity.

And, above all, he cared for Sam Christensen. For years he had been Sam's executive assistant and troubleshooter, and no Christensen executive dared claim either Rob's encyclopaedic knowledge of the company's far-flung operations or his privileged status in the eyes of its founder.

The two men's nocturnal telephone conversations had become the object of wry speculation on the part of the other executives. Rob's phone would ring at three or four in the morning, and he would rub the sleep out of his eyes as Sam's ruminative voice filled his ear.

'Rob,' Sam would say, 'I've been looking at our Florida sales and thinking about what you said this morning.'

In Rob's benumbed state the previous morning seemed light years from the present. He had to struggle to recall what his insomniac boss was talking about.

'Now, if that market is going sour because of the oil shortage,' the disembodied voice went on, 'the conventional wisdom would suggest that we cut our advertising budget down south and pull in our belts for a while. Am I making sense?'

'Well, sir, it depends…'

'My thoughts exactly, Rob. My thoughts exactly. Perhaps the conventional wisdom is wrong this time. Suppose Christensen were to hit that market for all it's worth, now that everyone else is unsure of what to do. We're strong enough in New England to absorb a bit of a loss…'

'Then,' Rob yawned, 'when the tide turns…'

'Exactly,' Sam laughed. 'We'll be stronger than ever in small industry. Let's talk about this tomorrow early, Rob. And Rob?'

'Yes, sir?'

'I'm just looking at the time. Awfully sorry if I woke you up.'

'Don't mention it, Sam.'

Thus a new idea would be born through Christensen Products' nocturnal hot line. As he brooded in his bathrobe over the reports and projections on his desk at home, Sam would reach reflexively for his telephone and dial Rob's number without a glance at the clock or a conscious notion of what he planned to say. But the sound of his trusted confidant's voice sufficed to unleash a stream of thoughts which often contained the key to the company's future.

Sam Christensen adored Rob Colwell for his loyalty and intellect. For Laura, then in her teens, her father's handsome young assistant had another sort of aura. With his strong, athletic frame and curly hair tinged with a fugitive tint of red, Rob was the image of youthful vitality and virile charm. Since he came to dinner often at the Everit Street house, Laura had more than her share of opportunities to cast diffident glances of admiration at him, and to blush with embarrassment when he smiled acknowledgment.

In those days Laura had not yet grown into the confident

and creative young woman who was to emerge from her college years. She was a pretty teenager whose laughing eyes and blossoming figure concealed a personality which still had rough edges. Though Rob might well have noticed the painfully romantic longings which tied her tongue in his presence, his attitude was anything but condescending. Whenever the intensity of his conversations with Sam allowed a few moments' breathing space, Rob drew Laura out on her plans for the future. He encouraged her interest in engineering, speaking knowledgeably on the subject himself.

To make matters yet more thrilling, Rob always noticed Laura's clothes and hair. His relaxed compliments, proffered in private so as not to draw attention to her in front of Sam, only served to increase his prestige in her imagination, for she attributed to them the same incontrovertible authority that Sam found in his invaluable advice.

Though the torch Laura carried for Rob Colwell dimmed as her adolescence gave way to college life and new ambitions, it left its mark upon her. The memory of Rob's quiet confidence and daunting male attractiveness hung at the back of her mind, and in comparison with it the excitable young men she met at school seemed oddly shallow. She found herself immersed in her academic work without second thoughts about the relative lack of romance in her life, inwardly confident that when the time was right a man of Rob's mature virility would cross her path.

When she returned to Christensen as an employee she became fully aware of Rob's enormous importance to the company, and felt a twinge of involuntary trepidation in his presence. He seemed even more handsome than four years before, for the passage of time had sharpened his incisive self-assured demeanour. A supremely eligible young professional, he was possessed of a business acumen which was more than a little intimidating.

To Laura's immense relief he welcomed her to the company with open arms, and made a point of visiting her small office at regular intervals for encouraging conversations. The four years that followed saw the blossoming of their friendship as well as their professional relationship. As Laura's own responsibilities within the corporation increased, Rob offered constant advice and moral support. The buoying caress of his smiling eyes became a virtual extension of the aura of happy camaraderie which emanated from Sam Christensen's irrepressible personality.

But today Rob's expression was hooded by concern, and his jaw set in deep concentration on the urgent business at hand.

'Zalman, I think you agree on which facilities will have to go.' Rob turned to Zalman Corey, Christensen's Vice-President in charge of Finance, who adjusted his horn-rimmed glasses nervously as he removed a sheet of paper from his briefcase.

'I'll tell you what I told Sam before his death,' Zalman said quickly. 'Our weakest points are Springfield, Albany and Rochester. If we close plants in those three places, sell the properties and eliminate the payroll, the financial benefit will probably see us through. Some of our product lines will, of course, have to be eliminated…'

'When you say "probably",' Laura interjected, 'do you mean that bankruptcy is still a possibility?'

Zalman Corey pulled at his tie. 'Only if things get a hell of a lot worse across the board in the next two quarters,' he said. 'Pardon my language,' he added sheepishly.

Laura turned to Rob. 'And you concur in this?' she asked.

'I think Zalman has said what needs to be said,' Rob nodded. 'Sam built Christensen into a very secure corporation, Laura. I wouldn't want you to think he in any way mismanaged the company. But he expanded our facilities during a more secure period. The point is that no one is safe nowadays.'

Laura frowned in consternation. She had hopefully conjectured that Andrew Dillon's alarming words were merely calculated to achieve some sort of psychological advantage over her. But now her most trusted colleagues seemed to suggest that Sam had left his company in a state of grave peril indeed.

'One more thing,' she said, intentionally keeping silent about Andrew Dillon's mention of Schell International. 'What about a merger?'

Rob shook his head. 'That's always a possibility for a company the size of Christensen, whose products have a good reputation. But in today's market the terms of a merger would not be favourable to us. No one will want to pay us what we're worth.'

Zalman Corey nodded ruminatively.

'However,' Laura pursued, 'if whatever cutbacks we make don't solve our problems, we might be forced to accept absorption by some national or multinational corporation somewhere down the line—and on even worse terms than we would get today.'

'Anything is possible, Laura.' Rob Colwell's eyes were grim. 'The worst eventuality as well as the best.'

'What I don't understand,' Laura said, 'is how we can be faced with such a choice so soon after Dad's death. I have the feeling that the whole picture has changed simply because he's been…eliminated from it.'

'I don't think Sam wanted to worry you with all this before his untimely passing, Laura,' Zalman Corey said. 'He knew there were hard times coming, but he was, or considered himself to be, in the prime of health. Sam was a brave man, and a very bright one. He simply assumed he would get us through this with a minimum of damage to the company.'

And perhaps he would have, Laura thought with a pang of grief for Christensen's lost leader. If Sam saw fit to run his company on a business-as-usual basis in the face of financial pressure from First Federal Bank, it could only have been because he had reason to believe his wit and guile would allow him to prevail. But the plans he had in his mind had followed him to the grave.

'Frank, you haven't said anything.' Rob turned to glance across the conference table's rich walnut expanse. As she followed his gaze to the chair in which Frank Jordan had sat in silence since the conversation began, Laura realised that a fearful instinct had made her avoid looking in his direction until now. In her own mind Frank still bore the sign of the monstrous Schell conglomerate whose power Andrew Dillon had evoked so blandly. She wondered whether the urgency of Christensen Products' predicament struck him as a novel experience after his years with the indestructible Schell empire.

Through his black eyes Frank made an inscrutable gesture which was neither agreement nor disagreement. But Laura could feel the quick turning of the wheels in his analytical mind.

'Well,' Rob turned back to her with a trace of discomfort, 'we'll all think it over. But there's one more important piece of business that has to be mentioned before we break up. I've been on the phone with some of our Board members, Laura, and we've found a curious amendment to our bylaws that Sam pushed through not long ago. According to this amendment, in the event of the company president's sudden death or departure, the majority stockholder becomes chief executive officer until such time as a new president is named.'

'I don't understand,' Laura said. In the hectic days since Sam's death she had not found time to dwell on Christensen's executive hierarchy, and had simply assumed that a new president would eventually be chosen by the Board from among the officers Sam had respected most.

'Well,' Rob smiled, 'since Sam left all his stock to you, Laura, you are now the majority stockholder. That means you are now President of Christensen Products.'

The shock occasioned by his words left Laura numb. She heard none of the casual remarks exchanged by her colleagues as they drifted from the room. But in a corner of her field of vision she thought she saw a slight smile curl Frank Jordan's tight lips.

It was a smile of amusement and of contempt.

CHAPTER THREE

Schell, Armand, mfr.; born Prague, Sept. 11, 1900; son of Janek and Sofia Schell; emigrated 1916; American citizenship 1921; B.S., Columbia University, Summa cum laude, 1919. With American Can Co., Forest Park, N.J. 1919-20. Successively member field sales staff, asst. district sales mgr., vice pres. sales. 1922 founded New Jersey Metal. Expansion throughout East Coast (incl. acquisition of American Can) 1920s. 1930 company name changed to Schell Inc. 1930s expansion incl. electronics, communications, construction, shipbuilding subsidiaries. 1937 company name changed to Schell International Inc., multi-national corp. with subsidiaries throughout W. Europe, S. America. 1940-5 weapons and ship mfr. for Allies; acquisitions incl. insurance companies, banks, hotels. 1940s advisor to Presidents Roosevelt, Truman. 1950 pres., NYC Fiscal Action Board. 1952 Special Envoy, European Financial Congress. President, Board chmn. Schell International Inc. 1937— company assets as of 1979: $33 billion.

Mar. Andrea V. Morgan, June 19, 1928. Children: Anton Schell, b. 1932 (q.v.), Roy Schell, b. 1938 (q.v.). Second marriage to Barbara Bond (cf. Andrew Bond, 1911-), Oct. 6, 1952. Divorced 1970. Daughter, Julia Bond Schell, b. 1958.

AN endless list of fellowships, memberships and honorary degrees followed, filling an entire page of the volume of

Who's Who in Finance and Industry which lay open on the desk before Laura. With a sigh she turned her tired eyes from the columns of fine print and considered the story of ruthless ambition hidden between their lines.

When still in his teens Armand Schell had completed his college education and begun a business career that straddled wars, depressions and recessions without a single false step. Turning world events unfailingly to his own advantage, he had risen to a pinnacle of political and financial influence unmatched by any single business figure since Rockefeller.

But the clipped biography made no reference to what was common knowledge in the business community. Armand Schell, a legend in his own time, was past his prime and in failing health. His two sons controlled the inner workings of Schell International and made most of its decisions on acquisitions. Most observers had concluded that with advancing age the conglomerate's founder had either lost interest in what he once termed his 'mission' as a manufacturer, or was simply too weak to resist the new generation of profit-oriented executives headed by his sons. As a result, Schell International was rapidly becoming a crazy quilt of unrelated companies whose interests often conflicted with one another. Yet its profits continued to grow apace, for dozens of governments around the world were beholden to Schell for important investments.

No longer a corporate innovator, Schell was now an essentially financial institution whose sheer dimensions defied precise description. Few sovereign nations could match its gross yearly product.

It was the last corporation in the world one would choose for an enemy.

Roy Schell and his brother Anton had their own short entries in *Who's Who*. Of Julia Bond Schell, the young daughter of Armand's unsuccessful second marriage, little was known. It was rumoured that the girl—whose delicate beauty shone forth from the rare news photos depicting her attendance at social and cultural events—lacked all interest in her father's business empire, and avoided the limelight intentionally.

Leaving the book open before her, Laura stared exhaustedly into space. The office was in darkness save for the fluorescent desk lamp whose beam illuminated the heavy volume. The digital clock beside the pen set Laura had given Sam six years ago read 11:36 p.m. Its large numbers, a balm for Sam's weak eyes, glowed emerald green against the obscurity behind.

No sound came from the corridor beyond the secretaries' empty office. Ernst, the elderly watchman with whom Sam had occasionally gone fishing on Sundays in summer, would be on a lower floor at this hour, mopping and dusting and emptying waste baskets with unhurried movements as he shook his head in disapproval of the fate that had torn his friend and boss from him.

Sam's huge desk was an unfamiliar landscape in the penumbra. Beside its old-fashioned blotter were Laura's graduation picture and an old portrait photo of her mother. The snapshot of Sam with his prize bass, taken by Laura on a carefree vacation in Maine, was a grey shadow on a distant wall. Surrounding it were framed pictures of Sam shaking hands with government officials, corporation presidents and friends. On another wall a profusion of testimonials and honorary diplomas reflected the pale light of the desk lamp.

As a child Laura had considered these accoutrements of a proud career as familiar furnishings, domestic and friendly. They were the cheerful background against which her laughing father took her on his knee, whirled her playfully in his huge swivel chair, and showed her off to his executives and secretaries.

Only when she came to work for Sam had she realised

that those pictures and diplomas testified to the full significance of his enormous achievements in business, and to the shrewdness and dedication with which he had built Christensen into an internationally respected corporation.

Now the walls, the smiling faces in their fragile frames, and even the lifeless pens in their marble stand had a bleak air of supplication. The spirit that had animated this office was gone forever. No one could bring it back.

And before long this office might not even exist in its present form. A new occupant and new, foreign furnishings might appear to wipe away the memory of Sam Christensen's sunlit life—unless something was done now to protect his legacy.

Why did you have to die? Laura thought miserably, a sudden upsurge of grief bringing tears to her eyes.

The contradiction of death seemed unbearably immediate. Sam was gone forever, and yet the cheerful rumble of his confident voice still echoed in all the corners of the room. Laura could almost feel his protective warmth enfolding her in the shadows, for the comfortable executive chair, tailored to his portly dimensions, was deliciously restful. Were it not for the crisis that had driven her here she might have lapsed into childlike slumber in its vast leather expanse.

She should be home in bed, she told herself irritably. Fatigue was tearing dangerously at her emotions. And heaven knew she would need her sleep.

But the revelations of the day had left her nerves on edge. She had come to Sam's office as President of his company, determined to get a feel for her new responsibility. Yet here she sat, paralysed by the irony of her situation. Sam had his wish: Laura had inherited his power and his position. But only his tragic and untimely death had made his dream come true, and his bereft daughter was far from capable of handling the job.

On the shelf behind her lay the financial reports on Christensen's plants in Rochester, Springfield and Albany. Their bland columns of figures told precisely the story Zalman Corey had outlined this afternoon. The three factories were running at half capacity, and since Sam had laid off as few workers as possible, they were generating huge losses. Rob had written them off bluntly.

Zalman, I think you agree on which facilities will have to go.

As a girl Laura had accompanied her father on visits to those branches. She had seen faces light up as Sam hurried along the assembly lines, shaking hands, joking with workers whose names he unfailingly remembered, accepting the friendly barbs directed at him, and enquiring about the health problems and academic successes of his employees' children. Everyone seemed to smile upon him with familial tenderness as they exclaimed over the extent of Laura's growth since her last visit.

Our weakest points are Springfield, Albany and Rochester. If we close plants in those three places, the financial benefit will probably see us through.

Now Laura was expected to lay off all those loyal, hardworking people. She could imagine their unsuccessful job searches in this day of high unemployment, and the long hours they would spend doing crossword puzzles or reading paperback books in the state unemployment offices while styrofoam cups of coffee cooled in their hands. The men in middle age would not find jobs to replace those they had lost at Christensen. Their pensions would be lost. In all likelihood the effects of their joblessness would quickly extend to the education of the very children whose names Sam used to recall so casually.

And when it was all over those idle workers would sigh philosophically and trace the origin of their misfortune to

Sam's death and his daughter's accession to control of the corporation.

Some of our product lines will, of course, have to be eliminated...

Alone in the quiet office, Laura shook her head.

'Something about this isn't right,' she thought, pursing her lips in frustration. Andrew Dillon's ultimatum, so shockingly absolute in the wake of Sam's sudden death, had an odd ring, as did Zalman Corey's seemingly ready-made suggestion to reduce overheads by closing factories. And there was the crucial fact that Sam himself had made no provision at all for such a move.

Sam must have known something important which allowed him to conclude that production cutbacks would not be necessary, despite his company's financial woes.

But what? What did he know?

'I have to find out,' Laura thought grimly, rebelling at the notion of being browbeaten into submission. Everyone seemed convinced that her inexperience required her to accept this blow to Christensen Products with suitable meekness. Only the shade of Sam's indefatigable spirit urged her silently to refuse to give in.

'They won't have me that cheap,' she murmured to herself in stubborn defiance. If she lacked the expertise to see a clear solution to her dilemma, she at least possessed the will to find it at all costs.

'Head spinning?'

With a start she looked up, frightened by the deep voice that had torn her from her reverie. Frank Jordan stood before her in the half-light, his jacket thrown over his shoulder, his open collar revealing the dark web of curly hair covering his deep chest.

She frowned, irked to see him loom so close to her when she had thought she was alone.

'I didn't hear you come in,' she said coolly.

'I knocked at the door,' he smiled. 'You seemed lost in thought.'

She had to look up into the blackness beyond the lampshade to see the face above his long limbs. A hint of mockery quirked his dark brow as he gazed down at her.

'What brings you here at this hour?' she asked, straightening a lock of her tangled hair.

'I was on my way out,' he said, 'and stopped by because something told me you might be here. I can see you're your father's daughter. Burning the midnight oil, just like Sam.'

She could think of no response, for the arrogance of his tone made it plain that he found her efforts at leadership amusing. She recalled the snide look in his eyes after Rob dropped his bombshell about her new position.

Having noticed the open book before her, Frank placed his large hands on the desk top and leaned closer to her. His clean male scent seemed to cover her suddenly, and she could feel the warmth of his breath. Reflecting that she had never found herself at such close quarters with him before, Laura had to force herself to meet the penetrating eyes fixed on her.

'Dillon mentioned Schell International to you, didn't he?' he asked abruptly.

'I beg your pardon?' she returned.

'Andrew Dillon,' he said. 'He talked about possible mergers when you went to see him, didn't he? That's why you were asking about the idea today, wasn't it? And he mentioned Schell, didn't he?'

Unnerved by his stabbing questions, Laura struggled to control her anger.

'What gives you that idea?' she asked curtly. 'And what difference does it make? You heard what Rob said.'

He leaned closer to her, the hard lines of his tanned face adding their force to his sharp words.

'It isn't hard to put two and two together,' he said.

'You're sitting here in the middle of the night poring over *Who's Who*. I can read upside down, Miss Christensen. It's a talent that's easy to develop. Now, what could make you so interested in Armand Schell? Someone must have drawn your attention to his corporation.'

'All right,' Laura sighed irritably. 'Yes, his name was mentioned. What of it?'

'And I did hear what Rob Colwell said,' he added. 'He said a merger would be disadvantageous to Christensen. That, by the way, was the only competent piece of advice you were given today.'

He sat down in the chair opposite Laura, his eyes appraising her reaction to his words.

'I'm sure I don't know what you're talking about,' she said, bristling at his arrogance.

'I can see that,' he agreed ironically. 'You have quite a problem, Miss Christensen. Your company is about to go down the drain, and you don't know what any of it is all about. Do you?'

Appalled by his condescension, Laura felt a rush of anger in her tired nerves.

'If you came up here to insult me…' she began.

'Not to insult you,' he cut her off. 'To warn you. And, if possible, to talk some sense into you. You're going to need all of it you can find, and in a hurry.'

Laura regarded him in silence for a long moment, determined not to allow his imperious demeanour to cow her. This day had been bad enough already without his invasion of her privacy. Yet something in his intense gaze dissuaded her from simply asking him to leave.

'Do you intend to explain yourself?' she asked at last.

'I'm going to try,' he said calmly. 'But it won't be easy, because you're not experienced enough to understand what is at stake in all this. I respected your father, Miss Christensen, but I think he made a silly mistake in setting things up so that you'd inherit a responsibility so far over your head. He loved this company, but in his ambition for you he may have destroyed it.'

Stung by his words, Laura would have loved to send him away with a comment to match his own insolence. Yet his accusation was not without its grain of painful truth. With an effort of will she resolved to find out what was in his mind.

'Leaving my incompetence to evaluate what you came here to say,' she said, 'why don't you just come out with it, Mr Jordan?'

'All right,' he responded without taking his eyes from her. 'Your friend Colwell and Zalman Corey have given you some bad advice. If you follow it, you'll be playing right into Andrew Dillon's hands. And don't believe he's bluffing. He's in earnest.'

'Why do you say that?' Laura asked.

'Because I know him. I know his type.' Frank's eyes narrowed. 'Dillon is expecting you to run scared by reducing overhead and cutting back production. That will weaken your company enough for him to flatten it when the short-term debt comes due—or before, if it suits him. He's gambling that your fear will blind you to the reality. And his gamble seems to be paying off.'

'I don't see…' Laura stammered.

'No, you don't,' he interrupted. 'That's obvious. But Sam saw, didn't he, Miss Christensen? Sam knew there was no reason to fear First Federal in the short run. That's why he had no intention of closing factories or dropping product lines. But now Sam is gone, isn't he?'

Carefully Laura scrutinised the firm lines of his handsome face. His gaze was pitiless, unforgiving. The careless waves of his black hair lent a roguish grace to his athletic form as he sat before her. His impertinence was unbearable, but the truth of his words was too penetrating to deny. In a trice he had probed to the essence of Laura's dilemma.

'As I see it,' he went on, 'your advisers have been living in too small a pond. They don't understand how corporate takeovers happen.'

'And I suppose you do,' Laura shot back.

'I've had some experience in the area,' he nodded, impervious to her sarcasm. 'I know Dillon, and I know Schell International. I also know something you haven't bothered to find out, and would probably never know if I weren't here to tell you: how the two are connected.'

'Connected?' Laura asked, taken aback. 'How?'

'Let me explain something to you,' he said, his hands motionless on the arms of his chair. 'A banker is not an impersonal institution, shrouded in old walnut and fancy board rooms, the way they like to pretend. A banker is an investor, no different from any speculator on the market. He puts his money into a lot of stocks, some more dependable than others. He can make mistakes, get in over his head, and lose money, just as you or I would.'

He paused, his dark eyes resting implacably upon her.

'Now, Andrew Dillon is in over his head right now,' he went on. 'First Federal's portfolio has been losing money for some years now. So Dillon is hanging on to the coat-tails of a man named Roy Schell. He's put every dollar he can find into a holding company called Beta Concepts, of which Roy Schell is the brains and major stockholder. The future of First Federal depends on that arrangement. Now, are you beginning to smell a conflict of interest?'

Laura frowned. 'You mean,' she said, 'that Dillon is beholden to Schell.'

'More than beholden,' he said. 'He practically works for Roy. He acts for Beta Concepts. Has to, in fact. That's where his money is, and where his tips come from. He's not the first banker to fall in with a conglomerator like Roy

Schell, and he won't be the last. Now, you can't expect a fellow like him to consider the best interests of a modest operation like Christensen when he has millions tied up in something so much bigger. Can you?'

'But where is the conflict of interest?' Laura asked.

'There wasn't any,' he said with a wry smile, 'until Dillon mentioned Schell International to you. That's when he gave himself away. If you knew Dillon, you'd know that his very mention of a merger with Schell proves that Roy had already told him he wanted to absorb Christensen. That's the only explanation possible.'

If Laura's head had not been spinning before, it certainly was now. Frank's revelations were as confusing as they were sinister.

'What makes you so sure of all this?' she asked.

'I wasn't at first,' he shrugged. 'It was a pretty solid hunch. But I haven't been working late today myself simply in order to impress my new boss, Miss Christensen. I've been doing a little checking, and I found out something that will interest you. Only hours after Andrew Dillon threatened you with bankruptcy, his bank was buying 50,000 shares of Christensen Products stock. It certainly looks as though he has more confidence in this company than he led you to believe, doesn't it?'

Laura shook her head in bewilderment. 'I don't understand,' she said.

'And not long afterwards,' he went on, 'a mutual fund called Barns & Porter, whose president is a close friend of Roy Schell, bought 65,000 shares of Christensen. For three days now there has been unusual movement in Christensen shares. Too much movement. Understandably, some of your long-time shareholders are nervous in the wake of Sam's death. So they're selling. But what is interesting is who is buying, and in such large amounts.'

'What does it mean?' Laura asked, hopelessly over her head in the welter of information he was forcing upon her.

'It means, young lady, that the raiders are upon you. Roy Schell is an expert at acquiring companies. He is quietly buying into your stock—using cover names to conceal himself—and influencing other speculators to do the same. These people all owe him favours, so when he tells them to buy or sell a stock, they obey. When he feels the time is right, he'll make a tender offer to all your stockholders at so attractive a price that they'll sell. Then he'll have enough of his people on your Board to force you to give up the company.'

'I'm sorry,' Laura sighed, 'but what is a tender offer?'

He shook his head in ill-concealed amazement at her ignorance. 'Let's suppose that Roy Schell has accumulated around 10 per cent of your company's stock,' he said. 'Now, he makes a public tender offer, either through full-page ads in the business papers or through direct mailings to your stockholders. He offers them either cash or equivalent stock in one of his own companies—say, Beta Concepts. The exchange rate he proposes is something they can't refuse, such as $1.75 to $2.00 for every dollar of Christensen stock they own. Since they're seduced by the quick profit to be made on the deal, they sell. And, of course, his personal friends like Andrew Dillon will sell when he tells them to. The result is that overnight Roy has taken over a huge block of your stock.'

'But doesn't he lose an awful lot of money by paying double for our shares?' Laura asked.

'His loss is tax deductible,' Frank smiled. 'That's just one of the loopholes that allows this sort of thing to happen in business today.'

Passing a tired hand over her furrowed brow, Laura fought to concentrate on the import of his words.

'But what about me?' she asked at last. 'I'm the majority stockholder. He can't make me sell *my* shares.'

'Good point,' Frank said. 'But he's thought of that, too. He's gambling that the short-term debt pressure you're under will force you to cut back production. Thus your price-earnings ratio will go down, and your stock will lose its value. Christensen Products will have a weak profile on the market. Then, of course, your shareholders will be all the more eager to sell. After Roy has accumulated enough shares for himself, he'll lower the boom by staging a nasty proxy fight in which you'll be accused of mismanaging the company since Sam's death, and of being the incompetent one-woman majority stockholder who's ruining the company through her stubbornness. At that point you'll own 51 per cent of nothing, Miss Christensen, and you'll be humiliated into selling out simply in order to save your employees' jobs. That's how the game is played. I've seen it many times.'

He shrugged indifferently. 'Of course,' he added, 'their jobs won't be safe. Roy will fire all your top executives and replace them with people who take orders from him. Christensen Products, as Sam knew it, will cease to exist. The company will be nothing more than a piece of paper in Roy Schell's portfolio.'

Horrified by the picture he had painted of her corporation's future, Laura gazed in dismay at his reclining form.

'But why?' she asked, unable to suppress the beseeching tone in her voice. 'Why is Christensen so important to him? Why us?'

'For investment purposes,' he responded blandly. 'Roy is a speculator. He deals in the hundreds of millions of dollars every month. He lives by manipulating stock prices, buying and selling companies, and taking losses for tax purposes while reaping profits on the Exchange. It's all a game to him—but a deadly one. He probably had his eye on Christensen long ago, but he must have known that Sam was too clever a man to let the company be taken over. Then, when Sam died and a crazy bylaw left Christensen without leadership, Roy saw his chance to move in for the kill. He called Andrew Dillon and a few other friends—and here you are, Miss Christensen, green as a calf, the ideal victim.'

'I suppose this is all a game to you, too,' Laura returned bleakly, hurt by his pitiless words.

'If you like,' he said coldly. 'I've been around people like Roy long enough to know the score.'

'Why have you bothered to tell me all this,' Laura asked bitterly, 'if there is no hope?'

'I didn't say there was no hope,' he said. 'There are ways to win a fight like this—if you have enough experience, and are smart enough to take some calculated risks.'

'Which I'm not,' Laura said. 'According to you, that is.'

'Time will tell,' he replied, raising an eyebrow speculatively as he held her with his stare. 'You're Sam's daughter. Sam was a smart man. You may be in over your head at the moment, but it's not impossible to rise above oneself if the situation requires it. In the meantime, Miss Christensen, you're not alone.'

'What do you mean?'

'I'm here to help you, if I can,' he said. 'I came to work for Sam because I admired the company he had built. Now he's gone, and through his own ill-advised plans for you he has put his life's work in jeopardy. But if you can be made to behave like an honest-to-goodness executive—which, as you say, you're not—we'll have a slim chance of forcing Schell to back off.'

'Wouldn't you feel more comfortable doing the job yourself?' Laura asked sharply. 'I'm sure the burden of my incompetence can't help the company.'

'You said it, I didn't.' His smile was sardonic. 'But to

answer your question, I have no interest in a company presidency for myself. Not at the moment, anyway. I came here to help Sam—not to take over. His death hasn't changed that.'

Infuriated by his complacency, Laura would have loved to find words to bring him up short. But the very axis of her existence had been hopelessly skewed by his frightening news, and suddenly it seemed that his shrewd intellect was the only ally that might save her from disaster. As she contemplated the straight contours of his powerful man's body, cursing the fate that had so suddenly made her dependent upon him, she resolved to swallow her pride and benefit as much as possible from his obvious expertise.

'All right,' she said at last. 'What do you suggest?'

He crossed his arms calmly. 'Dillon and Schell are counting on your inexperience and that of your advisers in defending yourself against a takeover,' he said. 'They're expecting you to react in fear to what happens. They correctly assume that if you drop assets and cut production, Christensen will be further weakened. The short-term debt is their main weapon. Therefore there is only one realistic way to defeat them.'

'What?' Laura asked.

'Don't react to what they do. Act, Miss Christensen. Make *them* react to *you*.'

His regard was inscrutable as Laura weighed his words. 'I don't understand,' she said hesitantly.

'They want you to make cutbacks. Therefore you expand. You produce. They want you to run scared. Therefore you act boldly. And most importantly, since they want you to behave as an impoverished corporation, the answer is simple: behave like the healthy and strong company Christensen really is. Make profit. Make the price of your stock go up, so that your own shareholders will be reluctant to sell. Make them understand that a merger will not be in their own best interest. If you do those things, Roy Schell will shrug his shoulders and look for a more pliant victim. He'll discourage easily when he sees that you're tougher than he thought.'

'But isn't that rather a tall order?' Laura asked in perplexity. 'You heard Zalman and Rob today...'

'It may be a tall order,' he said, 'but it's the only way. Either you make yourself some solid short-term profit and pay off those First Federal notes, or you're finished. It's as simple as that.'

He must have sensed her helplessness, for he went on in a gentler tone.

'I've seen it done before, Laura. A lot of companies have made fortunes overnight by keeping a sharp eye on the marketplace. It takes imagination and initiative, and a solid production base. You already have the base; Sam saw to that. All you have to do is use it for all it's worth. Look for the short-term profit Sam was too conservative to go after. Be aggressive. Take risks. It's your only chance, but it's worth a try.'

A quiet laugh escaped his lips as he leaned forward. 'I'm sorry,' he said. 'May I call you Laura? Or would you prefer Boss?'

Ignoring his irony, she pondered the logic of his recommendation. Though it seemed daring and even reckless on the surface, it might indeed prove necessary if the information he had brought her was correct. She would verify his claims about Andrew Dillon on her own. But to implement his advice was another matter entirely.

'And where is this short-term profit supposed to come from?' she asked.

'You'll find out,' he said. 'You've been here a lot longer than I have, and you've lived a lifetime with Sam. You know the company's basic strengths. Examine them. Go through your inventory and research analyses with a fine-toothed comb. Consult your advisers. Pick their brains. Talk to your sales staff. Look for that soft spot where the market will respond to a good, hard campaign. This corporation is a machine designed to turn production into profit. Make it work, Laura.'

He had stood up, and towered above her once more in the darkened office.

'But don't take too long,' he concluded. 'Time is short for you, and Roy Schell knows it.'

'You ask a lot,' she said, her tired eyes straying over the taut lines of his face and body. Clearly he was all dauntless strength and confidence, from his muscular limbs to his incisive mind. A perfect stranger to the fear that had coiled itself around Laura, he expected her to behave as he would in her situation.

'It's the job that asks a lot,' he corrected her. 'If you have to rise above yourself in order to fill it, then do it. I think I knew Sam well enough to know that that would have been his opinion.'

He glanced at the framed pictures on the far wall.

'Your dad was quite a man,' he said. 'He must have had a lot of faith in you, Laura, since he got you into this fix. You might as well give it your best effort, win or lose.'

His lips curled into a smile of amused sympathy as he looked down at her.

'But you can't go about the business of saving your company until you've had a good night's sleep,' he said. 'It's time you were in bed. Shall I walk you downstairs?'

Her fatigue dulling her senses, Laura stood up with a sigh. He had taken her coat from its hanger and was holding it for her. As she slipped her arms into the sleeves she felt the warmth of his large hands on her shoulders. The urgent power of his man's will was palpable even in the momentary caress of his palms, and for an insidious instant Laura felt a shudder of yielding steal down her back and through her exhausted limbs.

She fumbled in her purse for the office key, unnerved by the sexual ember that lurked behind Frank Jordan's incisive personality. He was the sort of man, she mused, who would offer encouragement only as a prelude to further demands. A man whose sympathy was in the service of his iron determination to have things his way.

And even now, as he held the outer door open for her with a smile, he seemed to have her in his power. Rebelling instinctively against her own vulnerability, she thought of the world of ruthless intrigue from which he had emerged when he came to work for Sam only a month ago. Now that unseen world had wound its tentacles around her own future in a cruel grip. Frank Jordan had offered to lead her through it to safety, because he knew its dangers and its challenges. But did this not mean that he was still at home in the heartless exterior which threatened her, and still belonged to it?

She hated to allow herself to be led by a stranger. Yet she had no choice.

Or was it Frank himself who made it seem that there was no choice? She could not tell, but she intended to find out.

They stood side by side in silence as the elevator rushed downward. The doors opened to reveal the empty lobby. A security guard sat quietly at his desk, viewing a bank of closed-circuit television screens which must have chronicled their descent from Sam's office. Laura greeted him with a forced smile as she passed.

The night wind blew her hair wildly against her collar as Frank held the door for her.

'Mr Jordan...' she began as she prepared to hurry home to bed.

'Frank,' he corrected, extending a long finger to arrange the silken strands of hair.

'Frank,' she said, struck by the novel sound of the name on her lips. 'I appreciate your…'

'Think nothing of it, Laura. I'm sorry if I was rough on you upstairs. Under the circumstances, it seemed necessary. Do you need a lift?'

'No, thanks. My car is right here.'

'Goodnight, then.'

He took his leave of her with an easy smile. But as she watched him recede into the darkness, the invisible depths of his own mind seemed as impenetrable as the night.

CHAPTER FOUR

THE two weeks that followed Laura's nocturnal encounter
with Frank Jordan were the most difficult of her life. Fighting the sinking feeling in her stomach at every instant, she
resolved to transform herself almost overnight into the
shrewd and experienced woman whose initiative might save
Christensen Products from certain disaster.

The process was agonising, for she could not suppress
her suspicion that the real Laura Christensen was being lost
in the maelstrom of her forced metamorphosis. Behind
every deliberate action she took she heard a stifled murmur
of protest from the frightened, grief-stricken girl she remained inside.

Yet oddly enough, she would later recall, the very desperation of her sudden corporate responsibility went a long
way towards distracting her from the throes of mourning
Sam's death. Though he was gone now, his spirit seemed
to summon her to pour her energies into the challenging
job he had bequeathed to her. Surveying from his own office the company he had built singlehandedly, she felt com-
fortingly close to him in her very solitude.

Systematically Laura moved from department to department within Christensen's headquarters, personally scrutinising every important page of the mountain of paperwork
in which the company's past and present were described
and catalogued. Immersing herself in balance sheets, contracts, payrolls, materials cost estimates and sales figures,
she fought to capture for herself some of the intimate

knowledge of the company as a living entity that had come so naturally to Sam.

Though the books and records could not predict Christensen's future, Laura began to discover dark corners in which surplus assets had been stored by Sam for just such a rainy day as this. Most were holdings in real estate. Some were blocks of stock held in companies across the country whose solid sales had attracted Sam's interest.

Laura wondered whether these surplus assets had figured in Sam's unspoken plans for safeguarding his corporation in this harsh economy.

She could not tell.

But even as she learned of Christensen's hidden resources, and saw the evidence of its strength and productivity, Laura made herself an unwilling expert on the company's short-term debt and its dangerous consequences. She saw how Sam's expansions had made the firm more healthy and vibrant while unavoidably leaving it vulnerable. It was like a growing child, sound and vigorous, yet still tender as it developed towards its full potential.

Now Laura understood why Christensen was in so sudden a crisis. Its fate was knitted into that of the entire East Coast, and even of the nation. The recession had forced factories to close everywhere—factories whose production lines would have required precision parts supplied by Christensen Products. And as factories had closed, workers had been laid off—workers who would have spent some of their wages on small appliances manufactured by Christensen.

It was a vicious circle. And there was no way to escape it until the economy improved. On that point, Rob Colwell and Zalman Corey were undoubtedly right.

Their mistake was to underestimate the true urgency of the situation. As Laura familiarised herself with the subtleties of cash flow, penalty interest rates and undercapitalisation, she realised that Andrew Dillon had had more than enough ammunition for his threat. There was no guarantee that First Federal's short-term notes could be paid on time without crippling Christensen as a competitive manufacturer.

As the days passed, every division manager within the company's New Haven headquarters received a visit from Laura. When not on her local rounds she telephoned those in charge of Christensen's subsidiaries and plants across the country. Concealing the urgency of her questions as best she could, Laura gently forced those under her authority to reveal the precise condition of their facilities in terms of profit and productivity.

The facts she gleaned were ambiguous. Most of her colleagues candidly spoke of slack sales while protesting their optimism about the future. Laura was left to wonder whether the looks of pained sympathy in their friendly eyes referred to Sam's death alone, or to his grieving daughter's painfully inadequate attempt to fill his shoes. If they knew the company as a whole was in imminent danger, they gave no sign of it.

Laura alone bore that burden.

She had already put the Everit Street house up for sale. The memories haunting its empty rooms would be too disturbing for her to cope with. Besides, she had left the house many years ago, and had become used to apartment living.

When she went there to pick up mail, she cast a loving glance at the Bosendorfer piano which had been one of Sam's rare concessions to his considerable personal wealth. For years Sam had spent quiet hours fumbling his way through simple classical pieces at the beautiful instrument. For his sake Laura had sharpened her performances of the Mozart sonatas and Debussy preludes she had learned as a piano student. Even today she could play some of them from memory, for Sam had never tired of hearing them after his long work days.

The piano would be sold with the house. Having already removed her personal memorabilia, Laura decided to keep a framed watercolour by Franz Kline for which her father had paid thousands of dollars during the first years of the artist's growing fame. Claiming that the abstract composition told a hundred stories, Sam loved to point them out one by one with his short finger. Laura could not bear to give the picture up now, for it was permeated with memories of Sam's bright imagination.

It was with virtual relief that she left the house keys with the estate agent and went back to her immersion in the company. There she crossed paths often with Frank Jordan, whose watchful eyes told her wordlessly that he was waiting for her response to the gathering storm which underlay the apparently routine doings which filled her days.

Occasionally she found herself at close quarters with him in an office or conference room. Though his behaviour was polite and even distant, she could not forget the way his powerful male virility had seemed to loom over her the night he had warned her of the menace to Sam's corporation. Even in his cynical effrontery there was a male assurance that fascinated her. Despite herself she felt beguiled by the sheer strength tensed behind his every word and gesture.

Yet she cursed her own susceptibility, for he had made no secret of his condescension towards her. She was determined to show him that she was not the ineffectual corporate novice he thought her to be. At the same time she intended to evaluate and verify each of his claims about Christensen Products' true peril, for she was not sure she trusted him.

So it was that Laura, when her exhausting days at Christensen Headquarters ended, spent her evenings learning the arcana of corporate mergers, and coming to understand how greedy entrepreneurs succeeded in taking over unsuspecting companies through high-pressure *blitzkrieg* tactics. Underneath the confusing vocabulary of fractional warrants, subordinated convertible debentures and cash tender offers which danced before her eyes, Laura saw the blunt reality. Frank had been right. The danger to Christensen Products went beyond the short-term loans brandished so menacingly by Andrew Dillon.

The sinister activity on the Stock Exchange left no doubt that someone intended to accumulate enough Christensen stock to take over management of the company. Whoever it was possessed enormous influence over the bankers and mutual funds in whose names large blocks of Christensen shares were now registered.

For the moment the process was moving with furtive slowness. Who could know when it might suddenly accelerate?

Laura had managed, through her days of frantic self-education, to see past the trees of her company's inner workings to the forest of its true identity. And the picture that emerged confirmed Frank's frightening assessment of the situation. With its solid reputation, its brilliance in product development, and its momentary fiscal weakness and low stock price, Christensen was the ideal takeover victim.

Profit, as Frank had said, was the only sure answer. Laura must find a way to increase profits dramatically, and with them the price of Christensen common stock—and she must do so almost overnight.

On a windy Thursday evening the answer began to take shape in her mind.

It was nearly midnight. Once again she was alone in Sam's dark office, the silence of the building around her contributing to the concentration she felt she needed. During the

last two weeks she had learned to suspend her judgment of
the company's long-term fate as she dealt with each day's
immediate problems. At night she liked to ruminate in solitude about what her work had taught her.

In less than a week the Board would meet to vote on her
accession to the presidency. The result was a foregone conclusion. It amounted to a vote of confidence more than a
serious debate. But Laura intended to merit real confidence,
come what may.

She had spent the last week poring determinedly through
her Research Division's files. At least two dozen new products were at the prototype stage. No one knew better than
Laura that the vast majority of these were small machine
parts destined for sale to industry. Their hurried manufacture could scarcely increase profits within the next two
quarters, with so many domestic factories closed down or
running at half capacity.

Laura's only hope lay with consumer products. If Christensen could reach the public with an affordable and efficient household item within a matter of months—and if
profits rose quickly in response to the campaign—the company's peril could be lessened and perhaps eliminated.

But the product must be more than attractive in itself. It
must be well suited to working families in the depressed
economy of the day. Families with two breadwinners, with
children in day-care centres…households without a lot of
money to spare.

On Sam's desk lay design sketches for the dust filtration
system her department had worked so hard on over the past
year. She had half-persuaded Sam that the device would
sell successfully, but she herself was scarcely convinced it
could be mass-produced in a short time with large profits
in mind.

It was a simple machine whose electric motor drove an
intake fan which drew air through a specially designed filter

and expelled it free of dust. Thanks to the properties of the fan mechanism, which were the work of Laura's brilliant and somewhat eccentric co-worker Randy Powers, the portable unit was capable of keeping an entire apartment free of dust for lengthy periods of time. Its removable filters, whose extraordinary sensitivity was Randy's greatest brainstorm, could be washed by hand, and were made of a synthetic material which dried with amazing speed after washing.

As Laura sat staring at the sketches her mind wrestled silently with the implications of the decision before her. Randy's clever invention, still only a promising prototype, might well be the answer to her company's prayers. But it had been one thing to lobby Sam for its manufacture. It was quite another to throw all the corporation's resources into this project on her own initiative. She alone would be responsible for its success or failure. It would be a calculated risk on which the fate of Christensen Products would hang; a risk Sam had refused to take even in happier times.

Nearly paralysed by the prospect of such personal accountability, Laura perused her own sales projections in tense silence. As the figures blurred before her eyes, her hand moved as though of its own volition and opened the company's xeroxed employee directory to Randy Powers' name. In a sort of concentrated daze she watched herself dial his phone number.

'Hello?' came an irritable voice.

'Hello, Randy,' Laura said into the receiver without taking her eyes from the plans before her. 'I'm at the office, and I was just wondering about something...'

'Laura? What are you doing downtown at this hour? You ought to be in bed. I'd be asleep myself, but I'm having a fight with my wife.'

'Give her my best, will you?' Laura murmured distractedly. 'Randy, I'd like to ask you a hypothetical question about our filter system. What do you think it would take to market it right away?'

'...'

The silence on the line was familiar to Laura. Randy was in the habit of falling into catatonic bemusement when a question took him by surprise.

'What I'm getting at,' Laura went on, 'is this. If we wished to sell this machine, say, in the spring, we could contract out the work on the plastic housing and on some of the motor parts. But the assembly would be up to us. I have a feeling our Springfield and Meriden plants could be refitted to take care of some of that work. But the next question is the filter. That's your design, and the essence of the machine's originality. Do you think you could set up the hardware to mass-produce that filter—say, right here in New Haven—in a matter of weeks?'

'Laura, there's nothing to that filter. You can buy the plastic from any synthetics company for five cents. It's how it's moulded.'

'I know. That's what I mean. Can you set up a shop here in town to mass-produce those filters?'

'Well, I don't know,' Randy yawned. 'That's not exactly my line. I dream the stuff up, and Sam—well, you, Laura— you'd have to get somebody to build the pressers and cut the filters and so forth. It could be done...'

'But to scale up your lab tools in order to mass-produce,' Laura persisted, 'would not be too tall an order for the Engineering Division, would it?'

'I don't see why it should,' Randy said. 'There's nothing that fancy about the mould...'

'One more thing, Randy,' Laura said, herself stifling an exhausted yawn. 'Is Shielah still working for her accounting firm?'

'Yes,' he growled. 'That's what we're fighting about. They're trying to transfer her...'

'And is Jason still in day care?'

'Where else would he be, with us both working?'

'Let me ask you one more question,' Laura said. 'With your combined incomes being what they are, how much would you be willing to pay for a portable machine that would free Shielah from having to dust the house?'

'I do the dusting, Laura.'

Laura smiled to think of Randy's punctiliousness. Though his labs at Christensen were always a mess, he kept his personal effects in a state of extravagant orderliness.

'Well,' she asked, 'how much would you pay for an item like that?'

'I don't know, Laura. Maybe seventy-five. Maybe a hundred. But I'm something of a cheapskate.'

'Thanks, Randy. And one more thing. I'm just looking at the time. Awfully sorry to call you so late. Tell Shielah I'm sorry I interrupted your fight.'

'Never mind. It was probably for the best. She's gone to bed now.'

'And kiss Jason for me. Goodnight, Randy.'

After replacing the receiver Laura sat in silence, her eyes closed. Inside her mind a slow revolution was taking place.

She had spent the last eight years of her life performing roles determined for her in advance—first as a college student, then as a corporation employee. Her personal contributions and ambitions had always been superseded by the larger entity of which she was a part.

Now, for the first time, she had an inkling of how Sam Christensen had felt as sole steward of his company's future. Rather than seek a place for himself in the world's existing structures, Sam had forced the world to make room for him through the products he invented and produced.

If Laura could inject Randy's dust removal system into the marketplace, people who had earmarked their household money for other purposes would change their minds and buy this new Christensen product. They would make room for it in a corner of their home or apartment. Competitors would try to duplicate it, paying royalties to Christensen for use of its patent.

Apartment dwellers without central air conditioning would have dust-free air for the first time. Homeowners could benefit equally. Thus an age-old problem would be solved for thousands, perhaps millions of consumers.

And if the product sold, Andrew Dillon and First Federal would have their short-term loans paid in full. Christensen's stock would go up quickly.

The order of things would have been changed. The world would have to make room for Christensen Products, rather than to absorb it.

Act, Frank Jordan had said. *Don't react. Make them react to you.*

For the first time in her life Laura understood what it meant to be a true executive, responsible for an entire company.

The feeling was both scary and wonderful.

Laura had arisen and reached to turn out the light when she recalled the sinister movements in her company's stock on Wall Street. Suddenly the lessons she had learned about corporate takeovers brought an idea to her mind with startling clarity. She left herself a note to call a number tomorrow morning, turned out the light, and moved exhaustedly towards the elevators.

On her way she left a memo for her secretary to schedule an urgent meeting with Randy Powers and Meg O'Connor, along with three of Christensen's materials and engineering managers.

And with Frank Jordan, she added on an afterthought.

As the office receded behind her she never thought to smile at the fact that Sam Christensen's tradition of nocturnal phone calls had just been restored.

Twenty minutes later she was home in bed, her somnolent body fighting for sleep against the plans thronging her mind.

Dream thoughts were beginning to vie with the probabilities and contingencies she weighed sleepily.

'We'll need a name for it,' she mused. 'Not Dustaway or No-Dust or anything prosaic like that. Something catchy. Something amusing and easy to remember—something to humanise the product.'

The image of an aged cleaning woman danced before her closed eyes. An irascible, temperamental lady who had worked for Sam when Laura was a little girl. The power struggle between employer and employee for control of the Christensens' domestic arrangements had led to an angry rift after less than a year, and the woman had left in disgust, calling Sam a fool and a hopeless mess-maker.

But Laura had liked her, for she had a pretty name: Molly Mahoney.

Molly, Laura thought with a smile.

Then she fell into a dreamless sleep.

CHAPTER FIVE

THE Directors' meeting took place on a rainy Wednesday afternoon. Rob Colwell held the door open for Laura, and gave her hand a furtive squeeze of encouragement as she entered the Board room. The seven members of Christensen's Board looked up expectantly at her through the haze of cigar and pipe smoke which filled the room.

Their faces were as foreign and as familiar as Sam's office, which Laura had occupied uncomfortably for nearly three weeks now. They were men in their fifties and sixties, stockholders and bankers whom she had known as a child, and to whom she had served cocktails at the Everit Street house when a teenager. A hint of their old avuncular smiles was visible on a face or two now, but most of them seemed to conceal their fears for the company under deadpan expressions.

Near the end of the table sat Frank Jordan in his capacity as non-voting observer and consultant. His eyes were upon Laura as well, their gaze intense and inscrutable. Laura thought she saw the shade of his familiar arrogance, as though Frank believed he was her true judge and adviser. Like an irritable director anticipating the audition of a struggling actor, he waited for her performance.

'Good afternoon, gentlemen,' Laura said, swallowing her emotions with an effort. 'Our first order of business, as you know, will be to confirm my nomination as President under the bylaws. Do I hear a motion to that effect?'

'So moved,' came Rob's voice.

'Seconded.'

The show of hands was unanimous, but rather bleak. Virginia recorded the result on her memo pad.

'Now,' Laura went on, 'we do have some important business to take care of today.'

All eyes were fixed on her, expectant and worried. By now it was common knowledge among the Board members that the company's falling sales dictated the cutbacks proposed by Zalman Corey. No doubt they were resigned to that fact, though unwillingly, for they all must feel that Sam would somehow have solved the problem of the company's debt. Laura could feel their larger fear that, over and above the immediate financial danger, her presence in the powerful role her father once played might bode ill for the corporation's whole future.

'I'm sure you're all aware,' she said with studied calm, that my father had been negotiating on a tentative basis with Paltron, Inc. of Massachusetts, with a view to Christensen's acquisition of that company.'

Eyebrows were raised around the table. Clearly everyone had expected Laura to open the meeting with the news that she would agree to close several Christensen factories. And here she was talking about acquisitions!

'I have spoken to John Slowicki and his colleagues at Paltron,' Laura said brightly, 'and I am happy to report that we have seen our way clear to close the deal. Christensen will acquire Paltron as of this week. The purchase price will be 750,000 shares of unissued Christensen common stock.'

Shock waves went silently through the room. Rob Colwell's features were clouded by perplexity. In a corner Zalman Corey sat pale as a ghost, his nervous hand adjusting the horn rims of his glasses. The Board members were staring at Laura, their lips pursed in blatant disapproval.

'And how do you propose to capitalise this idea?' asked

Ralph Simpson, the oldest and most conservative member of the Board.

'Certainly not by closing our facilities in Rochester, Albany and Springfield,' Laura said firmly. 'Those plants will stay open at reduced capacity until we are able to bring them back to full production. We will finance the Paltron acquisition by divesting ourselves of some real estate properties which my father had acquired for just such a purpose as this. The unissued stock is already authorised. I might add, though, that each of us top Christensen executives will take a 20 per cent cut in salary as of next week. The inconvenience will be temporary, I can assure you.'

Angry mumbles of protest filled the room. Laura's actions seemed absurd, and quite irrelevant to the company's current woes as understood by the Board.

Only the face of Frank Jordan expressed a fugitive glimmer of approval. Laura's hooded glance in his direction acknowledged it.

'Now,' she said, 'let me end with some further good news. We are going ahead with a new project, tentatively called Molly. This consumer item was designed by Randy Powers of our Research Division. Virginia will pass out the projections we've done on it. The major electronic aspects of its assembly will be handled by Paltron in Massachusetts, with whom I have already discussed the situation.'

A pained silence had descended on the Board. Flabbergasted by Laura's unaccountable decisions, they stared at each other in bewilderment as Virginia placed the folders before them.

'We'll be doing some contracting for materials and parts manufacture,' Laura went on imperturbably. 'As you know, we can count on Rob Colwell's expertise in that area. As for finance and marketing, I will be personally involved, along with Frank Jordan and Zalman Corey. We expect to be in production by the end of February. I believe (*I pray,* she thought silently) I can promise you and our shareholders a strong first quarter and a brilliant second quarter of the new year once this product hits the market.'

With her fingers crossed, Laura called for discussion on her proposals. The shocked Board members, having finally digested the enormity of the changes she was suggesting, began to ask for clarification. For nearly two hours she parried their questions, arguing carefully for her plans while avoiding any reference to the desperate motives which had made them necessary.

In the end Laura's own power as Board Chairman and majority stockholder, combined with the cleverness of her arguments, won the day. The issue of Christensen Products' imminent peril under the pressure of its unseen adversaries was not discussed. Only Frank Jordan shared that terrible secret with Laura.

After the meeting Frank accompanied her to Sam's office.

'Very smart,' he said when the door was closed behind them. 'You've managed to create 750,000 new shares of stock which will be in friendly hands at Paltron. That will give you leverage against Schell in a proxy fight. What gave you the idea?'

'Randy's system,' Laura said as she watched him throw his jacket on a chair and loosen his tie. 'It seemed smarter to acquire Paltron than to contract out the electronic work to them. And, as you say, there was the stock to consider.'

He had sat down in the chair opposite her, his long limbs dwarfing its modest dimensions. Despite the urgency of the moment, he seemed extraordinarily at ease within himself, as though the drama that had just drained Laura of her resources of guile and courage were an everyday occurrence to him.

'There's one important thing you'll want to consider before the weekend,' he said. 'Under disclosure law you ought to report your acquisition of Paltron to the Stock Exchange right away. When Roy Schell hears about that, he'll know two things: that you have a big block of stock in friendly hands now, and that he may face anti-trust litigation if he tries to take you over now that you've already merged with a company in the same market.'

'I've already done that, Frank,' Laura said from Sam's chair.

'Well, well,' he smiled, his eyebrow raised in admiring surprise. 'You have been doing your homework, haven't you?'

Laura nodded, proud of her own initiative and more than a little flattered by his approval.

'Just to drive the point home more forcefully,' he added, 'a half-page announcement of the acquisition in the *Journal* might be a good idea. It will impress your stockholders as well as Schell and his friends.'

'Already done,' Laura said. 'The ad will be in Friday's edition.'

Frank crossed his arms and gazed across the desk at her, a trace of gentleness in his probing irises.

'I'll be damned,' he said. 'You're made of tougher stuff than I thought. So you believed me about Schell all along.'

'The movement of our stock on Wall Street doesn't lie,' Laura said. 'Someone is preparing to take us over. Whether it's Roy Schell or someone else, we have no choice but to fight now. In another month it might be too late.'

'You're taking a chance, you know,' he said. 'You're gambling everything on this product you call Molly. If it sells, and Christensen's stock goes up, Schell will give up and look for greener pastures. But if it doesn't sell, or moves too slowly, you'll be so overextended by March or April that this company will be a sitting duck. Doesn't that scare you?'

'Of course,' Laura said. 'But a certain amount of fear goes with this job, unless I miss my guess.'

'You know something?' he asked, a laughing sparkle in his caressing eyes. 'For a little slip of a thing, you fill that chair pretty well.'

Laura felt herself flush under his gaze. Her weeks of frantic work had convinced her that she was equal to the tasks he had set her. But her memory of his hard man's body, poised in that same visitor's chair the night he stunned her with his warning words, had dimmed in the intervening days, and was coming to life in her senses now with fearsome immediacy. She could see muscles strain under the white fabric of his shirt as he clasped his hands behind his head. A lock of his dark hair hung carelessly over the tanned flesh of his brow. To hear him refer to her body, however teasingly, sent an odd little quiver through her slender limbs.

She had half accustomed herself to the mental image of him as an arrogant tormentor bent on exhorting her to bold actions of which he did not deem her capable. But his grudging praise seemed to open the door to an unforeseen view of him as a handsome, virile being whose lips might attract one's own, whose powerful limbs one might like to touch, to caress...

She banished the guilty thought with a shudder. But the hot flush which had come over her creamy complexion was worth a thousand words, and she had to hope he would attribute it to mere modesty.

For his compliment had meant a lot, whether he knew it or not.

'Now,' he said, reclining comfortably before her, 'why don't you tell me how you propose to get this Molly of yours off the drawing board and into the department stores by the first week in April?'

As she began to speak, the Board members had gone

home to their respective institutions, thunderstruck by the
boldness of their new Chairman and Company President.
No one understood what she was up to, or knew how to
stop her. Having expected her to accede docilely to the
proposed closing of three Christensen factories, they were
mystified by her decision to acquire Paltron and by the pay
cut she had so imperiously imposed on Christensen's executives. Laura seemed to have received her marching orders from another world, a world foreign to their expectations and concerns.

But Laura was majority stockholder. No one could stop
her in her tracks, for Sam had bequeathed her his power
along with his shares. One could only swallow one's in-
dignation and hope that she knew what she was doing.

'Hardly the way Sam did things,' one Board member
grumbled to another in the elevator. His interlocutor
shrugged a smile in answer, for he could recall many a
surprise unveiled by Sam during Board meetings in years
past. Perhaps, he mused, the girl was her father's daughter
after all.

And they went their separate ways never realising that
under the guise of a routine acquisition and a new product
line, a trench war against a corporate takeover had begun.

CHAPTER SIX

By early December Molly, the portable dust removal system designed to ease the odious household chores of millions of consumers, was no longer a drawing-board prototype in the bowels of Christensen Products' Research Division. It was a top priority for immediate production and test marketing, intentionally shrouded in mystery by the handful of planners Laura had assembled to hasten the process of its development.

Among them were Randy Powers and his hardheaded research colleague, Meg O'Connor. For the past several years Christensen insiders had called Meg Randy's 'better half', for it was Meg who knew how to cajole Randy from his eccentric, uncommunicative daydreaming and force him to put hard facts on paper for his superiors. A plump, cheerful woman in her early thirties, Meg had a sharp tongue and ready wit to match her bright red hair and sparkling eyes. Though Randy had tasted the sting of her Irish temper on more than one occasion, he knew she doted on him with maternal tenderness, and would protect him against those Christensen executives foolish enough to doubt the practical benefits of his seemingly inchoate designs.

Rob Colwell was in charge of materials for Molly's manufacture. Laura's contact with him during these hectic weeks had been mainly by telephone, for he was constantly travelling from one factory to another, examining plastics and metals whose characteristics must assure Molly's light weight and durability.

Laura well knew that Rob was anything but confident about her refusal to cut back Christensen's overhead and her huge investment of precious time and money in an untried product. Yet, once the die had been cast, Rob had responded to the new initiative with his accustomed aplomb. Upon his return from the far-flung outposts he visited in her behalf Rob would appear in her office or meet her for lunch, his robust good looks seemingly accentuated by the busy routine he was now following. His reports were laconic and to the point, just as they must have been in Sam's time. He never failed to take every contingency into consideration, and his recommendations were always thoroughly researched. Laura thanked her lucky stars for his invaluable skills.

Rob had eyed Frank Jordan with ill-concealed suspicion after Laura dropped her bombshell at the Board meeting. Clearly his sharp intuition made him aware of Frank's influence on her decision, and he was concerned as to whether it was in her own best interests and those of the company. But his own business acumen must have told him there was solid strategy behind the bold moves Laura had undertaken. So he had turned in upon himself and gone about his work like the thorough professional he was. Laura even thought she sensed in him a grain of admiration for an idea he might have liked to have invented himself.

But the troubling atmosphere of tension between the two men, both so virile and incisive, seemed to persist underneath their polite exchanges, and might have become a real dilemma in itself had they seen more of each other. As things stood, however, Rob spent his days on aeroplanes destined for plants in Florida, Montreal, or Baltimore, while Laura and Frank kept their fingers on the pulse in New Haven.

In charge of finance for the urgent new project was Zalman Corey, who soon came to anticipate his new boss's nocturnal phone calls. Having immersed herself in the miasma of her company's liquid assets and overheads, Laura importuned Zalman with one financial gamble after another in her determination to somehow underwrite Molly's production and distribution without crippling the corporation's overall balance of payments. For Zalman, who much preferred a quiet life with his wife and three cats, the new routine was torture. Time and again Laura had to use her hastily acquired financial expertise to reassure him, when she inwardly wished it was he who might calm her frayed nerves.

For her own part Laura supervised every aspect of Molly's development, and did her best to hurry the corporate process designed to make the new product available to the public before the spring deadline enforced by First Federal. Each morning she met with her personal staff to apportion the day's labours. There were phone calls to make, contingency plans to collate and adjust, contracts to be signed, and new strategies to discuss.

The most urgent priority was Molly's price. If the machine could not be made affordable for financially beleaguered apartment dwellers and homeowners, it would never sell. Therefore every aspect of its manufacture had to be scaled to the budget of the middle-class consumer who had long since given up expensive luxuries, but whose busy career made a time-saving device like Molly an attractive item.

And the best way to spread the burden of Molly's attendant overheads economically was to use as many Christensen workers and plants as possible—along with newly acquired Paltron—to make the item. Outside contract work must be kept to a minimum.

To accomplish this purpose while simultaneously overseeing the many other disparate activities in Christensen's dozens of factories was a dizzying task. More often than not, her head spinning, Laura felt as though her ten fingers were trying to stop a hundred holes in the massive dike that was Sam's company. For every phone call she made about Molly, five were coming in about other Christensen problems around the country. Through an effort of will she had to tell herself each night that her day's work would suffice until tomorrow, and that six or seven hours' sleep were more important than the piles of reports which conspired to keep her in her office until the wee hours of the morning.

'Hold on,' she told herself grimly. 'Just don't panic. Keep calm.' And she laughed to think that that was the most impossible thing of all to accomplish.

Sometimes her sense of humour abandoned her altogether, and she was convinced that each and every decision she had made was hopelessly inadequate. How comfortable it would be, she thought, to forget this miserable corporate rat race and live out one's days as a worker or teacher somewhere, unburdened by responsibilities one was incapable of handling.

At such moments Frank Jordan became the most important figure in Laura's life—and the most maddening.

Frank must have been keeping in close touch with Virginia about the rhythms of Laura's busy schedule, for he seemed to appear without an appointment just when she had a few moments to spare, or when his intuition told him her confidence must be particularly shaken by recent events.

Laura could hear the deep, confident tones of his voice as he bantered with Virginia in the outer office. In spite of herself she would glance hurriedly in the office mirror, touching her sandy hair with an urgent finger and cursing her silliness as she noticed the odd expectancy in the green eyes that looked out at her. A moment later he would appear at her door, his lips quirked by the wry smile she had come to expect, and throw his jacket unceremoniously over a chair.

'So,' he would say brightly as he sat down before her. 'Everything under control?'

In his enigmatic eyes she often saw the same look of condescension that had so irritated her when he first joined the company. Mercilessly he seemed to tease her, indicating by his every word and gesture that she was in well over her head and was paying the painful price for Sam's ill-advised decision to thrust this enormous obligation upon her.

When she saw that look, her stung pride forced her to answer him with glib confidence, despite her fears. She found herself studying the intricacies of the company's structure, and the most remote fiscal calamities which might befall it, just so as to be able to stop Frank Jordan short with a witheringly competent reply when he tried to point up her inexperience and ignorance.

'I understand Engineering is helping Randy to refit the presses on our local lines,' he said one afternoon as he sat comfortably on the edge of Sam's desk. 'Don't you think you're going to have to do some extra hiring when he finishes? That will cost money.'

'Not if we use numerical controls on the machines,' Laura said with a straight face. 'Computer-linked, of course. My father bought and paid for the soft technology last year, so we might as well use it. Besides, we can retool for quality control whenever we like.'

When his brow raised in teasing admiration as he stared down at her, she was satisfied that once again she had passed his test.

Frank was a pitiless taskmaster. It was he who advised Laura on the budgeting of her time and that of her staff. With an uncanny instinct for executive planning, Frank explained what choice must be made first among the welter of options facing Laura at each stage of this complicated game. He seemed to possess an encyclopaedic knowledge of Christensen's own plants and suppliers to match the financial expertise he had brought from his years in what Sam called a 'bigger pond', for none of Laura's reports on unsuspected problems in materials or assembly seemed to surprise him.

His aplomb amazed Laura. Thriving on pressure, taking everything in his stride, he managed to avert one crisis after another with unflappable calm. His coat thrown over his shoulder, his open collar revealing the crisp tangle of hair beneath his throat, Frank walked through the corridors of Christensen's headquarters like a relaxed tourist. Yet his sharp eyes missed nothing. At a moment's notice he straightened his tie, threw on his jacket, and was the image of daunting executive aggressiveness in the tense meetings that required his presence.

'He doesn't know what fear is,' Laura thought in wonderment as she contemplated him. 'Thank heaven.'

How she needed his peerless self-assurance at a time like this! The word troubleshooter could have been invented for him.

But he expected an equal daring from Laura herself, and was markedly impatient when she failed to show it.

In December Frank accompanied her to Christensen's Meriden facility. She watched intently as he entered into complex deliberations with the plant manager about strategies for mass-producing Molly's motor module at a minimum of expense.

'We can't handle this in the time frame you're talking about,' the worried manager said. 'We'd need too much overtime. The union won't hear of it.'

'Not if you fit smaller moulds into the lines you already have,' Frank said, his tanned hand pointing to a computer print-out he had brought with him from New Haven. 'We'll make you the moulds in Albany next week. And Laura will talk to the union membership. Won't you, Laura?'

She nodded, making a show of confidence while wondering just how Frank expected her to negotiate with a union whose officials she had never met.

Yet, when she explained the profit-sharing plan devised by Frank and Zalman in anticipation of Molly's sales, the union reluctantly agreed to a temporary overtime arrangement at increased wages. Frank had been right again—if only because the membership remained loyal enough to Sam Christensen's memory to go along with his daughter's plans.

Frank's recommendations had in common the fact that they were easier said than done—and uniformly effective once put into place. Under his demanding guidance Laura found herself constrained to play the aggressive, self-possessed role her father had created for himself and passed on to her. More often than not she felt herself more an actress feigning executive competence than a true corporate leader.

But as time went on she found to her surprise that her carefully modulated performance seemed to rub off on her own personality. Catching a glimpse of her energetic, preoccupied face in the mirror, she saw traces of the change her new way of life was bringing about in her. The modest, unambitious research assistant she had once been was slipping quietly into oblivion, eclipsed by a woman accustomed, willingly or not, to being in charge of things and people.

And behind this change, Laura was well aware, loomed the mysterious figure of Frank Jordan. It was he who had forced her to seize the reins of her company, rather than to see it swallowed by forces beyond her control. It was he who had insisted that she follow her own initiative rather than to react to events.

As she sat in her father's office, surrounded by traces of his buoyant spirit, and acutely conscious that it was his furtive amendment to the bylaws that had put her here, she knew that Frank Jordan was somewhere in the building, planning things for her to do, challenges to which she must rise. It was becoming increasingly difficult to know where the one left off and the other began, for both summoned her incessantly to rise above herself.

But if Frank was satisfied with her progress, he took pains not to show it. His exhortations to bold action always had a hard edge, whether or not there was a hint of affection behind them. Sometimes he reminded her of a demanding coach who browbeats his talented athlete into living up to her potential, even at the cost of exhaustion and considerable acrimony. At other times she thought such a comparison too flattering to herself, for his supercilious glances left little doubt that he considered her a spoiled child deserving of sympathy only because she had been forced to sleep in the bed her father made for her. Eventually, he seemed to believe, she would certainly have to step down and turn her position over to someone competent. Until that time he would see to it that her inexperience did not destroy the corporation entirely.

And sometimes Laura was simply too tired to second-guess him. She took his indispensable advice at face value, and stopped asking herself whether he was making fun of her or honestly trying to encourage her. As he stood behind her chair, massaging her tired shoulders with strong, warm hands whose calming touch soothed her nerves, his very silence indicated that this short break must suffice to give her strength for more work.

The mystery of the man maddened her as much as his teasing ways. Nevertheless she welcomed the change he had brought about in her at a time when it was desperately needed. She had Frank Jordan to thank for the fact that

Christensen Products still had a chance to survive and prosper.

Yet there was a dark side even to this state of affairs. For Frank was subtly making a new woman out of Laura. And that new woman, strengthened by adversity and tempered by new challenges, was far from indifferent to his charms. Even as the hard work he pushed upon her grew more satisfying, she found her senses responding tumultuously to the impact of his nearness.

Laura felt oddly out of place in her own skin, and frightened by a longing she had never experienced before.

The weather had grown colder, and the ocean breezes brought a preponderance of grim, rainy days to New Haven's tortuous maze of one-way streets. On regular occasions Frank joined Laura for lunch in the employees' cafeteria, or took her to dinner at a quiet restaurant near the Green. These encounters were intense affairs which seemed to rush by as the two sat absorbed in technical or financial discussion. Yet Laura could never entirely suppress her inner alertness to the physical side of Frank's virile personality. She noticed the clothes whose cut concealed the breadth of his back and shoulders, and the hard line of his jaw in which a tiny nerve quickened when circumstances darkened his mood.

And she came to admire the many resources of his humour, for he laughed easily when the complexities of their common work amused him. As though aware that the relentless pressure of her existence would be downright unhealthy if not interrupted at intervals, he insisted on celebrating each important step forward in Molly's evolution by bringing Laura flowers and ordering champagne at dinner. He seemed determined to throw a curtain of levity over the atmosphere of hectic gloom reigning in her life, for the more nerve-wracking things became, the more his acerbic wit found ways to make Laura laugh.

His cynicism about the business world perplexed Laura, for it harmonised poorly with the voracious love of life's varied challenges which shone forth in his every gesture and idea.

'If this is all just a "deadly game", as you called it,' she asked, 'why do you work so hard at it? Why are you putting so much effort into our problems at Christensen, when you could be doing something else?'

'The exception proves the rule,' he shrugged. 'Christensen is a damned good company. It makes products for people to use, instead of sacrificing everything to profit. That was your dad's work, and I'd like to see you carry it on. There aren't many companies like yours any more. The law of the jungle is money today, Laura. It makes for some interesting chess-playing with sharks like Roy Schell. And that amuses me. I want to see the look on Andrew Dillon's face when you pay off your short-term notes. I want to see Schell back off and look for another victim. In the end, it's their kind who will control the corporate world as a whole—but it's worth it to frustrate them this time.'

And he changed the subject with gentle determination, focusing his attention on Laura's own challenges while distracting her from himself.

But he could not have read the effect of his words in Laura's thoughts. To her they signified one thing only: that his tenure at Christensen Products was to be temporary. One day he would leave, putting the current battle behind him when it was won or lost, and continue his adventurous career elsewhere.

And when he left, would he take away a part of her that she could never recover?

Laura needed Frank Jordan now, more than she had needed anyone since Sam was alive. But underneath her prideful irritation at her dependence on him, she wanted to need him. Yes, she mused uncomfortably: a part of her cried out to give itself to Frank forever, so that she could spend all her days enfolded by the vital charm of his body and personality. And that persistent little part added its disturbing voice to all her other thoughts when he was near. Even as she asked herself what he wanted from her today, how he might help her through her newest crisis, a furtive inner voice asked, *Does he like me? Does he find me attractive?*

In consternation she suppressed the thought. But when next his smiling face appeared at her office door, its handsome features quirked in sharp, wry humour, that prohibited yielding in her senses came to taunt her anew.

It had been one thing to swallow her pride and accede to his harsh, threatening demands, cursing his impudent behaviour even as she admired the analytical mind which saw so clearly into the heart of her company's dilemma.

It was quite another to find her consciousness bound insidiously to the vibrant image of his tanned flesh, hard and sure, drawing closer to her with the same quick expertise that guided his steps in the perilous world of men, covering her luxuriantly, overwhelming her with its caress.

'Don't,' she told herself angrily. 'Don't even think about it.'

But when she looked inside herself in search of an answer to her own confusion, it was Frank Jordan's dark gaze that seemed to look out at her, holding her in rapt fascination.

CHAPTER SEVEN

FRANK had warned Laura that the key to Molly's short-term success would be an aggressive advertising campaign.

'I like the name,' he said. 'It's cute—and since the product is not exactly poetic in itself, we should humanise it. But the problem is that we're trying to sell people on the *idea* of Molly, as well as our specific product.'

After consultation with Christensen's advertising department, Laura was tempted to launch Molly through full-page ads in mass-market publications. Her advisers wrote a tentative text describing the machine's virtues.

'I don't think so, Laura,' Frank said with a frown. 'This sort of campaign won't convince anyone to take a chance on what amounts literally to a new invention. We need something more immediate. Something to grab people's attention and make them feel that Molly is the product they've been waiting for all these years. I think television is the only answer. It will be expensive, but worth it. We have to reach a lot of consumers quickly. After that has been accomplished we can go to magazines to bolster the impact of the initial campaign.'

The logic behind Frank's suggestion was convincing, but neither Laura nor the advertising staff could decide on an appropriate manner of presenting Molly in a television commercial. The little machine was not unattractive to look at, but was hardly photogenic in itself. Nothing about it offered possibilities for visual excitement, for it was designed to do its work quietly and unobtrusively.

There was no gainsaying the obvious: despite its amusing name, Molly was downright dull. In Frank's words, something must be done to make the product human.

One evening Laura lay somnolent on the couch before the television set in her apartment. On the screen was an old Hollywood movie depicting the stormy relationship between an eccentric millionaire and his uncontrollable children. The only sensible person in his opulent mansion seemed to be an irascible housemaid who reigned over the place like a friendly tyrant. Dressed in black with an abbreviated white apron, she excoriated her whimsical employer in blunt, strident terms when events forced him into hilariously ill-considered behaviour. She saw through all the story's characters, easily distinguishing those who were merely foolish from those whose motives were genuinely suspect. Often she expressed her judgments through subtle looks whose import was always borne out by the story.

Something stirred in Laura as she contemplated the matronly actress, whose face was as familiar as her name was unknown to the public. For decades she had played the role of the gruff, hardheaded housekeeper to perfection.

Instinctively Laura placed a videotape in the cassette recorder she had inherited from Sam and began taping the movie. When it was over she studied the list of players carefully. The name Marva Sims struck a distant chord in her memory.

The next morning Laura called Francie Tolliver, a bright young executive in the advertising department, and asked her to come to Sam's conference room. As Francie watched, Laura played portions of the tape she had recorded the night before.

'Watch Flora, the maid,' she said. 'Look at her authority. She's the only character who understands the household.'

'Her carriage is wonderful,' Francie murmured, her brow

furrowed in concentration. 'So erect. She seems a tower of strength. Who is she?'

'Her name is Marva Sims,' Laura said. 'I have no idea whether she's living. That film is at least thirty years old. But it's the idea that intrigues me. A clever, competent housekeeper who not only understands dusting and housework, but who is a shrewd judge of people.'

'You mean as a visual spokesman for Molly,' Francie said, tapping a pencil lightly against her briefcase as she watched the screen. 'I see what you're getting at.'

'Francie, I'd like you to do something for me. Leaving Marva Sims aside, if we could find someone like her, someone whose image is associated with good common sense... A character actress with a recognisable face.'

'We could show her as insisting that her employer buy her a Molly so that she could devote herself to more important work than mere dusting,' Francie said. 'Personally, I can't think of anyone who plays that sort of role regularly nowadays, but I'm sure I can find out. A little leg work with the casting agencies...'

'Exactly,' Laura said. 'I appreciate your help, Francie. And remember: we don't have much time to spare. I'm convinced that Molly needs a human image, and a strong one. A person people can identify with.'

When Francie had gone Laura returned to the conference room cassette recorder to rewind the tape. As the black-and-white film disappeared from the television screen replaced by a raucous game show, she reached hurriedly to turn down the volume. As luck would have it, the knob came off in her hand. In irritation she reminded herself that the TV set was growing old and must soon be replaced. Only a few weeks ago Virginia had sent it to the repair shop for work on its outmoded tubes.

A tiny glint of soldered metal caught her eye on the volume control post as she tried to replace the knob. She gazed distractedly at it for a moment, wondering whether it signified one of the repairman's efforts to keep the old set in working order.

A sudden glimmer of doubt told her the thing made no sense. The melted solder was shiny and new, and could have no place on a purely mechanical part of the controls. On an impulse she borrowed the magnifying glass from Virginia's desk drawer and returned to the silent conference room.

Recalling the lessons she had learned in microtechnology as a research specialist, Laura peered through the glass. A moment's careful scrutiny revealed a tiny circle of tooled metal nestled in the droplet of hardened solder. Barely visible to the naked eye, the device clearly had an electrical function and a purpose all of its own.

The improbable truth struck Laura all at once.

It was a microphone.

Loath to believe her own eyes, she knelt before the set, her finger keeping her long hair from her face as she stared at the minuscule contrivance. For weeks she had reluctantly accustomed herself to the notion that Christensen Products was the object of acute attention on the part of unseen strangers. But this almost microscopic evidence of a deliberate invasion of her own privacy and that of her colleagues seemed unutterably sinister.

So they care that much, she thought angrily, taking care not to put the idea into words.

She stood up and moved quickly towards her office, intending to use the telephone. But she was stopped in her tracks by the fear that that room was no more secure than this.

A moment later she was hurrying through the corridor towards the elevators, answering her co-workers' salutations with a forced smile.

She had to find Frank Jordan.

*   *   *

Two days later a dour group of top Christensen executives met in the conference room to discuss the discontinuing of three important product lines and the prospective sale of two Christensen factories.

'I think we're all in agreement,' Rob Colwell said from his position beside Laura, 'that the pay cut decided on at the Board meeting last month was necessary. However, it doesn't seem to have helped us that much.'

'I'm sure our shareholders will appreciate it,' Laura said.

'Yes, but the executive pool isn't happy about it,' Frank Jordan put in. 'I think there's a strong chance that we'll see some of our people looking for opportunities elsewhere.'

'I don't see what choice we had,' Laura said hesitantly. 'I'm sure it will only be temporary, Frank. Once we divest ourselves of some overhead and take care of our short-term debt, we'll readjust salaries accordingly. But for now a little belt-tightening seems the only safe course.'

'I agree,' Rob shrugged. 'We have to be conservative, particularly in the wake of the Paltron acquisition.' His voice betrayed a hint of reproach at what he obviously considered an ill-advised move. 'We'll just have to hope that sales pick up in the last two quarters of the new year. If they do, Christensen will be a stronger company, if a somewhat smaller one.'

'In the meantime,' Frank said, 'morale is an important issue. Laura, I think you should try to make this year's Christmas party the best in a long time. And some sort of bonus across the board would be a welcome token of appreciation for our people. Even if you have to squeeze blood from a turnip to do it, you should free enough cash to put a little something in everyone's Christmas envelope.'

A wry smile curled his lips as he looked from the page before him to Laura. Rob's eyes were on the silent television set, their tawny irises glinting with suppressed humour.

'Zalman,' Laura said, 'this is your field. Do you see a

way for me to give out bonuses at all comparable to what we had last year?'

Zalman adjusted his glasses nervously. He alone seemed oblivious to the concealed hilarity filling the room.

He was concentrating on his script.

CHAPTER EIGHT

'LAURA, how much of your French do you remember?'

Frank stood tall at Laura's office door, his coat thrown over the shoulder of the thick sweater which hugged the contours of his powerful chest and arms. The taut thighs under his slacks accentuated his aura of alert animal strength coiled for quick and efficient action. Looking up from her desk Laura was momentarily struck dumb by her sheer admiration for his exuberant male authority.

'My French?' she asked in confusion. 'I don't know. I suppose I could still read a newspaper. Or perhaps order a cup of coffee in a restaurant.'

'You'll have to do better than that,' he smiled, throwing his coat on the chair beside the window. 'I've just had a chat with Zalman Corey. You and I are going to Montreal on Friday. Rob Colwell will meet us there. We have to arrange to manufacture Molly in Quebec. And you know how some of those Quebecois feel about English these days.'

'Frank, are you sure about this?' Laura sighed. 'Can't we just export to Canada?'

'Not the way things are today,' he shook his head. 'With exchange rates and import duties the way they are, the product won't be affordable. We have to build and distribute it in Canada. It's going to be a gamble, because the Canadian operation won't be ready to go until late spring at the earliest. But we ought to lay the groundwork right now. Rob called this morning, and he has a plant in mind.

Once we've had a look at it, we can set the wheels in motion. And,' he added with a smile, 'we can mix business with a little pleasure for a change. I know a terrific French restaurant up there, and we might get in a morning of skiing before we have to get back. What do you say?'

'Why not?' Laura laughed. 'I can just as easily have a nervous breakdown in French as in English.'

'That's the spirit,' he joked, his ebony irises resting on the tawny swirl of her hair. 'Virginia has the reservations made. We'll leave Friday morning from Laguardia.'

A moment later he had disappeared, for an urgent meeting with Meg O'Connor and Randy Powers was to fill the rest of his morning. Laura sat alone behind her father's desk, her every fibre stunned by the fugitive trace of Frank's caressing glance.

Though Frank Jordan apparently remained unaware of the tormenting upset his nearness was causing in Laura's senses, she herself had come perilously close to breaking under the strain of her frayed emotions these past weeks. Frank's erect virility, once a mere image of tempting male attractiveness before her mind's eyes, had expanded insidiously to overwhelm her imagination. It was increasingly difficult to concentrate on the urgent tasks he persisted in bringing her when his every glance, the casual touch of his hand on her arm, his earthy male scent as he leaned close to her, tore at the heart of her resistance to his charms.

At first the intensity of her attraction to him had been a sly little imp that teased and taunted her when he was near. Feeling her knees go weak when he helped her on with her coat, his strong fingers brushing her back in their passage, she had tried to enjoy the private thrill which stole under her skin, as though it were nothing more than a furtive, momentary impression.

But now it was different. Now the vital, athletic form of Frank Jordan pursued her throughout her busy day, and haunted her dreams at night. Each time he arrived to take her to lunch or to a meeting, she realised with a shock that his handsome face and powerful body had not been out of her thoughts since last she saw him.

Though his cynical disapproval of her high position still peeked out occasionally from behind his friendly treatment of her, it was now clear to Laura that his respect for her initiative and hard work was sincere. In his careful, vigilant way he had come to like her as a person. True, she remained the mere pretext for the battle he had joined in her company's behalf, but something in his protective amiability told her that his bitterness about the corporate world did not extend to Laura herself. Frank Jordan had become her friend as well as her ally.

But friendship was the extent of his feeling for her. Of that Laura was convinced. Over and over again, through these tumultuous weeks, she had found herself taking extra care with her make-up, in the unspoken hope that an extra glow in her cheeks, a touch of colour above her limpid green eyes, would make her more attractive to Frank. Unconsciously she chose dresses, skirts and blouses whose trim and cut might make her appear a bit more feminine at work.

She cursed her own fruitless wiles, for Frank's wry gaze never lingered for long on the outfits designed to highlight her slim good looks. The bright compliments he offered were paternal in nature, and were obviously intended to encourage rather than to flatter. In his mind she was still the 'slip of a girl' whose fate had decreed that she try to grow into a big and difficult job.

To make matters worse, Frank always seemed to appear in her office at the very moment when her exhausting day's work had left her hair in tangled disarray, her make-up far from entrancing, her eyes dull with fatigue. Hoping in her guilty heart to attract his male interest, she succeeded only in appearing rumpled and ordinary when he approached.

Yet she could not stop herself from dreaming of him. Behind every hurried executive decision she made, behind every withering fear she felt for the future of her father's corporation, there lurked a secret eagerness for Frank's touch and smell, for his deep voice and sharp, knowing smile.

She had begun to feel herself a covert expert on every visible part of his handsome body, for her sidelong glances rested in fascination on the sinews of his neck, the hard length of his thighs, the curious glint of midnight blue in his dark eyes. She knew the ebony waves of his hair with an obsessive sureness. His body was becoming her personal talisman, filled with a dark allure that infuriated her. The wicked pleasure she took from the sight of it, when he took off his jacket to throw it on her chair, when he rolled up his sleeves for work, when he stretched his long limbs in moments of relaxation, was unbearably delicious.

But more disturbing yet was her idealisation of his image when she contemplated it in solitude. She had come to admire him with an adolescent's fervour, and found herself coveting every aspect of her familiarity with him. His voice on the telephone was a prized possession, and she listened to its deep tones with stealthy attention, wanting to know him better, to know all about him. In her girlish thoughts he had a stellar brilliance, a particular essence to which she clung selfishly despite her best efforts to put him out of her mind.

'Am I falling in love with him?' she wondered, shocked by the novelty of these strange feelings.

No eventuality could be more silly, more immature. In experience, if not years, he was far too old for her. She would never be more to him than Sam's young daughter, a helpless creature he wished to protect from financial sharks he hated. Even the blithe, joking consideration he showed her seemed to confirm that he thought himself worlds apart from her, that he reserved his amorous attentions for more sophisticated women he knew in New York or elsewhere.

Perhaps he had an intense love life of his own. A long-term affair... Perhaps he was a divorcé: Laura had never thought to inform herself on the subject.

She dared not admit to herself in all candour that it was love that inflamed her towards Frank Jordan. He was too enigmatic a figure, she told herself, to touch the centre of her woman's emotions. Ever since her youthful crush of Rob Colwell she had thought of true, adult love in terms of candour and trust. Charmingly outspoken as he was, Frank kept his feelings hidden behind the curtain of his indefatigable energy. If Laura had a place in his thoughts, he would have given her a sign of some sort, rather than to withhold himself so coolly.

Nevertheless, the dark intensity of his demeanour seemed to soften imperceptibly when he was alone with Laura. Occasionally he would take her hand with quiet affection, straighten an unruly lock of her sandy hair, his finger lingering for an instant on the downy surface of her cheek, a curious light of sympathy in his dark eyes.

At those moments the raw eruption in Laura's senses deepened vertiginously, and she told herself that love alone must be the source of the irresistible trust she felt for him.

Laura was living a contradiction, and its intensity was becoming unbearable. Frank Jordan had taught her a new self-reliance, and yet it was he whose initiative and expertise were responsible for the strides her company had made since Sam Christensen's death. And the more Laura felt herself capable of handling the company's future on her own, the more she doubted that her own future could contain a moment's happiness if Frank Jordan were not part of it.

Yet Frank manifestly took no notice of the feelings he kindled in her—feelings which grew each day in power and urgency, so that she felt she must die of frustration or throw herself at him with shameless abandon before another week was out.

As time grew short for Christensen Products, the fuse in Laura's emotions burned shorter and shorter as well. She knew its final flare would unleash a storm over which she would have no control.

The early flight to Montreal on Friday enabled Laura and Frank to meet Rob at an industrial park where Pirot et Cie. possessed a facility capable of producing the Molly in a matter of months. Rob had done his work well. Pirot's managers had already studied the blueprints he had brought, and concluded not only that there was a strong market for the product in Canada, but also that its cost could be held to a minimum by using existing machinery for production.

By late afternoon the major points of Christensen's leasing arrangement with Pirot had been ironed out. Amazed at the relative ease of the transaction, Laura and Frank were in a celebrative mood. Rob declined their invitation to join them for the evening, saying he had to fly back to New York for a luncheon meeting tomorrow. With a glance at Laura and a quick nod to Frank, he took his leave.

The executives at Pirot having surprised Laura by speaking to her in colloquial English without the trace of an accent, she had her first serious opportunity to speak French with the taxi driver whose vehicle bore her and Frank through the mad whirlwind of Montreal's traffic towards their hotel. To her amazement the small, dark man not only understood her hesitant questions about the unfamiliar city, but seized upon them as pretexts for airing his separatist political views. Though his pronounced accent and slangy turn of phrase made his disquisition difficult to understand, Laura gleaned that he blamed the government of Canada for all his city's problems. Delighted to hear that his passengers planned to manufacture a new product in his beloved province, he insisted on writing down its description, and promised to buy his hard-working wife a Molly when it became available.

Chez Victor, the French restaurant Frank had mentioned, was everything he had claimed it to be, although the ambience within its cramped confines was hardly what Laura might have expected. Only the flowers and fine silverware on its smattering of old tables suggested that it was anything more than a country-style *auberge*. The mimeographed menu handed out unceremoniously by a smiling, portly hostess was scrawled in a very French hand, and it was the chef-owner, M. Fasquelle, who appeared in his soiled apron to take orders from his well-to-do clients, whom he treated with grunting familiarity. His personal suggestions for dinner were communicated in so imperious a manner that Frank accepted them respectfully, his hooded glance at Laura glinting with amusement.

As it turned out, the blandly named terrine du chef, soupe de poissons, and boeuf à la moelle were culinary miracles whose subtlety and grace astounded Laura. For the first time in many weeks she found herself possessed of a genuine appetite, and Frank laughed to see her eat so heartily. 'Well,' he smiled as she somehow found room for the poire Belle Hélène which closed their meal, 'now I know how to put some flesh on that emaciated frame of yours. All I have to do is fly you up here every week-end.'

'I've been too worried to eat for so long,' Laura sighed. 'But I think under the worst of circumstances this place would make me hungry. It's a marvellous restaurant. Thank you for bringing me here.'

After another hurtling taxi ride through the city's frigid, windswept streets, they found themselves in the gleaming lobby of the hotel, behind whose shimmering drapes the lights of Montreal illuminated the night sky. The large, carpeted room echoed with the smooth strains of dance music from the adjacent lounge.

'I'll tell you what,' Frank said suddenly. 'We've had a good day, and we ought to finish it off with a little more celebration, if you're not too tired. Why don't we have a nightcap?'

The lounge was dark and lovely, its recessed lights glowing in corners decorated in subtle pastel greens. A few couples moved slowly on the dance floor while a trio played romantic songs in long, rhythmic phrases.

The brandy Frank ordered sent waves of delightful warmth through Laura's tired limbs. It had been a perfect day whose accomplishments, for a change, had not been marred by false starts and unpleasant surprises, and all at once Laura felt a curious surge of excited energy in all her senses.

'You know something?' Frank asked, his impish smile glimmering in the shadows. 'We can't go on like this, Laura.'

'What do you mean?' she asked, blushing in her perplexity.

'Just sitting here,' he said, 'without dancing, while all those people are enjoying themselves. You're the most beautiful woman in the room, and I should be showing you off.'

'Frank, I...' Despite his joking tone, his words sent a thrill of expectation through Laura's body, and she felt suddenly diffident.

'Come on, now,' he insisted, taking her hand to lead her to the dance floor. 'This is a special night.'

The enfolding touch of his warm, dry hand, abetted by

the brandy which tingled calmingly in her senses, sent a flood of yielding through her mind. All at once the most logical thing in the world seemed to simply place herself in his hands and forget the frantic emotions that had been tormenting her for weeks.

There was infinite gentleness in the strong body that led her in time with the quiet music. Frank's arm encircled her waist with easy familiarity, and her face drew close to his deep chest. She moved with him in a sort of charmed somnambulism, as though the dance itself were an impalpable element in which one could float without awareness of one's steps or of the song one heard.

She felt his hand graze her shoulder, her neck, her hair, in little strokes which had a magical power to silence the thoughts which troubled her happiness. The hardness of his thigh brushed her flesh soothingly, naturally. Though he held her with an almost ethereal softness, it seemed that this nearness of his tall, strong body was a steadfast edifice that buoyed her, lifted her liltingly atop swelling waves of sound and rhythm.

She was in his hands now, she told herself, and somehow their calm caress knew how to resolve the contradiction haunting her feelings for him—as though he knew how to be her ally, her friend, her protector, and also a strong, sensual man who could enjoy touching and holding her without insult to the mutual respect which was the essence of their relationship. And as he pulled her closer to the hard length of his body, so that his clean male scent suffused her senses, this bewitching contact itself seemed peaceful and secure, and not at all disturbing.

'That's my girl,' he murmured, the hard line of his jaw touching her temple. 'You do know how to relax, don't you?'

She nodded dreamily, lulled by the deep tones of his voice and by the delicate embrace which enfolded her.

And her sense of perfect well-being might have gone on indefinitely, had not a subtle flow of forces begun to tip her head backward—not so that her half-closed, unseeing eyes might contemplate him, but so that her soft lips might open to him, to accept his kiss with a great sigh of pleasure...

She arrested the impulse with a shock, unnerved to feel her body move with a will of its own when once her waking mind had relaxed its vigilance. And now it seemed that Frank's quiet touch was indeed an innocent and friendly thing, but that her own traitorous flesh could not be trusted to accept this intimacy without clamouring to make of it something more heated and insidious.

He had seen the rapt look in her eyes, and was smiling down at her as the song ended.

'My poor Laura,' he laughed. 'You're out on your feet. Let's get you upstairs to bed.'

Thank heaven, she thought in sudden panic. Thank heaven he had misunderstood. It was better this way, better that he should mistake her shamelessness for mere fatigue.

The elevator was sparsely filled with tourists and businessmen. Laura stood by Frank's side, still charmed by his relaxed cheer despite the tumult which had only begun to ebb in her senses. Her sidelong glances seemed to confirm that he had not noticed the effect he had had on her only moments ago.

But as they walked along the hushed, carpeted hallway towards her room, once again a great surge of warring thoughts overcame her. In a trice he would say goodnight, disappear to his own room and leave Laura to her confused, taunting dreams. Bitterly she longed for the day when, for better or worse, Frank Jordan would get out of her life. Simple loneliness would be preferable to this agony of wanting he kindled in her without being aware of it himself. So magnetic was he that it was torture to be in the same room with him, close enough to touch him with eager hands, and yet separated from him by an impenetrable gulf of her own making.

The door opened and she turned to say goodnight. In a frightening flash she visualised herself seducing him, throwing herself at him shamelessly, pulling him into her bed. The idea was so disturbing that she feared her last words to him tonight would be spoken in a voice shaken by desire.

'Now,' he said quietly. 'You're a lady with a lot of responsibilities, and you need a good eight hours' sleep. I don't want you to get out of bed until I call you. Then we'll have a nice breakfast and see what the day holds for us.'

His hands were on her shoulders. As he bent to kiss her cheek, she felt her fingers grasp his long arms with a hesitant languor she could not control. His lips touched her softly and receded as her eyes half-closed in involuntary delight.

But her slender hands had not released him, and it was with an inner sigh of resignation that she let her eyes rest pleadingly upon his own, her irises glowing pale green in the shadows as a nearly imperceptible tremor in her touch told him what she wanted.

She saw the sudden gravity in his gaze, the quick alertness which saw into her soul, the inevitable quirk of surprise and perhaps disapproval which frowned in his dark brow.

Then the door began to close, and she thought her heart would burst with wanting.

For she was in his arms at last, her slender form pressed full length against the hardness of his body by powerful arms locked firmly behind her back.

His kiss took her breath away, for it probed suddenly to the core of the heat she had vainly fought for so many days, allowing it to expand and carry her away in its triumph.

Somehow her hand must have found its way to the light switch, for a calming darkness engulfed her, banishing her long weeks of silent struggle with a sort of finality. At last she felt she could relax into the joy that was about to be hers, and she let her lips and tongue return the kiss that held her.

Awed by the terrible intimacy of that single kiss, so probing, so secret, she felt she belonged to him already. Her tongue met his own in a lithe dance of discovery, exploring and inviting. Her senses leapt dizzyingly as she felt his calm hands caress the soft curves they had never touched before. Their movement was unhurried, rhythmic, and the flesh of her back, her hips, her thighs came alive in little shivers of ecstasy under his caress.

She felt the ripple of his hard muscles under her fingertips as she pressed her hands to his back. With a sort of heedless joy she touched his neck, his broad shoulder. Her body moulded itself to his own, yielding in its every hollow to his hard flesh so that he would know she wanted him closer yet. Stunned by her own forwardness, she nevertheless exulted to feel his caress grow stronger, more heated.

So marvellous was this embrace which seemed to greet her body affectionately, lovingly, as after a long and painful separation, that she thought it might go on forever, inexhaustible in its perfection. But with a sigh she realised that her dress had come loose under his stroking fingers, her bra hung loose over the hand that grazed her breasts. And now, before she could quite realise that only her sheer panties still clung to her soft skin in the darkness, he was bearing her through the still air, placing her on the silky spread which slipped under her naked body.

She had not allowed herself to wonder what the reality of Frank Jordan's unclothed limbs might be. Now she lay in rapt anticipation as the muted sounds of his movements in the obscurity told her he was preparing to come to her.

And it was with a little gasp of pleasure that she felt herself encircled by his long arms and gathered against the warm expanse of his nudity. The harsh power of his body did not daunt her, for he knew how to harness and tame it, so that it cradled her gently even as its earthy touch and smell drew her to caress and kiss it in avid fascination.

His lips closed softly over the hard nipple poised for their approach. A spasm of ecstasy stirred her as she held him to her breast, her fingers buried in his thick hair. Languorously her silken thighs moved under him, slipping against his hips, sending messages of eager yielding to his coiled senses.

She shuddered to feel him strip away the last flimsy fabric separating him from her, and grasped him more urgently as her naked skin breathed the charged air of the room. Great billows of passion surged through her slender limbs as he explored every part of her, the gentle enquiry of his lips and hands teasing her to a mad height of wanting.

And even as he joined himself to her at last, the power of him forcing sighs of rapture from her lips, there was a core of quiet mystery in the body whose slow movements drove her to a wild excitement she had never imagined possible in all her guilty dreams about him. Leaving no trace of her unexplored, overwhelming her with the hot flare of his own need, he nevertheless held her intact, safe from harm in his embrace. Thus she could grip him, clutch him to her, fill her senses with him until she thought she would burst, for his touch never violated her.

But there was no time to wonder at the strangeness of this fiery intimacy with an unknown man who gave of himself so freely, so sweetly, from the very depths of his unseen heart; for already her passion was preparing to spend itself in the silent room. The great spasms which shook her seemed to rend the very fabric of her life, so that its countless days and hours were banished in a trice, and in their stead loomed a single face, filling her body and soul with the dark magic of its knowing gaze.

When all was still inside her once more, and she lay in his embrace, her gasps of pleasure having slowed to somnolent rhythms of blessed rest, she allowed herself to dream that she belonged to him now, forever. The part of her mind that knew he remained a separate being, come from an unknown past and destined for a future perhaps far from her, slept first. For a long moment her rapt imagination clung to its conviction that this calm closeness was forever.

Then she was asleep in his arms.

CHAPTER NINE

THE grey glow of dawn brightened gradually as the heavy boom of delivery trucks in the streets outside signalled the awakening of the metropolis.

Laura lay in silence, her eyes fixed upon Frank's sleeping form. Admiration for his handsome face in repose vied with a sort of awed fascination in her regard, as though she were contemplating an untamed and dangerous being whose awakening would be a thing to be dreaded.

Frank Jordan was no less a contradiction this morning than he had been last night, in those agonising hours preceding the charmed instant when he had kissed her for the first time. His unknown thoughts were as penetrating and alert as the taut body which had cradled her in its embrace only hours ago. But the change he had wrought in Laura could never be undone.

Here he lay in his quiet sleep, dark and inscrutable, far from her in the exterior world. Yet her whole body still bore the daunting traces of the enormous intimacy she had shared with him. And never again would she be able to contemplate him coolly, to wonder detachedly about his past, his desires, his plans. He was inside her mind now, and she could no more reestablish her previous view of him than one can turn back the clock.

She shuddered to think that he could have made such a difference in her by simply gratifying the passion he had inspired during weeks of apparently workaday coexistence. What must he think of her now? Did her image have a place somewhere in the dreams that passed through his sleep? Would he awaken to smile down upon her with a trace of contempt for her childish forwardness?

Laura suddenly knew all the shame of her vulnerability. He had given her the intimacy she craved so violently, and now she must pay the consequences. He could think what he liked of her now, and imagine himself possessed of some sort of ascendancy over her if he wished. Indeed, he had had his way with her all these weeks. Had she not done his bidding in nearly every detail of her struggle to save Sam's company from disaster? It was Frank who had pulled the strings from his obscure position behind the scenes.

Perhaps, already amply convinced of Laura's naiveté and girlish simplicity, he had long been aware of her guilty feelings for him, and had decided on a whim that no great harm would be done to Christensen Products if he mixed business with his own pleasure for once. Perhaps it seemed convenient and even amusing for so experienced a man to take pity on the callow girl he had condescended to help in her emergency.

If that were the case, he would undoubtedly awaken to his own impatient fear that, having thrown herself at him like an adolescent, she would now presume to importune him with childish displays of possessiveness, as though in her romantic mind last night's lovemaking had meant something deep and permanent.

These thoughts stole painfully through her mind even as her glance lingered involuntarily over the strong, hard lines of Frank's sleeping body. And as she caught herself furtively recalling the ecstasy she had known in his arms, she felt more shamed than ever, and closed her eyes with a little spasm of determination.

'Don't,' she heard a low murmur which shocked her.

He was gazing at her sleepily, a smile on his lips.

'Don't look away,' he said.

'How did you know I was…?'

'I could feel your eyes on me,' he said. 'It was nice.'

And with a calm softness which amazed her, he extended a long arm to draw her close to him. Reluctantly she allowed her naked body to nestle in his warm embrace, and listened to the rhythm of his breathing, her face pressed to his deep chest.

For a long, lovely moment he held her that way as sleep dissipated in his vital body. She could feel the energy of the new day coming to life under the warm skin that grazed her own. The hand that rested on the curve of her hip was dry and relaxed. His fingertips brushed lightly at the billowed maze of her hair, and it was with a thrill of recognition that she felt his lips touch her temple, her earlobe.

'Sleep well?' he murmured, an impalpable smile in his voice.

She nodded, her lips against the crisp hair of his chest.

'That's my girl,' he said, his hands running gently over her back. 'A good sleep was what you needed. A woman can't run a big company on strung-out nerves, can she?'

Against her better judgment she let herself luxuriate in the protective cradle of his limbs. Now that she had given herself to him he seemed more thoughtful and considerate than ever. His awareness of what had happened between them shone only in this warm, silent intimacy of his naked body which enfolded her so naturally.

Yet it was disconcerting to feel so at home in his arms, when her scruples about what she had done still thronged her mind. And perhaps he sensed the doubt which tensed her sleepy limbs, for he gathered her closer to him, his hands moulding her body to his own as though to protect her from her own thoughts.

How marvellous it was to feel herself wedded to his own nudity, even for one charmed moment! She could imagine a lifetime of such magic, and in her mind's eye she saw herself joined to Frank Jordan forever by bonds of trust and intimacy. What would happen, she wondered, if she could wake up every morning in his arms? What challenges could frighten her then?

But the dream vanished as quickly as it had come, and she cursed her wishful thinking. Her woman's intuition made her suspect the pious impulse towards trust and dependency that comes after an unforgettable night of love. She was still a responsible adult, and bound by her own maturity to behave like one. What had happened left behind it no obligation on Frank's part. Were she foolish enough to think that it did, she would be letting herself in for disaster.

'I'll tell you what,' he smiled, raising himself on one arm to look into her eyes. 'I'll bet you'd like a nice hot shower and a good breakfast. Then we can talk about what to do with this day.'

'You took the words right out of my mouth,' she replied, doing her best to match his own unflappable calm. If he could treat her with such relaxed equanimity, as though nothing had happened which needed to be discussed in any way, then she would do the same for him. Perhaps he was right, after all. What was there to say, or to worry about?

'You look so beautiful lying there,' he said, his eyes caressing her. 'Could a fellow have one kiss to wake up on?'

Her eyes half closed in involuntary rapture as he drew her to him once more. She could not help wondering whether this was the last kiss they were to share. Perhaps their indescribable intimacy of last night fell into the category of accidents which occasionally befall good friends, and are soon forgotten by both. If this kiss were the last she must savour it, then, and force herself to suppress her tragic sense that it was already a goodbye.

His lips joined hers, and with an ethereal sweetness he

explored the flesh he had known totally a few hours before. Laura felt herself all open to him, all pliant and acceptant, and it was with a great sensation of delighted yielding that she gratefully received the affection he bestowed. If her solitary tryst with Frank Jordan was never to be repeated, she would fix this last kiss in her memory as a secure link to the passion that had been hers in his arms.

Without embarrassment at her nudity or his own, Frank helped her up and watched her move towards the bathroom. She flushed slightly to feel his gaze on her body, and all at once hesitated to meet his eyes.

'Hey,' he called after her. She turned to see him standing with careless grace beside her bed. 'Hurry back.'

Despite their friendliness, his black eyes had never looked so deep, so penetrating.

The phone rang as she was struggling to tear herself away from him.

'Shall I answer it?' Frank asked, looking outrageously calm in his stately nudity.

'No, I'll do it.'

Concealing her shock at the sudden buzz, Laura sat on the edge of the bed and picked up the phone.

'Laura, it's Rob.' The voice was distant, the transmission hollow. 'I hope I didn't wake you up.'

'Not at all, Rob. Is there a problem?'

'Not really. It's about the contract we signed with Pirot. I told Mr Allard yesterday that our lawyers would be in touch about the details, but I forgot to give him the name of the international contract firm we hired to work with him. There's no sense leaving any confusion in his mind. I thought if you were going to be in touch with Pirot to-day…'

'Yes, I intended to call them this morning in any case,' Laura said, her voice catching despite herself as she glanced down at her own nakedness.

'I tried Frank's room, but there was no answer,' Rob's voice added.

For a stunned instant Laura saw herself naked between the powerful man who stood before her and the incisive voice on the line. Feeling atrociously vulnerable and embarrassed, she forced herself to speak in easy, businesslike tones.

'He's right here,' she said. 'We're just on our way to breakfast. Would you like to talk to him about it?'

'No. Just remind him, now that I think of it, to make sure Allard understands the import arrangement on the parts from Syracuse. Tell him to tell Pirot that we're handling the taxes ourselves.'

'Syracuse,' Laura repeated, fixing the word in her mind as she stifled her blushing glance at Frank. If Rob was at all aware of her nervousness, he gave no sign of it. 'All right, Rob. I've got it,' she said. 'See you Monday.'

She hung up the phone with a sigh. All at once she felt ashamed of her predicament. Like a heedless, defenceless girl she sat naked on the bedsheets which had felt the storm of her rapture last night. Yet she was the president of a huge corporation, here in this foreign place on important business...

When at last she looked up, Frank was smiling down at her.

'The Syracuse parts,' he said. 'He's worried about the duties.'

She nodded, her slight smile meeting his own.

'You take your shower, young lady,' he said. 'I'll call Allard from my room, and meet you here in ten minutes. All right?'

'All right.'

'And I want you to eat like a horse today,' he added. 'Breakfast, lunch and dinner. My God, what a slender little thing you are. If someone doesn't watch out for you, you're going to waste away to nothing.'

He watched in silence, his arms crossed, as she stood up. Outside the windows the huge city, frigid under its winter wind, teemed with speeding traffic and hurried pedestrians. Laura knew that in an hour or so she would step through the lobby's revolving doors to join that throng of busy people. And she would be on Frank's arm. Her day would undoubtedly hold a bit or two of unfinished business. And after that... With a last peek at the rumpled bedclothes beside Frank she wondered if there was a chance they might be lovers again.

'Am I thinking, or wishing?' The question made her blush. As she turned away, its answer quickened in the traitorous glow stealing under her skin.

With teasing persuasion from which all reference to last night's events was banished, Frank convinced Laura to accompany him to the Laurentians for an hour of cross-country skiing after their business with Pirot et Cie. was finished. The trip, past thickly forested mountains in which dozens of ski centres nestled, was like an idyll in a winter wonderland. Despite the rather intense cold, the wind had dissipated, leaving huge banks of snow glistening in the December sun. Threading his way through the Saturday traffic with quiet care, Frank met Laura's eyes with an amused smile.

'Are you sure I'm up to this?' she asked.

'If you can walk, you can cross-country ski,' he laughed. 'It'll do you good.'

To her surprise, he was right. After a few minutes of patient instruction she found that she was able to manage the regular rhythm required to propel herself over the grainy snow. They set off along a well-travelled trail, having memorised the map, and before long found themselves exploring lush forest corridors piled high with soft crystals which exploded as gently as champagne bubbles into the air as their skis slid through them. The stillness of the trails was remarkable after the busy atmosphere of the lodge. No sound broke the silence other than the hushed thrum of their skis. Only the faintest breeze stirred the snow-laden branches of the pines.

The intimacy of the experience was so bewitching that neither felt the need to speak. The woods themselves seemed to conspire to bring them together in this oddly private communication, witnessed by no human eye. Muted calls from nearby trails echoed softly as they approached a crossroads.

Laura felt wonderfully invigorated after her tumultuous night, and thanked Frank for bringing her.

'Cross-country skiing is the one sport for absolutely everyone,' he smiled. 'It doesn't matter how athletic you are, as long as you enjoy the great outdoors. All you have to do is drift along and watch the world pass by. When we get back home we can drive north to Connecticut and do this any time. With all your hard work, it would be just the thing for you.'

Frank must have calculated how long it would take for the route to tire Laura, for she was just beginning to feel a languor in her legs as the lodge came into view once more. After returning their ski equipment, they drank hot toddies before the roaring fire in the lounge. As she glanced at Frank's long limbs stretched before him, Laura could not help letting her eyes rest on him with admiration, and with a secret thrill of possession. That marvellous man's body had been entwined with her own only hours ago, and now she sat beside him as calmly as though he belonged to her.

It was not true, of course, but the fantasy was too intox-icating to banish as she exchanged quiet words with him, watched his easy smile curl his lips as he gazed into the flames, felt him touch her hand.

But as they arose to have a simple, bracing lunch before driving back to Montreal, a disturbing thought overtook her with stunning power. This simple closeness she felt with Frank, so clearly reciprocated on his own side, was part of a sinuous path leading through this sunlit day towards the night. And when the shadows fell at last, and they returned to their hotel for their last hours together before the flight home, what had happened once must surely happen again.

The thought coiled around Laura pitilessly, making her senses tingle with guilty anticipation. She wondered whether she alone was thinking it. Frank's dark eyes betrayed nothing of his feelings. He was every bit as cheerful and self-assured as always, though his demeanour was perhaps a bit more gentle, less exigent, since he deemed this brief vacation essential to Laura's health, and had no intention of renewing his incessant demands for performance until Monday. But could it be that he himself felt the deep, fulfilling afterglow of their intimacy?

Could it be that he would come to her again? That they both knew it, and could no more prevent it than they could prevent the sun from rising tomorrow?

No, she told herself angrily. This evening he would decorously leave her to her sleep, no doubt angry with himself for having taken advantage of her heedless seduction last night, and put the whole episode behind him. He would not wish to hurt her more than he had already. He was probably comparing her charming simplicity in his own mind with the sophisticated wiles of his women friends in New York or elsewhere.

It was already mid-afternoon when they emerged from their wild expressway and found themselves back in the city. They passed an array of enormous skyscrapers whose bulk concealed countless monuments to French explorations hundreds of years ago. The Notre Dame church, gigantic and beautiful, sprang into view as they approached the river. And behind every urban structure Laura saw, the mountain that had given the city its name seemed to loom in its magnificence.

At Frank's suggestion they decided to complete their day with a brief exploration of Centre Town. They walked along Sainte-Catherine Street, with its elegant department stores and crowds of Saturday shoppers, and gazed in the windows of the high-fashion establishments on Sherbrooke Street. Then Frank led Laura into a maze of underground passages lined with shops, restaurants and cinemas, which seemed an entire city under the frozen streets above.

'It's a relief after the cold, isn't it?' Frank asked as he strolled hand in hand with her. 'That's why they built it. Montreal stays cold until late April or so. The snow never melts.'

After returning to their hotel to rest and dress, they took a cab to Crescent Street where Frank introduced Laura to a restaurant which bore an uncanny resemblance to a Paris bistro. Patrons stood at the large zinc bar drinking *demis* of draft beer while waiters in waist aprons and white shirts open at the neck hurried from table to table. The jukebox rang with the sounds of popular French songs.

Laura's active day had given her a good appetite, and Frank watched in humorous approval as she finished the savory onion soup and *entrecôte* he had ordered for her.

'I think this old town agrees with you,' he said as they chose from the cheese tray brought by the waiter. 'Some day, when you're mistress of all you survey, perhaps you'll move Christensen's headquarters up here.'

'It's a thought,' she laughed, weighing his words inwardly. For the first time he had intimated that he truly believed her capable of running Sam's company indefinitely.

But the undercurrent of her thoughts was far more insidious than these bantering exchanges. She could feel the shameless language of her senses sending its lilting phrases into the warm air around her. And an insistent inner voice proclaimed that he, too, must be feeling this secret ferment. The day was almost done. Night was upon them, covering them with its sweet obscurity, drawing them inevitably closer to each other...

Bravely Laura tried to match Frank smile for smile, remark for blithe remark, to engage in the easy ebb and flow of conversation for all the world as though his nearness were not sending shudders of forbidden desire through her limbs. It was agony, that performance, and yet it was the only possible way to behave. She dared not admit to herself that in a few more minutes he would say goodnight and leave her alone. But what else could he do? He was too responsible, too much in iron control of himself, to let last night's wild scene repeat itself.

Behind his mask of good humour he must be concernedly asking himself whether this already dependent girl would draw the wrong conclusions from what had happened between them. He must be thinking of a way to let her down gently, so that she would not flatter herself about his future plans. After all, he must continue to work with her every day. Any lovesick airs she might permit herself would certainly make a mess of their business relationship.

She must not embarrass him by throwing herself at him again. It would be too humiliating. She must say goodnight blandly, coolly—just as though she were as adult as he, and knew full well that an unforeseen upsurge of physical need between friends meant less than nothing. She must be businesslike and mature, and let him know that he was still her invaluable adviser and colleague, that she harboured no illusion that he had become her lover, her love...

She fought to put everything out of her mind except that

one cool moment when she would bid him goodnight and close her door.

As they hurried from their cab into the hotel lobby, bound for the desk where the handsomely dressed clerks awaited, they passed the lounge where she had danced in Frank's arms last night. She sighed to think that he must be sharing her thoughts, for he did not ask her if she would like a nightcap, if she would like to dance. Doubtless he wished her to rest her tired legs after this day of strenuous activity. Perhaps he was tired, and in a hurry to sleep himself. Or perhaps, once he had taken his leave of her, he would go back out to keep a rendezvous with someone.

The crowded lobby and elevator passed as though in a dream, their turbulent sounds banished by her certainty that in five minutes she would be alone in her bed, dreaming pitifully of the man who had shared it with her last night. Let the tears of frustration flow, she told herself, after he had gone. Let her be as silly as she wished in her solitude. As long as she did not throw herself at him again.

Some day she would fall in love and marry, and this episode would persist in her memory as a strange sidelight of this terrible period of eleventh-hour struggles to save Sam's company. It would simply be part of that mad whirlwind of events in which normal rules were suspended by the unexpected. She would live it down, and never speak of it to anyone.

Without a word Frank walked her to her door, locked his arms warmly around here and kissed her hair. She rested her face against his chest, grateful for this contact which must give her the strength to let him go.

'Thank you for a wonderful day, Frank.'

'Thank you.' His voice was quiet against her hair. 'I'm sorry it's over.'

It was subtle, the movement of his arms that told her he wanted her. Impalpably light, the touch of his palms on her back; and yet never had her body received a message with such stunning force.

There was no time to think twice, nor did she want to. Quietly the door clicked shut, and the shadows enclosed them with an almost conspiratorial softness. Loosened by invisible fingers, Laura's dress seemed to fall away all at once, and she stood in her bra and panties, returning a kiss that sent a shudder of passion through her senses. Her slender hands slipped to Frank's broad shoulders, their passage easing his jacket off before they crept to undo the buttons of his shirt. In a trice she felt the warm skin of his back and hips under her fingertips, smooth and dry.

Their hands must have worked together in a mysterious complicity as she kissed the sinews of his neck, for the whole expanse of his loins fell under her touch with stunning suddenness, the crisp tangle of his man's hair brushing her palms as she caressed him. The last flimsy fabrics came away from her tender flesh, and she stood naked against his firm body, intoxicated by its aroused power.

An instant later she was beside him on the satiny spread, her quiet moan of delight greeting the lips which kissed her breasts, her stomach, her ribs. Had he wished it, she would have given herself to him in that one charged moment, for the wanting that had built up all day inside her was releasing itself in a violent storm. But his caresses were slow, and gently enquiring, as he explored the downy skin he had known last night for the first time.

Exulting in her realisation that he still wanted her, that his own thoughts must have lingered over her image throughout this charmed day, she felt her senses open to him in luxuriant eagerness. Her soft limbs grazed him in their sweet undulations, seeking with a will of their own to excite him. And now there was no embarrassment between them, no diffidence, but only the expanding joy of discovery.

She kissed his eyes, his brow, his hair as he held her closer. His large hands slipped under her back to her hips, and she felt the strength of male fingers capable of lifting her bodily to crush her against him. But she met him delightedly, her knees rubbing his waist, the skin of her legs filling itself with his touch.

Sensing the heat of his man's need, she welcomed it, her hands unafraid to explore him, their fingertips acknowledging and celebrating his desire. A groan stirred in his throat as he pulled her face to his, and she felt herself fairly levitated by the magnetism of him, stunned in air by the lips and tongue that held her.

She would never know whether that entrancing embrace had lasted seconds or long minutes, for even as they touched each other in euphoric release, savouring the novelty of their bodies' intimacy, the terrible momentum of their passion bound them together. In a flash she was his, her arms wrapped around him in ecstasy as every part of her strained to weld itself to him.

She felt his enormous heat gather under her skin, the wild potency of him firing her deliciously, and with a gasp her rapture bestowed itself upon the darkness all around. The past had dissolved vertiginously, and there was no time to think worried thoughts about the future. Only this eternal wave of pleasure existed, this expanding moment, rocking and buoying her forever, forever in his arms.

When at last the storm in their senses had spent itself, it was with an infinite delicacy that his hard grip softened, his embrace grew tender, his firm sinews relaxed around her, warmer and more intimate than ever as the sharp force of him receded, so that she was never bereft of him, never alone.

Her fingers grazed his neck, his broad shoulders with cooling gentleness as she lay under his weight, her body moulded to his own. He kissed her eyes, her cheeks, and

the soft scent of her hair suffused him. A tender silence
enfolded them both, for it seemed that in that one magical
moment nothing in the world had separated them. Perfect
oneness had been theirs. And now that it had happened,
nothing could take it away.

I love you.

The words stole furtively through her mind, tantalising
her at first with their lithe, pretty sound. A little poem in
three words, she thought dreamily. And though she knew
that in another moment the reality of Frank's separate existence would return to haunt her, she felt an impulse to
scoff at it nonetheless. She felt as though she had captured
the core of his male essence, known him entirely. A hundred years of living alone could never banish the memory
of that moment.

True, the three short words with their burnished, eupho-
nious sound had never passed her lips. But she had known
him and yes, loved him in that burning instant of utter
closeness. The dreamed perfection, the fulfilment she had
not dared to think possible, was now.

Her body tingled delightfully in his arms as the warm
obscurity of the room covered them. She felt him slip the
sheet over her nudity and hold her close. Outside the winter
wind whirled among the city's steel and granite towers,
cruel and vibrant. But here inside one knew the essence of
warmth, the purest intimacy.

Minutes passed silently as they held each other, their lips
and fingers touching softly. Though stunned into a wondrous languor by the force of her passion, Laura felt no
fatigue. Instead, a hidden swirl of excitement, of other-
worldly exhilaration flowed through her every nerve.

And as time passed that quick charge of physical joy
became indistinguishable from desire's inevitable reawak-
ening. The long arms that held her came alive, the quiet

kisses brushing her face grew more urgent, and she knew his passion was rising to meet hers anew.

Again it was perfect, whole and complete, though slower and more dreamlike, the rapture they gave each other. Her sighs coiled around him, and they were sighs of amazement, of delighted astonishment at the pleasure he could bring her. This time she gave herself in sheer bliss, dazzled by the sensations he kindled in her, and by his own responses when her hands crept to touch him, to increase his excitement. Again the mad, luxurious slipping of flesh upon flesh, hotter and hotter, drove her to a height of ecstasy unimagined in her guiltiest fantasies about him. And again he held her in his steadfast embrace, protective and strong, as her gasps whispered in the darkness, and as she relaxed into rapt somnolence in his arms.

She would remember that night forever as an iridescent dream in which fiery explosions of intimacy alternated with long, stunned periods of beautiful rest. How many times she was his she would never know. Whether she had truly slept at all remained a mystery. The night belonged to love, and from it the intervals of everyday time had been banished. For one perfect, endless moment the future had been held off, daunted and outlawed by an immediacy more powerful than the passing hours.

And with each new ecstasy, different from the last, too individual to ever recapture or forget, Laura felt a secret confirmation of the ineffable force that joined her to Frank Jordan.

A change had overtaken her in that enchanted night, and she accepted it in exultation. She would never be the same again. And in that very fact, which, she knew, might expose her to extremities of pain she had never experienced before, she took her pleasure.

For if time retained its cruel power to take Frank away from her forever, it had also brought her this night, whose place in her heart was permanent.

CHAPTER TEN

DAYS later the wintry world of Christensen Products' life-and-death struggle had engulfed Laura again. She was up to her neck in phone calls, blueprints and cost estimates. Frank was again haunting the corridors of Christensen's headquarters like a spirit, his quick glance looking for weaknesses in corporate organisation that might suddenly emerge to thwart Laura's plan to market Molly by late March.

The bespectacled face of Zalman Corey loomed before Laura as the weeks passed, importuning her to be more conservative in her contracting expenses, mutely begging her to be more traditional in her fiscal attitudes. Rob Colwell was in her office often, explaining the uncertain balance of payments governing Molly's parts and assembly, his eyes resting on the reports with the calm of a surgeon whose fingers tie delicate sutures inside the body of a dangerously ill patient. Laura marvelled at his self-possessed confidence in his ability to do messy and difficult jobs with alacrity.

Occasionally a touch of worry clouded his irises as he regarded her, and she wondered whether the secret change which had overtaken her was somehow visible to him. She could not help recalling the discomfort that had found its way into her voice when she had sat naked on the bed in Montreal, only a few feet from her lover, while accepting Rob's instructions over the phone. And she feared that when the three of them were together now at Christensen, her hooded glances at Frank and the tone of her voice in speaking to him betrayed a subtle alchemy that Rob must surely interpret correctly.

She knew that Rob would do anything in the world to protect her, for he considered himself *in loco parentis* and as such had fatherly concern for her. If he suspected for a moment that her youthful innocence was exposing her to hurts over and above those she had already suffered, wild horses would not prevent him from intervening on her behalf.

On the other hand, his respect for Laura must dictate that he avoid invading her privacy. And so he kept his watchful distance, showing by his supportive demeanour that he was always there if she needed him.

But Laura knew he could not be blind to the profound difference these past weeks had made in her. She could no more conceal the glow of fulfilment in her woman's body than she could hide the firm edge of her newfound confidence.

Frank Jordan had made her a new woman in more ways than one, and she felt that the process was almost complete now. Her lack of conviction in her own competence had taken a back seat to her determination to save Sam's company. She knew who her enemies were, and she felt a professional's visceral certainty that she would prevail against them. The facts and figures at her fingertips combined with the careful strategies in her mind to convince her that victory was attainable.

Each time an obstacle seemed to threaten Molly's marketability, or a financial reversal seemed to make the corporation more vulnerable, Laura no longer wasted time in fear and trembling. She acted. Those around her saw her concentration and her grim commitment. What they could not see was that she had stopped thinking of herself now, and thought only of the job before her.

Laura had become an executive, in her every nerve and sinew.

She alone knew the real secret behind her calm readiness for bold action. Her private self lived now in a secluded paradise of happiness, and had given up hoping or fearing for the future.

As winter had settled over the country in its cold triumph, Laura travelled its length and breadth with Frank, personally supervising every element of Molly's production. She came to know each mechanical and electrical part of the machine with an almost maternal familiarity, and she questioned her many quality control experts insistently in her effort to pre-empt cost overruns that might menace Molly's affordable price.

Her travels with Frank took her to Chicago, where savage winds roared across Lake Michigan and whirled turbulently through the busy streets of the Loop; and to Bangor, Maine, where icy snow lay in huge piles beside the plowed streets, and the thickly clustered pines seemed to wait patiently for man's era to close so that their roots could buckle the concrete roads and reclaim the land once more. They flew to Baltimore, where winter was a chilly breeze which brought grey days to the charming arrays of row houses whose old-fashioned elegance gave Charles Street its turn-of-the-century look. They drove the pretty parkways through Connecticut and New York to New Jersey, where sodden snow lay among busy factories and enormous oil refineries. They visited Paltron in Massachusetts, where Frank convinced Laura to try downhill skiing with him, and applauded her bravery as she fell flat on her back in the new snow of the beginners' run.

And everywhere they went, their tempered business relationship gave way in the dark of night to the heat of their passion.

Neither said a word about this prohibited undercurrent

of their life together. Laura came to feel that she was the possessor of a marvellous, almost mystical secret of which the world remained ignorant. Outside the windows of her hotel rooms the earth was cold, not only in the snow and wind but in the ruthless ambitions of the wilful men against whom her battle was directed. But inside, where no one could see, there was the incomparable warmth and closeness of her endless tryst with Frank.

Each time he touched her in the most casual way, she reflected that his strong hands knew her entirely. Each time she heard him speak, her secret heart told her that those lips knew every part of her. When she saw his muscled body in her outer office, in an airport, a hotel lobby, she knew that other women must be eyeing it with envy. And she knew it was hers.

Only for now? Perhaps.

Not hers alone? Undoubtedly. But Frank was her lover, and nothing could take that away from her.

Lover. The word had taken on an occult, allegorical meaning to her. It signalled their friendship, their respect for each other, and the depth of their intimacy. And above all it bespoke the one truth that she alone possessed, a truth never to be revealed even to Frank: that she had fallen hopelessly and utterly in love with him.

She refused to let herself imagine that the future might make of their affair something more open, more permanent than what it was now. Frank's very silence on the subject confirmed that it could never come to pass. And she had learned to love even that silence, for it acknowledged that their life together was real and beautiful, if only temporary. She shared his reticence gladly, for it brought her closer to him.

He had given her an emerald pendant not long after their return from Montreal, joking that its colour foretold the profits Molly was sure to bring to Christensen Products.

She wore it now as a talisman to remind her not only of the rapture she had known in his arms, but also of the courage he had instilled in her—a courage which must one day enable her to live without him.

She lived for the present, grateful for each day, each night she shared with Frank. The longer their time lasted, the more secure would be its place in her heart. The more dizzying the ecstasy he gave her, the more indelible would be the memory of it.

As they lay together in the shadows, relaxing in the lovely afterglow of their lovemaking, her eyes and fingertips lingered in fascination on all the handsome parts of his perfectly formed body. His dark gaze caressed her face languorously, and he ran a long finger through the glimmering strands of her hair.

He could not know that she was taking him in, filling herself with him in the concentration born of her understanding that tonight, tomorrow night, the next night might be the last time she would be his. She had realised that Frank Jordan was Now. That was his essence and his magic, and it made all ordinary modes of experience irrelevant where he was concerned. One could not try to hold him, to keep him, to second-guess his unseen mind or his unknowable future. One could not covet him conservatively, the way one collected assets or prepared a company for security in years to come.

One could only love him now. And that meant giving one's love without a thought for oneself. But if one gave unselfishly enough, renouncing all hope that he could be tamed and possessed, freeing him to be the vibrant, uncapturable thing he was through the very force of one's love, the result was ecstasy.

Yes, she must love him now. But if she loved well, now would be forever. The future without him could never harm her.

When the time came, she would marshal her woman's strength, for which she knew she already owed him a debt of gratitude, and let him go without a clinging word or a possessive gesture. That would be her final gift to him, and her repayment of her debt. And as he receded into his separate destiny, he would look back on her with respect. In his thoughts he would thank her for her renunciation and approve of her strength of character. She would have shown him in the end that she was indeed made of the tough and durable substance he thought he saw in her when she refused to give up her company without a fight.

So Laura accepted the challenge of her days and the indescribable joy of her nights with a clear mind. She looked upon the past without shame, and upon the future without unrealistic hopes. How could life disappoint her now? She knew a happiness she had never dreamed possible. How could fate wound her? She had no illusions left.

She did not suspect that the very world she viewed with her cautious thoughts could explode into a thousand fragments, like a fragile bubble made of dreams.

It was the last day of February. The hour was late, and Laura was even more exhausted than usual by her day's work. Yet her mood was cheerful, for only three weeks separated Christensen Products from Molly's initial marketing date. The quality control experts in New Haven had passed affirmative judgment on the machine's first mass-produced units, one of which was even now purring unobtrusively in a corner of Sam's office.

Laura was preparing to fill her briefcase with sales projections for study at home when Virginia's amplified voice emerged hollowly from the intercom.

'Miss Christensen, there is a Miss Schell here to see you. She has no appointment, but she says it's quite urgent.'

The name Schell rang in Laura's ear with a sinister novelty.

'I beg your pardon?' she asked, pressing the button. 'Whom did you say…?'

'Miss Julia Schell.'

'All right, Virginia. Send her in.'

Collecting her thoughts quickly, Laura rose to greet her visitor. She recalled having read that the reclusive Julia Bond Schell had no interest in her father's corporate empire. If this were true, what possible reason could she have to call on the president of a company which did not even have a relationship with Schell?

The door opened to reveal a slender young woman whose fine blonde hair was pulled back in a simple chignon. The mauve blouse under her matching skirt and waistcoat was of an exquisite silk, and its colour harmonised beautifully with the amethyst pendant she wore.

Julia Schell's great wealth shone in the very restraint of her clothes and accessories. But it was her delicate and even frail beauty which astonished Laura. The alabaster complexion around her hazel eyes, combined with the slim roundness of her limbs, made her seem a china doll which would shatter if handled too roughly. Yet Laura recalled having read somewhere that Julia Schell was a noted horsewoman. She wondered if this impressive aura of extreme fragility concealed a will as strong as that of Armand Schell himself.

'You're very kind to receive me,' the young woman began. 'I know you must be terribly busy, Miss Christensen, and I'm sorry to burst in on you like this…'

'That's perfectly all right,' Laura smiled. 'Please sit down. What can I do for you, Miss Schell?'

The dewy eyes under Julia Schell's long lashes were troubled as she perched uncomfortably on the edge of the leather chair opposite Laura.

'Well,' she sighed, 'this is very difficult for me, Miss Christensen. Very embarrassing, and...well, it all may seem far-fetched and ridiculous to you at first. But if you hear me out, I think you'll understand why I felt I had to come to see you.'

She hesitated before going on, and Laura smiled encouragingly, her calculations as to the reason for this unexpected visit well-concealed by her look of calm expectancy.

Julia Schell's hesitancy made her seem more delicate and vulnerable than ever. The tidings she bore seemed to pain her from within, so that she appeared virtually on the edge of tears.

'I might as well come right to the point,' she sighed, 'so as not to waste more of your time than necessary. I believe...I think you know a man named Frank Jordan.'

'Frank Jordan?' Laura raised an eyebrow in surprise. 'Yes, of course. He's worked for us since just before my father's death.'

Julia Schell nodded, her eyes meeting Laura's with a sort of frightened diffidence.

'Frank Jordan...is my fiancé,' she said in a small voice.

The effort to contain her shock cost Laura the last of her already spent resources, but somehow she managed to retain the attentive smile which had seemed so natural only a moment ago.

'My father is a man named Armand Schell,' Julia went on. 'He owns a corporation called Schell International, which you've...probably...'

'Of course,' Laura smiled. 'Your father's work is known and respected everywhere.'

'Frank Jordan...works for my father,' the other woman went on in a tone of agonised confession. 'He works for Schell, that is, as what they call a consultant—but I think t's actually more than that. What I mean to say is that he is quite close to my father.'

Laura's heart sank within her breast, and she realised with an inner sigh of despair that the blows her attractive visitor had just struck must now have left visible traces in her eyes.

'And how does this concern me?' she asked, the quaver in her voice belying her measured words.

Julia Schell turned even more pale at Laura's question.

'I...don't know much about business,' she said. 'My father and brothers understand corporate life. I've always been the only member of the family who was not involved. But I've been hearing things, Miss Christensen, about Schell International and your company. I know your father died just recently, and I'm very sorry about it. I may be doing the wrong thing, but I felt I had to come...'

'What sort of things, Miss Schell?' Laura asked. 'What things have you been hearing?'

'Please call me Julie. All my friends do.' Again a look of paralysed dread stole across the young woman's classic features. 'I overheard a conversation between my father and Frank...Frank Jordan. It had something to do with a take-over of Christensen Products, planned for sometime this spring. They were arguing, in a sense, but my impression was that they both agreed on this idea of a merger. Perhaps you already know about this, Miss Christensen. I'm so naïve in this area that I'm probably unduly worried.'

'Please go on,' Laura insisted. 'I'd be interested in anything you have to say, and I'll keep it in confidence, of course.'

'Well,' Julie sighed, 'for better or worse, here is what I thought I understood. If I'm not making any sense, don't pay any attention to me. It seemed to me that Frank had been instructed to strengthen your company so that it would not "lose its markets", or something like that. The idea was that a corporate takeover would not be advantageous to Schell International at this moment, while Christensen Products is financially troubled. But Frank's mission in all this—or so it seemed to me—was not to enable your company to resist a takeover by my father...by Schell. Quite the contrary. The purpose was to increase Christensen's hold over certain markets, and then to force a merger by applying some sort of pressure on the Stock Exchange. To drive the price of Christensen stock down, using investment specialists...to stockpile proxies... I'm sorry to be talking over my own head this way, but perhaps you'll understand anyway.'

She pursed her lips in concentration. 'There was a time-table...something about March 20th.'

The date of our stockholders' meeting, Laura thought in sudden panic.

'My brother Roy is involved somehow,' Julia added in distress. 'That's what Frank and my father were arguing about. My impression was that Frank's reward for this whole business was to be the presidency of...of your company, Miss Christensen. And a free hand in running it. This is apparently not what Roy had in mind, and Frank wanted assurances from my father that he—that Frank—would have his way in the matter.'

'You're saying,' Laura replied, unable to bear another word of the young woman's horrible news 'that Frank Jordan's actions are for the benefit of Schell International.'

Julie nodded miserably. The fugitive trace of a tear was visible in her eye.

'Frank Jordan is a good man,' she said. 'I wouldn't be engaged to marry him if he weren't. But the world of corporate finance is a cruel one. I can't escape this awful feeling that my father and his people—including Frank—are planning something that is not in your best interests or those of your company.'

She shook her head with a sigh. 'I'm smart enough to understand what I read about Schell International,' she said darkly. 'The corporation has changed since my brothers took over most of the responsibility. Personally, I don't have the impression that Schell is in business to help people any more, or to make the world a better and more modern place. It's all money and profit and tax losses now.'

Her charming features were twisted by worry as she gazed at Laura.

'I knew your father by reputation,' she went on. 'Christensen is obviously a very fine company. I'm sure you know best how to protect it, Miss Christensen. I'm only here because I received the distinct impression that there was some sort of subterfuge about Frank's involvement with you. Some sort of misrepresentation. If he's trying to make you believe he's helping you, and if his real intention is something else—well, he should be stopped. I can't bear to say this about the man I'm to marry, but there's no choice. Don't believe him, Miss Christensen. Don't…'

A sudden sob choked her, and she reached into her small purse for a linen handkerchief.

Thunderstruck by the revelations she had just heard, Laura fought to conceal her emotions. Though her world was falling apart around her, she concentrated her attention on the precise import of Julie's words.

'The intention of the Schell Corporation, then,' she said, 'is to take over Christensen Products late in March, through a stock manipulation.'

Julie nodded. 'If that makes any sense to you,' she said. 'And there was something about a new product… An important patent my father wanted to take over for some of his subsidiaries in Europe. They were arguing about that, too.'

Molly, Laura thought, her blood running cold. Her enemies intended to steal Randy's invention for themselves.

The plot in which Frank Jordan was involved clearly had a byzantine complexity. After all, was it not Frank himself who had denounced Andrew Dillon and First Federal as secret cohorts of Schell International? Why had Frank told Laura the actual truth about the bank, rather than to use all his wiles to hide it?

The answer was chillingly simple. Frank had told part of the truth in order to gain Laura's confidence. And his plan had worked. Not only had he convinced her of his own good will, but he had managed to penetrate to the inner sanctum of her own corporate plans, and eventually to influence and control them himself.

Yes, he had told the truth, Laura reflected in panic. But he had left out one critical detail: the fact that he himself also represented Schell International, that he himself was at the core of the plan to take over Christensen Products.

Had she wished to check out his story about collusion between Andrew Dillon and Roy Schell, Laura could have done so. And she would have found that Frank's story was true. Frank, of course, probably expected her to investigate his revelation.

But she had not bothered to do so. She had simply believed him.

And, in her naive innocence, she had ignored the one elementary course of action she should have taken from the beginning: to investigate Frank Jordan himself. A little careful checking would have revealed who he was and whom he worked for. But Laura had simply taken him at his word, taken him into her confidence, followed his advice, on the idiotic assumption that his pretended loyalty to Sam extended to her.

And, when it suited him, she had even taken him into her bed.

'Miss Schell…Julie,' she said at last, somehow stifling the flood of tears which grew inside her, 'you're very kind to go out of your way to inform me of all this. Please don't feel that you have betrayed your father, or his corporation, or Frank Jordan. I think you have done the right thing, and I'll certainly give careful consideration to what you've told me. Now I think you should put it all out of your mind and concentrate on looking forward to your...your marriage.'

Julie seemed more forlorn and defenceless than ever as she returned Laura's gaze.

'I...I feel so sick about all this,' she said. 'If they—if my father and Frank have done anything to hurt you, please accept my own apology for them. I just hope I've been of help. If everything I've said is nonsense, I hope you'll forgive a silly and ignorant woman for wasting your time.'

She stood up to leave, but hesitated before turning away.

'Frank...Frank Jordan is an intelligent and knowledgeable man,' she said. 'He is an expert in his field, and a very aggressive executive. What I'm trying to say,' she sighed, 'is that I imagine he can be ruthless in his actions. Oh, I don't suppose I can hold it against him personally. To him, and to all men like him, it's just business. But I felt you must be informed. In my own heart, I—well, I just don't know what to say.'

Despite her own distress Laura was touched by the figure of utter fragility she saw before her.

'You're right about one thing,' she said, forcing a smile. 'Business is business. We're trained to understand that. I would not blame Frank Jordan for acting on his company's behalf, Julie. And I don't think you should, either. I wish you all the happiness in the world. And please don't let his situation prey on your mind. Thank you for coming.'

Julie hesitated at the doorway, as though unable to tear herself from the moral support of the very woman to whom she had just brought such terrible news. For an instant Laura reflected on what she had read about this delicate young woman. No wonder, she thought, that Julia Schell remained aloof from the corporate world her father dominated. That world would have eaten her alive in a trice. She belonged in a protected environment, far from the machinations of wilful, cunning entrepreneurs.

And soon she would have her gilded cage, under the aegis of Frank Jordan.

With a last pained smile, Julie Schell closed the door behind her and was gone.

The digital clock before Laura showed 5:13. After a moment's thought she hurriedly opened a phone book and found the number she wanted.

'Schell New York,' came a pleasant voice after a single ring. 'One moment, please.'

The silence on the line hung like a pall over Laura's future. If it were all true, she was lost. If one could simply call Frank Jordan at Schell Headquarters, where he was known by one and all as a trusted lieutenant of Armand Schell himself...

'Mr Jordan's office,' another voice sounded in Laura's ear.

'Mr Frank Jordan's office?' Laura asked.

'Yes, ma'am,' the secretary answered. 'Who is calling, please?'

'I think I may be a bit confused,' Laura said. 'I left a message with Mr Jordan's answering service, but I'm not sure he has received it. The service is at 555-1717, isn't it?'

'Yes, that's his personal answering service, ma'am, but they don't forward those messages through us.' There was wariness in the secretary's busy voice, as though she were in the habit of protecting Frank Jordan against unwanted calls.

'I see,' Laura said. 'Well, I'm sure he'll get the message eventually. I won't bother you about it. Thank you very much.'

After replacing the receiver Laura stared blankly at the photos and diplomas on Sam's walls. Though she struggled to prevent all thought from entering her mind, a single damning idea leapt to her lips with fearsome insistence.

I never bothered to check him out.

Like a trusting child she had put herself in his hands. What was worse, she had even presumed to throw herself at him like a starry-eyed adolescent. Eagerly, gratefully she had done his bidding, played the pliant role of his puppet, his Trilby.

And she had flattered herself that the comedy she played had matured her, strengthened her, made her into a real woman and a real executive.

Inside she knew her heart was breaking. Yet she seemed to feel nothing beyond a cold knot in her stomach. She recalled the day of Sam's death, and thanked heaven for the human soul's defensive ability to cover over its deepest wounds with a blessed interval of artificial insensibility. For a matter of minutes, perhaps hours, she would resist the searing pain that must eventually overwhelm her.

During that brief time she must act.

There was much to do, and little hope of success. Nevertheless a sharp, desperate glow of rebellion shot through her veins. Her days of childish passivity were behind her now. And Frank Jordan bore most of the responsibility for that. Very well, then, she thought darkly. Let the woman Frank had created turn upon him now. She would weep her bitter tears over his loss later.

'Virginia,' she said into the intercom. 'Are you still there?'

'Just on my way out,' came the familiar voice. 'Is there anything I can do for you?'

Laura had taken off Frank's emerald pendant and put it in a Christensen envelope. Detachedly she watched herself address it to Frank Jordan at Schell's New York headquarters.

As luck would have it he was in Manhattan today for a financial meeting, and would not return to New Haven until tomorrow afternoon.

'Get me a standard resignation form,' she said, her finger on the intercom button. 'And call me a messenger before you come in, would you? I have something here that needs hand delivery.'

CHAPTER ELEVEN

LAURA sat in silence, her mind racing, as she waited for Virginia to come in. She knew that action must be taken now, this minute, to save Sam's company. Less than three weeks remained before the stockholders' meeting at which she had planned to announce Molly's distribution to markets all over the country.

Now she knew that that meeting was the intended scene of Schell's takeover of Christensen Products.

In a matter of hours Frank Jordan would know that he had been found out. He would immediately closet himself with Armand Schell or his son Roy and begin planning to hasten the timetable for their assault on her company.

Laura could see the truth in glaring colours now. Andrew Dillon's April 5 deadline for payment of Christensen's short-term notes had been a red herring all along. Schell's real intention had always been to take over Christensen well before that date. The essence of the plan was to drive down the price of Christensen common stock, and force its shareholders to sell in panic, on the very eve of Molly's distribution. Then, when unbearable pressure was applied in a proxy fight by Roy Schell and his allies just as Molly's production expenses had left Christensen Products in an overextended condition, Laura would give in and accept a merger.

The result would be that Schell International would pick up all the marbles overnight and triumphantly market Molly as its own product.

Thus all Laura's frantic efforts to make short-term profits through sales of a brilliant new appliance would have been in vain, for the attack on her company would take place before Molly could reach the marketplace.

Thanks to Frank Jordan's inside knowledge of Laura's top secret timetable for Molly's distribution.

It was a brilliant, cold-blooded plan, and almost impossible to thwart.

Laura was so preoccupied by these thoughts that she did not hear Virginia enter the office.

'The resignation form you asked for,' Virginia said hesitantly.

Without a word Laura folded the form and sealed it in the envelope with her pendant.

'I almost forgot to tell you,' Virginia said, her careworn eyes following Laura's hands, 'you had a call from Francie Tolliver in Advertising about ten minutes ago. She said she had urgent good news for you.'

'Virginia,' Laura said coolly, 'I'm going to need some help from you tonight. Can you spare the time? She pushed the envelope across the desk top without looking at it.

'Of course,' Virginia replied fearfully. Having seen Frank's name above the Schell Corporation's New York address, she eyed the envelope uncomfortably, as though it were a live thing that might bite her if she touched it. 'Laura, what's happening? Is it bad?'

'It will be unless we do something. Sit down, Virginia. I need you to do several things for me.' She took a deep breath and closed her eyes for an instant in concentration as Virginia produced her memo pad.

'While you're waiting for the messenger to arrive,' Laura began, 'I want you to get in touch with Peacock Associates in Manhattan, and ask for Larry Monk.'

'Larry Monk.' Virginia's arthritic fingers wrote quickly on the yellow paper.

'If he isn't in his office, find him,' Laura said. 'Tell his people it's urgent. Have him call me at any hour of the night, right here in the office.'

Larry Monk was a virtual legend in the business community. He was the most experienced and creative proxy solicitor in the country. He and his people were capable of wringing proxy ballots from the most disinterested stockholders in the most remote areas. Laura knew that her first line of defence against a takeover of Christensen was the loyalty of her traditional shareholders. She must convince them not to sell their stock, even if its price began to fluctuate wildly.

'That's number one,' she said. 'After you find him or get the message to him, I want you to find Rob Colwell. Ask him to come here to my office immediately. Then call Michael Sheldon in our legal department. Tell him I'll be here all evening and I'd appreciate it if he would drop in to see me.' Pushing her hair out of her eyes with a nervous finger, Laura pursed her lips anxiously.

'If you can get back to Francie,' she went on, 'tell her I'd like to see her here as well. As soon as possible.'

What am I forgetting? she asked herself desperately. There was not a minute to lose. The slightest oversight could be fatal.

'Now, this is very important,' she said. 'I want you to put all the copies of our stockholders' list in my safe. And all the pre-addressed proxy envelopes. I don't want a single stockholder's name lying around here in plain sight. Can you do that?'

'Of course.' Virginia shook her head in bewilderment. She could not know that the same people who had bugged Laura's conference room were more than capable of burglarising the office for the list of Christensen's stockholders.

Laura cursed herself for not taking that precaution earlier. Under the law Roy Schell or anyone else had every right to use those addresses to make a tender offer to those thousands of people through the mail. If the offer was as outlandish as Roy's wealth would allow—say, $1.75 or even $2.00 for every dollar of the current value of Christensen's shares, the stockholders would fly in droves to their brokers.

'One other thing,' she added. 'Call our security staff. Tell them that Frank Jordan no longer works for this company. He is not to be admitted to any of our facilities.'

'All right.' Virginia's pained tone made it obvious that her sharp eyes had not missed the telltale signs of Laura's true relationship with Frank. But she kept her speculations under control, for she realised that there was far more at stake tonight than the firing of one executive.

'When all that is done,' Laura said, 'I'd appreciate it if you would run down to the cafeteria and get me a sandwich. I won't dare leave the phone for the next couple of hours.'

A quiet knock came at the door. Virginia answered it on her way out. Rob Colwell entered the office, his overcoat slung over his shoulder.

'Rob,' Laura said, 'I'm glad you stopped by. We have something of a crisis here, and we have to move quickly. We're in danger of being taken over by Schell International or one of its holding companies. We have no choice but to get Molly on the market before our previous deadline.'

'Does Frank know about this?' Rob asked, unbuttoning his jacket as he sat down.

'Frank no longer works for us. I fired him ten minutes ago.' Laura's intent eyes betrayed no emotion. 'I'll explain all that to you at the proper time. What we have to do now is get in touch with all our people around the country and squeeze a week off Molly's schedule. We'll need finished units distributed by March 15th.'

Rob's brow furrowed as he gazed unseeing through the window at New Haven's rainy skyline. He drummed a finger quietly on the arm of his chair.

'Will do,' he said at last, turning back to her. 'I'll get on it tonight.'

Laura nearly sobbed with gratitude to see the unflappable loyalty of the man before her. What she had asked was nearly impossible, and he was prepared to obey without a word. Thank God for Rob!

'Michael Sheldon is coming here tonight,' she said. 'We have to delay the stockholders' meeting by one month, so as to give Molly time to sell before we have to report our earnings. Tomorrow you and Zalman and I will prepare a mailing for the stockholders. It will explain how important Molly is, and will also warn the stockholders that any proposed merger of Christensen with another company will not be in their best interests. There's going to be a manipulation on the Exchange, Rob, and we have to prepare them for it. This has to be the best proxy letter anyone has ever written. I'm trying to get Larry Monk in New York. He'll know how to help us write it.'

'All right,' Rob said. 'I'll be here.'

'Thank you, Rob. Thank you so much.'

She stood up to see him to the door. Before she could open it he took her in his arms. She felt a terrible weakness in her limbs, and had to fight off the tears of fear and frustration which quickened in her eyes.

'Courage, Laura,' he smiled, his hug warming her. 'You'll make it. We all will. What's life without a little excitement?'

His finger touched her chin as he held her out at arm's length. 'Sam would be awfully proud of you right now,' he smiled. 'As I am.'

Gratefully she returned his smile. A moment later he was gone.

Before she could collect her thoughts the phone rang. It was Larry Monk. By a miracle Virginia had caught him before he left his Manhattan office.

'Okay, Laura,' he said when she had explained her situation. 'You've done the right thing in locking up your shareholders' addresses. Schell will have to take you to court to get them, and that will take five to seven days when the time comes. But here's what I want you to do. Get some people together whom you absolutely trust—and I mean absolutely—and get to work on that list. Is it on a computer printout?'

'Yes.'

'All right. I want you to transfer all the names to three-by-five cards. Typewritten. Name, address, number of shares, and so forth. When you've done that, put the printout in a safety deposit box where no one can get his hands on it. Then simply shuffle the thousands of cards. Make a complete mess of them. Leave them in a cardboard box in your safe.'

'Why, Larry?'

'If Schell and his friends get a court order to force you to turn over the names—and of course they'll succeed—the law does not specify in what *form* you have to turn them over. So what you'll do is to invite them into your office and show them the box of cards. Let them have access to a small xerox machine. It will take them days to copy the cards. If they had the computer list they could make offers to all the shareholders overnight. This way you'll gain a little more time. Hours can count, Laura, so do what I say.'

'I'll do it.' Laura's tired hand wrote furiously on the pad before her.

'Good. Now, delaying your stockholders' meeting is crucial. 'You were smart to think of it. That month's delay might just save your company. Tomorrow, with your permission, I'll retain Sean Harris to work with your own legal staff. He's the best proxy law specialist around today. He's a good friend of mine, and I'm sure he'll be available to work with us. I'll bring him with me tomorrow. See you when I get there.'

'Great, Larry. Thank you so much.'

Her head spinning as she fought to recall the priorities before her, Laura looked up to see Francie Tolliver standing in her doorway.

'Come on in,' she smiled. 'What's your news?'

Francie swept into the room excitedly, her leather boots gleaming under the attractive skirt she wore. She sat down quickly in the visitors' chair and began rummaging through her purse.

'It's great news,' she said. 'You remember Marva Sims? The movie actress?'

'Flora the maid,' Laura nodded.

'Well,' Francie said, 'I've found her! She's right in New York. She lives in an apartment in Manhattan. I visited her today. Laura, you wouldn't believe her. She doesn't look a day older than she did in that movie. She's bright, alert, and still has all her showbiz instincts, and what's even better, she says retirement has been boring her silly. She'd love to help us out herself with a commercial for Molly.'

'You're sure she's feeling up to it?' Laura pictured Marva Sims in her mind. If she herself associated that angular, intelligent face with a thousand housekeepers, all the older people around the country—homeowners and apartment dwellers—were sure to recognise it.

'She has a touch of rheumatism, but she's absolutely fine. She still belongs to the union and everything.'

'All right.' Laura took a deep breath. 'Time is much shorter than I thought, Francie. I want you to get together with everybody in advertising tomorrow morning. We'll need a perfect script—and I mean perfect—in a matter of days. We're going to run this Molly ad in regional markets before the product is ready We'll have to go for advance orders. It won't be easy, Francie, but we must get something on the air right away.'

'No problem,' Francie said eagerly. 'I'll show you a tentative script in a day or so, and we'll work on leasing a studio.'

'And on buying TV time,' Laura said.

When Francie had gone Laura sat in exhausted concentration behind her desk.

Have I done enough? she asked herself desperately weighing all the contingencies facing her now. When Michael Sheldon arrived she would help him plan anti-trust litigation against Schell in the event of a proposed merger She did not need Michael to tell her that Christensen would lose the suit. But it would gain time, as would the delay of the stockholders' meeting and Larry's plan to make a deliberate mess of the list of shareholders.

But all those delays could only hold off the inevitable unless Molly reached the market immediately and earned huge profits.

The situation Laura found herself in was unlike anything she had ever faced before. None of the crises of the last four months could match it for sheer menace. She was alone. She alone must act.

Yet, she realised, in an unconscious way she had been preparing herself for this day since Frank Jordan first warned her about Andrew Dillon and Roy Schell. A thousand little doubts and fears had kept her alert to the possibility of an ultimate danger such as this.

Including remote, tiny doubts about Frank Jordan himself, which she had not had the courage to face consciously

Frank had been devilishly cunning. At every turn he had eluded her suspicions, gained her confidence. But his one mistake had been to arm her with enough of the truth arouse her defensive instincts, to sharpen her executive wits.

Now she would use those wits to defeat him.

'I can be cunning, too,' she thought with bitter determination.

Two days later a proxy letter describing Molly's enormous financial promise and the imminent danger to Christensen Products from a rapacious conglomerate was in the mail. The letter urged Christensen's thousands of loyal stockholders to hang onto their shares and, when the delayed stockholders' meeting took place, to vote against a proposed merger. The name and personality of Sam Christensen were mobilised to the hilt in the letter, and it was warned that in the event of a takeover no trace of Sam's guidance of the company towards service and innovation would remain.

Virginia and two trusted members of her own secretarial staff took responsibility for the mailings and for the transfer of the stockholders' names to index cards.

By Friday Laura was in New York with Francie Tolliver and two of her advertising colleagues, poring intently over the tentative script for Molly's television commercial. Seated in a chair beside Francie was Marva Sims.

'As I see this,' Francie said, 'we need Marva to complain to the camera that her employer is too cheap to buy a Molly for his house. Since Marva is the wise housekeeper, she doesn't want to be saddled with the chore of dusting.'

Laura's brow was furrowed in concern.

'I don't think that will work, Francie,' she said. 'Even if we present the millionaire as an eccentric cheapskate, the audience will get the message that Molly costs money—that Molly requires a financial sacrifice. We can't pose the problem that way. The real beauty of the product is that it is so inexpensive. Anyone can afford it.'

'And another thing,' Francie put in. 'So far we don'
have any real humour here. Marva can't appear as a mer
complainer. We have to underline her character as someon
clever, hardheaded…'

'Excuse me,' came a diffident voice. Marva Sims wa
leaning forward in her chair, her friendly eyes fixed o
Laura. 'I know I'm just the performer here,' she said, 'an
I ought to keep my big mouth shut, but I've just had a
idea…'

CHAPTER TWELVE

WITHIN ten frantic days of production supervised by Laura herself, a television commercial depicting Marva Sims as a millionaire's household maid was ready to be shown throughout the United States and Canada. Cleverly edited by Laura and her associates so as to communicate a gentle tongue-in-cheek irony, the film showed Marva working in exasperation with a dust rag on her employer's priceless antique furniture, while a narrator's voice deplored the boredom of dusting in general.

What came next had been Marva's own idea, and constituted the real brilliance of the commercial. After a quick cut the camera picked Marva up in her own modest apartment, where a Molly purred in a corner, freeing her from the onus of dusting at home. The simple appliance her employer had been too penurious to buy was clearly well within his maid's own budget.

In the final seconds of the short film Marva was shown in close-up, relaxing with a snack in a rocking chair before a television set on which a football game was in progress. With a wink to the camera Marva abandoned her irascible exterior and smiled for the first time. Her conspiratorial grin, not without its hint of sarcasm over her wealthy employer's cheapness, was a perfect coda to the commercial.

Having been charmed by the witty old actress during the exhausting days of filming she had supervised in New York, Laura viewed the final version of the commercial with some trepidation. But when she saw Marva's impish

grin, so perfectly timed and modulated in the final seconds
she felt a thrill of accomplishment. If any advertising mes
sage could convince consumers to buy a Molly for thei
own home, this was it.

As the editors went about preparing 15- and 30-second
versions of the commercial for time slots in markets around
the country, Laura added her own brainstorm to the film
It was a simple and effective idea, easy to implement. The
editors simply altered the image of the football game or
Marva's TV screen to show the favourite local team in each
region of the country where the commercial was to be run

Television time had been contracted for in all the majo
markets for Molly's initial sales drive. Completed by the
graphic *MOLLY: Coming This Month to a Store Near You'*
the commercial went on the air during the second week o
March.

Laura and her colleagues sat before their television set
the first evening for all the world as though their persona
fates depended on those sixty seconds of film. On tenter
hooks they watched as the first half of a popular situation
comedy wound towards it end. To Laura's satisfaction th
first half of the show was particularly amusing.

'Good,' she thought tensely. 'The audience will be in
good mood. They'll linger in front of the set long enough
to see Marva come on.'

At last Marva appeared, instantly recognisable in her fa
miliar role as the sour-faced maid. A hundred old movie
came to mind as one looked at her irritable features. He
performance was even more brilliant than Laura ha
thought initially. When the commercial came to a close sh
sighed with relief.

Marva Sims had made Molly human.

And now there was nothing to do but wait.

Laura spent the rest of that week beside her office an
home telephones, receiving call after call from her market

ing division. Sid Ritchie, Christensen's Vice-President in charge of Sales, became the most important man in her life. She importuned him to inform her of each and every bulk order received for Molly by retailers of any size. She spoke to each and every one of Sid's regional representatives by phone, and was gratified by the immense quantity of advance work they had done on the product's behalf. Each day Sid demonstrated Molly's virtues to visiting buyers from important chain stores, showing off his quality control reports with his accustomed brio.

At first the results were less than encouraging. A large East Coast retailer ordered a cautious 12,000 units of the new appliance, after lengthy negotiations with Sid and his lieutenants. A drug store chain closely associated with one of the Midwest's popular grocery outlets ordered 15,000 units.

In less sinister times, when short-term profit was not a matter of sheer survival, such initial results might have been welcome. But Laura knew that Molly's production and distribution costs, not to mention her unprecedented advertising budget, would outweigh all but the most sensational sales.

Yet with the passing days, as Marva's commercial was repeated around the country and followed up by full-page magazine and newspaper ads, the tide seemed to turn.

By the third Monday in March several important regional department store chains had ordered 80,000 units or more apiece. Not wishing to see themselves outdone, their competitors began to jump on the bandwagon, spurred undoubtedly by telephone queries from consumers about the new product's availability. Discount houses around the nation followed suit.

On Wednesday morning Sid closed a deal with a national mail order house for 200,000 units.

On Thursday the first of the country's best-known department stores shook off its natural inertia and ordered 400,000 units. A nationwide retailer, it commanded respect in the business community for its marketing decisions.

What followed was a deluge. Apparently convinced by their own eyes once they had seen Molly's simple and economical design, the major chain stores in the United States and Canada began beating a path to Laura's door in their haste to take advantage of her product's novelty. Sales of the few thousand units Christensen had been able to deliver already to selected stores were phenomenal.

Molly was a sensation. The retailing community sensed a windfall, and mobilised itself accordingly.

On Friday Sid burst into Laura's office, dragging Zalman Corey behind him.

'A million and a half units, Laura!' he bellowed, his face red with excitement. 'A million five already. And my people can't keep track of all the orders coming in. We've created a monster.'

Laura turned to Zalman, who had opened his briefcase with nervous fingers. She dared not breathe until he spoke.

'According to my calculations,' he said with the barest hint of a smile, 'that puts us over the hump. Well over. If we can get these units out, and if they sell in the stores the profit will not only wipe out our debt, but we'll have the biggest second and third quarters in the history of the company. At a risk of being hasty, I'd say you've done it, Laura.'

In the next week the most famous retailer in the country contracted to sell Molly under its own name. The deal was closed for 400,000 units with the proviso that the name Molly remained integral to the item.

A dozen offers were made to manufacture more sizeable versions of Molly for stores and offices, with handsome royalties to be paid for use of Christensen's patent.

Contract offers for production of the appliance in Europe

and South America were funnelled to Laura's legal department.

The response was so overwhelming that Laura felt a pang of worry over Molly's dependability. If the little machine broke down and required servicing, the losses to Christensen under its warranty would be catastrophic. But a glance at the Molly in Sam's office confirmed the quality control experts' enthusiasm. There were no apparent bugs in Randy's ingenious design. The machine functioned perfectly, and Ernst said he had not had to dust the office since it was put in.

Of more concern was the movement in Christensen stock on Wall Street. The first days after Marva's commercial reached the public were disconcerting. Christensen's common stock fluctuated wildly, and trading was so heavy that the Exchange was forced to close it off twice. Laura was convinced that her enemies, having seen the commercial and heard rumours of Molly's promise on the Street, were making their move in a desperate hurry. Each morning she waited anxiously for the financial newspapers, expecting to see full-page ads registering a tender offer to her stockholders.

But the passing days saw a settling of the confusion. The heavy action on Wall Street involved smaller blocks of stock. That could only mean that Molly's success had convinced Christensen's stockholders to hang on to their shares. The wild fluctuations ended, and the price of Christensen common stock began a steady upward climb.

Laura had brought Molly to the public in the nick of time. Her stock was too valuable to sell now. No conglomerator could accumulate a large enough block of it to threaten her.

On March 26th Laura opened the *Wall Street Journal* to find a half-page public tender offer directed to the stockholders of AMZ Manufacturing, Inc. of New Jersey. AMZ was an important mid-sized corporation which had long been a competitor of Sam Christensen in the machine tool trade.

The tender offer was made in the name of Beta Concepts.

So Roy Schell and his friends had backed off and found another victim, Laura mused with a smile.

On the last day of March Laura received a treacly letter from Andrew Dillon underlining First Federal Bank's many years of service to Christensen Products, and explaining the Bank's reconsideration of its intention to call in the corporation's short-term loans. The letter ended:

> 'We feel that our decades of financial cooperation justify a confidence in Christensen which the Bank unfortunately failed to demonstrate during the sad days following Sam Christensen's tragic demise.'

The letter amused Laura, for she and her colleagues knew that the short-term debt was meaningless now. The challenge before Christensen Products was expansion, not survival. Laura's long work days were spent in the effort to fill the orders deluging her many plants, and in plans for the acquisition of additional facilities. Within a year Christensen's assets would double, and they must be used to prepare the company for future innovations.

Nevertheless Laura, Rob Colwell and Zalman Corey appeared unannounced at First Federal's Manhattan headquarters the next afternoon. Laura passed through the same corridors and elevators that had been the scene of her initial panic in the wake of Andrew Dillon's threat five long months ago.

Seconds after his secretary announced them, Andrew Dillon hurried from his office, shook their hands warmly and ushered them inside, offering them coffee.

'No, thank you,' Zalman spoke for all three. 'We'll only be a minute.'

Laura watched in silence as he opened his briefcase and took out a large cashier's cheque which he placed on the desk top before Andrew Dillon.

'Twelve million dollars,' Zalman said. 'Penalty interest included. I think you'll find that everything is in order, Mr Dillon. The other short-term notes will be paid in full as they come due in the next few weeks.'

'Well, I...' Andrew Dillon stammered. 'This really wasn't necessary. I'm terribly sorry for the inconvenience to you. I thought I had made clear in my letter that the Bank was prepared to extend...'

'Miss Christensen prefers it this way,' Zalman said as Laura retained her silence, doing her best all the while to stifle the grin she would have liked to flash in Rob's direction.

'This cheque...' Andrew Dillon said.

'Yes,' Zalman interrupted. 'It's drawn on our new account with Concord Bank of Connecticut. We share your fond memories of our many years of doing business together, Mr Dillon, but Miss Christensen felt a change was in order—in today's changing times. We wish you the best of luck in the future with your other clients.'

A deadly pallor had stolen over Andrew Dillon's distinguished features. He had lost, and he knew it. Not only had his scheme with Schell International failed to produce the hoped-for merger, but he was now losing the account of a corporation whose enormous profits would require expansion that his bank could have financed.

As her colleagues held the door for her, Laura spoke to Andrew Dillon for the first and last time.

'There's always a silver lining, Mr Dillon,' she said. 'At least your bank still owns 50,000 shares of the hottest stock on Wall Street.'

As the door closed behind her Andrew Dillon stood frowning behind his desk.

She had been wrong, he thought ruefully. On instructions from Roy Schell he had sold First Federal's shares in Christensen Products two weeks ago.

CHAPTER THIRTEEN

Two hours later Laura was seated with her colleagues at a large table beside the shimmering drapes adorning one of the tall windows at the Four Seasons restaurant. Beside her were Meg O'Connor and Randy Powers. Francie Tolliver sat next to Zalman. Across the table's opulent expanse, between Rob and Sid Ritchie, was Marva Sims.

No one had had time to think of celebrating during these last hectic weeks. It had been Laura's idea to bring together the inner circle of Molly's creators for a victory dinner, and tonight had seemed the logical occasion.

'Well, what shall we drink to?' Rob asked cheerfully when the waiters had finished pouring champagne.

'To Molly,' Laura smiled.

'To Marva,' Francie said, 'for the best performance of the year in a starring role.'

'To Andrew Dillon,' Zalman suggested with a rare hint of levity. 'He gave us the kick in the pants we needed to get going—and we gave it right back to him.'

'First things first,' Marva said in her quiet voice. 'Here's to Laura. She was the brains behind it all, and the prime mover. I have my own reasons for gratitude toward her, you know. Without Laura I wouldn't have had the chance to work again—and I loved every minute of it. Besides, now that Molly is taking off, I'm looking forward to seeing my face all over the place.'

Laura's eyes rested happily on her friends as she raised her glass. Privately she looked back upon the one important contributor to Molly's success who was not present. Frank Jordan's role in the drama that had led to this happy moment was indeed a crucial one. Perhaps, she reflected ironically, she owed him thanks in the same sense she owed them to Andrew Dillon. Even in his chicanery Frank had spurred her to an achievement of which she would not have thought herself capable.

She found herself returning Rob's quiet smile as these thoughts stole through her mind. Even in his mood of celebration Rob was as restrained and dignified a figure as ever. As she contemplated him Laura could not imagine why he had not married in all these years. The incisiveness of his intelligence, combined with his ruddy, virile good looks, made him an irresistible man. Perhaps, she mused, he was as much a perfectionist about women as he was about his work. Nevertheless, he would one day make someone a marvellous husband.

The sight of his handsome face made her think of the one person, eclipsed now by time and events, to whom Molly's success would have meant so much: Sam Christensen. How poignant to realise that Sam died before the epic struggle of these past months had even begun, and that his death was in fact the calamity which set everything in motion.

In five turbulent months Laura had lost her father, and loved and lost Frank Jordan, whose betrayal she would never be able to forgive. But she had Christensen Products' crisis to thank for the constant challenges that had distracted her from her own hurts. Even now the fatigue and excitement thronging her nerves made grief seem a distant emotion.

Suddenly her reverie was interrupted by a pair of black eyes fixed on her with probing intensity from across the room. For a moment she could not place their familiarity, though the sharpness of their gaze disconcerted her.

Then she realised that the improbable had happened.

Frank Jordan was entering the room and had caught sight of her. On his arm was an attractive young woman whose wavy auburn hair set off her friendly eyes to advantage.

In trepidation Laura watched as Frank spoke briefly to the maitre d'hotel and moved toward her. The look in his eyes was neutral as he smiled a greeting to her guests.

'Sorry to bother you all,' he said, placing a hand on Zalman's shoulder as he faced Laura. 'I've been hearing so much about Christensen and Molly that it seemed congratulations were in order.'

He introduced his companion as Helen Rowings. Though everyone obviously knew by now why Laura had fired him, he seemed oblivious to the embarrassment which hung in the air. Thankfully, though, they were in too happy a mood to be impolite. Rob alone seemed poised in dark readiness, his eyes fixed questioningly on Laura.

'And this is Laura,' Frank said to Helen. 'I think we'd all agree that she's the real heroine in all this.'

'I'm so pleased to meet you,' the other woman said, smiling brightly. 'You're quite a story around this town, Miss Christensen. Not many people have handled Roy Schell the way you have, and got away with it.'

'I think our friend Roy may choose his enemies more carefully from now on,' Frank laughed.

'You're very kind,' Laura said with a pained smile. Helen Rowings seemed more attractive with each word she spoke. The gentleness and good humour glowing in her hazel eyes were really quite seductive. Sighing inwardly, Laura thought of unfortunate Julie Schell. Her fiancé was clearly dallying with yet another woman behind her back. Laura herself had evidently been neither the first nor the last.

A moment later they had gone. Despite her best effort to feel only bitter triumph on seeing Frank Jordan, Laura was tormented by the sense of loss his appearance had stirred within her. The sight of his sharp eyes resting on her in

simple admiration, without a hint of anger or defeat, had
disturbed her. He was a good loser, at least. One could say
that for him.

But that warmth in his regard had brought back haunting
memories of their many bewitching evenings together, absorbed in each other's company inside hotels and offices
while the winter wind raged outside in any of a dozen cit-
ies. It all came back in a fearsome rush, and the cold knot
of indifference Laura had coveted inside herself these last
weeks was softening into a hollow of grief that wrenched
her heart. She had not succeeded, after all, in accepting the
inevitable philosophically when time came between her and
Frank Jordan. She would never forgive him for his treachery, but she knew she would never be able to forget him
either.

As he disappeared around a corner with Helen on his
arm Laura wondered if she had seen him for the last time
in this life. The thought sent shocks of pain through the
corners of her mind whose existence she had tried to deny
for many weeks.

She did her best to contribute to the mood of levity which
continued throughout dinner, but she did not have the courage to accompany her friends on the night on the town to
which they were looking forward. Gently refusing Rob's
offer to take her back to New Haven, she sent them all on
their way with her best wishes and took a cab to Penn
Station for the train home.

An hour and a half later she was alone in her apartment,
dressed in her bathrobe, contemplating the Franz Kline watercolour which Sam had loved.

'Every corner of it tells a story,' he had often said, 'if
you look at it long enough.'

But tonight the abstract swirls of black and grey spoke
only of loss.

Though Laura had wanted to be alone with the feelings
warring inside her, the solitude of the apartment did not

seem to help. She sat on her couch in silence, waiting patiently for the flood of tears that had never come since she had learned the truth about Frank. But even now an inner defence held stubborn sway over the tide of pain which rose and fell in waves within her.

She could feel the strength in her veins. Tomorrow she would be at her father's desk, where a photo of Sam himself had replaced that of Laura. An interviewer and photographer from a national women's magazine had an appointment with her at two o'clock, and they were merely the latest in a series of visitors from the media. Laura was a celebrity.

'Then why do I feel like a lonely little girl?' she asked herself, her legs curled under her in the shadows. 'A miserable, heartbroken wallflower whose date has just invited someone else to the prom...'

The buzzer sounded suddenly at eleven-thirty. Laura supposed it was Rob, concerned about her abrupt change of mood in the wake of Frank's unexpected appearance. Grateful as she was for his protectiveness, she wished he had not bothered to come. He could not help her now.

She stepped back a pace in involuntary terror as the door opened to reveal Frank Jordan's tall form in the shadowed hallway. The look in his eyes was frightening. She could see powerful emotion in his black irises, along with an almost superhuman effort to control that emotion.

'What are you doing here?' she asked, gathering her bathrobe around her.

'I'm sorry to disturb you,' he said. 'I can see you're getting ready for bed.'

Despite herself she watched unmoving as he closed the door behind him. The suppressed violence in his demeanour made him seem unspeakably imposing in his dark business suit.

'I'll be honest with you,' he said. 'After we said hello tonight, I couldn't help wondering whether that was the last time I'd ever see you again. I didn't have the chance to say what I would have liked to say, in front of all those people, so something told me I should come to find you.'

'All right,' she returned coldly. 'Say it.'

'I want you to know,' he said, 'that there are no hard feelings about anything. You did a great job with your company, and now you have the success you deserve. I understand why you did what you did...'

'You understand,' she repeated bitterly.

'Yes,' he insisted. 'It was the only reasonable course. We couldn't go on forever the way we were. But I'd like to tell you how much I...enjoyed it while it lasted.'

'Enjoyed it!' she said, her anger threatening to overwhelm her. 'Well, that's wonderful for you, Frank. I'm glad it was a pleasure for you.'

'It was,' he responded simply. 'It was something I'll never forget. If it hurt you, I'm sorry.'

She stared at him, weighing his arrogance in wonderment. He spoke of the past as though it had been a honeymoon, rather than a betrayal.

'All's well that ends well,' she said ironically. 'Since you're so worried about hard feelings, you might tell Roy Schell the next time you have lunch with him that all is forgiven now that the best man has won.'

Perplexity vied with the odd intensity in his black irises.

'Speaking of that family,' she added sharply, 'I think perhaps you ought to be running along now, Frank. I'm sure your friend Julie must be worried about you. Which is understandable, to judge from your companion at the Four Seasons tonight. Your life seems to involve quite a few strands to keep track of. A real juggling act, so to speak.'

The reproachful words had tumbled out before she could stop them, and she cursed the grain of jealousy they contained. But the dangerous light flickering in his dark regard remained clouded by incomprehension.

'I don't get it,' he said. 'You seem to have me mixed up with the wrong people.'

She laughed bitterly. 'Do I? Well, never mind, Frank. It's late, and I have work to do tomorrow. I don't have time for your self-justifications.'

He had advanced upon her slowly as she spoke, and towered over her now. For an instant she recalled the daunting image of his tall frame in Sam's darkened office, the night he had first warned her about Andrew Dillon. His threatening posture, so virile and erect, had left its mark on her senses for weeks afterwards. Now she knew it had all been part of his own plan to betray her.

'If you're trying to blame me for something,' he said, 'you might as well come out with it.'

'Blame you? Never, Frank. You did what your instincts told you to do. Perhaps, in your own way, you saw no harm in it. Why don't we just leave it at that?'

He shook his head. 'I can see it's worse than I thought,' he said. 'I'm sorry, Laura. But your company is back on its feet again. I'm glad of that, at least.'

'No thanks to you,' she shot back, a black rage overtaking her as she regarded this complacent stranger, so foreign, so hated, who nevertheless carried an irretrievable part of her woman's heart in him, and would take it wherever his destiny led him.

Her words must have pushed him over an unseen edge, for he grasped her slender arms convulsively, his large hands like iron manacles.

'What's that supposed to mean?' he asked, his voice low, his lips close to her face.

'Take your hands off me,' she hissed, struggling ineffectually in his grip. 'Get out of here.'

'I can't leave it like this,' he said. 'I wanted to help you, not hurt you.'

'Tell that to Julie,' she said, tears of frustration coming

to her eyes. 'I'm sure she'd be interested to know that you
motives are so exalted.'

'Why do you mention her?' he asked. 'She's nothing to
me.'

'Good for you,' she said, hurting her wrists as she
writhed against him. 'She'd love to hear that. I'm sure the
same goes for Helen. You're quite the ladies' man...'

'Listen to me,' he warned, a terrible urgency in his voice
'A lot of things have come between us. More than I
thought, I suppose. But don't ever talk to me about other
women. You're...'

All at once he hesitated, suppressing his own words with
tight control. She felt the tremendous force of him, coiled
upon itself so close to her in the charged air of the room
and cursed herself for having let him in.

'You're wrong,' he said at last.

'Liar,' she retorted in dark triumph.

With stunning suddenness he pulled her against him, the
power of his arms forcing the breath out of her. Her angry
struggles had loosened the tie of her robe, and to her horror
she felt the crisp cloth of his jacket against her naked
breasts. The earthy male scent of him, palpable under his
elegant clothes, suffused her as he forced her lips open.
Madly she squirmed to get away from him, but so tight was
his grip that her efforts succeeded only in forcing her nudity
to rub itself jerkily against his hard body. In a trice his kiss
had penetrated her, his tongue caressed her own, and she
realised in panic that there was no place to hide from him.

She did not know what he was trying to prove in his
angry way, but she was horrified by her own response to
him, for already, in her every sense and sinew, she felt
tantalisingly at home in his arms, at home in this tense
embrace which held her soft flesh to the firmness of his
muscled limbs.

Fiercely his hands furled the warm terrycloth which hung
about her in disarray, pulling it up, forcing it aside so that

they could close around the gentle curve of her thighs, her hips. They were hands that knew every inch of her, every secret corner which had awakened to the ecstasy of love for the first time under his touch. And as she fought against him, aghast at the intimacy of his hold on her, the sly rhythm of her old passion was stealing over her naked skin, binding her ever closer to him, making her shudder with inviting female undulations, wanting and loving this bondage that infuriated her.

He was turning back the clock in that wild instant, abetted by her own flesh and soul, and she could not think how to stop him. The taunting heat inside her expanded dizzyingly as he pulled her hips to his own. She felt the hard force of him against the silken nudity of her limbs, and the taut tips of her swollen breasts quickened against his deep chest as his tongue slid over her own, lithe and knowing. All at once his anger seemed gone, eclipsed by a passion to which she was even more vulnerable. His fingers were on her back, her shoulders, the soft skin beneath her waist, alive with wanting, their touch a triumphant greeting after painful weeks of separation.

She was his woman, those warm caresses seemed to say. The strong woman he had fashioned from a self-conscious girl, and whose needs could only be satisfied by this man who was already part of her, too deeply rooted inside her to excise and banish, whatever his unforgivable perfidy. Well might she struggle, in her bitterness, to break the chains that bound her to him. Her very strength had come from him. She was fighting against herself, and her squirming could only lead her inevitably to his bed, and to the hard man's flesh that had known her eager caresses and gaze of fascination so many times.

But he hesitated, as though shocked by the fury of his own need, and withdrew his kiss without relinquishing his iron hold on her. His hand furled her sleek hair with a sort of awed enquiry as his gaze took in the swollen shadow of

desire in her features. He himself seemed amazed by the
occult power of this intimacy which joined him to her, by
the very softness which clung involuntarily to him, the vulnerable female flesh he fondled. With a slowness born of
unseen emotions he kissed her temple, her earlobe, her
neck, his lips grazing her skin with indescribable familiarity.

The gentleness of those sweet kisses tore at the heart of
her resistance to him, and when the hot flare of his need
brought him to part her lips once more, and his groan of
desire filled her senses like a deep caress, she thought she
was lost. She felt her own fingers slip over the hard ripples
of muscle under his shirt, traitorous fingers which longed
to slide around his hips to the crisp hair on his chest, his
stomach, to pull gently at his belt until it opened, to pleasure him like a pliant slave who knew that she could never
be whole without him, that no price was too high to pay
for the ecstasy he alone could give her.

But a saving impulse, from the depths of her mind and
heart, forced her to grasp him suddenly in an embrace of
entreaty, and to speak the only words that might stem the
tide of his passion.

'Don't,' she whispered. 'You'll kill me.'

The words had slipped out with a will of their own, and
in an instant struck their mark. She knew that at the very
centre of his lovemaking had always been a wellspring of
respect, a willingness to bring her pleasure while refusing
to violate her. Though his cruelty had known no limits in
the treachery he plotted behind her back, he would not dare
use his body as a weapon to torment her.

'Go now,' she heard herself say in a voice that beseeched
and commanded. 'Never come back.'

And as he released her, it seemed that she could at last
find her anger once more, and defend herself at the price
of a heart broken by her own refusal.

'I never want to see you again,' she said, avoiding his

eyes as she pulled the bathrobe around her with a shudder. 'Go away and live your life, Frank. Please.'

Her gaze was fixed on the shadows covering the walls. Awed by the finality of her own words, she fought to survive her last instants in his presence. Never again would she look into those black eyes behind which paradise had seemed to open upon her, unbearably delightful. Never again would she hold those warm hands, feel the caress of the wry smile which had buoyed her spirits when she felt so alone, touch the tanned skin whose virile fragrance had charmed her nights.

She heard him turn and walk away. The door closed upon him with a hushed brutality that made her feel faint. For a brief moment a hard inner voice congratulated her on the remnant of strength that had forced him away.

Then, in a tide that washed away all thought, her tears came at last to torment and comfort her. For what seemed an eternity she sat alone, quiet sobs shaking her breast, hot tears inundating her.

When at last she dried her eyes and hurried to her bed, she was a changed woman. The future opened out before her, calm and serene in its indifference. She felt that the metamorphosis which had begun the day of Sam's death was now complete. She was a hollow shell, and would remain so.

Life beckoned her to new challenges, and she intended to meet them. But in her expectancy there was no hope. Tomorrow her work would offer blessed distraction from this emptiness which, she knew, would never be filled again. Her heart belonged to a stranger, and she must now go about the bleak business of living in exile from her very self.

CHAPTER FOURTEEN

IT was May. Winter had long since given way to a rainy spring on the East Coast, and finally a few days of fresh sunshine were arriving to signal summer's eventual advent.

The face of Laura Christensen had become familiar on the pages of dozens of business publications. Her courageous and clever stewardship of Sam Christensen's company to unheard of prosperity was a story the media could not resist. Features on her had appeared in women's magazines all over the country, and she had even been asked for TV and radio interviews. Her selection as Businesswoman of the Year was a virtual certainty.

To Laura's relief her college graduation portrait had finally been eclipsed in the press by a recent photo which showed her as she was today: dressed in a simple suit, her sleek hair pinned back, her smile touched by diffidence and a trace of fatigue.

Molly's sales had grown apace since the first hectic weeks of production, and Laura was up to her neck in judicious expansion plans for Christensen. There were factories to buy and lease, related product lines to design and develop, materials to buy, and companies to acquire. Christensen Products today was a far richer company than the one Sam had left Laura, and she was resisting considerable pressure to move its headquarters to Manhattan.

Laura had never worked for fame, and the attention she was receiving made her uneasy. To her astonishment, it showed no sign of subsiding, for her youth and beauty once such an obstacle to recognition of her abilities, were now a journalist's dream come true.

But in recent days a single story had eclipsed all others in the business press. Armand Schell had died after a long illness, leaving his empire in the control of his sons and their allies. A host of dignitaries from governments around the world had attended his funeral in Manhattan. In a lengthy eulogy one of the President's cabinet advisers, himself a former Schell employee, had praised Armand Schell's contributions to America in war and in peacetime.

The press teemed with stories about the power struggles destined to shake the Schell conglomerate. It was known that Roy and Anton Schell had no intention of sharing power amicably, for only their father's presence had kept them from each other's throats during his lifetime. Of concern also was the enormous political leverage that had died with Armand Schell. His corporation had not lost a single important anti-trust suit in the last forty years, for no government dared incur his displeasure. With Armand dead, the questionable acquisitions Schell was involved in around the globe might no longer go unchallenged.

Laura had read this news with interest, not only because Schell's acquisition of AMZ Manufacturing brought its influence close to Christensen's own markets, but because she wondered where Frank Jordan would fit into the new scheme of things. She also wondered sadly whether his planned marriage to Julie Schell would soon become a reality. Though the welcome coldness in her emotions prevented her from dwelling morbidly on the prospect, she could not help scanning the business and social columns for news of the wedding.

But these thoughts were far from her mind one Saturday morning when she found herself on Fifth Avenue in Manhattan. She had come to buy clothes, for her wardrobe was pitifully inadequate now that her responsibility required her attendance at so many formal functions.

Summer in New Haven would be hot as always, and Laura was in search of some comfortable suits and dresses. Fifth Avenue was particularly attractive in the bright morning sun and, having ordered all her purchases to be delivered to her new and larger apartment in New Haven, Laura was strolling happily, unencumbered by bags or boxes, when a familiar face flashed across her vision.

She turned to see Helen Rowings beside her on the sidewalk. Helen also had stopped in her tracks, and was smiling.

'Remember me?' she asked. 'Of course I didn't have any trouble recognising you, Miss Christensen, with your face all over the papers.'

'How are you?' Laura asked, her friendliness covering over her acute awareness of the other woman's relationship with Frank Jordan.

'Oh, fine,' Helen smiled. 'Work, work, work. I imagine you're swamped yourself, with Molly doing so great in the stores.'

'I'm doing the best I can,' Laura laughed. 'It can be a grind.'

Helen hesitated, and seemed to be making an inward decision.

'I don't suppose you'd have a minute for a cup of coffee,' she asked. 'Now that I see you, there's something that I'd appreciate talking to you about.'

Laura glanced at her watch. 'All right,' she said, intrigued despite herself by Helen's invitation.

A few moments later they were seated in the corner booth of a busy coffee shop.

'You're nice to take the time,' Helen said, her friendly eyes regarding Laura. 'I probably shouldn't be bringing any of this up to you. It's on the confidential side, to tell the truth, and Frank would have my hide if he knew.'

Laura said nothing, but hid her irritation at the mention of Frank's name behind a polite smile. Despite her pangs of jealousy she could not help liking Helen's gentle, down-to-earth manner and self-effacing wit. No wonder, she thought, that Frank hesitated between a creature of porcelain delicacy like Julie Schell and this fine, attractive young woman.

'It's ancient history to you now, I'm sure,' Helen began. 'But from my position on the sidelines, I couldn't get rid of the feeling that there were some things you didn't know about Frank when you knew him—and when you fired him.'

I knew enough, Laura thought bitterly.

'You're right,' she said aloud. 'It is ancient history now.'

'Nevertheless,' Helen said, 'I hope you'll lend an ear for a moment. If what I have to say is old news, fine. If not, it might just interest you. Believe me, I'm not trying to interfere. If I hadn't bumped into you on the street just now, I never would have dared get in touch with you.'

She took a deep breath. 'I've known Frank for about five years now,' she said. 'I met him when I went to work for Schell as a junior executive. He had already been there for three years or so, and was quite a celebrity. He was Armand Schell's right-hand man, and everybody could see how brilliant he was. The rumours were all over the place about his future role in the corporation, and how he would handle Roy and Anton, and so on.'

She hesitated as the waitress brought their coffee. Laura could see the concentration in her attractive features.

'I'm getting ahead of myself already,' Helen smiled. 'Schell was not a fun place to work, and that's putting it mildly. But Frank was the head man where my section was concerned, and he, at least, liked my work and tried to encourage me. We used to play tennis sometimes—mixed doubles with a married couple from my floor—and Frank would take me out to lunch occasionally.'

She shook her head with an amused laugh. 'Of course, Frank is an incredibly handsome guy,' she said, 'but I never had any illusions about romantic possibilities where he was concerned. In the first place, I'm just not his type, and I knew it. He was a good friend, and I was satisfied with that. But most importantly, the accepted wisdom around Schell was that Frank was practically engaged to Julie Schell—Armand's daughter—and that he would marry her someday and assume an awful lot of power within the corporation.'

She looked at Laura. 'Here's where it gets interesting,' she said. 'People at Schell were so in awe of Frank that they didn't dare tease him about Julie. But I had become friendly enough with him that I took the plunge one day and asked him about her. His reaction amazed me. He was very angry. Not at me, but at Julie and her father. He told me that after his first year at Schell, he had become very close to Armand. Now, during that period the "old man", as we called him, was already becoming rather retiring, and losing his hold on the business. Meanwhile, he had this daughter by his second marriage—which ended in divorce—and he didn't know what to do with her because he was already so old. She was a shy girl, quite reclusive, and he felt guilty about the divorce. So he asked Frank, as a personal favour, to pay some attention to the girl, because she was so lonely.'

Laura listened in silence, weighing Helen's words carefully.

'That's where the rumours started,' Helen went on. 'People saw Frank and Julie at company functions, saw the two of them with Armand when he appeared in public, and drew the logical conclusion. It was supposed to be a relationship made in heaven. Lonely heiress and handsome executive—all that.

'But what people didn't know was that Frank couldn't bear Julie. That's what he told me the day we spoke of it. He said that her china-doll sweetness was nothing but an elaborate front for the outside world to see, and that underneath she was every bit as ruthless a person as her brothers.

She smiled. 'That amazed me, of course,' she said. 'But Frank explained how Julie had taken advantage of Armand's guilt about her mother, and had him absolutely wrapped around her little finger. Armand Schell himself! Stranger things have happened, I guess. Now, Frank was annoyed enough already at playing escort to Julie when she needed a date. But as time passed he began to realise that she had more ambitious designs on him. What she wanted, he said, was to marry him someday, and see him outstrip her brothers for control of Schell International.'

Seeing Laura's raised eyebrow, she nodded. 'Don't laugh,' she said. 'The idea was within the realms of possibility, because Armand trusted Frank more than his own sons. The only fly in the ointment was that Frank couldn't stand Julie, and was already looking for a way out of the company. The point is that Julie was a realist as well as a schemer. She knew how to take advantage of people's weaknesses. No one but Frank realised how ambitious she really was, and is.'

She frowned. 'I found out for myself about Julie Schell's influence,' she said. 'One day I was fired by an ax man from Personnel, without an explanation. Of course I was upset, but also relieved in a way, because Schell was such an unpleasant environment. They helped me find another job—thank heaven for small favours—and I thought no more about it. Then one day last autumn, Frank showed up at the accounting firm where I worked, and told me he had also left Schell. I couldn't believe it. He was giving up so much!'

She sighed. 'Then he dropped a bombshell. My firing had upset him, and he had talked to Armand Schell about it. To make a long story short, he wormed out of the old man the fact that he himself had had me fired, for the craziest reason: his daughter was jealous of me! Apparently

Julie had heard about my friendship with Frank and over-reacted to it. So she wheedled the old man into getting rid of me.'

A bitter laugh escaped her lips. 'Well, that was it for Frank. He had seen Schell International turning into a corporate snake pit during his years there, and this was the last straw. He could laugh off Julie's designs on him, but not her actions. He saw through her enough to know that there was nothing romantic about her attitude. Power was all she wanted from Frank. But she saw me as a threat, so she had me removed from the picture.'

Her eyes rested gently on Laura. 'Frank knew your father by reputation,' she went on, 'and loved the idea of working with him. His only concession to Armand was to retain his consultant's position long enough to see through the projects he had controlled over the previous years. He asked me whether he could help me find a better job, because he felt personally responsible for what had happened to me. I said I was happy enough where I was. We both laughed a lot that day, because ''Hell International'', as we called it, was finally behind us.'

Laura sat in silence, shocked by what she had heard. If Helen was telling the truth, the lovely young woman who had so tearfully denounced Frank Jordan to her in Sam's office was not only a dangerous schemer, but also a brilliant actress.

'Now, Laura—may I call you Laura?' Helen asked.

'Of course,' Laura smiled.

'Now, I think I've given you the overall picture. I'm not going to pry into your own affairs, because it's none of my business. I don't know why you fired Frank, and I don't have to know. I saw him a couple of times during the months he was with you, and he was terribly excited about your work. He considered Christensen a breath of fresh air after eight years at Schell.'

Her brow furrowed in concentration, Helen seemed to

search for words to express her thought. 'Let me put it this way,' she said. 'Julie Schell lost a great deal when Frank walked out on her and her father. Frank was her only chance for the influence she wanted, and, like all the Schells, she wasn't in the habit of taking no for an answer. I truly believe she was actually jealous of me. Not out of love, but out of ambition. If she is really the sort of woman I think she is, her need for revenge would go deep. She wouldn't want Frank to be happy anywhere else—or with anyone else—and she'd act on that basis.'

Laura had turned pale at her words, and Helen was looking at her curiously.

'Did I strike a nerve?' she asked. 'I'm sorry, but...'

'No, never mind, Helen,' Laura said. 'It's just that...well, if what you're saying is true, I may have made a big mistake.'

'Laura,' Helen said, touching her hand, 'Frank would kill me if he knew I was telling you this, but I can't help it. I heard him talk about you when he was at Christensen, and I saw the look in his eyes the night we ran into you at the Four Seasons. It was a look I had never seen before. I know Frank, and I know you meant something very special to him. If I thought the long arm of Julie Schell had succeeded in coming between you two...'

The truth was coiled pitilessly around Laura. In the last year her credulity had brought her close to disaster on more than one occasion. First she had taken Andrew Dillon at his word when he threatened her with bankruptcy. Then she accepted Frank's version of events without checking out his own background.

And finally, she had taken Julie Schell's accusations at face value, without establishing their validity on her own.

One fact emerged now in a new light. In the end, Christensen Products had actually been saved from bankruptcy or takeover. But had it been saved by Laura alone? Was it not Frank whose advice had been the driving force behind the strategies whose ultimate success was now touted in the newspapers? Were not Frank's initial warnings about Roy Schell the key to everything?

If Helen was telling the truth, Julie had been diabolically clever. She had simply denounced Frank in the vaguest possible terms, using information she could easily have gleaned from any of a dozen sources about Christensen's dangers. She might have known of her own knowledge that her brother wished to acquire Christensen. All she had to tell Laura was that Frank himself was implicated in the plan.

And Laura had believed it all, and had fired Frank without asking him to explain.

'Let me ask you something,' she said to Helen. 'Did Frank ever mention a proposed takeover of Christensen Products by Schell?'

'By Armand Schell?' Helen shook her head. 'Impossible. The old man was through with acquisitions by the time Frank came to Schell. That would be Roy's game, or Anton's. It was their little competition. Each one would take over companies unilaterally, and use his own power on the Board to force through the mergers. If Roy acquired an electronics company in Maryland, Anton would do the same in Brazil or Belgium. It was that crazy policy that turned Schell into the mess it is today. But Armand himself was out of that part of the business. All he ever did was entertain heads of state and work on his memoirs.'

'If someone at Schell was interested in Christensen,' Laura asked, 'would Frank know about it?'

'Nothing escaped Frank when he was still with the company,' Helen said. 'Afterwards, I don't know. But I'll tell you one thing, Laura. If he did know of a takeover plan when he was at Christensen, he would have done everything in his power to stop it. He hates Roy Schell and his brother, and all they stand for.'

Laura shook her head in an agony of indecision. She

recalled the words Frank had spoken the night he had come to her apartment.

I wanted to help you, not hurt you.

If Helen was right about everything, it was easy to understand why Frank had seemed perplexed by Laura's angry remarks about his relations with Roy and Julie Schell.

Why do you mention her? he had said. *She's nothing to me.*

You seem to have me mixed up with the wrong people.

But why then had Frank accepted Laura's firing of him without saying a word in his own defence? If his efforts on her behalf had been sincere, he should have been furious at being fired.

Furious, and deeply hurt...

A decision began to take shape in Laura's mind, irrevocable and urgent.

'Where is Frank?' she asked abruptly.

'In Nassau,' Helen said. 'That's where he lives since he left you. As a matter of fact, that's the end of the story. He finally convinced me to leave my accounting firm and go to work for him. He's a consultant to several big corporations. But he can't stand the Coast any more, so he stays in the Bahamas while I act as his liaison. I fly down there once every three weeks or so to go over things with him.'

Helen hesitated, her lips pursed. 'I'm going to open my big mouth for the last time, Laura,' she said. 'He's not happy there. He's closed in on himself, and I'm worried about him. If it has anything to do with you...well, I don't know what to say.'

'Is he there now?' Laura asked. 'Today?'

'I assume so,' Helen replied. 'He was here last week for Armand's funeral. For old times' sake, he said. I haven't seen him since, but I'm in constant touch with his answering service. If he went anywhere, I think I'd know about it.'

'Have you got his address?' Laura asked, seized by an

impulse she could not control. She must get to the bottom
of her relationship with Frank Jordan now, today. And in
order to do so she must see him in the flesh.

Helen's integrity was too obvious to give rise to suspicion. She must be telling the truth. And if she was, Laura
had not only fired the man whose every effort had been on
her behalf for four months, but she had told him to his face
that she never wanted to see him again.

She dared not allow herself to hope that her personal
relationship with him might be saved. But she could not
live with the idea that she had rejected him on the basis of
the accusations of the scheming woman who had already
made his life miserable at Schell.

Laura did not allow herself second thoughts. She took
Frank's address from Helen, thanked her quickly and expressed her hope that they would meet again soon. Then
she hurried to the nearest telephone to call her travel agent
in New Haven. A reservation was booked for her on the
next flight from Laguardia to Nassau. She informed her
answering service that she could be contacted at Frank's
address, and took a cab to the airport.

An hour and a half later she was on a non-stop flight to
Nassau. She had no extra clothes with her, and had not
even thought to bring any personal effects. If she stayed
the night she would buy whatever she needed. She had to
see Frank.

As the plane soared high above the Atlantic Laura turned
the facts over and over in her mind. There was no doubt
about it: Frank's actions had all been consistent with the
idea that he wanted to help her. And in fact he had succeeded.

But how had Julie known when to denounce Frank? How
had she known which weapon would strike at the heart of
Laura's trust in him? Why had Frank not defended himself
the night he came unannounced to Laura's apartment?

There were too many questions. Closing her eyes, Laura tried to put all thought out of her mind.

But one idea hammered insistently at her. Julie Schell's story of her engagement to Frank had destroyed a gloriously intimate relationship on which Laura had placed a thousand unspoken hopes. That had been the cruelest blow of all.

And even now an impish voice inside her wondered out loud whether there was the slightest chance that Frank still cared for her. She banished the thought desperately. She had been hurt too often in the past year to entertain absurd dreams about the future.

She had loved him once. Now she intended to clear the air with him, and apologise if apologies were in order. That was all.

It was late afternoon. Outside the window Laura could see the sun descending slowly towards the horizon. The captain's amplified voice pointed out Grand Bahama Island below. Laura could see catamarans and sailboats in the water near beaches which glowed like crescent moons in the golden light.

New Providence came into view minutes later as the plane descended. Possessed by a terrible urgency, Laura did not hear the stewards' welcoming words. Though she had never seen these beautiful islands, they were merely a bland background for her final destination.

Tiny Nassau International Airport flashed quickly before her eyes as she hurried towards the taxis and buses waiting to pick up arriving passengers. The tropical air was delightfully scented with the fragrance of sea and flowers. A smiling cab driver whose white teeth gleamed against his brown skin in the afternoon light nodded amiably after a glance at the address Laura showed him. He whistled soundlessly as the cab drove along the left side of the street past groves of trees festooned with bougainvillaea, hibiscus and oleander.

The cab left the inland airport and soon reached the coast road. Limestone houses with wide verandahs and overhanging upper porches passed by, their windows protected by louvres from the glare of the setting sun.

His intuition having told him Laura was a stranger to the islands, the driver pointed out the many cays along the horizon. Laura was momentarily charmed out of her reverie by the sight of a flamingo strutting calmly on a deserted beach—the only such bird she had seen outside of a zoo in her whole life.

No wonder, she thought, that Frank had chosen such a lovely place to live in solitude, far from the rush of Manhattan.

Tactfully the driver avoided asking Laura whether she was here on business or for pleasure, or for a visit. Had he done so she would not have known how to answer him.

The sunset was beginning to spread its fiery spectacle across the entire sky as the driver slowed to a stop beside an isolated mailbox. After peering at it for a moment he edged the cab into a narrow dirt road which descended toward the ocean.

A lengthy trek through dense foliage led at last to a circular drive beside a comfortable house nestled under tall trees. The thump of the surf was clearly audible from behind it. Though the sky was still bright, the thick leaves cast dark shadows over the drive. It would soon be night, and Laura had made no plans at all for a hotel reservation or even transportation. Momentarily unnerved by her impulsive arrival in this far-flung place, she had to steel herself to see her plan through.

A jeep was in the driveway. Behind it stood a small sports car. Laura wondered abruptly whether Frank was alone here, and whether her appearance might interrupt a business or social meeting, or perhaps something more intimate. She began to regret her spontaneous decision to

come, and had to recall Helen's assurances in order to give
herself courage.

After paying the driver she took a deep breath, walked
to the door and rang the doorbell. A muted tinkle sounded
inside the house. For a moment she heard nothing else.
Perhaps Frank was outside on the beach.

At last soft steps were audible behind the door. With a
hollow click the latch came loose. The door opened slowly.

Laura's heart nearly stopped.

Julie Schell stood before her, dressed only in a man's
bathrobe, her delicate eyebrow arched in surprise.

'Miss Christensen,' she said calmly. 'What a surprise.
Do come in.'

CHAPTER FIFTEEN

In a state of shock Laura entered the house. Its lean, attractive furnishings passed before her eyes in a blur. Behind a large picture window the surf fell heavily against a lovely little beach. A sandbar brightened the water a few yards from shore.

'Frank isn't in just now,' Julie was saying. 'He's in town. Would you like something to drink?'

'No, thanks,' Laura said, her breath catching in her throat. 'I mean, yes. Whatever you have.'

'We have soda, fruit juices, all kinds of alcohol—whatever you like,' Julie said with a proprietary shrug. 'Frank likes to keep the place well stocked.'

'A glass of soda would be fine,' Laura said, perching uncomfortably on the edge of a handsome wicker chair. 'Miss Schell, I'm…I was terribly sorry to hear about your father. Please accept my sympathy.'

'That's nice of you,' Julie said without emotion, moving unhurriedly in her bare feet toward the kitchen. Her silvery blonde hair was splayed in careless waves over the robe she wore. 'It wasn't unexpected, of course,' she called back, 'but we were all shocked nonetheless.'

A moment later she emerged with a tall frosted glass and placed it on the table beside Laura.

'I didn't realise you were coming,' she said, 'Frank is great to be with, but he can forget to tell me the most basic things. Is it business?'

'Yes,' Laura stammered, feeling a flush of embarrassment come over her in the warm air. Though a lovely breeze furled the curtains beside the window, the atmosphere seemed unbearably claustrophobic. Julie lounged comfortably on the couch, apparently unperturbed to be seen in her nudity. Her demeanour was far from that of the diffident, frightened girl who had visited Laura in Sam's office. There was a palpable hardness in her beautifully rounded limbs, her voice, and above all the clear eyes that regarded Laura.

'Actually,' Laura admitted, 'Frank wasn't expecting me. I'm terribly sorry to burst in on you like this. It was some business I wanted to discuss with him. Something rather urgent. I suppose I should have called.'

'Not at all,' Julie laughed. 'We're very informal here.' She seemed determined to present herself as the mistress of the house, and Laura dared not ask whether she herself was visiting Frank. In pained perplexity she tried to think of something to say.

'It's beautiful here,' she said at last in a wan voice.

'Yes, isn't it?' the reclining girl answered with a quick glance toward the beach. 'A romantic setting. Just the thing for Frank.'

Laura wished she could find a way to get up and leave gracefully, for the absurdity of her position was coming home to her with increasing force. She had invaded the privacy of a couple which could scarcely welcome her. She cursed the impulse that had made her take Helen at her word about Frank.

'So Frank doesn't know you're coming,' Julie smiled coolly.

Laura shook her head.

'I wouldn't want to be presumptuous, Miss Christensen,' Julie said. 'If you're serious about being here on urgent business, that's well and good. I thought I understood that you and Frank were no longer one. In any case, I might suggest that if your business is personal, you may have made your trip for nothing.'

The venom in her words was unmistakable. Laura's embarrassment was reaching a fever pitch. But something in Julie's ill-concealed cruelty struck a strange note, and she resolved to hear her out.

'I'm not sure I understand,' she said with studied neutrality.

'I suppose we shouldn't talk behind Frank's back,' Julie sighed, 'but he makes no secret of his many... involvements. He is a very masculine man, and, to put it bluntly, a promiscuous one. It's the nature of the beast, and one has to forgive it. I did long ago. I do think, though, that it would be tragic for any of his acquaintances to assume his flings are any more than just that.'

Laura said nothing. She knew her emotions were colouring her face. Her impulse to come here seemed to have brought her straight into the maw of Frank Jordan's sinister life. But no matter what happened now, she decided, she would do what she came here to do. She would not leave before finding out exactly where the truth about Frank lay.

'I can forgive him a lot,' Julie went on. 'I decided years ago that the advantages of being with him outweighed the disadvantages. And I know the feeling is mutual, because Frank never strays far. My poor father wanted us to marry before his passing, but neither Frank nor I felt the time was right. I enjoy my own independence, and Frank...well, Frank would like to get the wild oats out of his system before we settle down and raise a family. I can't really blame him, you see. It's a purely physical thing, after all. He and I see eye to eye in so many ways. We really knew we were made for each other when we first met. Birds of a feather, as they say.'

'I'm happy for you,' Laura said with a forced smile. 'But this doesn't concern me. As I said, my visit is on business.'

'As you like,' the other woman said, getting up with a

sigh. 'I thought it might interest you to know where things stand. I'll be back in a moment.'

With a distinctly contemptuous turn of her head she walked from the room.

Moments passed in atrocious silence, accented by the hushed boom of the surf outside. The cry of a sea bird echoed distantly. Laura could hear a clock ticking somewhere in the house.

Her misfortune was almost farcical, she reflected as she sat alone by the window. Julie had taken cruel pleasure in treating her like a lovesick woman scorned who had flown here in a desperate attempt to regain her lover's affections. And was there not, in fact, a terrible grain of truth in that notion? In her guilty heart Laura had dared to hope that more than her professional friendship with Frank Jordan might be saved today.

Why, she wondered, had Helen lied about Frank's involvement with Julie? Why had she made such a capricious effort to plead for him, behind his back? Perhaps Helen felt that Julie was bad for Frank, and had decided on a mad whim to play matchmaker by propitiating Laura. Or perhaps Helen's motives were as inscrutable as those of everyone else in Frank's life.

Nevertheless, Helen's description of Julie's character seemed amply borne out by the spiteful display Laura had just witnessed.

Even now she heard a radio turned on somewhere in the house. Julie was obviously content to let her visitor stew alone while she went about her business.

A single question remained: was Frank innocent of involvement in the plot that had nearly destroyed Christensen Products?

'What difference does it make?' Laura thought miserably. If Frank were innocent, her apologies could hardly interest him now. Her firing of him was undoubtedly ancient history in his mind, as was their short-lived affair.

In humiliation she wondered what to do. Her pride dictated that she call a cab and return home immediately. But the prospect of embarrassing herself further, and confirming Julie's suspicion about the reason for her visit, immobilised her. She could not sit here like a fool, waiting for Frank to come home to his mistress. Neither could she bring herself to turn tail and flee.

After what seemed an eternity of silent waiting she prepared to find Julie and ask to use the phone. The crunch of automobile tyres on the gravel outside stopped her in her tracks.

So the worst was to happen, she thought. Frank was here. She would have to play this painful comedy through to the end.

To her surprise the doorbell rang. Julie emerged nonchalantly from the bedroom wing, still clad in Frank's bathrobe, and walked to the door without a glance at Laura.

What she saw when she opened it must have surprised her, for she stepped back a pace and watched in silence as a man entered the room.

For the second time Laura turned white in shock.

It was Rob Colwell.

Ignoring Julie, he advanced upon Laura, his expression grim.

'Rob,' she exclaimed. 'What are you doing here?'

'It's all right, Laura,' he said. 'Your answering service gave me this address. I may be out of line, but I thought I could help.'

Her first impulse was to fly to him as her saviour. Steadfast and loyal as always, he was here at her service. He could take her home, take her away from this miasma of ominous intrigue surrounding Frank Jordan.

'Rob,' she said, 'I'm at a loss. I don't understand.'

'Where's Jordan?' he asked, wary determination in his eyes.

'He's not home,' she replied.

'You haven't seen him?'

She shook her head. He shot a dark glance at Julie, who was standing in the doorway, a speculative look on her face.

'Come with me now, Laura,' he said in a low voice. 'I don't know what possessed you to come here like this, but this man Jordan and his friends are no good for you. Hasn't he done enough to you already?'

'Rob,' Laura asked, still trying to collect her thoughts, 'what made you come all this way? Why are you here?'

'I came to stop you from dong something stupid, Laura. I don't want to see you hurt more than you have been already. What business could you possibly have with Jordan after what he's done to you?'

Laura stared at him in confusion. Every sinew in her body longed to cling to Rob for protection now, and to let him take her away from this strange outpost in which she felt so defenceless. But the very idea that he would have rushed here the minute he found this address seemed out of character for him.

Nevertheless her second thoughts could not compete with Julie's cruel revelations. The hopes Helen had raised in her were dead now. The best course was to leave with Rob and try to forget Frank Jordan's alien world. She must leave it behind her forever.

Only this morning she had been a confident young woman, proud of her work and content with her existence, as she shopped on Fifth Avenue. And now here she was, a few short hours later, trapped like a victim in a foreign clime, the tentacles of Frank's endlessly jarring existence wrapped around her. Rob offered a quick, clean route of escape.

'All right,' she said, rising to her feet. 'Let's go, then.'

Rob took her hand with a smile. She prepared to give Julie a lame excuse for their departure.

Before she could find the words, the sound of a car stopping came once more from the driveway.

All three stopped in their tracks, their glances darting from each other to the darkness behind the screen door. Quick footsteps sounded in the gravel outside.

Dressed in tan slacks and a t-shirt which hugged his deep chest, Frank Jordan entered his house with long strides. He frowned to see Julie's deshabille, and looked quickly from Rob to Laura.

The words he spoke were like a knell of catastrophe over Laura's whole world.

'I don't believe I have to introduce Mr Colwell and Miss Schell,' he said with a hard smile. 'I believe they know each other already.'

A stunned silence hung in the air. The four people in the room stood uncomfortably, unseen forces raging among them. Julie's glance at Rob was irritable. Rob avoided Laura's shocked gaze. Having spoken his unexpected words, Frank had eyes only for Laura, their expression darkly probing.

'Get your clothes on, Julie,' he said at length. 'There's someone here to take you home.' Though he did not bother to look at her, the command in his voice was so imperious that she hurried towards the bedrooms.

'Laura is leaving with me,' Rob said, finding his voice at last. His face was red with anger. 'If you stand in her way, Frank, or bother her again, I'll kill you.'

'She didn't come here with you, did she?' Frank asked, ignoring the other man's threat. Laura shook her head.

'Then you'll decide for yourself, won't you?' he told her grimly. 'You came here to see me, and you're going to see me.'

All at once the robust energy that had seemed part and parcel of Rob Colwell's male essence appeared to dissipate. He stood in the middle of the living room, his eyes turned now towards the darkening ocean outside, oddly crestfallen and deflated.

Laura turned back to Frank in utter bewilderment. He had not moved from his place by the door. Though his powerful limbs were tensed for action, he seemed determined not to approach Laura, but to speak his piece from a distance.

'I spent a lot of hours wondering why you fired me the way you did, so suddenly,' he said. 'I knew it had to be something that had nothing to do with my work for you. Something outside. The only clue I had was that you sent your messenger to my office at Schell. But, in the end, that clue was enough. I knew someone from Schell must have gone to you behind my back and misrepresented me to you. Since I was already through with Schell forever, there was only one person who fitted the bill. It couldn't be Armand, because he and I understood each other. It couldn't be Roy or Anton because they were both delighted to see me go.'

He crossed his arms, his eyes never leaving Laura.

'It had to be Julie,' he said. 'I recognised her style. Always behind the scenes, always conniving. But a question remained. Julie knew I would never come back to Schell. She knew that as well as Armand did. So what did she have to gain by compromising me with my new employer? Not much. Would she frame me out of pure perversity? I don't think so. Not unless she found out somehow that my relationship with you was more than that of employee to employer. That would make sense. Julie could never bring me back to Schell, but she could do her damndest to see that I was never happy with another woman.'

Laura stared at the long lines of his implacable man's body, hardened by anger and by his iron control of himself. He was a terrifying sight, and an indescribably handsome one.

'But Julie couldn't know how I felt about you,' he went on. 'Not unless someone told her. Someone who was in daily contact with both of us. Someone who could see that the looks passing between us were those of a man and a woman. Someone who had a reason, a personal reason, to want to kill that relationship at all costs. Someone who cared so much that the very sight of us together was more than he could bear. Only one man was in that position.'

His eyes left Laura to dart a glance at Rob, whose back was now turned as though in ineffectual defence against the blows struck by Frank's words.

'He had to act,' Frank went on, 'but he couldn't risk trumping something up against me himself. That would make him look bad in your eyes, Laura. A friend should never be the bearer of bad news. So he did some checking and found out that someone already existed who was more than motivated to come between us, and guileful enough to do so efficiently. Julie Schell. He contacted her, no doubt in an apparently accidental way, and let her understand that I was involved with Sam's daughter. Then he sat back and waited. In a matter of days she made her move, and I was fired.

'As it turned out,' he said, 'your company was saved after all, and he must have been delighted. Frank Jordan was out of the picture, and the status quo had been restored. Until you ran into Helen Rowings today in Manhattan and flew down here. When he heard about that, he rushed to stop you, and almost succeeded.'

Laura had sat down in a daze, shattered by Frank's words. Rob was staring out at the waves, his eyes bleak and empty.

'I wouldn't blame him too much, Laura,' Frank said. 'He did what he did out of love. He was loyal to Sam Christensen and to his company, and he was a big enough man not to feel threatened when I was hired. He knew his value. I don't think he even felt betrayed when you took my advice over his about First Federal. He's a professional, and wanted what was best for you. But his world fell apart when the woman he had loved and waited for since she was a teenager chose a stranger named Frank Jordan to love instead of him. That was the last straw.'

Laura watched in horror as Rob turned and walked from the house without a word. The screen door closed quietly behind him, its clink a fatal sound thrown over her entire past.

An engine burst into life outside. A moment later its hum was receding into the trees, drowned by the thrum of the surf.

'Why did you...?' Laura asked in a breathless voice.

'Let him get away with it?' Frank smiled bitterly. 'I thought you belonged to him, Laura. I thought you two had an understanding, with Sam's blessing. I knew how he felt about you the first day I came to work for Sam. I could see it in his eyes. I considered myself the fifth wheel in the whole picture, since I had just come on the scene from another company.'

He shrugged. 'I was head over heels in love with you from the first moment I saw you,' he said. 'And I'm afraid my jealousy made me behave a little coldly toward you, those first weeks. I couldn't resist you, and I was sure you loved someone else. Well, that night in Montreal, and afterwards...'

He exhaled sharply, as though the memory were too intense to bear.

'As I say,' he went on, 'I couldn't resist you. You were so beautiful, such a woman... But I couldn't bear to put any strings on you. That's why I behaved as though nothing had happened between us. When you did the same, I assumed it was because you loved Colwell all along. I felt guilty as hell for taking advantage of you behind his back, but I told myself you weren't a schoolgirl. You were a woman, and knew what you wanted.'

An infinite sadness had stolen into his black eyes.

'At least,' he said, 'I tried to make myself believe that.

All along I worried that I was hurting you, tearing you… In the end I gave up on the future and tried to hang on to the present, for as long as it might last. It ended when you fired me, of course. The best idea seemed to bow out gracefully, even though I suspected there was something behind that pendant wrapped around my resignation form. Whether you blamed me for what we did together, or never cared at all, the result was the same.'

A tender smile curled his lips as he went on. 'Besides,' he said, 'I knew by then that you were strong enough, and smart enough, to see your company through without any more help from me. I had served my purpose. And you and Sam had restored a lot of my faith in human nature after eight years in that Schell snake pit. I knew I would never be the same without you, but I was damned proud of you, Laura, and proud to have known you. I had the memories of our time together… They say it's better to have loved and lost than never to have loved at all. I just prayed to God that I hadn't hurt you…'

A movement in the hallway interrupted him. Fighting her impulse to throw her arms around him, Laura watched in silence as Julie Schell returned from the bedrooms, her suitcase in her hand, a look of malignant anger in her limpid eyes.

Frank went to the screen door and motioned with an upraised hand. Steps sounded on the gravel outside, and a man Laura had never seen before entered the room. He was dressed in a finely tailored business suit, and the hint of grey at his temples made him look particularly distinguished. But as he stood between Frank and Julie, Laura gazed in awed fascination at his eyes. They were the coldest, most inhuman eyes she had ever seen.

All at once a spark of recognition made her glance from the stranger to Julie.

'Roy Schell,' Frank said neutrally. 'Laura Christensen.'

'Come, Julia,' the other man said after a hard, evaluative glance at Laura. 'We're going home.'

He took Julie's suitcase and held the door open for her. Hatred and defeat mingled in her eyes as she darted a look from Laura to Frank. Then, with a shrug of contempt, she strode out of the door, her head held high.

At last Frank sat down. His eyes scanned the ocean. Laura regarded him in silence, her nerves racing.

'Julie cornered me at Armand's funeral,' he said, 'and begged me to let her fly down here for a few days. She said she was depressed and needed to think. I let her come—out of regard for the old man, I suppose. He had really loved her after all. That's why he let her get away with so much.'

His smile was rueful. 'It was my mistake,' he said. 'As soon as she got here I could see she felt no grief over his death. Her kind can't feel a thing like that. She just wanted to see what I was up to. I think she wondered whether I had a woman here.'

With a sigh he locked his hands behind his head. 'After a decent interval,' he went on, 'I had it out with her about you and Christensen. She admitted what she had done, in a flood of phony tears, and threatened to harm herself in some way if I kicked her out. Comical as that idea was, I believed her capable of just about anything, so I called Roy in Manhattan. I told him if he didn't get on one of his private jets and get the hell down here to take his sister out of my hair, I would make use of a few things I know about his financial dealings of the last few years.'

He laughed. 'That made him jump,' he said, 'because with the old man dead the government is going to be a lot less pliant where Schell International is concerned. I was waiting to pick him up when I got Helen's message that she had talked to you and that you might be on your way here. That's why I was a little late getting back. When I walked in here and saw you with Colwell, I wasn't sure what to think. But when I found out you hadn't come together, I knew I had been right about him all along.'

He turned to look at Laura, his dark gaze alive with passionate enquiry.

'Now he's gone, Laura,' he said, 'and you're still sitting here. Was I right about you?'

Tears had quickened in Laura's eyes as she listened to his words. For months, unbeknownst to her, Frank had been feeling the same pain, the same longing that had tormented her unmercifully. He too had clung to the present in his belief that the future was sure to separate him from her, and had seen his worst fears confirmed when she exiled him violently from her life.

Now he sat a few feet from her, unable to convince himself that time had truly brought her back to him. Could it be, she asked herself in wonder, that only those few feet of mere space now stood between her and the man whose place in her heart was more permanent than life itself?

'I loved you, Frank,' she said quietly. 'I...love you.'

Tears blinded her as the words came free at last, the dream they carried shimmering unseen in the darkened room. Her woman's soul leapt within her breast, delivered at last of the burden it had suffered and cherished alone for so long, and she thought she would die to see that secret fly from her, triumphant in the night, towards the stranger she loved.

But his arms had encircled her, warm and protective as home itself, and she heard the words on his lips now, a whisper that stole through all the corners of her past, banishing their pain as it opened her to a future beyond her hopes.

'I love you, Laura.'

She felt his smile as he kissed away her tears.

'Laura Jordan,' he said. 'How does that sound?'

The gemlike syllables stunned her in their novelty, for she had never dared to say the name to herself. Yet it wa natural and beautiful, like a charmed destiny that had waited long years for her steps to lead her to it.

For an answer she hugged him to her with hands that seemed to discover him for the fist time, dazzled by the firm reality of these handsome limbs which would recede from her no more.

The hushed rhythm of the distant surf conspired softly with the long arms that cradled her in the darkness. She let herself rest at last in this wordless intimacy which seemed to grow and flower with each passing instant. Strong and sure were those steadfast arms, and eternal as the waves of time which opened before her now.

She tried to recall the young woman whose impassioned gaze had scanned the sleeping limbs of the man she loved, forcing herself at every moment to give him up even as the very sight of him filled her heart to overflowing. He was Now, she had told herself. That was his essence, and her agony, for she dared not hope to belong to him.

But already that young woman was slipping quietly from her memory, along with the anguished days and private tears she had endured with all her courage.

Yes, she mused. Frank was Now.

And Now was forever.

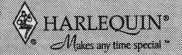

*The only way to be a bodyguard
is to stay as close as a lover…*

STAND
BY ME

The relationship between bodyguard and client is always close…sometimes too close for comfort. This September, join in the adventure as three bodyguards, protecting three very distracting and desirable charges, struggle not to cross the line between business and pleasure.

STRONG ARMS OF THE LAW
by Dallas SCHULZE

NOT WITHOUT LOVE
by Roberta LEIGH

SOMETIMES A LADY
by Linda Randall WISDOM

*Sometimes danger makes
a strange bedfellow!*

**Available September 1998 wherever
Harlequin and Silhouette books are sold.**

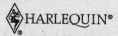

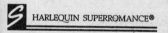

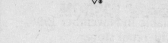
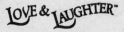